Boomerang

To: Doug Fisher

Enjoy

Adam. W. Wiktorek

Sept 2, 2001

Oregon State Fair

Boomerang

Adam W. Wiktorek

Writer's Showcase
San Jose New York Lincoln Shanghai

Boomerang

Writer's Showcase
an imprint of iUniverse.com, Inc.

For information address:
iUniverse.com, Inc.
5220 S 16th, Ste. 200
Lincoln, NE 68512
www.iuniverse.com

ISBN: 0-595-15926-5

Printed in the United States of America

BOOMERANG

In 1919, a sleepy little town in Western Idaho changed its name from Boomerang to Payette. In the grand scheme of things the name change did little more than honor a pioneering fur trapper, François Payette, a rascal who apparently tickled their fancy.

During the great migrations of the 1850's through the 1890's, Boomerang was an important stop along the Oregon Trail for settlers traveling further west, but many early travelers recognized the area's beauty and opportunity and halted their migration in the Snake River Valley community.

ORPHAN TRAINS

"Orphan Trains" were an institution in this country from 1854 to 1929. During that 75 year period more than 150,000 children, made homeless by epidemics, accidents, poverty and neglect, were gathered from Eastern cities burdened by their numbers, to be sent to Christian homes in the country. It was a blessing for many of them. However, it has been said, "Not every child was justly served. This is a story of one such family.

Chapter I

Jacob Mead shivered and swore at the incessant chill. It would be a couple of hours before the sun would warm up the night air trapped in the parlor where he and his mother had been sitting since before dawn.

He desperately wanted to stand and stamp his feet to get the blood circulating again but he also felt he'd rather endure the discomfort than attract his mother's wrath. He looked down at his feet. "Lookit there, Pa's shoes," he mumbled to himself. "He'd have a fit if he could see me wearing these damn things. He chuckled to himself as he remembered what ma said when she handed them to him.

"Put 'em on. Company's coming and I won't have you running around like a damn dog without no shoes on."

His clothes were the same togs he wore every day, but freshly cleaned: bib overalls, a tad too short, a flowered shirt with frayed cuffs and with the elbows worn nearly through, and then there were his father's shoes.

He glanced out the window at the early morning mist beginning to disappear down along the creek below the house.

Looking over the edge of the coffin, he could see the tip of the old man's sharp nose, a wisp of gray hair plastered to his forehead, and his bearded chin jutting from the bottom of his face as if still defying anyone to cross him. Thanks, he thought, ya sure as hell saved me the trouble 'a killin' ya, by dying, ya old bastard. First respectable thing I ever remember you doing. He stared fiercely at the coffin cradling his father's body, and rubbed the small scar above his right eye unconsciously. Yes sir, you probably saved me a whole lot of trouble.

No older than perhaps 17 or 18, the young man looked as if he were still growing into his bones. His hands were massive with large bony wrists sticking out of the shirt his mother had made from feed sack material. A shock of thick brown hair, only half tamed and slicked down with water, crowned a usually pleasant clean-shaven face with a strong chin. His unusually thick black eyebrows furrowed into a glowering scowl, his cheek muscle, taut with fury, rippled as his dark eyes swept over his father's coffin.

His feet were crammed into shoes a size too small and they were beginning to be a source of considerable discomfort. Dead man's shoes at that, but his ma had said it didn't make no sense burying a good pair of shoes. Anger at the old man lying stiff and cold in the plain pine box, or perhaps the frosty morning air, caused him to shiver.

He glanced around the parlor and at the odd assortment of chairs and at their old worn davenport his mother had arranged for their expected company. No one was sitting in Pa's big leather chair with the little table holding a candle beside it. Neither Jacob nor his mother had ever ventured near it for fear of drawing Pa's wrath. There was a fireplace, dark with accumulated soot, but no fire in spite of the chill. The windows, one facing down the hill towards the creek, the other facing towards the barn, were covered with feed-sack cloth tacked up to hide cracked panes. There were no pictures on the walls, nor had paint been wasted on them. In the center of the room lay a worn rag rug upon which sat two wooden saw horses supporting the plain pine coffin slapped together by Mr. Butler, the undertaker from down in Boomerang.

Looking over the coffin, Jacob studied his mother; she was too thin. She looked weary and old; her black homemade dress hung listlessly on her as if it were as tired as she. Her hair, in a tight bun at daybreak, was already coming down, a wisp of gray escaping behind her ear. Sitting stoically beside her husband's bier, her face betrayed no emotion. She hadn't said two things to the young man since he had found his father dead in the barn the day before.

Shortly after the discovery his mother had gone into town in the buckboard to fetch Doc Highsmith, leaving the boy to sit in the barn with his Pa.

Waste of time if you ask me, the boy thought ruefully. Pa's dead, and it sure don't take no doctor to come up with a reason. He either died of being ornery or the good Lord finally got sick of his bad temper and done him in.

While she was gone, he'd hauled the old man's body back into the house and stuck him in his bed. Jacob's nose wrinkled in disgust at the foul odor the old man's corpse emitted as the day matured. He decided that he might as well clean Pa up some before Ma got back; maybe then she'd think a little more kindly of him, not that he expected much from her either.

Least I never wanted to kill her like I did Pa, Jacob thought.

Doc Highsmith, 55 years old, trim of torso and sporting a luxuriant beard, had come riding in alone later that afternoon. Alighting from his surrey with the grace of an athlete, he tied his horse to the hitching rail, grabbed his black satchel, turned to the lad and said in a deep, almost musical bass voice, "Your Ma's at Butler's getting a casket built, son, she'll be along directly. Let's go see to your Pa."

They walked into the bedroom strewn with the trapping of Pa's life; an old buffalo rifle leaned against one wall, his clothes hung from a nail on another wall, his boots were flung carelessly on the floor with other clutter. It was dark in the room because the window was covered with an old unidentifiable animal skin.

He'd covered the body with the feather tic after washing him, commenting out loud to himself, "Yer as cold as stone, and ya ain't never gonna warm up again on this earth, but I know for sure it's plenty warm where ya are now."

The doctor thoroughly examined the thin pasty body and remarked, "You did your mother a real favor cleaning him up like you did, boy."

Jacob shrugged despondently, "Only reason I cleaned him up was so Ma wouldn't have to do it. I figured she was having a pretty good day so far, so's they's no sense to ruin it by her having to wrestle with the old man."

"How'd you find him?"

"I went down after breakfast to finish my chores, and there he was, dead. Had a holt of the wheelbarrow, kinda tipped it over on hisself. I calculate he fell and grabbed the handle to try 'n pull hisself back up."

"What time was that?"

"About sunup. He was still warm when I found him."

Doc looked at the boy through narrowed eyes. "You know why your Pa died, son?"

"Yes, sir. Meanness."

"You're closer to the truth than you think. He smiled wryly, "Did you know your Pa had been shot?"

"Shot?" The boy raised his hands in defense. "I didn't shoot 'em, Doc, honest. I didn't hear no shots neither."

"No, I know you didn't shoot him. What killed your Pa is what made him so mean. Right here, you see this hole next to his hair?" Doc pushed the old man's thin hair up off his forehead and pointed at the old war wound. "He's been carrying a mini ball in his head ever since Abe Lincoln's war."

The young man looked closely. His pa always wore a hat, low down, so's you could hardly see his eyes most of the time. Doc pushed the shock of thin hair up a little further, revealing a small round pucker of gray flesh, smaller than the tip of a finger.

"That's a bullet hole?" the boy gasped in astonishment.

The doctor nodded thoughtfully and said, "Yep that's a bullet wound. He almost got through the war without a scratch, till this. Told me the name of the battle years ago, but I disremember it now. The shot should have killed him right then and there, but it didn't. When he woke up he was a prisoner and eventually ended up in Andersonville, I think he said. He was so dirty and covered with blood, they didn't know if he was shot or cut. Not that it mattered they weren't into wasting money on fixing Yankees up anyway. Them Rebs didn't have enough supplies to fix their own wounded at the time.

"That was pretty near the end of the war. Good thing too, or he'd have been dead for sure. He's been carrying that mini ball in his head for more than forty years.

He looked from the wound to the boy's wide eyes and continued, "For the last couple of years, I suspect that the ball has been festering, causing him hellish pain, and I'm sure that's what made him so damn mean lately, though you could hardly tell the difference. As long as I've known your pa, he's been unkindly.

"Is that the reason he was getting weak?" the boy asked.

"Yes, that's sure a sign. How'd he show he was losing his strength?"

"Last week he took me to town to help load the buckboard. He's was never wanting to take me to town. Then, the other day he said he didn't want to be lifting no heavy loads no more. Never did get to lift nothing though. Pa started trouble first. Ya hear 'bout it?"

"Well, I heard he got thrown in jail for being drunk and hitting a woman. What happened?"

"He wasn't drunk, Doc. He never touched no strong drink. Said it made him sick. He was just naturally mean by his own self. Ya know that was the first time he took me to town since two years ago or so when we had to run some cows out here that come in on the railroad.

We was getting ready to leave, and a lady was settling up with Mr. Hermann, when Pa came up beside her and yelled at her, 'Get the hell out of my way!' 'Fore she could move, he whacked her up side her head and knocked her down. I thought he was gonna kill her. That's when Sheriff Carpinelli come and took him off."

"More'n likely, as I said, your pa suffered pretty bad these last months." Doc said gently. "See son, when things start going wrong in your head, all kind of things can happen. Part of that is the way your pa started treating everybody mean-like, not just you and your ma."

The boy continued, "After Pa got throwed in jail, I didn't know what to do, so I hightailed it back home. Ma went back inta town and got 'em out'a jail.

"He was madder'n hell at me for leaving him in jail all afternoon. Like'd beat me to death down there in the horse barn where I found him dead this morning. Good place for him to die, right there where he beat me."

The young man sat looking over the edge of Pa's casket. The old bastard was gone and now it was just him and Ma to run the place now. He could take care of the outdoor work all right. Been doing most of that around there anyway since they took him up at the railhead. Ma might have a harder time of it since neither of them had been to town much. Who we suppose' to trade with, and what other business is there that Pa never told us about? He wondered.

He cursed his shoes again. He'd ease them off, except now he could hear company coming. Horses and wagons rattled across the wooden bridge below the knoll the house stood on. The bridge had always been Pa's warning when uninvited guests arrived.

But they hadn't had company at the ranch for as long as he could remember, except for when the sheriff came by or Doc stopped to look in on Ma. That was just to make sure Pa hadn't killed her or her son. Ma talked about a couple of sisters and a brother from time to time, and the boy thought Pa had some kin, but no one was welcome at the Mead place. Pa had said many times, "I don't want no one snooping around here, tending my business when they got business of their own to tend."

Doc Highsmith came into the room, nodded at the boy, and went over and comforted Ma. They were talking so low he couldn't hear what they were saying. Don't matter no how, he thought angrily, while he stared at the old rag rug. I ain't sticking around this place no longer than I have to.

When he looked up, Doc was standing beside him.

He whispered, "I'd like you to walk with me, boy. I been talking with your ma." They strolled out into the sunshine across the front porch and down to the weedy front yard. "Are you thinking of leaving now that your pa is dead?" Doc Highsmith asked bluntly.

The boy looked up at the doctor then turned quickly and fixed his gaze on an empty field. He was startled by the doctor's intrusion into his thoughts. Damn right I am, he thought. As soon as this is over, I'm grabbing my stuff and heading out. Ma can figure out for herself how to run the place. It ain't nothin' to me. I ain't even her own kin. Just some orphan rat they picked up at the railroad. His brow knitted in anger at recalling his father's threats. They could send me back to the railroad any time they had a mind to. He must'a threatened me a hundred times with that.

He looked back at the doctor sheepishly. "Don't have no full plans to go, but now that Pa's dead," he hesitated, looked at the ground and mumbled, "I been thinking on it some."

"Listen, boy," Doc said sternly; "you just listen to me. Your ma is scared to death thinking that with Jess dead, you'll run off. You've both been through a lot of bad years putting up with your pa, no question about it. So she's asked me to talk to you now about staying on awhile until things settle some.

"Why?" the boy demanded, glaring at the older man.

"That's a fair question, but the answer's rather complicated. They ambled over to the stone fence that that ran from the corner of the house down along the drive to the creek. "Let's sit."

"Son, what do you know about the Orphan Train and where you came from?"

"The only story I know is I come from the railroad and that if I didn't do what Pa told me, I was going back there." He paused, "Doc, I read in the Bible about slaves. You know about them?"

Doc Highsmith looked at him quizzically. "I do," he answered.

"Yeah. Well, so do I." A bitter scowl clouded his tanned face. "That there is what I am, Doc, a slave. Fact is, I been a slave since I got a memory. All I've ever done is work this here farm. I plowed; I sowed, rode line, broke horses, cut hay, picked apples, and hunted game. I done everything on this farm for nothing but the food I 'et and the clothes I had to wear." His voice rose noticeably higher. "These here shoes, they ain't even mine, but they's the first real shoes I ever had on. Ma always made me moccasins, which ain't no damn good in the winter, 'less you ain't got nothing else.

"Pa now, he had these here shoes, 'n he had boots, good ones. Came clear up to his knees. Wore 'em every day, and kicked my ass with 'em 'bout every day, too. Hell, he near wore 'em out kicking my ass. That the story she told you, or some other story." His breathing was growing heavy, "'bout how she's been so good to me?" His face, even under his dark tan, was beginning to turn red.

Doc patted his shoulder. "Now settle down boy, don't go getting a temper on me. I'm here to help you and your ma over these rough times. The worst of it's over for now, but let me explain a few things to you."

The youngster shook his head and took a deep breath trying to control his temper and all the while looking at Doc with penetrating eyes under thick furrowed eyebrows

"To start with, there was some bad sickness, real bad, years ago, back East," Doc began his story.

Taking in the sun's warmth, the young man leaned cautiously against the stone fence and waited for Doc to continue.

"In 1887 and '88, there was a terrible sickness in most of the states east of us, Illinois, New York, Pennsylvania, and the like. They called it the grip or the flu, and it was killing folks by the thousands. Lots of kids were dying, and so were grownups." Doc Highsmith paused to sort his thoughts and watched the boy pulling at a stalk of dry grass and stripping the seeds into the palm of his hand. Continuing, he said, "When grown-ups got sick, their kids sometimes were taken away and put in quarantine until their folks were well enough to take care of them again.

"Well, it happened that not all the youngsters got back to their folks for various reasons. With lots of them, their folks died. There were some children that just got shuffled around and the parents couldn't find them. Records weren't kept as carefully as they should have been. There was fraud, corruption, and there were even young people who were sold. Maybe the saddest was the poor folks; so poor that they just left the children hoping that they would somehow have a better life."

The young man began to listen more intently, studying Doc's face, unaware of the seeds in his hand drifting to the ground.

"The heartbreaking result of all of this is that the orphanages became full, and there just wasn't enough to take care of them all. So when some do-gooder came up with the idea of loading orphans on trains and parceling them out, the orphanages got rid of hundreds, maybe thousands of hungry little mouths. About the only thing you had to do to claim a child was show up at the railroad station.

"Your ma, married to your pa for about four years, read about the Orphan Train in an old newspaper just a few days before the train, carrying what was left of some two hundred youngsters out of New York, was due to pass through Boomerang. She never consulted with Jess. She knew he'd never agree to her taking up a strange child." The older man rubbed his chin thoughtfully. "Let's see, you're," he paused, "about eighteen or so, I reckon. That about right?"

"I guess so, Doc," the boy said flatly with slight shrug of his shoulders. "Don't really know much about my age."

"Didn't you ever celebrate a birthday of some kind?"

"Nope, never."

"I'll be damned," he said with a humph. "Well, let me finish my story. Then you make up your mind if you need to leave the ranch. Let's see, where was I?"

"You said Pa'd never let her have no strange baby."

Doc nodded, saying, "Yep, that's it. Your pa had a reputation as a hard man; hard worker, hard on his folks, hard on his animals."

"Yeah, that's Pa all right," the boy agreed vigorously.

Doc hushed him with a hard look. "As I was saying, he was rough on everything and everybody, and he was hard on himself, too. But worst of all, he was awfully hard on your ma. She had just turned seventeen when she married Jess. Plenty old enough for hard work and raising a family, but nothing could have prepared her for your pa.

"Jess was a widower early on. Worked his first wife into an early grave is what they say. Then he just disappeared for about 10 or 15 years. When he showed up again he was with a new young wife—that's your ma—and enough cash to buy this spread.

"Didn't talk to town folks except to buy stock or dried goods. He always paid in cash and he never owed any debts. To this day folks can't figure why during the lean years in the '90s your pa always had money when so many folks were struggling just to eat.

"Now, here is where we get into what you might call none of your business." As he talked, the doctor rubbed the heat from the morning sun into his legs. "Folks here abouts never met the new Mrs. Mead, and we all kind of wondered about her. But old Jess, he just kept her out on the ranch. He never even bought one yard of cloth to make a new dress or anything else a woman might need. I tell you, son, we were all mighty curious." Doc fell silent with a faraway look in his eyes, but then he continued in a softer tone, forcing the boy to lean in closer.

"It was about this time there came into your ma's hands that wadded up newspaper with the story of the orphan babies in it. Something bought at the store had been wrapped in it and I expect your ma was hungry for anything from the outside world and read every word.

"She never said anything to Jess, as I already told you, she just waited till he was out of sight somewhere on the ranch, hooked up the buckboard and showed up in town, much to the delight of us all. Every lady in town came to chat with her, but your ma was scared to death so she wasn't much company. It didn't take long before folks began to figure she was just like Jess. He never wanted to talk to anybody unless he was buying or trading, and so they left her alone.

"I introduced myself, but she brushed me aside like she was afraid to talk to me. I tried hard to be friendly to her because I knew Jess, and I felt there might be trouble with him before the day was over, but he never showed up.

"So, I stood back and watched her waiting at the station most of the day, clutching that old piece of paper and looking across the prairie for the train to come in from Boise.

It was about three hours late when it did finally get in, and to make matters worse, she didn't have much to look at. They'd been giving young'uns away for over twenty-five hundred miles, and it looked like all the good ones were taken.

"But there you were, the youngest of the bunch to start out and still no takers. Folks just naturally didn't want babies, they wanted young'uns who could pull their own weight. They were looking for workers. Besides that, it was common for babies to die, and there they'd be with no worker and a funeral to boot.

"There was actually three of you left on the train. The other two, both older boys, had been spoken for right off the bat, which left just you. Shy as your mother was, she was the last one to look, so she was gonna have to take you or go home empty handed.

"I watched as she picked you up," Doc said, smiling warmly at the boy. "I thought I was looking at an angel the way she stared at you. She turned to me and said, 'Doc, this here is my boy. Mine and Jess's. I want you to meet him. His name is Jacob, after Jacob in the Bible. See, it's here on the tag," and she held you up so I could see you and the tag.

"Ain't he just the most wonderful thing you ever saw?'"

Confused, the young man interrupted, "What's this story have to do with me, Doc. I don't know no Jacob."

"Yes, you do, boy. That's your given name. You are Jacob. But then, there was Jess, ranting and a raving that he wouldn't stand for a Biblical name on waif. 'Probably a damn bastard 'fer all we know!' Is what I believe he said. I guess from what you and your mother are telling me, he never did call you by your right name and neither did she."

"He just called me boy, just the way you call me. 'Boy, fetch this, boy, do that, boy, you're gonna get a whipping," he said imitating Jess' angry expression.

He stopped suddenly, his face becoming serious. "Jacob. Do I have a last name, Doc? I'd love to get shed of the name of Mead. Stinks far as I can see. How old was I when she took me up?"

"Patience son. I'll get to all your questions fast as I can. Don't know about your last name. I suspect your mother can help you there. But you know Mead's not such a bad name. Any name is good far as that goes. A name is mostly like a handle on a tool, say a shovel. You use the shovel to clean the gutters in the cow barn, you get done, and of course the shovel stinks. Next person comes along can clean that shovel up and it's as good as new."

Doc took a deep breath and glanced back at the rundown house. "You need to understand your mother and why she treated you like she did. Let me tell you what happened when she came home with a wee babe. You see, I got mixed up in the middle of it right from the start.

"You were less than two years old, I believe. I don't really expect you to remember anything about it. Jess was waiting for your mother and he was furious. What he didn't know was he was waiting for two folks, not just one, that is, considering the babe in your mother's arms. He'd been down in that horse barn picking out just the right strap with a brass buckle on it to settle up with her for leaving without permission. 'Ain't no animal allowed to stray off the place!' is what he kept yelling at her as he whipped her. As I recollect, he didn't take into consideration she was holding a baby, and you caught a couple licks with the buckle before she could throw you off to the back of the buckboard. That's how you got that scar above your eye. I stitched you up myself. Your pa was raging crazy."

Doc shook his head, his brow furrowed in anger as he recalled the tragic events of that terrible night. He continued, "After the beating, he just went inside like nothing happened and went to bed, leaving her bleeding and hurt, laying on the ground. When she woke up, it was the middle of the night, and in spite of expecting another beating, she climbed back into the buckboard and made it to town. She thought she would either die from the beating or he would kill her the next day anyway, so she came to me. I stitched both of you until daylight. I was worried that she might not make it, she was cut so bad, and he had actually fractured her skull. She'd lost a considerable amount of blood to boot. But she's a powerful strong woman, Jacob.

"We had to get the law involved, but there's not much the law can do about a man beating his wife, just so long as he doesn't kill her. The only thing that saved her another beating then, is the sheriff told Jess if he beat her or the baby to death, he was going have to run him in. Jess offered to shoot the sheriff's eyes out if he didn't get off the place, but he did heed the message and allowed her to come home a few days later, and to fetch you with her.

"That wasn't the end of it, though. Jess still felt the need to whip her into shape now and then. I'm sure you saw that. What you didn't see was what it was doing to her inside. Now she's whipped nearly to death. If you leave, I doubt she'll last two months. You any idea of what she might die of?"

"No, sir," he said, his eyes focused on the ground.

"Grief. Pure grief from losing her son. You're all that's been keeping her alive these past fifteen years."

Jacob looked up and snapped, "Go to hell Doc. She treated me almost as bad as Pa. Slapped me around, yelled at me every time I got near her. If she's got anything in her heart for me, it's regret we ever crossed paths. She'll be happy to get rid of me."

"You couldn't be more wrong. Dear God," Doc said looking skyward, "give me the words to explain to this child how wrong he is."

"Who you talking to Doc, me or God?" Jacob demanded. "I know farming and cow-poking. And I know there are lots of roads away from here that's got to lead to some place better'n this little bitty speck of cow shit covered ground."

"There no question she treated you pretty rough." Doc held his hand up to stop Jacob from interrupting. "No question at tall. But don't you understand her reason for it. It was on account of Jess. Every time she showed you some affection, Jess would knock her around and then light into you. She knew that treating you good brought bad to both you and her. For herself, she could take it, but it nearly killed her to see some of the beatings you took.

"As you got older, you figured out ways to stay away from him some, but if she even said a kind word about you, he'd get that strap out and limber it up. Don't you see son? She didn't want you hurt, and the only way to protect you was to hurt you a little bit herself. At least that way you weren't cut or laid up, like you were when Jess whipped you. Bad as it was, your ma saved your life.

"One time, she tried to get some folks in town to take you, to get you away from Jess. A family by the name of Hazeloff was willing to take you right around a year after she first brought you home. I wish it could have worked out.

"But Jess caught wind of the scheme, so your ma, you, and the Hazleoffs all suffered at his hand. He nearly killed Myron with a club. Mrs. Hazeloff was laid up for a week, and you and your ma weren't heard of for a couple of years except for when the sheriff would stop by to make sure you were both alive. The law is mighty heavy on the side of the husband and it don't hold with any interference in family matters. I'm sorry, maybe it's not right, but that there's the way it is.

"Your mother has brought the both of you through some bad times over the years, and in most ways, she's a strong woman, Jacob. But right now she's in the poorest state a human can endure. The yoke of Jess being lifted from her and her feeling that you'll leave is gonna kill her quick unless I can convince you to soften your heart long enough to go in and talk to her. She's not the same woman who got up out of yonder bed yesterday morning for another day of drudgery and mistreatment. No sir, son, she surely isn't."

"What're you asking me to do, Doc, forget all them years of being treated worse than we treat our animals just 'cause Ma's your friend?" Jacob gave a half chuckle. "Least she usually had a reason fer dusting me. Pa, he'd hit me fer nothin', sometimes without me even a knowing he snuck up behind me. That's why I was gonna kill him, 'cept now, he's saved me the trouble."

Doc appeared surprised at Jacob's confessed intent to murder his father but managed to keep his voice level. "I know that you've read the Bible Jacob, because you know about slaves and such. Remember what it says in Matthew 5:39?"

"No Doc, I don't," Jacob sneered. "What's it say. Let your ma beat on ya whenever she takes a mind?" He snorted in contempt. "Sure I read the Bible, some. Ma taught me to read and cipher my numbers," he said with some pride, recalling that his father could neither read nor write. "But I never put much stock in that there book."

"Well, in the Book of Matthew, it tells you to turn the other cheek when someone strikes you. It also tells us to forgive those who've hurt us. Jacob, for the life of me, I can't see why you haven't gone bad based on what you been through. You got real strength of character, son, and I expect that it'll direct you to do what's proper. Now I'd like you to go in and just stand by your mother. You don't have to talk to her that'll come later. Will you do that for me?"

"All right, Doc I will, but," his voice was tight with reluctance as he sighed and left the thought unsaid. He went back into the sitting room and stood by his mother.

Steel-shod hooves clippity clopping across the wooden bridge announced that folks from town were arriving. There were plenty of the curious as well as couple of Pa's relatives and Ma's too. All seemed to be bringing in food. Jacob could see the men, along with several children, checking out the barns, the stock and the machinery.

Well, if you're going to steal from a widow, this would be the best day, he thought.

Jacob watched several youngsters' bare feet flashing in the grass and wading in the creek. That was forbidden. Pa'd knock hell out of them if he was here.

But he was here. Standing, Jacob could see the pinched nose, gaunt cheeks, and that lower lip that was a forecaster of a coming thumping. Try scaring Satan with that fat lip of yours, you old bastard, he thought. Your damned old lip ain't gonna scare me and Ma no more, old man.' That thought startled Jacob. Here he was thinking of Ma being scared of that lip too. Maybe Doc was right, maybe she had been scared of her husband.

When we get to be alone, I'll have to ask her, he decided.

From the cold of the early morning, the room had eventually turned pleasantly warm, but that was hours ago. Now it was stifling. Folks kept waltzing up to Jacob and his mother.

"We're so sorry about your loss," they would say.

Not us, Jacob thought in silent reply for Ma and himself.

"Thank you, dear," the widow always replied.

"Did he suffer long?" asked a plump old biddy in a dress much too tight and stained with sweat from the day's heat and her exertion.

No, but Ma and me did, Jacob thought, covering his mouth to contain his mirth.

"Not that we know of. He never complained," Ma answered, ever so politely, her face a mask, showing no emotion.

Toward late afternoon it came time for the burying. Earlier, in the cool of the morning, some of men had dug a grave next to the stand of aspen below the corral where Mrs. Mead had directed them.

As they gathered around the grave, Jacob discreetly studied the temporary grave marker Mr. Butler had clapped together; charcoal letters on a plain wooden board with the words, "Jessie O. Mead, B. Oct. 22, 1828, D. Mar. 29, 1906".

"That's about all folks needs to know about old Jess Mead," Jacob mumbled to himself under his breath. "'Specially that last part, 'bout being dead."

He could not remember ever being around so many people at once. He stood quietly, not wanting to attract attention.

The preacher finished reading from the Bible, looked towards the sky and in his high pitched, raspy, but solemn voice began blathering on and on about the poor old man and how his folks were going to miss his cheerful manner and generous spirit. He obviously didn't know Jess Mead at all, because he was quite sympathetic in assuming that Pa was up there looking down on them with a "gladdened heart" at the sight of all his friends gathered to see him off.

When the preacher was done, everyone threw a handful of dirt onto the casket and wandered back toward the house and the sumptuous dishes brought by the ladies.

Hanging back in order to be the last to pay his respects, Jacob grubbed in the pile of fresh dirt until he came up with a sharp stone about the size of his fist. He tossed it deliberately on the casket. It plopped exactly where he aimed it, right over Jess' cold, dead heart. Nice chuck, he thought, and headed for the house.

Looking westward toward Oregon and Sugarloaf Mountain nearly a hundred miles away, shimmering in the distance, he spoke aloud to himself, "Me and Ma, we got some talking to do."

CHAPTER 2

At dawn, Jacob stood at the barn door as the day approached. It wasn't his habit to just stand and watch the sunrise, in fact he had never noticed daylight coming before: too many chores to do before breakfast, too much work to do after. As the light slowly revealed the roughhewn out buildings, he stretched and breathed deeply.

He was still pretty tired, having stayed up late last night waiting for company to leave. Some left before dark, but more than a few lingered until they had to light lamps to help find their way home. Jacob had watched from the front porch as folks drifted off, lanterns brightly shinning, floating slowly across the wooden bridge and out toward the prairie, looking in the distance like fire flies that couldn't turn off. Voices more than a half mile away were clearly heard as they called their good-bye's back and forth to one another, their tiny lights spreading out as they went on separate trails.

Jacob noticed that there was already a light in the window back at the house. Ma is up fixing breakfast for Pa. Jacob caught himself and realized that Pa was gone. Smiling grimly, Jacob went back to his chores. He tried to practice what he was going to say to Ma. If he stayed or not would depend on if she would let him take a horse. If he were going to get a job, he would need a horse and a saddle too.

"Maybe I could offer to work for her to earn enough to buy one of the nags we got 'round here. No, that won't do," he mumbled as he spread fresh straw in the stalls. "I've been a slave here all these years; that won't change. Wonder if I could sneak into Oregon, up around the

Owyhee country and catch one of them wild cayuse they got running around?"

With such thoughts, he finished cleaning the barn and got the plow team harnessed and ready for the day's work. He fed them some grain to chew while he went up to the house for his own breakfast. Carrying a half-bucket of fresh warm milk, Jacob entered the kitchen through the back door.

Ma, dressed in the same worn dark dress she wore at yesterday's funeral, motioned him to set the bucket on the drain and to go clean up. Neither spoke.

Out on the back porch was a pitcher of warm water to wash in. That was unusual. They usually washed in cold water. With the morning chill still over everything, the warm water felt good.

When Jacob went inside his mother was pulling a platter of biscuits from the oven. "How'd you want your eggs?" she asked gruffly as she set a plate of steaming fresh biscuits in front of him.

"Just fry 'em," he said softly, not meeting her tired eyes.

"Everything okay down in the sheds? Anything missing?"

"I didn't see nothing missing. Didn't make no special effort to look, though."

"Boy?" she questioned. "I'm sorry, I mean Jacob. You got any special plans for this morning?"

He looked closely at her for a moment. "Well, I got Harry and Chub all hitched, grained, and ready to do some plowing after breakfast."

"Would you unhitch 'em. We're all needing a little rest, even the horses, and if you'll give me the time, I'd like for you and me to talk.

Jacob had been waiting for this, he just didn't expect a showdown so quickly. We might as well get on with the hanging, he thought. "Yeah, sure Ma," he sighed. "Right after breakfast."

She had fixed a breakfast that Pa would have kicked her to hell and gone for, just for wasting so much on him. Thick bacon, eggs fried sunny-side up, biscuits, and hot coffee. Jacob smiled, and thought, I wish Pa'd died more often. Not a word passed between them as Jacob ate.

After eating, he went back to the barn, unharnessed the horses and turned them out into the corral. They must have sensed they were getting a day off as they galloped in circles kicking big clods of dry dirt in the air. Old Chub, lay down and started rolling in the powder dry earth, kicking up a cloud of dust in apparent joy. "Well, I got to go face the music, fellas, enjoy yourselves," said Jacob. His breakfast suddenly felt like a lead weight in his belly.

Reluctantly, head hanging, Jacob trudged back to face his mother. I ought to tell her right out I want to leave, he thought. But leave, for where. Outside of Boomerang, he couldn't even remember ever being anywhere besides this ranch. I'm gettin' anyway, he decided, clenching his teeth, the muscles in his cheeks rippling. "I want to get as far away from here as I can. And I don't give a damn if she loses the place or not. It ain't never been nothing to me but whippings and hard work."

Jacob doffed his wide-brimmed hat and slapped dust off his trousers as he entered her parlor. There were strict rules about wearing hats in the parlor. Jacob felt he was facing enough without her screaming about that too. He settled on the wooden stool by the fireplace and waited for her to come from the kitchen.

"Be right there," she called. When she entered, she was toting a steel box about a foot square, and a small black leather notebook. "Sit there," she said as she motioned Jacob toward Pa's big leather chair. "You're the man of the house now, that's your chair.

Jacob sat glued to the little wooden stool.

"Go on, get yourself in it so's we can talk. We've got some important things to discuss, and I want to get on with it."

He forced himself to comply, sulking to the chair. As he eased himself down, he flinched, half-expecting Pa, or even Ma, to raise a fist against him.

She studied Jacob's face, struggling for the right words, and causing Jacob to squirm in his seat. "Jacob, there ain't but one way to start what I have to say to you, and that's to say, I'm sorry we ever met."

Well, you're ahead of me on that, but you can't be half as sorry as I am. He kept his thought silent as his fingers curled so forcefully into the leather arms of Pa's chair that his knuckles turned white.

"When I first come on you, it was in my mind that just the sight of you would soften your pa's heart. That's one reason I wanted a baby so bad. I wanted your pa to see he didn't have to hurt everything he came up to just to get by. But I was wrong. I was wrong to go get you, and I was wrong to bring you home. Jess couldn't help himself, but till I talked to Doc, I didn't know it.

Turning away with watery eyes to regain her composure, she returned her gaze to her son, who sat uncomfortably in his father's overstuffed chair, looking as if he could thrash her. She continued, "If I hadn't brought you here to the ranch, you surely would have had a better life 'n you had. Doc told you how you come to be on the train and the trouble after, didn't he?"

"He told me," Jacob said, his tone flat, his expression as hard as stone.

"Son, the reason I said I'm sorry we ever met ain't what you think. You've been a good son, and I'm right proud of you and the way you turned out. It's 'cause of the hard life I've been forced to give you. I had to beat you just to keep Pa from beating you, and it almost killed me every time. I'd rather have cut off my own hand. I can't expect you to understand so soon after he's gone, but I can promise you that you'll not get beat around here again. Never."

"Ain't going to be around here long enough to get beat," he said flatly. "First chance I get, I'm heading out."

"I knew you was thinking that'a'way, that's why I asked you to spend time with me today, so's when you do go, you'll have some place to go and a reason to go there."

"Meaning?" he inquired with narrowed eyes.

"Meaning, you're free to leave anytime you've a mind to. But there's things you 'n me got to settle 'fore you run off."

"I suppose," he grumbled.

Ma looked at him imploringly. "Son, you got a right to hate me and your pa. Lord knows, between us you been misused all your life. I can't take away all them bad years, but I can help you some with the years you got ahead if you'll let me."

"First, is this here book," she said, holding it up for Jacob to see. "It come wrapped with your belongings and clothes when I come to fetch ya from the train. I never showed it to Pa, and I ain't hardly more'n glanced at it myself. He'd a likely taken it and burned it. So I hid it over at Doc's place all these years. He brung it back to me yesterday. She laid the book on her lap and continued.

"It's got names in it of some folks, and the name of a town back in New York. I can't even say the name of the place or the people.

"Reason I think it's important is what two little boys told me when I come to fetch you from the railroad station back in 1890. They'd been traveling with you, and when they first seen you, you was with a older sister and two brothers, but they said your brothers and sister was took somewhere along the line and you was overlooked. You might consider going back East and see if you can't find you some of your blood kin."

"You saying I got brothers and sisters?" Jacob blurted.

"That's what them two little boys told me."

"Do you know where they are so's I can ask 'em about them kids?"

"Jacob, after Doc fixed us up and Jess let us come back home, I didn't get back into town for years. Honest truth is, I don't have any idea who them little boys was or where they got to. Near as I can remember, they went to two families over in Oregon who come to Boomerang to claim 'em.

"The other thing we need to talk about is this here box," she said touching it lightly. "It was your Pa's. There's enough here to get you started anywhere you want and a little bit to help me get a hired hand."

She carefully opened the old metal box. Jacob stared into the strong box in utter amazement. He had never seen more than two dollars in the daylight at one time before in his life, and here was more money than he could count lying inches deep in a battered old container.

His mind still reeling with the information he just heard, he involuntarily, he reached toward it. She handed him the entire box. I can buy a real good pair of shoes with what's in this box, he thought. He carefully leafed through the contents. There were several packs of one hundred-dollar bills. They rested on top of a bed of coins. Gold. What the hell's a dirt-poor farmer in the middle of Idaho doing with so much money? Jacob wondered.

"Ma, you're rich," he exclaimed.

She smiled wanly and said, "I ain't rich, Son, you are. I 'spect I ain't entitled to a penny of it. You earned it all, with the years of working for nothing and doing without. If you want, I'll keep watch of it for you, but it's all yours."

"Where'd it come from, Ma? He steal it?" Jacob asked apprehensively.

"It come from over in Oregon and up in Washington State, maybe Montana. Your pa was selling stock to the army back during the Indian wars. He done real good, buying cattle, then driving 'em to the Army depots for slaughter. The Army was desperate for beef back then. He sold 'em horses too. Jess was real smart that way and he took advantage.

"Jacob," Ma looked at Jacob intently, "a widow can't inherit from her husband in Idaho if he has a son."

Jacob's puzzled look assured her that he didn't understand the enormity of what she was trying to say. "You understand what I'm saying to you?"

"You mean he can't leave you nothing." Jacob couldn't believe what he was hearing.

"The ranch—it's yours—all of it. When you leave, I'm asking your permission to live here and run it for you. If you want me to go, I will, that be up to you. But if you was of a mind to go to a real school and get some education, I'd see to it you'd have a ranch to come back to."

Jacob's mind was whirling. He could have her off the place and she would have to go. And what of the money, was it really his? Twenty minutes ago, he was about to rebel and demand his freedom from this dried up old woman who was now handing him thousands of dollars and the ranch. Not only that, she was looking to his mercy for a place and a reason to live. This is a bigger chaw than a seventeen year old, uneducated, ignorant backwoods farm boy should handle in one bite, he thought.

She sat staring at him and he stared back, looking into her pale blue, sadly tired eyes. Jacob had never noticed her eyes before, they were a beautiful light blue. He looked away feeling embarrassed.

The clock tick-tocked loudly in the background, Jacob could hear birds flying by and singing outside the open front door.

"Ma, I've got some harness to fix," he said suddenly in his embarrassment and bolted from the room, leaving her sitting in the parlor where yesterday Pa had lain.

Jacob didn't go back into the house until well after dark. He had plowed over eight acres that day, a good day's labor for man and beast. The hours had passed almost unnoticed because of the turbulent thoughts that assailed him. When he finally quit, he felt guilty for not having taken a break at noon to eat and to rest the animals. He brushed them carefully and gave them an extra ration of grain before turning them out for the evening.

As he entered the kitchen, Ma glanced up and smiled. "You been working hard today. Hungry?"

Jacob nodded.

"Fixed you something special, lookit here." On the table was a chocolate cake with thick brown frosting and a candle smack dab in the middle.

"What's that for?" Jacob asked.

"For you—to eat." she said with a girlish grin. "Today's your birthday. It's time you turned eighteen years old, and you ain't ever had a birthday party before."

"My birthday?" he asked incredulously. "How come?"

"Because, everyone's got a day they was born on, that there's their birthday. We don't know for sure what day you was born on so today is as good as any. April first will be a easy day to remember too, coming like it does just two days after your pa died. Since you already got your birthday presents, the money and the ranch, all that's left is for you to have a cake."

After dinner, Jacob stuffed nearly half that cake into his face. Ma was smiling from ear to ear watching him eat. He found he was beginning to feel more kindly toward her as the evening wore on while they talked and laughed.

No thought of her leaving ever again entered Jacob's head. He was still a little cautious. He had years and years of healing to do, but Ma was at least making life enjoyable.

Fall was coming on and most of the crops were in, with the help of Everett, their new hired hand. He had come on the place a couple of weeks after Jess died, looking for work.

Everett Koons had drifted West about 25 years ago looking for new opportunities after fruitless years of sharecrop farming in Kansas and Iowa. He lost his farm to the bank and his lovely wife to childbirth. The West was his refuge, though he mostly just managed to survive.

He was a barrel of a man, about 50 years of age, with a ruddy complexion. His hair and eyebrows were the color of new snow. But it was his eyes that fascinated Jacob and his mother. Shaded, they were light blue, but when the sun was in his face, his eyes were startlingly pink. Everett was an albino. With a wide easy grin and wry wit, there wasn't a day long enough or work hard enough to tire the man out. He even wore Jacob out trying to keep up.

One day, Ma called Jacob back to the house early in the afternoon. "Got a letter a while back concerning your education. You interested, or not?"

"What's it all about?" he asked curiously.

"When you didn't kick me off the place, I thought I better start earning my keep and being a real ma to you. What I went and done is inquire, with Doc's help, how to get you educated. You ready to leave the ranch for a year or so?"

"Leave the ranch, for what?"

Sensing his dismay, she took his hand and held it gently. "Jacob, when I first saw you, I knew you was a smart boy. Could see it in your eyes. I first figured on learning you myself and then sending you off to a good school for finishin'. Well, Jess, he had other ideas 'bout what to do with you, and that was mostly to work you to death. I was lucky to be able to read the Bible to you from time to time, and you picked up on that real handy. So you see, I know you got a good set of brains in that knot of yours. We just got to see to filling it properly."

"Are you figuring on settin' me off the place now 'stead 'a me settin' you off?" he said in a tone that was meant to tease rather than threaten.

"Yep," she said excitedly, "that's exactly it. Everett and I can run this place by ourselves till you get back."

"Back, back from where?"

"Back from New York, if we can talk you into it. Doc's arranged a private teacher to help you get ready fer schooling. There's a real good school back East where they teach all about ranching and farming and livestock and such, called Cornell. Doc says it's near that other town we was talking about right after Jess' funeral. See this here paper?" Ma offered a document to Jacob. "It's from the school. You can spend a year or two learning how to really make this ranch pay. While you're there, I'd like to see if you can look up your real family."

At his mother's suggestion Jacob saddled up and rode into Boomerang the next day and visited with Doc Highsmith. About halfway to town he noticed two young riders following a short way behind him. Even though they were wearing western boots, Jacob thought they looked more like city boys than cowboys because of their store-bought pants with no wear holes and their low-brimmed caps. They didn't seem to be paying much attention to him, and he soon forgot them.

He and Doc palavered all afternoon until it was time to get home. When Jacob stepped aboard his horse, the animal reared up, terrified by the unfamiliar sound of an automobile chugging by. After he regained control over his horse, Jacob noticed the two strangers who had followed him into town. One, a stocky lad was a head shorter than the other and now wore a red and black bandanna around his neck. Jacob hadn't noticed the bandanna when they were out on the road. They were standing in front of the Falk Mercantile store and seemed to be eyeing him furtively. Jacob nodded to the taller man, whose long yellow hair seemed out of place on a man dressed in city clothes. Neither of the men moved a muscle in return greeting. Jacob urged his horse to a trot toward home.

As Jacob's retreating figure grew smaller, the taller of the two strangers glanced knowingly at his partner and motioned for him to move. They sauntered to their horses, keeping a close eye on the departing Jacob.

As Jacob rode home he savored his new life. The bad years were slipping into dim memories, replaced by friends like Doc and Everett. Ma was now a real mother and important in the smooth running of the ranch.

He watched the passing prairie, lazily caught up in his thoughts until he heard the pounding of hooves coming up behind him. He turned to see the two strange young men he had seen earlier on the road and then later standing in front of the store. They were in an apparent hurry to leave town. One split to pass Jacob on his left the other to his right at a full gallop.

A thundering explosion erupted in Jacob's head, and he had a peculiar feeling, as though he was flying. A blinding light, a mouth full of dirt road and total unconsciousness followed in the next instant. Hours later as he struggled to regain his senses, he became aware that it was nearly dark and he was trussed like a yearling ready for branding. A short distance away he could hear the muttering of two men talking as they approached him.

"Well, buddy boy," the shorter one said. "You ain't dead after all. Pretty good hit, Neil."

Jacob realized who they were—the two riders from town. Even in the fading light Jacob could see that the one named Neil had a grim face. A thin blond mustache below flaring nostrils bedecked his upper lip, his mouth looked like it was in a perpetual sneer, and his eyes squinted like shuttered windows hiding a foul secret.

Jacob shuddered at the look of the man.

"Shut up, you stupid bastard. I told you, don't use no names," a wave of rage crossed Neil's face as he turned on his undersized companion and pushed him roughly.

"What the hell difference it make. You're gonna kill him anyway, ain't ya?"

"Course I am. Just don't go calling out no names. Somebody else might be around and hear ya." He turned and snarled at Jacob. "What's your name boy?"

"Jacob Mead," answered Jacob in a dry raspy whisper.

"I knowed it. I know'd it was that Mead boy," said the shorter of the two. "His pap died and left him a heap of gold, way I heard. Bet his Ma'd pay plenty to get him back, even if he had a couple a new holes in 'em."

Neil cut him off sharply. "We better move 'em away from here till we can figure out how to get the money out'a his ma. She's liable to have someone looking for him when he don't show up."

"Gawd damn it Neil, we're gonna be rich off this," the shorter man cried, grinning and revealing a wide gap between his front teeth. "This is the best thing we ever got a holt of."

They hauled Jacob up by the armpits and forced him up on his horse. Missing the stirrup with his toe, Jacob, hands tied, toppled off the other side and landed hard on his back knocking the wind out of him.

His patience completely gone, Neil rushed to the fallen man and delivered a swift kick to Jacob's ribs and with a sneer ripped a hand across his face sending his senses reeling. Jacob, hurt and utterly confused, drifted semi-consciously back to his afternoon talk with Doc Highsmith. Doc had gone to Cornell. He talked grandly about the maple-covered hills, cool summer evenings, the little town—Ithaca, he called it—and the school itself. As Jacob drifted between being awake and unconsciousness, he dreamed of being far away from the danger he was in now. He wandered those hills looking for—

When Jacob awoke again, he was soaked and freezing. In the dim light of a dying campfire he could see both men faintly silhouetted against the eastern sky. Shorty, the smaller of the two men, had a canteen in his hand that he had just emptied all over Jacob. It looked like it was near dawn and the outlaws were preparing to get an early start to the ranch and collect their money.

The men carelessly broke camp. There were no cooking utensils or bedrolls, Shorty simply kicked a little dust into the campfire and called it good. Attention was then turned on Jacob to once again get him mounted on his horse.

The sun was just breaking over the eastern hills as they neared the Mead ranch. Fear choked bile up into Jacob's throat. This could be the end of Ma, Everett and me. I got to warn them, but how, he questioned silently. As they crossed the wooden bridge, Jacob let out a bellow in rage, frustration, and fear.

Neil turned in his saddle and hit Jacob with a thud in the back of the head with a rifle butt. Brilliant stars lit up Jacob's universe as he slumped forward, struggling to maintain his balance, pain shooting through every fiber in his body.

He was unable to maintain his grip and he fell awkwardly from his horse, hit the edge of the bridge, and fell the three feet into the shallow trickle of water. He felt himself being pulled under the bridge by strong arms. A hand slapped across his mouth. Jacob looked at the biggest pair of eyeballs he had ever seen. It was Everett crouched down looking as uncomfortable as sack of potatoes jammed into a dark corner. He waved his pistol and motioned Jacob to be quiet as one of the outlaws dismounted above their heads and tromped to the edge of the bridge looking for the escaped prisoner.

"Looks like he's trying to slip away under the bridge," the man called "I'll get 'em."

Jacob saw Shorty's legs and his gun hand as he jumped off the bridge next to the creek. Shorty peered into the darkness under the bridge. The last thing he saw in his life was the flash of Everett's gun as it exploded in his face.

Neil probably terrified by the sudden turn of fortune and still on his horse, turned and fled in panic.

Later, after Ma had fixed Jacob's cuts they sat at the kitchen table and talked about his experience while they ate a late breakfast.

"How'd ya happen to be under the bridge, Everett?" Jacob asked.

"I didn't just happen to, boss. I heard ya'll coming from way down the lane." Everett dunked a thick piece of homemade bread into his coffee. "Last night when ya didn't show up your ma 'n me was worried 'n so I took a lantern looking for you. I found where you was been down and bleeding. I figured you was in trouble on account you was shedding blood and I knowed your horse wouldn't throwed you. And there was signs that made me suspicious, but it was too dark to trail, so I came back to watch out for your ma.

The burly man took a gulp of scalding hot coffee, then continued. "I was just going back out to look for you when I heard them fellas a'coming. So, I just looked for a place to watch from. When I seen ya was all tied up, the bridge was 'bout the only place I could find to ambush 'em. Didn't figure on ya being such help though. When you bellered like a stuck hog, ya like'd to make me shit my pants. That was real smart of ya, jumping off your horse and into the creek like ya done."

Ma asked, "What was they after with you anyway, Jacob?"

"They wanted the money," Jacob said, chewing a mouthful of eggs as he talked. "They was talking about how they heard Jess left a heap of gold, and they was figuring on you to paying to get me back. Only they was planning on a couple of extra holes in me 'fore they turned me loose."

"One of us has to get into town and drag that carcass back to the sheriff," Ma said coldly. "Everett, I think that'd be you. I believe Jacob's going to need a little rest till that head wound heals. You've got a hard head, boy, just like Jess, else-wise that rifle barrel would'a caved ya like a pun'kin, " she chuckled at her own joke, while Jacob grinned back at her.

Jacob went in to his bedroom and lay down, his head tormenting him due to its recent misuse. His mind was whirling, digesting all that had happened in the last twenty-four hours. As he lay resting, he pondered about going back east to school.

"A few months off the place might not be such a bad idea," he said aloud as he lay looking out the window at the blue Idaho sky.

CHAPTER 3

"Past lunch time, I reckon." Everett squinted at the sun and than down at the grim cargo in back of his wagon. "I'll sure be glad to git rid of you, son. Should'a took ya to town yesterday." He had delayed getting away from the ranch to make sure the escaped outlaw wasn't coming back.

Everett's horses seemed to be nodding their heads in assent as they plodded into Boomerang. He felt his guts churning as he drove. It wasn't hunger that was causing his discomfort, and it wasn't the ripening carcass wrapped in the back of the buckboard. What bothered him was the town itself. No self-respecting drunk ought to ever go to any town without trying every saloon, at least until the money ran out.

"Lucky I ain't got much on me," he said and chuckled, as he spied the sheriff's dingy little jail.

Everett slowed the plodding team in front of the jail and called, "Sheriff, you in there?" No answer came from within the darkened, sand colored structure.

"You seen the sheriff?" Everett inquired of two ladies passing toward the mercantile store. "I need 'em."

"Sorry, no," said a young blond woman. "We haven't seen Tom since yesterday. Did you try the store? He usually leaves word there when he has to leave town."

"Much obliged ma'am," Everett said, touching the brim of his straw hat.

Climbing down on stiff legs, he hit the ground with a soft thump, a little cloud of dust rising knee high. Sure could use a little rain 'round here, he thought. Everett turned and followed the ladies heading toward Falk Mercantile.

Falk Mercantile was the largest building in town, at least measuring the wide way. The two churches, one at each end of town, were taller by far. Inside the cool darkness were displayed the innumerable variety of the goods necessary to supply a frontier town and its outlying farms and ranches and to assure a fair profit to the proprietor. There were tools, buckets, plows, and cloth for the ladies candy for the youngsters, and all manner of hardware, canned food and dried goods.

Inside the comparatively cool darkness Everett's eyes adjusted to the dim light as he took in the smell of the place. It was an aroma repeated in hundreds of similar establishments where he had replenished his supplies. Fresh cured leather, tobacco, dried fruits and vegetables, seed and fertilizer all mixed together.

From behind a stack of oaken buckets and bundled shovels, a burly man holding a hundred pound sack of corn meal asked gruffly, "Well, you want something, or do I drop this sack and throw you outta my store?"

"You're a friendly cuss ain't ya?" Everett shot back at him. "How's business? Not too good I 'spect, if you talk like that to folks."

"Oh, sorry mister," the man said, squinting at Everett. "Couldn't see you so well. These old eyes of mine been getting dimmer and dimmer every year. I thought you was Wiff Bass. We got kind of a joke going on between us. What can I do for you?"

"I'm looking for the sheriff. He around?"

The voice took shape as a mountain of a man stepped up to Everett, offering a generous paw. He wore a bib apron of heavy brown cloth generously stained and fitting snugly across his ample belly. Tousled gray hair, small silver rimed eyeglasses perched on his forehead, and a bristly full beard, topped a set of wide shoulders that seemed to have no neck. "Name's Hermann, Harold Hermann," he said as a wide happy grin split his beard. "Own this here store and the hotel across the street. If you need a room we can put you up real good, with a bath and everything for fifty cents. Dinner's thirty-five cents extra, paid up front. You need a room?"

"Everett Koons, hired-man on out at the Mead place," Everett said shaking the man's hand. "I was kinda figuring on getting back home tonight, but I need the sheriff so it 'pears I'm forced to change my mind."

"You got someone to lock up or something?" he asked as they strolled towards the door. "The sheriff leaves the keys here with me when he has to go out on business. Sometimes I got to lock a feller up, sometimes I got to let one go."

"I got one all right, but he don't need no locking up. He's dead."

"Dead?" Harold raised his eyebrows. "What happened, he have an accident 'er something?"

"Ya might say he had an accident, a couple of 'em in fact." Everett smiled, wrinkles in his weather worn face looking like some of the smaller canyons over near Weiser. "First, he accidentally tried to kill my boss, then he accidentally looked down the barrel of my pistol just when I took a notion to pull the trigger."

"Laws, ya don't say," the big storekeeper exclaimed mirthfully. "Let's get a look at 'em. He from around here? Imagine that, looking down the barrel of your pistol." With peals of laughter he followed Everett out to the resting horses and their gruesome cargo.

As they approached the wagon they could already smell the putrid corpse, though the old canvas cover Everett had thrown on it helped mask the smell some.

"I don't know who he is, Mr. Hermann. I was hoping someone here abouts might be able to come up with a name. We was wanting to find his partner too, 'cause he was in on the plot to grab the boss and kill him. Gotta warn ya, though, this one ain't too pretty. He got a real close look at the working end of that gun just before his accident."

Mr. Hermann reached over, shooed a cloud of blue blowflies hovering over the corpse and tugged at a ragged tail of blood-soaked cloth. In the next instant, he gagged and spun, spewing thick, bile-laden spit into the dust. Presently, he recovered and wiped his mouth with the back of one hand while gripping the buckboard for support with the other. He gasped, "Go get, ol' Butler, up at the undertakers. We got to get him in the ground 'fore he stinks up the whole dang town. Why didn't you warn me he was so rotten. How long's he been dead, a week?"

"Three days," Everett said in a casual tone.

"Well, laying in that buckboard in the hot sun ain't done him no good."

"You ain't told me, Mr. Hermann. Do you know 'em or not?"

"Can't be sure with his face swollen and busted up like it is. I sold a bandanna, maybe that same one, to a young cowboy Monday morning. There was two of them together. Didn't get their names but I kind'a kept an eye on 'em 'cause I thought they was aiming to rob the bank, or maybe even my store, the way they was hanging around. There was just something about 'em that didn't sit right. Later I watched as they drifted out, heading east. Just trotting along, didn't seem like there's any reason to concern myself with 'em no more so I forgot about them till I seen that bandanna."

"I think it'd be a good idea to get him out of the wagon and the hot sun. You able to help?" Everett asked.

"I think it'd be best to leave him right there and haul him over to the funeral parlor. That's the building," Harold Hermann pointed to a building with a black hearse parked in front. I'll go fetch Doc. He's supposed to look at the dead folks 'round here and he writes down what kilt 'em."

Hermann headed off looking for the doctor while Everett led the reluctant horses down the dusty street. It was heating up fast. He paused at the watering trough situated in the center of the little town's commercial section, near the blacksmith shop with its noise and fire pit. A horseless carriage, the first he had ever seen, was demanding the attention of the smithy and several curious onlookers. The obvious owner of the machine, a slender man, impeccably dressed and with neatly trimmed hair and beard, was standing back, politely allowing admirers access to his contraption.

While the horses were satisfying their thirst, Everett climbed back on the wagon seat for a better look and sat pondering the automobile. What the hell does a body do with a contraption like that. Might's well have an extra— His thoughts were interrupted by the shout of a young boy.

"Hey look, everybody. There's a dead man in the back of this here wagon. Can we see him, mister?"

Suddenly, curious though seemingly friendly folks surrounded Everett.

"Geeze, he stinks awful. Hey mister, why're ya carrying a dead man around?" the barefoot boy asked.

The owner of the horseless carriage, curious as the others, peered at the cargo in the back of Everett's wagon. After a quick glance, he grabbed the blacksmith's arm and they disappeared into the blacksmith shop, then reappeared almost instantly. He was armed with a pistol that he pointed directly at Everett's head.

"You better have a good reason for killing my nephew, mister." Turning to a youngster nearby, he commanded, "Son, go get the sheriff. Be quick about it."

"Sheriff's gone, Mr. Moss. Nels Hermann told me 'n pa yesterday that he'd be gone at least two days. Nels' pa has the keys. Want me to get 'em so's we can lock 'em up?"

"Get down from there, mister," Mr. Moss turned to a bystander, saying, "Bruce, disarm him."

Bruce, a lank, pocked-faced man, reached up and pulled Everett roughly from his perch. Wordlessly, he grabbed Everett's rifle and gave him a shove up against his wagon.

Stunned by the suddenness of his dilemma, Everett struggled for words of explanation. "Mister, if this is your nephew—"

Bruce slammed Everett with the barrel of his own rifle right behind the ear, stunning him and sending him to the ground.

"Damn it, Shotwell, none of that!" Moss shouted. "Pick him up."

"I want to know why my sister's boy lays dead in the back of your wagon, mister," he demanded as Bruce Shotwell hoisted Everett's limp body up and into a standing position.

"Ow shit. What the hell'd you hit me fer?" Everett struggled free and wheeled to face his attacker, but Shotwell had dropped Everett's gun, ducked into the crowd, and was quickly out of reach.

Turning back, his face grimacing with pain and rubbing the back of his head vigorously, Everett barked a reply to Moss. "You say that's your nephew I got in the back of my wagon, mister? He ain't got no face, so how come you think he's kin 'a yours?" Everett was quickly back in control of himself in spite of the pain in his head and the ringing in his ears.

Mr. Moss, pistol in hand, was livid. Through clenched teeth, he said, "That's my nephew all right. I bought him that pair of boots not two years ago over in Boise when he turned twenty. He and his cousin, I bought them each a pair of the same boots."

"His cousin named Neil?" Everett asked, as he picked up his rifle and scanned the crowd once again for the man who had assaulted him.

"Yes," Moss said his face dark with anger. "Why? Did you kill him too?"

"Not yet, but the day ain't over yet."

"What the hell's going on here?" Doc Highsmith demanded, shoving his way through the crowd. "Moss, what the hell you doing. Put that damn gun down. You all right, Everett?" When Everett nodded, Doc turned to Mr. Moss. "This here's Everett Koons, hired hand out at the Mead place. What ya got there, Everett. Harold told me you'd run into some trouble." He turned back to the well-dressed Mr. Moss and addressed him in a stern voice. "Christian, I asked you to put that thing away. Now put it the hell away!"

While Doc was taking charge of the situation, Everett climbed back to his perch on the buckboard and pointed at a saloon across the street with a sign that announced that it was the Primrose Saloon. "I'll meet ya'll at that saloon soon's I deliver this fella over there." He nodded in the direction of his intended destination. "I ain't running off. Fact is, Mr. Hermann is holding a room for the night for me. I'll be needing to talk to the sheriff tomorrow when he gets back. And Moss, I'd like you to know how come yer nephew ended up sucking a gun." He gently slapped the reins against broad black rumps, encouraging the horses to complete their grisly delivery.

Doc called to Everett, "Tell Butler to clean him up, and I'll be by later to examine the body."

Everett waved in understanding.

"No sense arguing with me, Mr. Butler," Everett insisted. "You're either gonna take this carcass, or I'm dumping it right here. You can collect from that Mister Moss, or his sister, or whoever, I don't care, just I ain't hauling him another step. My horses are already pretty upset by the stink and havin' to haul him all day. Ya see, I gotta live with 'em for several more years, and it just don't pay to have ol' Harry upset, Chub neither."

Mr. Butler was only half dressed, having left his long black coat hanging in the funeral parlor. He was in his bargaining and working clothes, long-sleeved black shirt rolled up to the elbows and unbuttoned at the neck, no tie, with black pants tucked into black high top-boots that shone like mirrors through a light coating of fine dust. His head was nearly bald except for long wisps of thin black hair blowing about his ears.

Butler was used to wheedling money out of grieving folks, but he wasn't having much luck with this unsympathetic old bird. "Just ten dollars, sir. After all, you kilt him, least you can do is help send him off."

Conscious of his lack of funds, and wanting to turn his lonely ten-dollar gold piece into a good binge, Everett wasn't about to budge. Grasping Shorty by the boots, he tugged him to the very end of the buckboard. The cloth covering the body snagged on a splinter and failed to slide with the body, revealing the black and bloated, shapeless form that used to be Neil's sidekick. Bet yer buddy'd never recognize you now son, he thought. I'd bet my whole ten dollars.

Mr. Butler hastily agreed to accept the body.

Doc held court at one of the large poker tables in the Primrose Saloon. Flies buzzed lazily out of arm's reach and shafts of light supported by a haze of almost invisible dust stretched from the bare windows to the floor. There were five men waiting with Doc: Mr. Moss, Bruce Shotwell, Harold Hermann, Wiff Bass, and the burly blacksmith.

Moss grumbled, "He better be treating my Randall with respect."

"If you're so concerned 'bout him getting treated respectful, whyan't you go with 'em?" Harold questioned. "You 'fraid of getting stuck with the bill? You're gonna have to pay it anyway. Your sister and Jep ain't got money to bury that boy, and you know it."

"Of course you are correct about that, Harold," Moss said dejectedly. "Where the hell is that farmer, Doc? You said we could trust him to get right back."

"He'll be here, Moss. Likely he's stuck making arrangements, seeing he's the one that killed him. You know old Butler, he'd squeeze a nickel out of a dried up widow if it took him till noon the day after doomsday."

Everett finished his business with Mr. Butler, drove his team back to the Primrose Saloon and tied them in the shaded alley beside the establishment. As he pushed aside the batwing doors, he quickly summed up the situation. "Looks like a hearing to me," he said, as he approached the seated men.

Mr. Moss replied suspiciously, "You familiar with small town courts, Koons?"

"Ain't saying I am, ain't saying I ain't. Just got the feeling you was all here to judge me. Moss, you said you got a nephew name of Neil. That right?"

"Before you start spouting off about Neil, I want to know what happened to Randall. His mother and father have fallen on hard times. Jep, that's his pap, is cripple, and this is just about going to kill his mother. She's my sister."

Everett told the bewildering tale to the six men, omitting nothing Jacob had told him of his night of terror.

Minutes later enlightened but deeply shaken, a contrite Christian Moss hung his head. It would be his sad duty, not only to tell his sister and her husband how they had lost their son, but he also had to tell Jep's sister that her boy was in trouble too. He apparently was responsible for Randall's death.

"Mr. Hermann, I need a couple of favors from you. Can we talk in private?" Everett asked as he guided the big man away from the others.

Harold Hermann was used to granting credit and doing favors for nearly everyone within twenty miles. He could be gruff and throw a bum away faster than a can of bad peaches, but nobody asking a favor was ever turned down.

Hanging an elbow over the edge of the massive mahogany bar, Everett motioned for Mr. Hermann to lean closer. "See this gold eagle. I want you to change it for me, and keep a dollar to pay for a room for tonight and a couple of meals. Can you do that?"

"Why sure, but that's no favor, I do that for cowboys all the time."

"I ain't done yet. I'm going to get roaring drunk tonight, and I want you to see to it that I don't hurt nobody and that I get to bed when I'm broke."

Mr. Hermann, warming up to this sunburned old farmer, nodded in acceptance of such light chores.

"One last thing. See that skinny fella with all them holes in his face sitting there, next to Moss?" Everett gestured casually to the table.

Mr. Hermann nodded lowering his voice to nearly a whisper. "That there's Bruce Shotwell. Yeah, I see 'em."

"Well, he's earned a little extra attention from me. Slapped me up side 'a my head with my own rifle whilst Moss was holden'a gun on me over at the smithys. I'm going over now and coldcock the son of a bitch right between the horns, and I'd appreciate it if you'd see I don't get no interference."

Turning to the short, skinny bartender and smiling as if he was about to burst at the coming attraction, Mr. Hermann said, "Clarence, you got change for this ten?" The small coin rattled and spun around three or four turns as he dropped in on the bar. "What do you want, Everett, hard dollars or paper?"

"Let me have the silver dollars. I like to feel something in my pocket and I like to hear a little jingle."

Clarence changed Everett's ten-dollar gold piece for Mr. Hermann, and Mr. Hermann carefully counted the remaining nine battered silver dollars into Everett's rough hands, keeping one of the coins for himself, as agreed.

Everett stuck one silver dollar in his breast pocket. He smiled looking up from beneath the brim of his old hat at Harold Hermann. "I like to keep one back, case I got to buy my breakfast in jail." He winked. "Old habit I guess." He stacked the remaining coins into two even piles on the bar and turned to the barkeep. "Clarence, keep an eye on these for me, will you partner? I'll be back for 'em in a minute."

Clarence nodded with mock seriousness as Everett stepped away from the bar and strode purposefully towards the sitting men.

Bruce Shotwell was watching Everett intently. It didn't help; he still never saw it coming. A lightning-quick swing of Everett's huge paw connected squarely with the center of Shotwell's face.

"I hope his head aches as bad as mine when he wakes up." Everett nudged the unconscious man, sprawled like a rag doll in the sawdust, with his foot. "He'll sleep pretty good for awhile I reckon. Damn that felt good. I believe my own head feels better now."

Bruce's stunned companions made no move to help their fallen comrade. They kept a wary eye on Everett.

Mr. Hermann, rocking with mirth, picked up Everett's money and handed it to him as Everett examined his knuckles for signs of wear and tear. Detecting none, he took his eight silver dollars and slipped them into his pants pockets; four in the left and four on the right.

"Reckon I better get something to eat 'fore I start drinking. Other'n that, I think business is closed for the night." He pushed through the batwing doors into the fading light of the setting sun. Gonna be a hell of a cool night, he thought as he headed for Mr. Hermann's hotel and a hot supper.

The Bancroft Hotel, named after the original owner, served free beer with meals to those who would drink it. It was a strong drink, dark and musty, smelling from the over-abundance of hops preferred by Mr. Hermann's cousin, who made and shipped barrels of the foul-smelling stuff over from Boise. To Everett, the dank liquid was like honey. Before his meal arrived, he had consumed three large tumblers and was on his fourth. The plate of steaming potatoes and vegetables and a platter of beef, burnt crisp and black was soon set in front of him. He was already feeling the glow of the elixir he had consumed.

A half-hour later, he rose unsteadily, satisfied he hadn't insulted the cook. The other guests seated nearby were not disappointed to see him weave his way out of the dining room and onto the street. Standing erect but a bit infirmly, Everett looked for his next destination. There were five saloons in this town, and he had nine dollars. Let's try that one. He stumbled off the wooden sidewalk into the dusty street heading toward the lighted Lucky Steer, across the road.

"That malt 'ol Hermann puts out is pretty handy if'n a man wants to get drunk cheap," he commented out loud to no one in particular. "Wonder if you can get it for breakfast too?"

Pushing aside the batwing doors, Everett swung into the place like a man familiar with such establishments. Several drinks and two dollars later, he decided to move on in an effort to find more interesting company. A couple of hanger-oners, hoping for a free drink, tagged along, trying desperately to be friendly.

"Git you two. Go find someone else to support your habit. I'm taking care of myself tonight, and I don't need no help spending my money."

He sauntered into The Dollar, a smaller dive filled with smoke and noise. There were only eight or ten cowboys, but they filled the small room with their stink and boisterous yelling, each trying to overcome the other with noise and laughter. Everett plunked down a silver dollar, the third since he had eaten.

The greasy unkempt bartender snatched it up quickly and held it to his chest. "What'll it be, partner?"

"Whisky. What's all the ruckus about?"

"Nothin'. They's like that every night. Practically the same bunch every night too. Guess they just like to hear some noise after being out all day where there ain't nothing to hear."

Suddenly, a crash filled the room as two men started swinging at each other. Someone bumped into Everett just as he lifted his glass to take a sip. The entire contents splashed to the sawdust floor.

"Care for another one?" the bartender asked quickly to take advantage of the situation.

"What the hell you talking about," Everett shouted. "I ain't had the first one yet. Since you don't seem inclined to control them yahoos, I believe you're obliged to repair the damages."

"Not my fault, mister. If'n you can't hold your liquor better'n that, then there's a charge for another drink, and the faults all yourn."

It was too noisy to argue, and Everett wasn't about to drop another dollar on this bar.

Back outside, he heard the tinkle of music coming from the Primrose. He recalled they had a piano over near the wall and stairs leading up to a second floor indicating there might be women there, too. Stepping once again into the dusty street, Everett headed unsteadily towards the brightly-lit hall.

All the lights in the Primrose suddenly blinked once, and then went out just as he stepped up onto the wooden sidewalk. Then, pain penetrated his alcohol-soaked brain, a blinding pain that traveled on steel rails up the back of his neck, to meet and finally to crash into the other railroad train traveling in the opposite direction in the vast space in back of his eyeballs. As he lay on his back, Everett caught a glimpse of Bruce Shotwell grinning down at him and holding a bar or club in his hand. The pain in his head and the alcohol in his system worked together in robbing him of will and Everett slipped into unconsciousness.

"No doubt he's gonna live," Doc was bending over Everett's prone body, " although I've seen men take hits like that before and not make it. He's got a pretty severe concussion, and probably a skull fracture. He'll be lucky if he ain't laid up a month or better."

Everett could hardly make out what Doc was saying. Who you talking about Doc? No words formed on Everett's slack, dry lips, as he lay immobile.

Mr. Hermann stormed into the room. "Caught the son of a bitch. He snuck back to his place and was grabbing stuff so's he could hightail it out of the county."

"He in jail?" Doc inquired.

"Not yet, we just got back. He's trussed up in back of the freight wagon. Wanted to check with you first and see if old Everett was still alive."

Of course I'm still alive. Take more than a bump on the head to kill me. He lay still and pale.

"Say, Doc, when'd the sheriff say he was coming back?" Harold asked. "This town's going to hell these last two days. First, Everett bringing in that dead boy, then Moss finding out it was his nephew got kilt and getting all upset; now here's Everett getting his egg cracked. We need Tom to stick around more, and I'm for asking the council to insist on it."

"Couldn't agree with you more, Harold. Fact is, this is a mighty stretched-out county, and Tom could use a couple of deputies to help him. Don't forget we've still got that other fellow, what's his name? — Neil somethin' or other—to worry about, too. He's still running around out there somewhere."

Ya'll can sure depend on my help to catch that damn skunk. Everett wasn't giving up. They'd have to acknowledge him eventually.

"I'll go back and get Shotwell settled in the lock-up so's Tom can talk to 'em when he gets back," Harold said. "Ought to be here 'fore long. It's near noon now."

Near noon. I got six dollars to spend yet tonight. How come it's noon already. Everett made an effort to turn on his side. Pain shot through his head as he strained to move.

"Look Doc, I seen him move his hand," Harold said, staring at Everett.

"Might be coming out of it," Doc mused as he pulled up an eyelid and peered into the limpid, unresponsive pool of Everett's eye. "Some folks recover pretty fast with this kind of head bashing. The trouble is, if they wake too soon, there hasn't been enough healing. It can cause them to suffer awful headaches until they mend some on the inside. I just hope he lays still for three or four more days."

Bruce Shotwell, tied up tighter than a schoolgirl's diary, lay in the back of Hermann's freight wagon. His mouth was dry with fear. He had never locked horns with the law before. That is to say, he had never been arrested.

They're gonna hang me sure. That thought had preoccupied him ever since Hermann and the citizen posse had captured him out at his shack hours ago.

Men approached the wagon, but the high sides obscured his view. In his mind's eye he could see the heavy hemp rope they were carrying. Bruce suddenly became a Christian. Closing his eyes as tight as he could so as to block out any light or the sight of his executioners, he started praying and sobbing, slobbering spittle down the side of his face as he begged his maker for mercy. Hearing the commotion in the back of the wagon, Mr. Hermann and his companions peered over the sides. The sight they beheld set them all to laughing, further aggravating the panicked prisoner. Bruce had wet himself, out of fear and the fact that he had been held trussed tight for several hours.

"Let's get 'em in jail 'fore he shits hisself too," someone yelled.

Another man climbed up on the driver's seat and drove the short distance to the little jailhouse. When the wagon stopped, the tailgate dropped with a crash, again startling Bruce who by now was reduced to a quivering lump. Rough hands grabbed him and threw him to the ground.

"What the hell's the matter with you, boy?" one of the men who had been in the posse demanded. "Cut that damn whining and blabbering. We ain't gonna hurt you, but you're gonna have to wait in this here jail till the sheriff has a chance to talk to you 'bout that pinch bar you whacked Koons with. You near killed him. Can't have crazy people like you getting away with that kind of treatment on folks."

"He's gonna live?" Bruce stammered. "That means I didn't kill him. The bastard hit me when I wasn't looking. He had it coming." Bruce was decidedly braver than he had been ten seconds ago. "They don't hang you for knocking out folks." He was almost euphoric in his relief that there would be no hanging. A couple of days in jail was all.

"Aw shit. Lock this idiot up. Get him out of my sight." Doc whirled in disgust and headed back to look in on Everett.

Everett strained to open his eyes again, but the light was too intense. He had struggled upright which caused him intense pain, only to find he couldn't hold his eyes open. Muttering, he asked aloud, "Where the hell am I?" He reached and felt the soft down cover over his legs, and the straw mattress underneath. "In bed?" His perplexed mind still couldn't grasp enough facts to sort out his confusion.

Gingerly, for it hurt to move even his arms, he felt his face and head with both hands. Thick stubble coated his cheeks and chin, and a heavy bandage swathed his throbbing skull. "It was that there Bruce Shotwell that hit me," he whispered hoarsely. "I remember now. Snuck up behind and hit me with somethin'.

"Didn't I hear Doc and Harold Hermann talking in here just a few minutes ago? Wonder where they got to?" The strain of sitting up and the heavy pain in his head caused Everett to slump sideways and drift into an exhausted sleep, his questions unanswered.

Doc, upon finding Koons slumped over, called for help and got him stretched flat again. "He'll make it, all right," he said to the girl who helped him.

Everett didn't wake up for another twenty-four hours. Rested and hungry, he requested food of the towheaded boy sitting beside the bed. When the boy returned with the food, he said, "Sheriff wanted me to call him the minute you woke up, but you oughta eat first. Doc says we got to get some grub into ya 'cause ya ain't et' in three or four days."

Everett squinted to focus on the boy. "Go along and call the sheriff. Might's well get the show on the road. I got to get back to the ranch and outta this town. Seems like they treat folks a little rough around here."

Everett was just wiping a little dribble of chicken soup from his stubble chin when Sheriff Tom Carpinelli made his appearance.

Carpinelli looked born to his job. He was well over six feet tall, straight and lean as a ramrod. At 49 years old, he looked ten years older with his snow-white hair and mustache carefully trimmed. "Mr. Koons, I'm Sheriff Carpinelli. Just call me Tom. Everybody does. Doc told me what he could, about you bringing in Mr. Moss' nephew and all, and about the beating you took last week."

"Last week?" Everett interrupted. "How long have I been here, Sheriff?"

"I think three days, might be four, but today's Monday, and you been sleeping all weekend. As I was saying, Doc, he was trying to save you the trouble of having to plow the same ground again being's how you're pretty stoved up yet, but I got to hear your version. Feel like talking? If not, it can wait."

Everett waved and nodded indicating that he felt strong enough to talk.

"I got Shotwell in the jail, but I can't hold him much longer. It don't pay anyway. I think he likes it in there, because we got to take care of him and feed him and such. Worthless cur."

"Go ahead and let him go then," Everett said. "Quick's I get so I can stand, it's gonna be payday. Wouldn't want him forgettin' me. We hit one another often enough, sooner or later, he's bound to give it up."

"Doubt you'll get the chance right away. He was packing to hightail it out of here when they caught him. He's got kin over in Montana somewhere. I 'spect he'll be wanting an extended visit with them." The sheriff pulled a stiff-backed chair over to the bed, sat down, and continued, "Listen Everett, about Browning, you sure that it was him with Randall Alsman out at your place?"

Everett recounted the events that led to his being in town these past several days. Since he had never seen the outlaw who got away, the only way he could identify him, he told the sheriff, would be by his voice. He had heard him clearly in the stillness of the early light as the outlaws had approached the house intent on their morning mischief. "Jacob heard his name mentioned, I never did."

With the report completed, Sheriff Tom Carpinelli stood and shook Everett's hand. "I'll be going out to the ranch in a few days. I'd like you to go out with me if you've a mind to linger a couple of more days and get your strength back. Been meaning to drop in and say howdy to the widow Mead and Jacob for a while now. How they getting along, outside fighting off outlaws?"

"They're gettin' by, Everett said smiling. "Fact is, young Jacob is heading back east for some schooling in a few days. His ma and me will run the place ourselves till he gets back, but for sure we'll miss 'em."

"Fine boy," the sheriff said with a thoughtful nod. "Turned out to be a fine boy. And after what Jess put him through you'd a thought, he'd a turned sour or mean like his pap, but I guess some folks is just born meaner 'n hell and some, well," he gestured with his hands as if to say he didn't understand people, " they just ain't. You go ahead and rest now. I'll come by day after tomorrow and fetch you home."

CHAPTER 4

Neil Browning was terrified when he heard the shot explode underneath his horse's hooves. Randall, arms flailing, his face a red splotch, had burst from under the bridge in the gathering light, and crumpled in a heap.

Cold, stunned nerves, and terror caused Bruce to lose control of his bladder and he pissed himself as his big horse, startled by the gunfire, whirled and galloped off, not needing encouragement from his rider. Neil had expected to feel a bullet penetrate his back with each second. He hunched low, attempting to make himself a smaller target, thankful for the growing distance and hopeful that his companion's horse, now running riderless and aimlessly, would attract the shooter's attention.

Four days later, horse and rider, exhausted by the grueling indirect route through the back country, Neil slunk into Boise, Idaho, using every shadowy alley he could find to avoid being seen. Darkness had covered the city for more than three hours by the time he dismounted and tied his horse behind his mother's house. Out front in the street, he heard an automobile chugging by.

Neil's horse perked up his ears, nervous at the unusual sound of the puttering horseless carriage, the whites showing in his eyes. Neil grabbed the nag by the nostrils, squeezing cruelly. "Shuddup, you," he whispered through clenched teeth.

He had left home just a week ago, he and Randy. They were going to look for some work or excitement over toward the west. They planned on scouting out Ontario, over in Oregon, until what looked like easy pickings showed up.

Now Randy was dead. Neil was sure of that. The frightening image of Randy's demolished face floated in front of his eyes in the darkness. Neil's mind diagnosed for the hundredth time the reason for the disastrous and sudden turn of events. It wasn't Neil's fault at all. It was that damn Jacob Mead that killed 'em, he thought. Must'a had a gun hid under the bridge. "I'll make the son of a bitch pay for that," he whispered. "I'll kill that bastard if it's the last thing I ever do."

His thoughts moved to the money. A cowboy, quite drunk, had revealed to Neil, in the strictest confidence of course, that there was a ranch twelve miles east of town, owned by a family by the name of Mead, and they had more money than they needed. Neil and Randall had done some scouting around, and were heading out to the Mead spread when they happened on Jacob Mead heading into town. They hid beside the trail until he passed and then followed him. "This is almost too easy," they had agreed between themselves as they prepared to trap their quarry.

After following Jacob to his destination, they simply sat and waited. It was a small town, and he wasn't liable to slip out without them. When Jacob finished his business and mounted his horse, Neil and Randall were standing in front of Falk Mercantile. Neil looked right into Jacob's eyes with a bemused sneer when Jacob's horse, startled by a passing horseless carriage, reared, nearly throwing his rider.

Taking Jacob had been easy. They had simply ridden up to him in a gallop with Randall slightly ahead. As Randall passed and distracted Jacob on his left, Neil passed on the back right of Jacob and hit him on the back of the head with a stout stick he had picked up for just that purpose.

"Yes sir, I am a natural born leader." Neil had bragged at the time. He wasn't so sure now. Randall was dead, he didn't get any money, and now he was going to have to face his ma and Aunt Tess, Randall's ma. Fear softened his steps as he glided through the shadows towards the back of the family house.

Boise, Idaho, in 1906 was by most standards of western towns a prosperous city. A center of commerce, with a good north-south graded road, and the Union Pacific Railroad switching yards, Boise was destined to become a great metropolis. Churches, saloons, blacksmiths, mercantile stores, schools, and the like were in sufficiently plentiful supply to take care of Boise and the surrounding smaller towns a hundred miles distant.

Into this bustling community in 1886 had been born to Elmer and Martha Browning an infant named Neil Browning, brother to Elmer Jr., and their sister Verna May Browning.

By the time Randall was born, Neil had already established himself as a willful child. Elmer Browning Sr. died in 1889 at the age of 39, leaving the mother to raise three children on a clerk's pay. Not an easy task in that time, but she managed to keep the family together and fed, with some help.

When Randall Alsman was born in 1888, his mother had been generously helping her husband's sister with the raising of the Browning cousins in spite of their own hardships. After all, they were family.

As the cousins grew, they spent a great deal of time together and their mischief grew with them. It was a constant battle to keep them in school, especially Randall, who seemed to have no ambition other than to be gaming with older boys and young men at the saloon. Neil had his own set of problems, having developed a mean bullying personality that caused him to intimidate anyone smaller or weaker than himself. He seemed to have a sixth sense when it came to smelling out victims. Not surprisingly, both became well acquainted with the local law enforcement establishment by the time they reached their late teens.

Neil entered the old clapboard house through the back door, careful of the loose board near the stove. That board could wake the dead if you hit it just right. He quietly entered the loft bedroom.

"Mother's been looking for you. Where you been?" Elmer Jr., almost invisible in the dark, was propped on an elbow in his bed.

Not caring to get into it with his older brother this late, Neil chose to ignore the question. He would face mother in the morning.

"Police come by," Elmer said sitting up. "They talked to mother, and she left with them." Tilting his head in question, Elmer asked, "Is Randall with you? Because if he's not with you, then it appears something's happened to him." Neil remained silent, so Elmer continued. "Mother came back home after about an hour, and now she's over to Uncle Jep and Aunt Tess' place."

Panic filled Neil's heart. "You shut up, you twit. And don't tell Mother you even saw me, you hear?"

Elmer sighed. He wasn't afraid of his little brother, and this wasn't the first time the police had come to talk to their mother, and subsequently Neil, after a day or two's absence.

Dog tired from long days in the saddle, Neil nevertheless bolted out of his bedroom after grabbing a handful of necessaries and a carpetbag to pack them in.

His horse, nearly spent, refused to gallop as Neil flogged him with the reins in a futile attempt to speed him up. His luck was holding, though, and he fled safely.

He had traveled one hundred and twenty miles in less than five days. His rear hurt, and he had to find some place to hole up until he could get some help; then he was going back, getting that money, and taking care of that "damn Mead kid." Neil considered his options. His best bet was some of his friends right in Boise. Danny Davenport would like to get in on a big killing like this. "Yeah, it'll be a killing all right in more'n ways 'n one," Neil said bitterly.

Danny Davenport listened to Neil Browning with deliberate interest. Danny was both big and small at the same time. He was nearly six foot three inches tall, but you could almost close your hands around his skinny waist. His height and lack of weight had always been a cause for teasing, and even worse, it caused his inability to get a job.

"Can't take a chance with ya, young fellow. Ya might break if I was to try 'n work ya hard, and hard work is the only kind we got around here." He had heard that excuse or something similar ever since he dropped out of school seven years previously. Forced to live by his wits, Danny was ready to try almost anything.

"Danny, listen, I'm forming a gang. I got a lead on some big money up in Boomerang. Only thing, they don't want to give it to us so, we gotta take it. I got it all scouted out."

The dingy saloon smelled good to Danny. He had been forced to stay away for over a month because he had no money. Neil's offer of a couple of beers was much appreciated.

"Randall in on this with you?" Danny wasn't especially fond of Randall. In the gang, usually there was honor among them, but Randall had once stolen three bucks from Danny, and Danny never forgot.

"Naw, he chickened out. Listen, you in or out. Come on Danny boy, this is the big one we been talking about forever."

In a few hours, Neil had his gang. No one turned down the offer. He was a good salesman.

Willie Frey was riding double with his brother Ed, and while he wasn't totally sold on this adventure, he would not only follow Ed anywhere, he also didn't want to be left out of anything that promised mischief, adventure, or the kind of money Neil was talking about. As much as anyone in this gang, Willie resented rules. He especially hated the rules at home that had dominated his life.

Willie looked like a small copy of his brother. Both boys wore clothes that had seen too many washings. The patches on their pants covered almost the whole of the original fabric. Willie's pants as well as his shirt had belonged to Ed three years earlier, and they weren't new when Ed had gotten them. Both boys were of fair complexion and average build.

Willie was 14 and Eddie 20. When Eddie was about 14, he had broken his lower leg jumping into a swimming hole. His father thought money spent on a doctor was wasted money and as a consequence Eddie walked with a slight limp.

The Frey boy's father, Ormond Frey, had come out to Boise with nothing but an ambition to succeed and the will to work day and night. And succeed he did. Through a discipline of thought, word, and deed that brooked no nonsense, he had acquired considerable wealth. As his six children came along, he applied the same strict rules of discipline to them that he applied to himself.

In addition to being a stern disciplinarian, Ormond Frey was a selfish father. Other than strapping his children for perceived wrongs, he paid them little heed. He provided shelter, but there were no other signs that this was indeed a wealthy family. Whereas neighbor children would have pennies to spend for candy or trinkets, the Frey children might as well have been born into the poorest family in Idaho.

A short while later, five young men left Boise, heading north towards Emmett. They had plans to cross the Payette River and travel down-stream sticking to cover to avoid drawing attention. They should make it to the Mead place in just a couple of days, and "It shouldn't be no trick to clean up that kid and his ma. Maybe less than an hour." Neil had assured his companions they could get an extra horse along the way. Isolated farms and ranches had provided him and Randy with mounts before, and under the cover of darkness there was no chance of getting shot, he guaranteed.

Willie shifted his weight to get a better grip of the horse. "Hey Ed, stop a minute, will ya? I gotta piss."

"Sure, runt. Hop off." Ed Frey eased his horse up next to a boulder and Willie slid off, rubbing his thighs in relief. "Hey Neil!" Ed called out to the rider some distance ahead.

Neil came trotting back. "What's wrong with the runt?"

"Aw nothing, he just has to take a leak. I ain't et all day, none of us has. We gotta round up some grub 'fore I faint plumb off this horse." Ed squinted at the hot sun, which had begun its decent in the western sky hours ago.

Danny Davenport and Pat Brackett, also riding double, cantered up to Ed and Neil.

Pat Brackett slid off his horse and adjusted a stirrup. Tall, dark-complexioned and muscular, Pat Brackett was reluctant to work at a regular job. He usually supported himself by preying on beautiful women; however slim pickings of late prompted him to consider Neil Browning's offer of easy money attractive. And so he found himself traveling with the same boys he had hung around with during his brief days in school.

"Where's the runt? He fall off your horse, Ed," questioned Pat.

"Naw. We's just thinking about getting something to fill our guts. Neil here's fixin to tell me how that's gonna get took care of. Willie's over yonder takin' a leak. Here he comes now."

"We're gonna go hunting fellas," Neil announced.

"Hunt, with what? We ain't got no guns," Ed said dejectedly. He and Willie, courtesy of their skinflint father, did indeed have no guns.

"Can't let a little thing like that stop us. You do the hunting, I'll do the shootin'." Neil had figured all along to just shoot a cow somewhere along the way, another of the tricks he and Randall had devised in their younger mischievous days together.

The gang spread out away from the hard-packed road and started looking for signs. Within minutes, Ed was motioning to Neil to come running. Neil, intent on his own search, wasn't aware of Ed's frantic waving until a rock pitched by Ed landed at his horse's feet. Glancing up, he saw Ed and Willie crouched in the sage brush gesturing frantically, pointing beyond Neil's field of vision. He looked for Danny and Pat. They were nearly out of sight off to his left in the tall pungent sage.

If I get a shot, they'll come a running, Neil thought as he dismounted and headed for Ed and Willie.

Pat and Danny, startled by the booming discharge of Neil's rifle in the stillness of the afternoon, aimed their horse toward the sound. Reining up in a cloud of dust beside the carcass, they dismounted and joined in the gleeful celebration like young children about to have a picnic.

Neil started directing his comrades to gather wood, bleed and butcher the cow they killed, and to set up a crude camp. Chores were well under way when, without warning, they were startled by a booming voice.

"What the hell you boys doing on Double Bar X land?"

As unexpected as the voice was, none of the gang could tell which direction it came from, and like a covey of quail, they panicked and ran into the trackless semi-arid desert.

Willie, his heart pounding like a trip hammer, ran right into the horse and the rider who startled them so unexpectedly.

Instinctively the cowboy grasped the frightened boy firmly, then dismounted, hauled him into camp and called for the rest of the gang to come back in and face him.

"We gotta go back," Ed whispered to Neil, as the boys reassembled in a dry creekbed a hundred yards from camp. "He's caught my brother."

"Shut up, damn it; we'll get him back. Just let me think," Neil ordered.

After a moment he said, "Pat, you and Ed just go walking back up there, but wait some, so's Danny 'n I can circle around. He'll likely be expecting us to give up on account he's got the Runt. When you can, distract him somehow. We'll come in and jump him."

Slipping through the lengthening shadows, Danny and Neil moved quietly and cautiously out of sight. Ed and Pat waited a time, then started heading back toward where they had last seen Willie and the dead steer.

"Hey mister!" called Eddie Frey. "Don't shoot. We come to get my brother. Can we come in?"

The old cowboy called back reassuringly, "Come on in, son, ain't no one going to hurt ya. Come here and let me get a look at ya."

As the two young men approached, the man studied them closely. "You youngsters oughten ta' be out here killing other folk's cows" he admonished the three apparently contrite young men while he looked around the area nervously. "Where'd 'yer pal get to? They's another one with you, ain't there?" His grip on Willie's shirt collar tightened noticeably while he scanned the area. "I thought I seen another one running off into the brush with ya."

Pat stood, his heart beating furiously, looking down at the toe of his worn shoes. Ed, equally terrified, stared at his little brother in the big cowboy's grasp. He was supposed to create some kind of diversion, but he just stood there quivering. Willie looked at his friends with hope that they would get him away from his captor, but they had no guns, and the cowboy had gathered up their horses when they panicked and ran.

Finally Pat answered. "They took off running with Ed and me. Ain't seen 'em since."

"They's two out there?" the cowboy questioned. He hollered out over the darkening prairie, "Come on in, fellers. I got your pals here. You might's well give up."

The unexpected roar of a rifle shattered the stillness of the descending night air and sent the cowboy slumping to his knees, pulling Willie with him. His eyes mirrored the stark terror of imminent and unstoppable death.

A second explosive bullet tore through his neck, tearing away flesh from spine to ear. A splash of blood, like a cup of coffee tossed on a dead campfire, washed over Willie's head and neck as he turned away in a reflex reaction to the death grip of the dying cowboy. The man made one last attempt to draw in fresh air through his shattered windpipe, failed and slipped away, his cowboying days finished.

Screaming in terror and soaked with blood, Willie fell to the ground. Ed and Danny were shocked, frozen in their tracks. They watched Danny and Neil appear like phantoms from behind a nearby sage bush, Neil's rifle still smoking from the discharge. Crouched and rolled up on his hands and knees, Willie continued his wild screaming, unaware of the others gathering around him.

Neil shoved his rifle into the scabbard on his horse's saddle and, exasperated at Willie's screams, delivered a swift kick to his ribs. "Shut up, ya little shit. Ed, you shut the runt up or I'll shoot him too."

Shocked out of his trance, Ed stooped to comfort his little brother.

"We got us another horse and a couple of guns, Neil declared. "Lookee here what this cowboy was carrying." Neil wrestled the pistol and gun belt from the body and retrieved a rifle from the saddle scabbard. He began rifling the saddlebags he had pulled from the man's horse. A silver flask containing a pint of whiskey appeared from out of the dead cowboy's necessaries. Neil twisted off the top, took a swig, and handed it to the whimpering Willie. "Here Runt, it'll put some iron in your belly."

In less than five minutes, the contents of the flask were gone. Bucked up by the fiery liquid, they all began feeling considerably bolder and their appetites, destroyed by fear, had returned with the fierceness that only hungry young men can experience.

It was getting darker by the minute, and the evening chill was beginning to settle over the prairie. Setting up camp near the dead cow, Danny, at Neil's insistence, had begun the job of cutting a slab of beef to roast.

"Hey, Pat," Neil called, "gimme your matches."

"I ain't got no matches," Pat replied. He called to his companions, "Hey, Eddie, Willie, Neil wants to start a fire, you guys got any matches"

Both answered in the negative.

"Shit," Neil burst out. "Someone go roll that stiff over and see if he's got any. Hurry up, it's getting cold."

Pat walked over to where the dead cowboy lay sprawled awkwardly on his stomach, a pool of blood spread from beneath his body onto the desert soil. He searched the dead man's back pockets and found nothing. Warily, he grasped the corpse by the shoulder and rolled the man partly over onto his back. A rumble of nausea surged through his guts as he slid his fingers into a sticky, bloody shirt pocket. He felt something—matches. He pinched them between his index and middle finger and let the body drop back to its original position and scurried back to Neil.

"Geezus, Neil, he was bloody as hell," Pat shuddered, as he gave the matches to Neil.

"Forget it, gimme the damn matches." Neil grabbed them and stooped to scratch a match on a rock at his feet. "What the hell!" he exclaimed, as the tip of the match crumbled against the stone. "These damn things are wet!" He examined the matches in the fading light as anger welled up inside him. The matches were blood-soaked and useless.

Danny walked up to Neil with a bloody slab of meat. "You gonna get a fire started?"

The rest of the gang had gathered what wood they could find in near darkness. They might as well have saved the effort because as the last of the light faded they realized that there would be no fire.

As the biting night chill descended, the cold, disheartened bunch of misfits attempted to hunker down for sleep. They were a gang much different from the confidant and cocky young friends who had set out from town just twenty-five miles and a few hours ago. Dreams of adventure and money were now replaced by fears of the dead cowboy lying sprawled on a bed of sand not thirty feet away, and of the consequences of being caught with a murder to their credit.

As the evening turned pitch black the gang was forced to sleep within a few feet of the murdered ranch hand. Perhaps shivering from shock as much as from the cold night air, Willie snuggled against his older brother's back and cried, not caring if the others heard him or not. They heard him. They were all feeling sorry for themselves, and fearful, cold and hungry.

Before dawn the next morning they were on their way

"We gotta get the hell away from here," Neil said. "Not likely they'll spot the body, but someone might see us if we hang around too long."

As light overcame the shadows of the night, the little band of bad boys headed directly west toward Boomerang and the Mead ranch. Luck was with them this morning because Danny, riding alone now on the dead cowboy's horse, discovered several pieces of dried beef jerky wrapped in a bandanna in a pouch on the saddle. Satisfying their hunger with the welcome victuals and with the rising sun warming their backs, yesterday's nightmare became a forgotten dream. Neil began to regale them with tales of the gold coins and greenbacks hidden on the Mead place that at this time tomorrow would be theirs.

By the time it got nearly dark, they were sitting on their horses in the small stand of trees that grew about a quarter of a mile from the Mead ranch. They watched a man, apparently doing chores go into the house and back out to the barn.

"No sense stumbling around there in the dark 'less we know where we're going." Neil decided they should stay back one more night and make some plans. "Them bastards tricked me once, and Randy got kilt over it. Ain't going to happen again."

"What?" Danny thundered. "You told me Randy chickened out. Now you saying he's dead? I never would of come if I'd a knowed that. What the hell you got us into anyway?"

The others watched in dismay as Neil suddenly struck Danny with a sneak punch that split his lip and drew blood. "You're in this, Danny boy! Ya hear me? You're in it up to your neck, you and the rest of ya." His jaw set, his cold hard eyes swept over the frightened youngsters, criminals no doubt, but with the exception of their leader not yet hardened in spite of their felonious deeds.

"We can take this place like a Sunday school. There ain't but two of 'em, the kid, and his ma. You want out, Danny? I'll put you out. Clear out of yer misery, that's how I'll put ya out. You understand Danny boy? Do I make myself clear enough for ya?" Neil's pistol was quivering in his hand within an inch of the shaken Danny Davenport's broken lip.

Totally cowed by Browning's viciousness, they drew back to find a place to spend the night and make plans for the next day.

CHAPTER 5

Everett sat on the edge of the bed that had served as his nest for the past week or so. With Doc's okay, he was leaving for home today. Sheriff Carpinelli would drive the buckboard. When Everett had been attacked, word had been sent out to Ma and Jacob, via Nels Hermann, not to expect Everett for awhile, that he had been hurt but would be healing and home within the week.

Everett drew in a breath of the fresh air wafting through the open window, crisp, cold, and mind-clearing. He looked out the window facing north. Miles of bright early morning sunshine swept across the sage-covered earth stretching beyond the edge of town. Low areas between him and the horizon contained pockets of silvery ground fog that would hold for about another hour, disappearing as the sun reclaimed the precious and scarce moisture from the desert air.

Everett loved this time of year. A hard worker all year long, the coming of fall was his chance to rest and gather strength for the next spring and summer's backbreaking chores. He was especially appreciative this fall, having had the comfort of a steady job with the Meads, who treated him like family. He had been knocking about the territory for twenty-five years without much direction, working some here, some there. There was always work available for a good handyman and cowboy. He had even tended bar for awhile in Caldwell, thumping his share of unruly drunks. Nothing else, however, had satisfied him as much as helping the Widow Mead and her son, Jacob. Everett was happy to be going home.

Someone knocked at Everett's door. "Come on in. It ain't locked."

Tom Carpinelli filled the frame of the door, nearly touching the transom. "Bad news travels fast, Everett. There's been a killing over near Emmett. Quick as I get you home, I'm to join up with Hiram Quinabe, town marshal over there. He asked me to help 'em sort it out."

"Who's kilt?" Everett asked, sitting up straight on the bed.

"One of the Double Bar X, riders. Buzzards found 'em, first, then one of the hands found 'em. 'Pears he must a stumbled onto some rustlers. There was a dead steer and signs of where they tried to get a fire started. Gunned the rider down in cold blood and left 'em to rot. Yolanda, down at the central telephone office, hailed me this morning not more'n twenty minutes ago with the news."

"Damn, don't that beat all. Listen Sheriff, whyn't you go ahead and take care of business. I can wait another day or get someone else to take me out."

"I'll take you," The sheriff reassured him. "I'm wanting to check on the widow anyhow. Got a lot of years of watching out for invested in her. Won't stay long, and I know you're anxious to get back. Quinabe's young but he's a good man. He's probably got the matter solved already anyway. He'd appreciate me not taking credit for any of it if he can clear it hisself. And if he ain't solved it by the time I get back, he'll appreciate the help that much more. You got your gear together?"

"No gear to look out for, just the buckboard and what I'm wearing. I generally travel light when I expect to be back by sundown the same day I left."

"All right," he chuckled, "I'll fetch my horse and your rig and meet you out front of the hotel in half a hour."

Everett cautiously swung his legs out of bed, reached for his pants, and commenced to dress. A wicked pain wracked his head and eyes at the effort. "Whew!" he exclaimed. "Weaker'n I thought. That son of a bitch, Shotwell, better be in Montana like the sheriff said, 'cause that's where he's gonna light when I catch up to 'em." He finished dressing and carefully descended the stairs to the lobby, deserted except for the duty clerk. "Come to settle up. What'd I owe ya, young feller?" Everett asked the pale young man, who was wearing a wrinkled white shirt with a string tie. His trousers looked like they'd been slept in too.

"Morning, Mr. Koons. Let's see, you paid for the one night. That was Thursday, a week ago. Today's Friday, so you owe for a week that'd come to three and fifty. No charge for your meals. Mr. Hermann said you ain't 'et nothing but soup 'n hardly enough a that ta keep a bug alive."

Everett counted his remaining cash onto the counter. Six dollars. I'm missing a dollar, he thought. Nope, here it is, in my shirt pocket. Well, except for one rotten apple, this town seems pretty honest. Could of been robbed, laying in the road like I was, for who knows how long.

"Thanks young feller, here's four dollars. I've been well took care of, don't want no change. Listen here, I want you to fetch this two dollars down to the livery stable where they took care of my rig and horse. Will ya do that fer me?"

"Sure Mr. Koons, anything else. You got any bags you want me to carry?"

"Nope, just me and what I got on s'all I got. You take care now, ya hear?"

"Yes sir, Mr. Koons. You take care of your ownself, too."

Everett strolled out the front door and into the bright sunlight. He had to squint his eyes almost shut to dampen the pain caused by the sun's brightness.

Tom Carpinelli was just dropping the team's hitching block when he noticed Everett. "Not too late to haul up and stay another day, Everett. Might do you good."

"Naw, I want to get back. I'll rest better in my own bed." He settled his hat over the bandage to break the sun's rays. That helped some.

"All right, old timer, it's your funeral" the sheriff said sympathetically. "Climb aboard and sit, I'll do the driving, and if you get feeling too poorly, I talked the livery out of a bail of straw so's you can lay back if you need a rest."

With the sheriff's help, Everett managed to get himself seated on the high seat of the old wagon. The sheriff had tied his own mount to the back.

"Looks like it'll warm up right nice 'fore noon," Carpinelli stated as he flicked the reins across the backs of Everett's team.

Willie Frey, his worn clothes wrinkled and filthy from two days of traveling and sleeping in them approached the ranch cautiously. He had been scared out of his wits ever since he left sight of his companion's hiding place in a stand of cottonwoods nearly a mile back. He had just stepped onto the bridge crossing the creek below the ranch house when he heard a shout.

"Hey, you, what you doing 'round here?"

"Oh!" was all the startled Willie could utter. He froze in his tracks.

"What's the matter, ain't you got no ears?" a man standing near the barn yelled.

"Sorry, m-m-mister," Willie stuttered. "I'm lost. I seen your outbuildings and thought you might help me out. Please mister, I been out all night."

The man trotted to where the quaking Willie stood petrified with fear and introduced himself with a reassuring and friendly smile

"G'morning boy. Where'd you come from and who might you be?"

Stuttering badly, Willie replied "W-W-Willie Frey, from over at Boise. I got separated somehow from my brothers last night in the dark."

"You need to come on up to the house and get warmed up. You probably ain't had no breakfast neither has ya?"

"No sir, seems like I haven't eaten in a long time." Willie's fear was beginning to subside as he followed Jacob. He glanced up at the ranch house where friendly smoke curled from the chimney. Looking at Jacob's back he felt a little guilty, knowing that this man, who appeared to be about the same age as his brother Ed, would be dead before noon. The plan called for Willie to scout the place for guns, extra folks and anything else he could find that would help the cause. The lie about being lost from some brothers was thought up to allow all the other outlaws to approach unopposed——if he handled it right.

Willie, growing more confident by the minute, appeared to age about two years, if Jacob would have turned and noticed. Still a small boy, he had somewhat matured on the streets of Boise and had gotten himself noticed a time or two by the law. His father had taken care of the law, and Willie too, with generous applications of the razor strap. Nothing in this world exceeded Willie's fear of his father with that razor strap in his hand.

"Ma," Jacob announced as he entered the kitchen door, "this here's Willie Frey, lost boy. Found 'em down by the bridge just a minute ago. Got lost from his brothers. Willie, this here's my ma, Miz Mead. Think we can rustle up another settin', Ma?"

"Land sakes boy, where'd you come from?" Ma fussed with wiping dust from Willie's worn jacket. "You look plumb miserable. Poor little critter. Take him out back, Jacob, and the both of you wash up. Don't look like you been very friendly with a bar of soap for awhile, young'un." Ma began grabbing down platters and utensils for the three of them while the boys went to clean up.

When they returned, she barked a friendly command, "Sit," and began spooning heaps of food onto their platters. The flask of cold milk promptly disappeared as they washed down biscuits, gravy, eggs, and bacon. "Jacob, when'd that Hermann boy say Everett'd be back?"

"Not exactly sure Ma. Might be a couple a days yet."

Willie took that bit of news in with a satisfied sigh. There were only two of them, just as Neil had promised.

"Now tell me, young'un, where you from so early in the morning, and where was you going so late in the day?" Ma asked. "Your family from around these parts?"

Willie, happily engaged in satisfying his raging hunger, didn't appear to be avoiding the questions, he was just busy eating while she was busy questioning. Ma smiled to see him eating so eagerly.

When they finally pushed away empty plates, Willie was in full control of himself. The terror of the killing of the cowboy, and the misery of trying to sleep on the cold desert floor for two nights without cover, were distant memories, not worth considering.

"Ma, I got chores to do," Jacob said. "Willie, you want to come with me? Quick as I get done in the barn, we'll saddle my pony, and we can go look for your brothers."

"Let him sit and rest till you're caught up with your chores, Jacob. Poor boy's been up all night. I 'spect you're pretty tuckered out, ain't ya, boy?" Ma asked the boy kindly.

Willie yawned and appeared to be fighting heavy eyelids. With the good food in his belly and the warm cook stove at his back, he was having a difficult time staying awake. He nodded drowsily in answer to Ma's suggestion and watched Jacob depart to his chores.

"Now young man how about telling me how you came to be lost," Ma said, taking Jacob's seat at the table. "You wander off in the dark from your brothers, or was it the other way around, and they lost you?"

"Not real sure, ma'am," he said, looking away from her prying eyes. "We was riding double, me and my brother Ed. I had to get down and go in the bushes for a few minutes, and when I got done, I couldn't seem to find my way back out the same way I went in. I called and called, and I could hear 'em answering me back, but they just kept getting farther away. It was like we was all turned around with echoes or something mixing us up. Next thing I knew, it was dark and I couldn't hear 'em no more. I just sort'a wandered all night mostly. I was too cold to sleep, and my stomach hurt something fierce from being so hungry. Sure do want to thank you and your boy for helping me out and feeding me 'n all." Willie mumbled the last few words.

His eyes were closing drowsily as he fought to stay awake. Ma watched as he involuntarily laid his head on the table and slipped into a deep sleep sitting in his chair. She turned to her own chores and let him sleep.

"Jacob'll be here in a minute, youngster. He's coming to fetch ya to your brothers." She shook Willie gently by the collar. Nearly an hour had passed, and Jacob had tied his pony outside and returned to the barn. "Wake up now. Laws, look at your neck. You ain't washed it in a month. We can't send you back to your ma looking like that."

Willie did not respond. She stepped to the stove where a kettle of water simmered and wet a clean cloth in the hot water, soaped it with her good lye soap, and gently washed the black accumulation from the sleeping boy's neck.

"My land," she exclaimed as the cloth turned deep red in her hand. "Oh my land, that's blood. Terrible lots of blood." Shaking Willie vigorously she asked the half conscious boy "You been hurt, Boy. How come you got blood all over you?"

"Blood?" Willie mumbled. "It ain't mine. It's the dead man's blood." Willie snapped fully awake, mumbling half aloud and in full panic. "I think someone got hurt. Wasn't me that done it, honest."

"Done what boy? What you got yourself into? Where'd this here blood come from?" Ma stepped back from him apprehensively.

Willie's eyes widened in fear as he realized what he'd said.

"Are you gonna tell me what this is all about?" she insisted, wariness in her voice.

Looking for an escape, Willie jumped up, sending his chair flying backwards with a crash. Ma reached for him, just as he swung around looking for the door, his elbow clipping the woman sharply in the ribs and throwing her off balance. She gasped in surprise and grabbed for his worn jacket to keep from falling over the chair, the sharp pain of a broken rib robbing her temporarily of breath.

"Jacob! Help me Jacob." She was groaning more than screaming.

"Shut up. Shut up, damn it?" Willie reached for the heavy frying pan drying on the stove. He closed his eyes as he swiped at her blindly.

She raised her arm to protect herself from the blow taking the full force on her forearm. Bone snapped, and she fell halfway across the room as Willie threw the pan at her and bolted out of the kitchen, through the front door and away from the house. The pan glanced off the floor and spun harmlessly into a corner.

Ma was struggling to her feet just as Jacob came rushing in. "Ma. What happened?" he exclaimed, rushing to her side

"It's that Willie. Go fetch him. He took off out front." Her gasping voice alarmed Jacob, but she continued. "He's into something dreadful Jacob. Go catch him, I'll be all right."

Jacob, not realizing his ma was seriously hurt, and not comprehending exactly what she was saying, raced out the door he had just entered. His horse was tethered and waiting. Willie was just reaching the wooden bridge when Jacob hit the saddle and whirled his horse toward him.

Willie had run less than thirty steps past the bridge when he looked up and spied four riders approaching a few hundred feet away. Jacob reached Willie and dismounted almost on top of the boy, throwing him to the road.

"Help Ed, help me!" Willie's terrified screams pierced the still morning air.

Jacob stood over the fallen boy. "What the hell's come over you, Willie? Who's that you hollering at over there? Them your brothers?"

Willie groveled, whining in the dust of the road, the cockiness and bravado knocked out him.

Jacob was going to repeat the question when a shot was fired by one of the four horsemen. The round glanced harmlessly between the legs of Jacob's horse.

Another round followed that missed Jacob, but caused him to take action. He reached down, grabbed Willie and pulled him up, just as the gunman squeezed off a third round. Jacob threw Willie up on his horse and mounted behind him racing for the barn's open door. Inside the darkened structure there was safety.

"I don't know what the hell's going on here, but I got to get up to the house and help Ma." Jacob dismounted and pulled the strangely quiet, ashen faced Willie off the horse, his eyes wide and staring. The fight was gone from Willie.

"Mister, just let me s-s-set." Willie sunk weakly to the floor of the hay barn.

"Get up, you. Get up and get your ass up to the house!" Jacob demanded.

A shot rang out as the four riders surrounding the barn door blocked the morning light.

Jacob rolled for the cover of the thick hay recently stored for the coming winter. Another wild shot hit the rafters. Jacob thought yearningly of Pa's guns in the house. He was defenseless in the barn. Scrambling to the hay chute, he threw himself to the lower floor of the horse barn and tack room ten feet below, just as the gunman fired again. The bullet, feeling like a white-hot brick, hit him just above the belt, piercing his side. Robbed of breath, he spun as he slipped down the hay chute out of control, landing on the back of his head and neck. Still recovering from the recent head bashing by Neil Browning, the fall was too much of an insult to his skull and his eyes rolled up, locked open in convulsion.

"Willie. Runt. You all right?" Ed was shaking his little brother.

Willie groaned with pain as his brain released its deadly messages of a concealed wound. A smoldering spark of pain began burning out of control. "Ed, I think I'm hurt. He hurt me when he threw me up on his horse. I can't hardly breathe."

Neil meanwhile looked down the chute at the prostrate Jacob, lying with eyes staring blankly skyward. "That's for Randy, you bastard," Neil hissed, as he fired at the figure lying still on the floor below. The bullet passed harmlessly through Jacob's coat and shirt leaving a scratch on his ribs. Jacob didn't flinch and appeared to Neil to be dead.

Neil's attention returned turned to his gang. "The money's up at the house guys, let's go!" He turned to Willie, half sitting, half lying in the hay. "Get up, Willie. Ed, get him up. What's it like inside the house, Runt. You see any guns?"

Ed grabbed his brother's arm and started to lift the boy. A gut deep groan escaped Willie's throat, along with a trickle of blood from the corner of his mouth.

"Willie. Neil, come're. Willie's hurt." Ed felt wetness in the fabric of his brother's coat. Withdrawing his hand, he was horrified to see it soaked with blood. He suddenly realized that his brother was shot, and that it had been Neil who had recklessly fired the only shots.

"I'm freezing, Eddie. Help me, I'm so cold," Willie gasped, his face turning a sickly shade of blue-gray."''

"Neil, you bastard, look here what you done. You shot my brother."

Willie sunk back to the floor of the haymow, frothy blood gurgling from his dying lips. "Quit, Ed. Don't do it." His voice was barely audible. "These are good people. Don't do it."

"Come on Willie, let me help you get your coat off. You're gonna be all right." Ed struggled to pull the coat off the stricken boy. As Willie's injured arm slipped out of its sleeve, the extent of the damage leaped from its hiding place. Willie's upper arm was shattered, his punctured lung had collapsed, and bloody bubbles pumped from the bruised, fleshy hole in his chest with each beat of his heart.

"Leave him sit and let's go." Neil slashed at Ed's head with an open hand then turned and motioned Pat and Danny to get going. Ed sat with his brother's head in his lap as cold sweat ran from the Runt's scalp and the final beats of his heart faded from his body.

"Dammit it, Ed, I said leave him. Get your ass outta here!" Neil stomped toward the open barn door where the frightened Pat Bracket and Danny Davenport had stopped and waited. The crashing explosion of a heavy gun sent Pat Bracket sprawling back into the shadow of the hayloft. He lay dead in the hay, his heart shattered his eyes frozen wide open.

The sound of the booming gun penetrated Jacob's brain. His mouth was dry, and the pain in his head was thunder and lightning fighting each other in a wild match that both appeared to be winning. He rolled onto his stomach and retched his breakfast while he struggled to understand what was happening. That wasn't thunder, he realized, that was Jess' old-fashioned buffalo gun. He glanced back toward the ceiling and the hay chute he had tumbled through. He recalled dodging pistol shots. He remembered Willie and the four men astride horses blocking the sunlight coming through the barn door. Jacob stood shakily against a beam, and the world began to slow its spin. With no other weapon available, he reached for the three-pronged pitchfork, not sure what good it would do, but he felt naked, empty-handed.

The barn was a two-story affair, with the south end of the lower floor only fifty feet from the house. The dugout entrance extended more than twenty feet toward the kitchen door. If I hit the door running, I can make it to the house 'fore they know it. He peered out the door just as a grubby man with long blond hair shot five or six times at the house, emptying his guns. There was no return fire.

"He's shooting Ma," Jacob screamed as he leaped the berm at the entrance and charged around the corner of the barn, running madly to the wide door of the hayloft and scattering the outlaws horses, ground-tethered in front of the barn.

Neil Browning was reloading his pistol when Jacob, pitchfork in hand, came around the corner of the barn door. Before the man could close the chamber of his gun, three tines of cold steel pierced his gut as Jacob plunged the pitchfork completely through the gunman's body.

Jacob, his mind in chaos and his body pain wracked, was only dimly aware that the wounded figure in front of him was somehow familiar. He leaned over him and snatched the man's pistol, then glanced at another gunman hunkered down in the hay, cradling Willie's head in his lap. He appeared harmless, holding boy's head so tenderly, tears streaming down his dirty face. Jacob then turned his attention to the one man who was standing, gun in hand. Slowly, the gun slipped from his fingers to his feet. He sank, vanquished, to his knees. Their leader lay bleeding in the hay; their adventurous spirit was shattered.

"Don't shoot, mister," was all the man could say.

Jacob scooped up the rest of the outlaws' weapons and ignored the probability that they would flee. Clumsily he ran to the house to check on his mother. Inside, he found that the feisty Widow Mead had just finished her struggle to reload the antique, fifty caliber, breech loading buffalo gun Pa had kept and used long after more modern cartridge rifles were popular.

"Ma. You all right?"

"Oh, thank God, it's you, Jacob. I thought you was dead." She grabbed him with one arm and hugged him fiercely.

"I just killed a man, Ma," he gasped. "I killed him for sure. I stuck him clear through with the pitchfork!" He was shaking like a leaf. "I think it's that same fella that busted me up last week, the one that was gonna kill me."

"You done what you had to do, son. It can't be helped. It ain't your fault."

"Son, my arm's broke. Broke bad. That young'un done it with the fry pan." She groaned as she tried to shift the broken limb to a more comfortable position. "Ya got to help set it and then get to town and have Doc come and try 'an fix it proper."

Mother and son patched wounds and comforted each other, while warily watching the barn in case the remaining outlaws recovered enough to try something else against them.

A piercing scream came from the barn causing them both to jump with fright, followed by absolute silence. "Some one must'a pulled that pitchfork outta him," Jacob whispered as he crouched near the door armed and ready for another a go around. As time passed and it remained quiet Jacob turned his attention back to his mother.

He was feeling totally helpless as he eyed her shattered arm when suddenly Danny Davenport, with his hands raised, appeared at the kitchen doorframe.

"Git!" Ma commanded.

Jacob reacted by aiming the leader's confiscated pistol at the man's heart. He was barely stopped in time by his mother's hand on his arm.

"Please, help us," implored the devastated outlaw, "Neil's still alive, and he's hurt bad. Real bad."

"Haul him somewhere," Jacob said, grim lipped, his eyes blazing with fury. "We ain't lifting a finger to help that son of a bitch. You show your head in that door again, and it's gonna get blowed off. Now get off our place 'fore I start shoot'n." Jacob threatened him with the cocked pistol, daring him to argue.

Davenport backed away cautiously and stumbled down the steps. With the outlaw gone, Jacob turned to his mother, "Ma, I got to get you some help for that broke arm. But how?"

"Go fetch Doc, Jacob. I'll be all right for a spell here by m'self."

"I cain't leave with that crew in the barn, and they're all too hurt to go." Jacob glanced toward the barn. It was deathly quiet.

The morning haze had lifted and the sun was beginning to bear down on the earth and its inhabitants. Jacob had gotten Ma's arm splinted as best he could and convinced her to rest until he could figure out what to do about the outlaws and about getting her help. He looked up at the old mantle clock. Ten minutes past eight o'clock. He found it hard to believe that it was only little more than two hours ago when he had spied the troubled boy walking across the wooden bridge leading up to the ranch. Two hours had produced two dead men, a gut-ripped outlaw, and two young men who would probably pay for the morning's mischief with years of their lives spent behind prison bars. There was no question in Jacob's mind that one of the men would not survive. He had seen the pitchfork tines go completely through the man's body.

"I know they got to git sooner or later," Jacob remarked to Ma hopefully. He sat near the kitchen door with all of the guns he had taken from the outlaws and a couple from his pa's old arsenal. If they wanted to leave, they were welcome to get. But if there was any movement in the direction of his house, there would be hell to pay.

Blood seeped from Jacob's side. He had been too excited and distracted to notice it before.

He was somewhat startled when he pulled up his shirt and his saw the wound. Spasms of pain were starting to build in that fire-pit of blood and broken flesh. He and Ma were in more trouble than he had reckoned. With his mother's arm shattered, possible broken ribs and with his bullet wound and the blow he took to the head, he wasn't sure if they could fend off another attack.

Jacob tried mightily to stay alert but found himself dozing in the warming midmorning air. He was awakened by the sound of hooves clopping across the wooden bridge and he watched through the door as the outlaws retreated from the Mead ranch.

Willie and Pat Davenport's bodies were tied across the saddles of two separate horses, while Ed and Danny were mounted double on a third. The double mounted riders were leading the horses carrying the dead boys, and the mortally wounded Neil.

"How far's town, Neil?" Danny asked apprehensively. To quit the Mead ranch, Danny had scoured the tack-room for straps to bind Neil to his horse so they could escape. "How long you think it'll take to get there?"

Neil was in excruciating pain and hardly able to comprehend Danny's question, but as the only one of the bunch to have ever ridden in this country, his knowledge was needed if they were to escape or to get help.

"Come on Neil, you got to tell us how to get to town."

Neil finally gasped out directions, pointing painfully toward the west and the road to Boomerang.

Everett had had to lie down in the back of the buckboard after about an hour and a half of traveling. Sheriff Carpinelli stopped and spread the straw bale for Everett, and he waited for nearly an hour while his passenger slept. Now fully rested, they were both seated atop the high wagon seat enjoying the late morning sun as it built its temple of heat.

"I reckon this here is about the best time of the year, don't you think, sheriff?" Everett remarked with a contented sigh.

"Yep, you can say that again, old man. You got all your haying and such done?"

"Well, sure Sheriff, 'bout like you got all your sheriffing done."
Everett pulled off his hat and wiped his forehead with his sleeve. "You
got that matter of the murder over at Emmett, and I got mending and
patching to do to get ready for spring plowing and planting. It's an easy
time 'a year, but there's always work a-waiting."

The miles rolled under the wheels unminded by two friends passing
time and distance in peace.

Everett suddenly sat straighter in the seat, looking intently ahead.
"Here, Sheriff, look yonder. What's that look like?" Everett had spotted
four horses that even in the distance appeared queer to his eyes.

"Looks like someone riding double—and that ain't sacks of grain
over the back of them two horses." Tom half stood and handed the reins
to Everett. "Can you handle the team. This looks like trouble. I'd feel a
lot more comfortable if I was on my own horse."

"Go ahead, I'm just fine. Never knew a day I couldn't handle a team."

Sheriff Carpinelli eased off the buckboard, untied his horse, and
mounted. With an easy gait, he headed toward the strange group, wary
of trouble. With his hand on the butt of his pistol, he approached the
riders.

By the time Everett drove up to the knot of men, the sheriff had
frightening news for him.

"They shot up the ranch, Everett," Carpinelli said in a flat tone.
"'Pears Ma and the boy are all right, but they sure as hell tore up this
bunch. See that poor bastard bent and strapped in his saddle?" The
sheriff pointed to the man folded nearly in half in his saddle. "Gut stuck
with a pitchfork. Guess Jacob done it to 'em. You better get on home. I'll
have to turn back and get these fellas to the jail. Soon's I get back to
town, I'll send Doc out. Ma or Jacob might be hurt. These fellas weren't
sure."

"Sheriff, this bunch didn't have anything to do with that killing over
at Emmett, did they?" Everett asked.

"Damn, Everett!" The sheriff exclaimed. "You're one hundred percent right. I'll bet next month's pay they did it." Turning to Danny and Ed, then eyeing the brand on the horse the wounded Neil Browning was strapped to, Tom Carpinelli asked the suddenly pale riders, "You two been over near Emmett the last couple of days?"

Chapter 6

Fall was upon the high country a little early that year. By the tenth of October there were mornings that boasted of frost lingering late into the forenoon shadows of buildings and trees until the sun was able to wrest the cold from its protective cover.

Jacob and Everett worked silently in the still early-morning coolness, cleaning stalls, milking the two milk cows, and readying Harry and Chub for the day's work. Winter wheat was nearly all sowed, save for about four or five acres that Jacob intended to finish plowing and sowing before he was to leave for the East.

The docile team of black draft horses munched their hay patiently as Jacob threw the heavy harness on their backs. The pain in his side had subsided to where he hardly noticed, except when he twisted as he threw the harnesses. He wasn't about to ask Everett to do his job, though. Throughout the weeks of healing, neither was willing to admit any weakness to the other. Everett, as proud and uncomplaining as his young employer, forked manure into the wooden wheelbarrow, ignoring the frequent twinge within his head that felt often like an imprisoned demon kicking his brains out in a vain attempt to find an exit route.

"Think we'll be seeing the sheriff soon?" Jacob asked as he threw fresh straw into the stall.

Everett continued forking manure for several minutes before speaking. "Reckon we will. Them three hooligans is supposed to have their trial next week."

"Between being laid up then and waiting for the law to settle up with that bunch, I'm gettin' kind'a anxious to get on that train in Boise and head east." Jacob pulled a chinch strap tight and tied it down as he asked, "You think they'll hang all of 'em?"

Everett stopped throwing and leaned thoughtfully on the dung-fork. "I wouldn't be surprised. I reckon they'll be includin' that Browning fella too, if he don't croak from what that there pitchfork done to 'em." He glanced at the tool leaning against the far wall. "Damn, I thought he'd be dead by now, way you run him though. That guy's tougher'n leather." Everett forked the last of the pile in the wheelbarrow. "Let's get up to the house and get breakfast. We got us quite a bit work left to finish up a'fore you go traipsing off to New York."

As usual, Ma had prepared ample victuals. While Everett and Jacob discussed the day's chores ma fluttered around the kitchen filling plates with delicious food and cups with steaming, strong coffee.

"Jacob, you sure you're feeling good enough to work behind that team today? I don't want that gunshot opening up again," she said, her voice filled with concern.

"Don't worry Ma, me and Everett is gonna share the work. I'll plow awhile, then he'll take over."

"Miz Mead, I tried to get him to take it slow." Everett said, shaking his head. "Might's well talk to a hoe handle. But I think we got it worked out so's the work'll get done and his pride won't be hurt none." Everett chuckled.

"Everett, I swear if you hadn't already proved how hard your head was I'd thump it for you again, 'cept I know it'd just be a waste of time," Jacob retorted jokingly. "Ma, don't listen to him. Fact is, he practically begged me to help him. It's him that's still hurting. I'm healed perfect."

"Don't care which one of you claims to be healed the most, you're both a couple a knot heads, and I got to take care ya," she declared holding her bandaged arm up for them to admire.

They were indeed a sorry bunch, running the ranch with all of their hurts and complaining to no one, for there was no one to complain to, and the work had to be done. "Don't work past noon boys, please. I want you to come in and rest like ya done yesterday. Ain't nothing on this ranch that's got to be done so bad that you need to go out and hurt yourselves a-doing it."

"We promise to take it easy, long's you do, Miz Mead. Your boy 'n me think it'd be plumb foolish of you to work yourself to death trying to tend to us."

The sun rose as it did every day, its warming rays wiping away the night chill. Jacob and Everett headed back to the barn.

"It just don't pay to argue with your ma, does it?"

"Naw, it sure don't," Jacob said in a serious tone.

"Well, we might's well get to it. I'm heading over to Cottonwood Canyon; there's a couple of heifers that should have dropped their calves last night or the night before. Been keeping an eye on 'em. Need to get 'em closer in so's the coyotes don't bother 'em. You get more'n ten or twelve passes cut, get down, and rest the team and yourself, ya hear?"

"Hey. Who's supposed to be boss around here, you or me?" Jacob asked with a smile.

"Why Jacob, you forget already?" Everett swung gracefully into the saddle, grinning ear to ear." Shucks boy, you're the boss. I'll be back 'fore ya know it.

Jacob always did like to plow. Especially in the spring when hungry birds with babies to feed would sometimes fly right between his legs to get at the worms and grubs turned up by sharp angled plow.

But plowing in the fall had its own sort of pleasure. He enjoyed listening to the sound of the plow cutting the dry earth, kicking up light dust that smelled of the promise of a new year's crop.

The soil parted easily behind the strong team. Jacob walked in the furrow, guiding the plow in straight furrows 20 rods long. The draft horses knew their job as well as Jacob, and plodded stoically from one end of the field to the other. At the end of the return trip across the wide field, Jacob rested the horses and himself for about ten minutes. He was almost at the end of his second round when he spotted the sheriff trotting toward him from the direction of the house. He turned the team around to face the trip back. "Whoa!" The team stopped like well-trained soldiers and assumed a position of rest by lifting one hind leg in a slightly cocked position.

"Howdy, Sheriff," Jacob greeted the man warmly.

"Good to see you, Jacob. Everett about?"

"He'll be back directly. He's down to Cottonwood Canyon to fetch a couple of fresh heifers back up to the barns. Expected him back by now."

"I don't mean to alarm you none, Jacob, but I got some awfully bad news. I want you to get back up to the house, arm yourself, and stay with your ma. I'm going down and fetch Everett."

"What's the bad news, Sheriff, or do I have to guess?"

"It's that damn Neil Browning. Here we been waiting for him to die, then last night he come up missing. But not before he killed Mason Crabtree."

"I thought he was to go on trial in a few days."

"That there's what was supposed to happen—if he didn't die. Didn't look too promising for him to live. Why, even yesterday Doc said fever was eating him up. Had him lodged at the hotel with Crabtree guarding 'em. Couldn't expect much trouble, man as sick as him. Had him trussed up in the bed too. He must'a worked his way out of it.

"Poor ol' Mason Crabtree was a hell of a good man, well liked too. Somehow I should of took better care, but that damn Browning was so near dead…" the sheriff's voice trailed off and Jacob could see depth of Sheriff Carpinelli's grief. "You go on up and watch out for your ma. Remember what I told you, arm yourself and keep a close look out."

Jacob found his mother struggling with the Sharps buffalo gun again.

"Sheriff come by," Jacob said.

Ma handed Jacob the old Buntline pistol. "Here, strap this on, and don't go nowhere without you got it on."

She had managed to cock the heavy lever open on the Sharps, but was having trouble inserting the large cartridge into the chamber and balancing the gun at the same time. Jacob took it from her and slipped the bullet home. This rifle was accurate for up to a half mile, but it weighed over 14 pounds and you had to prop it between aiming rods to hold it still enough to hit anything

Looking west toward town, or to the south, they would be able to see a body coming for a couple of miles. If Neil Browning was planning on sneaking back out here, he would have to come from the north to take advantage of the barns blocking the view. Walking around the end of the barn could easily cover even that direction. There was no danger of being ambushed, but the sheriff's advance warning, and his being in the neighborhood, was a comfort. There was no fear of Neil, but as Jacob stated to Ma, "To tell the truth, I'd be happy to skip another meeting."

Since Ma was fine, Jacob went out to take the harnesses off the team and turn them out. He checked with Ma one more time. That old one-shot buffalo gun had a couple of companions in the form of a Colt forty-five, and a Remington repeater. Jacob strapped the Buntline to his leg and tied it down. They had ended up with a couple of good guns taken off the outlaws, and no one had ever asked them to give them back.

Jacob led the team into their stalls. Harry, as usual, led like a pet on a rope, while Chub, untended, walked right on into his stall. Each received a good ration of oats, and Jacob began rubbing them down, just enjoying the sound of the horses grinding the oats, and the smell and comfort of the barn.

Everett walked in leading his cow pony. "Sheriff's up to the house visiting with your ma. He don't figger we'll have any trouble, just wanted us to watch so's we don't get took by surprise." He pulled saddle and bridle from his horse and turned it out into the corral.

When he returned, Everett remarked about the hog leg Jacob had strapped to his leg. "That sure reminds me of the old days, when all the cowboys was carrying guns. Sure was easy to get shot in them days. It ain't been the same since about '92 or '93 when the law got so it was more bother to carry a gun than it was worth. Used to wonder about that. Didn't seem right. Hell, I carried a pistol from the time I was weaned, but I reckon they's a lot more cowboys living today on account of they ain't all armed no more. Just the same, you carry that thing until we're damn sure Browning is put where he belongs."

"We both ought to carry a gun, don't ya think?" Jacob asked. "What if Neil Browning catches up with you 'stead 'a me, then what. Would you take a crack at him?"

"Nothin'd pleasure me more," said Everett with a devilish grin. "But then again, if he don't never show up on this place, that'll be too soon. If he's dumb enough to stick his nose anywhere around here, he'll leave sticking his toes straight up at the moon, just like his cousin did on his last ride back to town. You can bet my paycheck on it."

Tom Carpinelli strolled into the barn chewing on a stalk of dried straw. "Miz Mead's mighty worried 'bout this here turn of events. One of you boys has got to stay with her, that is, within sight of the house, till this gets settled."

He turned and looked Jacob in the eyes. "I'm sorry, son, but I got to ask you to delay your plans again till we know what's going on. In the mean time, nothing's changed. We're meeting at ten o'clock Monday next and trying them two we got in jail. I expect ya'll to be there." He turned to Everett. "That means you too Everett, and Miz Mead. Shouldn't take more'n a day, maybe two.

"Then, when we've located Browning and got him corralled, we got to give him a trial. Soon as that's settled, then you'll be free to go," Sheriff Carpinelli said to Jacob. "She's anxious for you to get out in the world, see something, and get your education. At the same time, she's a bit skittish with that outlaw running loose."

"I ain't leaving, Sheriff," Jacob assured him. "Not now anyway. That waster shows up 'round here, Everett an me'll see he don't hold me up with no long trial, lessen they try corpses. Ain't that right, Everett?"

The older man nodded sharply. "The boy speaks the truth, Sheriff. If we see him, and he causes us any trouble at all, we'll likely take the opportunity to save the county the trouble of feeding and cleaning up after 'em." He emphasized his statement by snapping a twig he had picked up.

The Sheriff paused a moment, studying Everett closely. "Everett, I know how you and Jacob feel about Browning, but I don't want to have to be calling on you for killing him and having to arrest you for murdering him. Ain't saying don't kill him if you have to. Fact is, I'd rather have him taken alive. But if you can't catch hold of him without gunplay, any bullet holes in 'em better be in front. That way they don't ask so many questions back in town. Clear?"

"Clear as creek water," Everett said with a wide grin. "You staying for dinner, Sheriff?"

"No, I better not. Don't want to put no burden on Miz Mead, and besides that I got to get back and finish getting a posse together. Got a fella riding over to Emmett to fetch the marshal. Don't that beat all? Remember back when I's bringing you out, and I mentioned young Hiram Quinabe had asked me to help 'em with that murder over on the Double Bar X? Now here I am, needing to ask him to help me." The sheriff pulled his wide brimmed hat down snugly. "Listen fellas, I appreciate the invite, but I got to skedaddle. See ya'll at the trial next week. And ya'll keep an eye out for trouble, ya hear?"

Jacob and Everett finished rubbing down Harry and Chub and turned them out into the corral with Everett's riding pony. The horses recognized that their day's work was done early again, and they showed their appreciation with a good roll in the fine powdered dust.

Jacob had been getting stronger every day, and if Everett hadn't insisted on both of them going up to the house for victuals and rest, he would have been inclined to repair a few tools or harnesses while enjoying the warm Indian Summer afternoon.

After chow, Jacob and Ma retired to the parlor. Jacob lay on the davenport half-asleep, mulling over the escape of Neil Browning while his mother fussed with her sewing basket. "Ma, what would you do if you was him?" he asked quietly. "That Browning fella I mean?"

"I sure wouldn't head for home," Ma answered. "The law would look there first. Coming out here to the Mead ranch would be just as dangerous. Nope, if I was him, I'd hide under their noses. What was it Everett told us about Browning having some kind'a kin in Boomerang?"

"That's it Ma!" Jacob exclaimed excitedly, sleep banished completely. "That there's where I'd hide if I was desperate. He said, Browning's cousin had an uncle there in town, an important kind a fella. What if that man was uncle to both of 'em, he'd be obliged to take in his own kin, wouldn't he?"

Jacob got up and in stocking feet quickly crossed the room to Everett's door. It was open an inch or two and he could hear Everett snoring softly. "Everett," he called. There was no reply. "Everett, wake up."

"Eh. Jacob, that you. What's wrong?" Everett's cracking voice called.

Jacob shoved the door wide open and said excitedly, "Everett I think I know where he's hiding."

"Who. Who's hiding where?"

"Browning!"

"How the hell do you know where he's hiding?" Everett grumbled, sitting up slowly in bed.

"Sorry I woke you up," Jacob said defensively. "You sound a little grouchy."

"Don't fool with me, Jacob. How come you think you know where he's hiding when the sheriff's in town getting a posse together and they're gonna comb the whole county?"

"We figured it out. See, I was laying there talking to Ma," he motioned at the couch, " and thinking what kind of chance he'd have trying to get away if he was sick and hurt so bad he couldn't ride a horse. He'd need a place close, and someone who wouldn't turn 'em in right away. Then Ma mentioned that cousin of Browning's. I ain't saying this place is perfect, but it's the only place to hide real quick, and it's right in the middle of 'em. They likely wouldn't even think to look for him in such a place."

Everett squinted his eyes in thought and said, "Sounds as if it might make sense, but who'd take him in. How'd he get there. And why in the hell would anybody take in a son of a bitch like him in the first place less'n they's kin or something?"

"That's it!" Jacob exclaimed. No one would take him in 'cept kin. Didn't his cousin have kin, an uncle that lived there in Boomerang?"

"By damn!" Everett declared, flinging his wool blanket off his legs. "I'd bet a month's pay, hell, two months', you're right. Mr. Moss is uncle to that young feller I kilt under the bridge, and him and that Browning was first cousins to one another."

"What're we supposed to do about it?" Jacob asked. "If he's hiding in town and they're all out riding looking for him, no telling where he'll get to, 'less he just holes up to heal."

"Sheriff said Doc looked in on 'em just yesterday, an he was running a fever then, so he's likely still mighty sick. He'll more 'n likely hole up till he gets his strength back. Best if I go into town and talk to Tom, whilst you tarry by your ma and see to it she's taken care of."

"Damn it Everett, there you go taking charge again," Jacob said forcing a scowl on his boyish face.

"Shucks, boy. Ain't that what you was planning on telling me to do?"

"That don't matter if it was. I'm supposed to the make the plans around here."

"Sure that there's the truth," Everett said, gesturing wildly with his hands. "And you have, I just anticipated 'em to save you working your knot so much. Just trying to help. You're the boss. Yes-sir-re-sir, you're the rooten tooten shooten boss of this here outfit. Any body argue 'bout that'll have to answer to me."

Jacob leaned against the doorframe. "Everett?"

Everett looked at his boss sheepishly, "Yes, sir?"

"Go saddle up and git."

Christian Moss lay awake looking at the shadows on the ceiling. Sleep often came only with great difficulty, and just as often was interrupted by the ghosts that haunted him. I must be dreaming he mused silently. I thought I heard Abby down in the kitchen. No, of course not, he realized, as his thoughts began to mesh with reality. Abby's dead. Why won't she let me sleep?

He raised himself and sat on the edge of the bed. He shoved his feet angrily into his slippers and snatched the robe from the bedpost. Anger was one of his two constant companions. Anger at the death of his beloved Abby. Anger at his failure to recognize her frail mental state. Anger at Abby for taking her own life. No, not Abby. He couldn't be angry at his cherished one. She had been ill; it wasn't her fault.

For forty years, except for her private demons, they had been the most perfectly mated pair. His success in business had allowed them to retire and travel the world, a distraction he had hoped would allow Abby relief from the darkness she was haunted by. Instead, it provided her with the means to end her life one night by leaping from the deck of the *Provincial Princess* into the cold, dark waters of Biscay Bay off the coast of Spain.

Christian's sister Tess was the one person left in the world who still needed him. Jep, her husband, had suffered a crushing injury in a gold mining accident up near Cambridge back in '85, five years after he and Tess had married. That Jep had survived the accident was a miracle, that he could support his wife and son was an impossibility. Consequently, Christian had helped the family in the intervening years. Were it not for Tess Alsman, Christian surely would have followed Abby into the ocean on that fateful voyage.

But tragedy, his other frightful companion, wasn't done with Christian Moss, or with his sister. Randall Alsman, Tess' only child and Christian's adored nephew was killed, apparently while attempting a robbery of the Mead ranch. Tess wasn't handling it well, which wasn't surprising in light of facts that came up subsequent to Randall's death.

Aimlessly, Moss wandered downstairs in the darkened house, through the kitchen and into the formal sitting room with its heavy dark green drapes surrounding tall windows that looked down upon the little town. Abby had decorated the room herself. The walls were of dark oak with large dark oil paintings hung on various walls. Even the plush rug was dark. Christian had thoughts from time to time of changing the decor to lighten up the room but always abandoned the idea. He picked up a cigar and lit it. As he blew out the match, the darkness pressed in around him again except for the faint light from the gas streetlights and the glow of his cigar.

"Mr. Moss." A voice floated seemingly from out of nowhere. "Don't get riled, Mr. Moss. I ain't here to hurt ya."

Startled nearly out of his wits, Moss sat bolt upright on the edge of his chair. "Who's there?" he listened intently, "Who is that?"

"It's me, Neil Browning. Ya gotta help me, Mr. Moss. I'm sick. I'm hurt real bad and I ain't got no one to turn to 'cept you."

Moss strained to penetrate the shadows of the great drapes near a front window where Neil Browning had cleverly concealed himself.

"What do you mean sneaking into my house, you damn cur? Get the hell out of here. You hear me? Get out!"

"Mr. Moss, you don't understand," Neil said, his voice a high pitched whine. "I didn't mean for nothing to happen to Randy, honest. That damn Mead, he's the one that done it. Had a gun hid, he didn't give Randy a chance, not one damn chance. Don't ya see, it wasn't my fault."

Christian sank back into his chair. Exhausted from lack of sleep, and angry at the intruder, he grumbled, "I'm in no mood to listen to your whimpering. Just get the hell out of my house before I take the law into my own hands."

Silence filled the room until Neil spoke in a deeper, stronger tone. "I guess I didn't make myself clear, Mr. Moss." Neil stepped from the darkness, the gas light from the street gleaming faintly off the barrel of a pistol. "You're obliged to help me, seeing as how you 'n me's kin. Randy's my cousin, and you're his uncle. That makes us kin, and kin has got to help one another."

"You—my kin?" Moss exclaimed indignantly. "Not by a damn sight. No, by God, we are not kin!" He stood suddenly and strode purposefully to the gun cabinet.

Neil ran across the room and intercepted him, pushing the barrel of the pistol viciously into the older man's neck. In a hard-as-steel whisper, Neil threatened, "I pull the trigger this close to your ear, 'an you ain't even going to hear it."

Moss looked at Neil disdainfully. Even in the pale light he could see that Neil's long blond unkempt hair was knotted in a greasy mess from lying in bed for over a month. His sallow face was nearly covered by a scrub of a beard; his eyes, dark coals in sunken pits, were flashing from place to place in a look of anger, fear and confusion. Moss, with a great sigh, drew himself up, and with challenge in his eyes invited Neil to fire.

"If you're to kill me, get it done. I'll not hear the shot, but the whole town will, and you'll be doing me a favor, you son of a bitch. Go ahead and shoot, you cowardly bastard. Shoot!"

Neil, realizing Mr. Moss was right about the whole town hearing a gun shot, obliged him instead with a malicious pistol blow to the head, knocking him semi-conscious to the floor.

"Mr. Moss, I ain't feeling too good. I don't recommend you go upsetting me no more." He stopped as a wave of coughing wracked his body. "I think the best thing for you is to quit trying to argue with me and help me get out of town. I got to get back to Boise. My ma'll take care of me. I recollect you have one of them automobiles. I can hide in the back, and you drive us to Boise, that's all. Won't be no more trouble 'n that. Just get me to Boise, get me home, and you're shed of me."

Moss rolled to his back and looked up at the menacing figure standing above him. His head hurt with the worst pain he had ever felt. He felt the lump in his hair, and the slippery wetness told him his scalp had a serious laceration. Anger welled up in him again. Anger and tragedy seemed to dog him like old friends. No, old friends go home occasionally, these two just hung around like stray hounds looking for handouts.

"You want me to drive you to Boise?" he whispered. Why don't you just steal a horse and ride over there by yourself? Why bother coming to me?" Moss' mind was clearing as the pain subsided.

"I cain't sit a horse, I'm too stove up. That Mead bunch run me through with a pitchfork, and my guts ain't healing so good. 'Sides, like I said, you 'n me is kin. Who else I got to turn to?"

"Well, seems as if I don't have much say in what happens, so I may just as well drive you to Boise as lie here rubbing my sore head. The minute we get to your house, you are to leave my automobile. Is that understood?"

Neil grinned menacingly. "That's all I'm asking for, just a little help to get clear of this town. It ain't healthy for me here, with or without being gut stuck."

"You'll need patience. We'll have to wait a day or two, as I'm out of petrol until some is delivered. I'm expecting fifty gallons to come in by freight tomorrow."

"What the hell do you mean wait a day or two?" Neil shouted, his grin gone. "You fooling with me? What the hell is petrol 'er what ever you said?"

"Petrol is the fuel that makes the automobile go. We're not going to Boise without it."

"We ain't got time to wait for no petrol, we need to get outta here now, before the town wakes up and starts looking for me. You can just get a wagon and drive me there."

"Not in a manner that would help you. I don't own a wagon or buckboard, and thus I would need to contract a conveyance from the livery stable. Since I have my automobile, the liveryman would naturally want to know the nature of the dilemma that would cause me to abandon my auto and disturb him in the middle of the night. Have you a good story I might tell him. Perhaps we might tell him I'm forced to ferry a desperado to Boise. That would certainly satisfy his curiosity, don't you think?"

Neil paced nervously back and forth for a minute and then stopped, pointing the gun at Moss once more. "Mister, I think you're fooling with me, and I ain't in a mood to be fooled with. Maybe you think this ain't serious. I got to get out of this town pronto, and killing you, if you can't help me, wouldn't worry me none."

"I've already encouraged you to kill me, but so far you've only managed to give me the worst headache I've ever experienced. No, I am not fooling with you, on the contrary, I am quite serious about wanting you out of my house and gone. However, at your insistence, I will consider that circumstances force me to comply with your wishes, and to avoid further damage to myself, I will assist you. If Boise is your goal, the means to get there will have to be left to me."

He paused, waiting for Browning to respond. Neil, standing slightly stooped in pain, said nothing.

Moss continued, "If you will allow me to go to the kitchen, I'll pre-pare coffee or tea, and then we'll need to institute a routine that will allow us to further your plan of escape. Will that be satisfactory?"

Neil looked balefully at Moss and pondered his offer. "Can't let you outta my sight, lest you go running on me. How you gonna get me out of here and get the rig ready to drive too?"

"Not much trust in you, is there?" Moss said with a twisted smile. "I said I would assist you, and I will. My *word* is your guarantee. Your deliverance to Boise, God willing, is assured."

At that, Moss stood and slowly left the room. He could hear Neil as he began retching in dry heaves in the sitting room but he made no move to help him. Moss simply continued preparing strong tea for both of them.

Daylight found both men sitting, eyeing each other in cold silence. Christian Moss watched the glazed eyes of his guest with interest. Neil appeared awake, but was unresponsive and harmless. "I promised you safe delivery to your home," he said, knowing Neil was incapable of hearing him. "There, however, I suspect you'll find little comfort from either your family or the law." Moss had been talking to Neil for over an hour without a response from him. A man of his word, he would see that Neil would arrive home as promised.

A shout, horses' hooves, and men calling to each other suddenly filled the early morning air. Boomerang was alive with activity.

"He must'a stole a horse and run 'fer it," a voice yelled.

"Kin he ride, shape he was in last night?" questioned another voice.

Moss went outside and stood on the verandah listening and watching the activity in the center of the village, which was not far from the old Whitney House, his Victorian style home. Sheriff Carpinelli seemed to be holding a gathering near the small jail that housed his office. From his vantage point Moss could see the sheriff had gathered many of the town's male citizens. Harold Hermann, standing in a freight wagon, was waving his arms and shouting down at the crowd. They were all talking and shouting back.

The sheriff called to Hermann during a lull in the boisterous commotion, "Harold, you deputize who you want, and have 'em ready when I get back from the Mead place. Should be back just before noon, if'n I don't catch him out there. He's carrying a mighty strong dislike for young Jacob, and I kind of figure he might head that way looking to get even, damn fool that he is. And, get a holt of Butler and Doc and have 'em take care of Crabtree's body. I don't want Lottie Crabtree seeing him all busted up like he is. Damn, that Browning's bad." The sheriff shook his head sadly.

Christian Moss stood transfixed. Butler was the undertaker. His thoughts froze the blood in his veins. He knew of the death of his nephew Randy Alsman. Everett Koons had shot the young man in a robbery attempt. That perhaps was not entirely Neil's fault. He was present, and he was involved in the robbery, but he didn't directly kill his own cousin. He also knew that Browning and two members of his gang were involved in the death of a range cowboy and a young lad named Willie Frey but neither of those deaths were blamed directly on Neil Browning—yet. The pending trial that was promised if the outlaw lived would determine if he had any further involvement. This reference to Mr. Butler and Mason Crabtree frightened Moss because it could only indicate that there was another death for Mr. Butler to attend to. Was there another death to attribute to Neil Browning?

Returning to the parlor, he looked at the sick man sprawled in his setting room, hallucinating blankly on his chesterfield. "If you live, young man, it will only be long enough to face the hangman. It would be better indeed if you were to expire where you sit."

Moss' words somehow worked through Neil's fevered mind. Lucidity, a fleeting thing for him in these last weeks, brought back brightness to his eyes. "You ain't thinking I'm gonna hang, are you Moss?" he croaked. "No, damn you. Neil Browning ain't meant to swing from no rope. Ya hear me?" He began raising his voice.

"Hush." Moss said, stepping quickly across the room and shutting the door to the verandah. "You'll call the town up here yourself. I simply conjectured your future. You are, of course, in full charge of the direction your life will take. I stand here only as an observer and as an assistant under your command."

"Speak so a fella can understand ya, damn it. What the hell are you talking about?"

"I'm saying I will help you as promised. Beyond that, you're on your own."

"That means you're taking me to my ma in Boise, right?"

"You understand correctly," Moss said, nodding patiently. "Now rest. You'll have to trust me to the arrangements of your escape. I am concerned for myself in that I may be viewed as your accomplice should my cooperation be suspected. I have no wish to share your fate with you. You must agree, do you not, that you have complicated my life?"

"Just get me out of this town, and your complication ends, pronto," Neil sighed.

CHAPTER 7

Sheriff Carpinelli hailed Harold Hermann as he neared the jail. The Mead ranch was quiet and a normal routine prevailed. The three residents were healing well and all appeared in good spirits. Now that they were forewarned, Sheriff Carpinelli felt sure they wouldn't be taken by surprise. Especially in consideration of the condition Browning was in when Doc looked in on him late yesterday.

How in hell did he manage to overcome Mason? Carpinelli wondered. That fool should be dead as badly injured as he was. He shook his head in wonder as Hermann stepped out of the small jail. He dismounted and tied his horse to the old worn hitching rail in front of the jail.

"Got 'em all deputized and armed, Sheriff. They're over to the Primrose getting a bite. I told 'em to meet us here soon as you showed up."

"Thanks, Harold. How many wants to go?"

"Hell, every man-buck in town wants to hunt down that killer, clear on down to Mason's nine-year-old great-grandson, Matt. Anyway, we got thirteen good men, not counting you and me. Where you figuring on starting this?"

"Ain't but three ways he can get out of town. He can head north and try 'n cross the Snake up at Weiser, or he might head direct for the Snake west of here and try 'n cross into Oregon 'round Ontario. Or he can head south and try and get into Oregon through the Owyhee country, that there's the most desolate godforsaken country in the world. I pretty well covered east toward Boise and the Mead place, no sign of him in that direction.

"My bet is the Owyhee country" the sheriff speculated. "It had a fair reputation back in the 80's 'n 90's as badlands. Remember the Kindred gang that used to hole up out there? He's likely heard of 'em too. There ain't but a few dirt-poor dry ranches out there, kind of isolated like. He might find a sympathetic soul to take him in till they find out what trash he is."

Checking his gun again, the sheriff slipped it neatly into its holster and continued, "You can get lost in less 'n a half a mile in any direction out there even if somebody was a watching you. I might put my money on him heading there; then again, I might have to reconsider, just because right now, he's pretty damn desperate." The sheriff paused to think. He shook his head, "Geez-sus, Harold, I don't know which way to look. We'll just have to split up and each take a heading till we come up with something."

Harold Hermann's posse came directly across the road to the jail from the Primrose. "What's up, Sheriff?" Whiff Bass called. "We got us a good bunch, and there's some daylight left to burn if'n you ain't had no luck a-finding that bugger out at the Mead's."

Whiff Bass walked with the bandied swagger of someone who was much more comfortable aboard a horse than walking on a dusty street. His face was coated with about a week's growth of gray whiskers, and his old felt hat sat on the back of his head, allowing a shock of salt and pepper hair to hang into his eyes. His perpetual grin was nearly devoid of teeth.

The sheriff recalled how Whiff had come by his name some years previously after an encounter with a pet skunk. Bass had brought a kit home, orphaned by his trap line. It turned out to be half-tame after a fashion, and hung around Whiff's place for over a year.

One day, Whiff's old dog Hoot decided that he and that skunk could-n't live together anymore, and they commenced to fight it out right there in the front of the house. Whiff, hearing the commotion, came onto the two of them just as old Hoot was set to kill the little critter. Whiff grabbed the skunk in one hand and the coonhound in the other at the same time the skunk decided to save himself. Next thing you know, Whiff acquired himself a new name. He came hollering and running through the middle of town blinded by that skunk stink and rubbing his eyes because they hurt something fierce. Then he dove headfirst into the horses' watering trough. He had been called Whiff ever since.

Sheriff Carpinelli waited until the rest of the men gathered and smiled at the memory of Whiff and his pet skunk. Today was a grim day. A humorous thought was as welcome as water to a parched garden.

"Been out to the Meads," he said, pushing the brim of his hat back and wiping his brow. "He ain't there and I don't expect he's headed that way. I've been talking it out with Hermann and it looks like we'll have to split into three groups. Whiff, take Jose, Leroy, and Lloyd with you and scout over west of here toward the Snake. See if you can pick up any sign that he's made it to Oregon."

"Right, Sheriff. We can cover both crossings and ask a few questions around the settlement. Should be back a half hour after dark." Whiff and his men mounted. "See y'all 'round seven, seven-thirty at the latest."

"Good, but hold up a minute," Carpinelli turned to a tall, slender young man who was checking his revolver. "Ike, I need you to head north, up around Weiser. Keep a close eye out for sign. Who you want to take with you?" Without waiting for an answer, he continued, "Remember, all of you," he said, as he cast his gaze at the assembly, "this man is dangerous. He's not afraid to kill, and he's desperate to get away. 'Sides Crabtree, he's been involved in at least three other killings we know of."

Ike pointed out four or five friends to ride with him. "We'll get started pronto, Sheriff. That Mason was a good man, a damn good man. We all want that killer's hide."

"All right, Ike, you too Whiff, get started. The rest of you, we'll head down toward the wilderness south 'a here. I'm still thinking Browning's gonna want to get out of Idaho fast. He'd be able to get over the border 'round there with damn few folks around to question him. Harold, you gonna be able to stay in town?" Sheriff Carpinelli asked, turning to the big storekeeper standing on the jailhouse steps. "I'd just as soon you hung around here and keep an eye on things till we get back."

"Got plenty to do right here," Harold replied. "You be careful of that egg-sucking snake. He's liable to bite ya from ambush. You be back late tonight likely?"

"I expect so. We're none of us packed for a night on the prairie this late in the year, but it'll be after dark 'fore we get in. Sun sets 'bout seven o'clock now. We'll be in an hour or two after that. By the way, Harold, did you happen to check around town to see if any horses was missing or wagons or such?"

Harold hitched up his pants and said, "Yeah, I thought 'a that too. Ain't nothing missing. If he's run, he's afoot, or he's got a friend snuck in to help him. You ever think there might be two of 'em out there?"

"Damn, no, I didn't," Sheriff Carpinelli said, rubbing his chin thoughtfully. "Hey, Whiff, Ike," he yelled at the departing riders. "Hold up a minute."

The three leaders gathered, and the sheriff warned them of the possibility of Neil having an accomplice. With the warning, the three teams split up and headed out on their assigned missions.

Everett looked around at the small village as he rode in. "More saloons and churches than they's regular businesses," he mused to his horse. He pulled up in front of the Falk Mercantile store. Big Harold Hermann could be seen inside standing near the cash drawer, jawing with someone obscured by the piles of dry goods. A trip into town this late in the day was tiresome and caused a man to be mighty thirsty. Everett hailed Harold as he dismounted. Harold helloed back and hastily completed his business with his customer.

Sauntering out, he approached Everett with an outstretched hand. "What'cha up to, Everett? Late for you to be getting into town ain't it? You staying here tonight? I got'cha a vacant room if you was deciding too."

"Howdy, Harold," Everett said grinning at the brawny storekeeper warmly. "Ya might say it was a mite late to find myself just getting here. 'Spect I will be forced to spend the night. Mighty thoughtful of you to kick someone out'a my room. How'd ya figure you'd be needing a room for me? You some kind'a ghost reader or something?"

Grinning from ear to ear, Harold lead Everett across the road to the Primrose, but not before he posted Nels by the cash box with the admonishment to, "Watch close now, you're in charge, ya hear?"

"Yessir, pa, I kin handle it," the boy replied puffing his chest out. "Don't you be too quick a-coming back, I kin do it just 'bout's good as you."

"Good boy ya got there Harold," Everett said as he and Harold crossed the road.

"Takes after his father," Harold replied, appearing to swell with pride.

"Well then, maybe I better hold judgment on 'em for a few more years 'n we'll see if he really takes after you, in which case he'll likely go bad. Then again, he might just take after his ma, who everyone in these parts knows for certain is what keeps you in line and a-going straight."

"Everett, dog-gone you. How'd you get to be so smart and live so long. Beats me how you know so much an ain't got kilt fer it." The jovial storekeeper and hotel owner swung the batwing doors of the Primrose open and held them for Everett.

They sat at one of the round, felt-covered poker tables and held their conversation while the bartender brought them each a huge, frothy beer. Harold said, "Thanks Clarence." He flipped two bits on the table, picked up his beer, and blew the head off onto the freshly saw-dusted wooden floor. The room had the pleasant smell of cigar smoke, beer, and sweaty cowboys associated with most saloons. Everett loved the atmosphere and slouched deep into the wooden captain's chair and relaxed.

"Harold, I ain't said why I come to town, 'cause I been noticing there's lots of folks missing, and what I got to say might upset the apple cart."

Harold Hermann sat a little straighter and told Everett, "Near anyone who can carry a gun's headed one direction or the other a-looking fer that killer what done in 'ol Crabtree. Ya should'a seen the job that worthless bastard done on the defenseless old cuss. Couldn't hardly recognize his face. Doc helped Butler clean him up some so's his widow could look at him. But fact is there weren't much to work with. Just get the blood off, that there's about all they could do."

"Well, listen, Harold," Everett lowered his voice to a whisper. "The town's deserted right now, and from what Jacob an me's figured out, that might be a bad sign." He leaned forward and continued. "Jacob and his ma has calculated that if you cain't find Browning outside of town by dark tonight, ya better start a-looking fer 'em in town."

"Why's that?"

"'Cause he ain't never left town, that's why!"

Harold squinted across the table at Everett. "You think he's hiding right under our noses?"

"Yep, right in amongst the lot of ya."

Harold exhaled loudly. "Don't that beat a hole in the pond. Then, if they ain't caught him already, we'll likely have to turn this town inside out ta find 'em."

"Might not be that hard if you think about it like Jacob did."

"Why's that?"

"Jacob figured that if Browning's so stoved up he can't run, he probably cain't sit a horse neither. That's from what Tom told me 'n Jacob. So, what's that leave?"

"Guess he'd have to hole up someplace," Harold answered. " But who in the hell'd put up with him. I ain't noticed anybody a-yelling and a-screaming they was being held prisoner. And if he's that sick, how'd he manage to find a body who'd take him in volunteer?"

"The answer's plain as horseflies. How about Christian Moss?" Everett paused to let the idea sink in. "Moss is kin to the one I kilt out at our place. This here Neil Browning is cousin to that dead boy, and probably claims kin to Moss 'cause of it. Least ways that's what me 'n Jacob figures. He's hid right there." Everett nodded out the window in the direction of the Victorian house that dominated the town.

"Damnit, if you're right, we might 'a lost him already!" Harold exclaimed.

"You see him leave?"

"No, but early this morning I seen Christian standing out front of his place whilst we was forming the posse. He just stood there and didn't make no effort to come on down and see what we was up to. Shucks, I never gave it a second thought. Later, I guess I still wasn't paying too much attention, but I looked up and that big ol' automobile of his run right past my place maybe two hours or so 'fore you showed up. I didn't look to see if anybody was with him.

Harold leaned forward in his chair, his expression changing to one of alarm. "Hell, even if he had him hid in the back, that automobile is so big ya wouldn't see nobody. Generally he drives alone. Looked to me like he might be heading for Boise to visit his sister and her husband. He goes over there couple times a week since their boy was kilt.

"I was surprised to see him going by in that he'd been waiting for some petrol for a couple of days, so the darn what'ch-a-ma'call it'd run.

I got freight into my store right after noon, so likely his petrol came too. Let's inquire down at the livery."

They finished their drinks and left the Primrose, headed for the blacksmith shop and livery stable.

Sylvanus Ruse was pounding out horseshoes the same as he had been doing for the last 25 years. His broad back, thick chest, and brawny arms attested to his strength, earned from hammering metal into horseshoes and tools for more than a quarter century. He looked up as Everett and Harold Hermann entered the shop. With a grimy rag that he pulled from his back pocket, he wiped the sweat from his face and arms. "What can I do for ya, Harold?"

"Howdy, Sly. Hot in here, even for this time 'a year," Harold said, wiping a palm across his forehead. "You remember Everett Koons here, don't ya?"

"Sure do. Howdy Mr. Koons." The blacksmith proffered a gigantic sweaty paw.

"Howdy." Everett shook the man's hand and grimaced as his own hand was nearly crushed in Sly's grip.

"Some different than the last time you come by my shop, ain't it. I thought there was gonna be a hanging right then and there."

"Yeah, me too, for a little bit," Everett smiled a reply. "Anytime someone wants to throw a necktie party, I'm in favor of not being the guest of honor. I was right happy to refuse the offer."

"Listen, Sly," Harold said, "you seen Mr. Moss today?"

"Why sure, he was in here couple of hours ago. Met the freight wagon. He'd been waiting fer some petrol to put in that contraption of his to make it run. Took two five-gallon cans of it with him. Smells a little like lamp oil. I guess his rig burns it somehow. Don't know much about automobiles, as you probably guessed. Look over there," Ruse glanced towards the back of his shop and its clutter of tack, hardware and tools. "See them cans. They's his. I keep 'em for him. He claims it smells too much to store out at his place."

"Did he say if he was leaving town, or going over to his sister's place or anything?" Harold asked.

"Naw, he never said nothing much to me. We jawed a little just like we always do, 'bout the weather and such. Why?"

"Reason we're inquiring is, Everett here thinks Moss might know something about the disappearance of the fella that killed Mason. That kid Everett kilt was running with a cousin by the name of Neil. He's the bastard that kilt Mason last night. Now Browning ain't no real kin to Moss, but whatever Moss would do for one, he'd do for the other, just like they was brothers.

"I follow all that, but what you getting at, Harold?"

"Appears Mr. Moss might be mixed up with 'em, him being kin and all."

"I don't believe that for a second, fellas," Ruse said defiantly, his dark eyes blazing. "I've knowed Mr. Moss for years. It ain't like him to help a outlaw like that, kin or no kin."

Harold raised his hand defensively. "We ain't saying for sure he is or he ain't. Ain't even saying he wants to. But if he's being held against his will, he might be forced to help. You happen to see if he left Boomerang or did he just drive around a little?"

Ruse's face softened as he carefully thought about the situation. "I believe he left for Boise. Damn, I hope he ain't mixed up in this."

"Thanks, Sly. The sheriff'll be back in a couple of hours, in the mean time, keep all this under your hat. We'll let him go over to Mr. Moss' house for a look when he gets in. Come on over to the Primrose when you close, I'll spot ya to a beer."

"Yeah, thanks. I'll see you later, Harold, you too, Mr. Koons."

"It's Everett, Mr. Ruse," Everett said with a grin, emphasizing the blacksmith's last name.

Ruse chuckled and waved at the departing men.

As the sun descended in its final minutes of daylight, the warmth of the day escaped rapidly into the crystal desert air, inviting the early evening breeze to chill the earth and all its inhabitants. The few wispy clouds overhead hungrily soaked up the dying rays in blazing hues of red, gold, yellow, and gray. The mountains to the east, already crowned with an early dusting of frost and snow, glowed as pink as a school girl's lips, while to the west, towering rounded mountains became silhouetted hunchbacked giants guarding the sun's nighttime hiding place.

"It'll be cold tonight," Everett mused to his companion, as they sauntered towards the Primrose.

Harold Hermann nodded in agreement. Stopping in mid stride, he turned to Everett. "Sheriff could be heading in a mite earlier with this cold coming on like it is."

"Damn fool if he don't. They'll be ice in the bucket inside a couple hours, way it's cooled down."

"Look, Everett, I gotta help Nels close the store. You hungry yet?"

"Since you named it, yeah I could go for a bite. You got the same cook you had before?"

"What the hell you think? I married her near 20 years ago, I can't fire her now. She's just learning to get it right."

"That there was Mrs. Hermann doing the cooking last time I was here? Well, I never. Might lucky man is what you are, Harold."

"Well, she's actually too good for me," he said sheepishly.

"I know that."

"Hesh!" he said with a scowl, then smiled at Everett. "I'll meet you and Ruse over at the Primrose for a couple of brews soon's I get closed up. Then if you take a room at the hotel for the night, supper's on me. Time we finish eating, the sheriff and the rest of the boys ought to be gettin' in."

"That there's an offer I'll not turn down. Now it 'pears you're too good for me. Ah, but I'll learn to accept you, if you just let me get a-holt of some more of that dark ale I had last time I supped at your place."

The Primrose was nearly empty and appeared to be waiting anxiously for the evening's doings. Everett leaned against the mahogany bar and raised his foot on the brass rail.

"Beer?" asked the bartender.

"That'll do." Everett watched as the bartender poured a mug of beer, then asked, "Any of them boys looking for Browning come back yet far's you know, Clarence?"

"They ain't come in here," he answered as he slid Everett's beer in front to him.

"Mr. Koons," Sylvanus Ruse hailed as he entered the bar. The bat wing doors, now reinforced by full-length doors as guardians against the evening chill were slight hindrance to the thirsty blacksmith, anxious to wash the day's dust from his pipes. "Hermann with you, or has he gone back to his store?"

"He's gone back to help his boy close up."

"Wish I had me a boy like his," Ruse said wistfully. "Both my boys took off soon's they could. No dirty blacksmithin' fer them, they says. Now, my oldest, Alfred, we call him Al, is mucking a thousand feet down in the ground digging gold for some big-shot for a dollar, two bits a day up near New Meadows, north of here. Sometimes he don't see the sun for a week at a time.

"My young'un Tom, he ain't doing much better 'n his brother, seems to me. He's out in San Francisco loading freight on ships. Last time we heard was last year when we got a letter from 'em. He says he works every day till he near drops. Says the dock boss'll give your job away in a minute if you don't do just what he says, and you got to pay him too, just for working. Then the fool kid claims he's making good money. I tell you, Everett, them boys is missing a good thing by not working for their old man."

Harold arrived shortly and the three men stood talking and sipping their beer for nearly an hour before anyone from the posse showed up.

It was after dark when Whiff Bass came through the front door, slamming his arms around his sides attempting to warm himself. The three men behind him all looked as if they were freezing.

"Clarence, set us up a bottle of that Jamaican rum there," Harold Hermann requested. "You got four clean cups?"

The barkeep scowled at the big shopkeeper.

"Just funning ya, Clarence. We know you keep a few clean ones around just in case you want a drink your own self."

Harold turned to Wiff. "Ya been out longer than expected, Whiff. Run into some trouble?"

"Hell, you know if something can go wrong, it'll happen whilst I'm in the middle of it," Whiff sighed. "After we lost our light, I was about blind in the dark, and 'n damnit, I steered ma' horse off the trail and inta a hole and 'bout broke her leg. She was down, 'n all four of us couldn't get 'er back up. Shore didn't want to shoot the poor bugger, so we kept at 'er till she finally hoisted up her ownself. Then we walked her clear back ta town, a-limping the whole ways, more 'n five miles. Her leg's tore up some, but it ain't broke. Least it don't appear to be. We'll check it in the morning. I put her in a stall, and Moses grained her fer me over 'ta your place, Sly. That all right with you?"

The brawny blacksmith nodded.

"Cain't ride her on home tonight no how till I find out how bad she's hurt."

Turning to one of Whiff's men, Harold asked, "Ya'll scour that country over by the Snake?"

Jose, his swarthy cheeks pinched with cold, stood looking into his cup at the fiery liquid remaining after a long swig. He drawled, "We hit every ranch, farm, ferry, and goat house twixt here 'n that river. Nobody ain't seen him ner any other strange rider. Sure do wish I'd a knowed it was gonna get this cold tonight. We liked to froze ta death the last two or three miles. It's beginning to look like we might be in for a remembering winter, and it ain't even snowed yet."

Whiff added, "We watched for tracks that might have wandered crooked or something. Being he was so sick, it'd make sense he let his horse wander some, least that's the way we figured from what Doc told us."

Everyone piped in with a comment about the future of Neil Browning in a general commotion of talk, the multiple conversations getting livelier by the minute.

Heavy boots out on the wooden sidewalk signaled the arrival of the sheriff and his bunch. The biting cold swirled in uninvited with the four searchers and wrapped itself around the men inside, reminding them again of their recent cold journey back to town.

"Clarence, if that bottle ain't full, set out a fresh one," called the sheriff, as he strode into the room. "Me 'n the boys are 'bout froze clear through. Hey there, Everett," he called when he saw the Meads' hired hand. "How come you ain't out to your place taking care of Miz Mead 'n Jacob?"

"Evening, Sheriff," Everett said, raising a hand in a wave. "They's fine, I 'spect. Jacob's got a-holt of things out there."

"Then how come you come to town?"

"Well, I declare, Sheriff, ain't you glad to see me a'tall? Suppose there's no sense in asking ya if you had any luck?"

"No, I ain't glad to see you. Your job is out at the Mead place." The sheriff looked over the thawing men surrounding him. "We looked around out there in the bad-lands till it got too dark to see. If he come that way, he done it as a ghost 'cause no man slipped through us or them ranchers." Sheriff Carpinelli looked around the room and asked, "Where's Doc. He been in?"

"Ain't seen 'em since before noon," answered Harold. "He said he was gonna sit a spell with Lottie Crabtree 'n try to calm her. Poor old gal left alone so sudden like that. She 'n the old man was married over sixty years. Hell, ain't that many folks even reach fifty years old in this country. They was both something special."

"Sheriff, I don't think Browning ever left Boomerang," Everett suddenly blurted. "At least not last night or this morning."

"How do you figure that, old timer?"

"Tain't hard to figure. It just took time." Everett took a sip of his beer, looking over the rim at the sheriff. "Young Jacob's the one what come up with the answer, not me. I just come to town to see how good his figuring was. It appears his figuring was dead right. He figured Browning was too sick and hurt to travel much. The way you and Doc said he was feeling yesterday, that makes a lot of sense. So, if he's too busted up to set a horse, he's probably too sick to steal a wagon and harness a horse, too. It just sorta figures then, the only way he can get to cover is hide right here in town. We calculated he'd pick Christian Moss, being as how he's kin to him some."

"Sheriff," Harold interrupted, "Moss is gone. Loaded up his automobile with petrol soon as the freight come in. I seen him drive by 'round two or two-thirty, and ain't none of us seen him since."

Murmuring filled the saloon as the news was discussed amongst the newcomers.

Carpinelli pulled his silver turnip watch from his vest pocked, flipped it open, and announced the time, "Near eight thirty. Ike 'n his bunch should of got back by now. Maybe they run into 'em. Damn, I hope so."

"Sheriff, I told my wife to hold something back for supper fer us," Harold said. "Figured it'd be late. What say we retire over to the hotel and get some grub in our bellies. Maybe Ike and the boys will come in with some good news."

"You fellas go ahead. I'm going over to the jail and get something warm to wear and I gotta go looking for Ike and his posse. They might need help."

"I'll go with ya," Whiff said.

"Me too," said another.

"We're all going with ya, Tom," Harold announced. "Give us a few minutes to get something warm. Ten minutes'll do it."

"Thanks, Harold. Men," the sheriff called to get their attention, "meet me in ten minutes in front of the jail. We're going back out."

"No need of it Sheriff, they're coming just now," a voice spoke up. "Someone's with 'em."

The front door opened again, admitting the cold night air. It was Ike's posse with unexpected company: Hiram Quinabe, the young marshal from Emmett and a stocky, muscular-looking stranger wearing a badge indicating he was with the Boise, Idaho, police department

Hiram Quinabe didn't look old enough to carry the responsibility of riding herd on a rough and tumble town like Emmett, Idaho, but he had earned the town's respect through his willingness to face several unpleasant situations when he first arrived. He was of average height, pleasant looking, with dark brown hair, dark eyebrows, strong chin, and an enormous walrus mustache which he wore trying to add a look of age to his young face.

The real surprise, though, was the unexpected appearance of Christian Moss.

Harold Hermann was the first to break the stunned silence. "Mr. Moss. You all right. We all thought you was took by that outlaw."

"Hello, Harold. Evening, Sheriff," Moss said quietly, nodding to each man. "I'm fine now, Harold.

"Luckily these two good fellows came upon a wretched happenstance in which I was the victim. Were it not for them, I would have certainly perished out on that desolate road tonight. Clarence," he said, turning to the barkeep, "we are in desperate need of something to warm us."

The barkeep set additional whisky tumblers up for the new arrivals.

The sheriff turned to Hiram. "Glad ya come up tonight, Marshal. Who's this you got with ya?"

"Sheriff, this here is Wade Leigh, of the Boise Police. He was pretty anxious to come and see if he could help us lasso Browning. Him and Browning have had several run-in's. Better let Mr. Moss tell you everything, Sheriff. He's got a real yarn to spin."

Turning to Christian Moss, the sheriff stated matter-of-factly, "You seen him, then."

"Oh, yes, yes indeed," Moss said nodding vigorously. "He was, let us say, my guest since before daylight this morning. I've seen about all of that blackheart that I care to, unless he's behind bars. He left me this afternoon when a washout stalled us and the driving mechanism failed in my Apperson."

"Wait. What the hell is a Apper.... What'd you call it?" Everett asked, his face screwed up tight in confusion.

"Apperson, Mr. Koons. That's the name of my automobile. The man who built it named it after himself. I believe it is the only one in the West.

"When the vehicle broke down, Browning became a madman. Of course, he threatened to kill me if I didn't continue on to Boise. I found it necessary to teach him something about automobiles before he finally believed that the vehicle was incapable of further travel. Then since I posed no immediate threat to his recapture, he spared my life and left me. He simply wandered down the road a short distance.

"About dark, he vanished completely, just wandered away. I'm not even sure what direction he took. During the time we were stranded together he would walk toward Boise, perhaps a quarter mile, stop, rest, then come back and threaten me. Later, he wandered in the other direction and repeated the process.

"I thought I was going to die from the very moment the automobile became disabled. After he left, I became concerned about being exposed to the elements. Your friend, Marshal Quinabe here, and this kindly police officer from Boise brought me in. I'm afraid I was forced to abandon the vehicle."

The sheriff offered his hand to the stocky newcomer.

"Glad ta meet ya, Sheriff," the police officer. "Your reputation travels well ahead of ya. Hiram here called me over from Boise on account both him and me have tangled with Browning before. I came over to see if I could be of some help. I 'spect I know Neil Browning better'n anybody. Hell, I started arresting that boy when he was still in knickers. He wasn't but in grade school first time he come to our attention. He's been trouble on two legs ever since he got up on 'em, even way back. Damnedest bully fer a kid you ever saw. Whole town knew he'd end up no good someday."

It was eventually decided that the best course of action would be to launch another search for the wounded outlaw at first light. Volunteers were assigned tasks and a time to assemble which would be in the hour before daylight.

Some of the men, exhausted from the cold ride and hungry, excused themselves for rest and victuals in the comfort of their respective homes. The sheriff, Hermann, Koons, Hiram Quinabe, Officer Leigh from Boise, Christian Moss and a couple of others retired for a late supper at the hotel.

The platters of fried potatoes, black slabs of burnt steak, and steaming mugs of hot coffee, as well as a pitcher of bitter beer for Everett Koons, were in place. The men were chowing down when out of the cold night, Doc Highsmith, sad of the face, came in.

"It ain't too late to set ya up a plate, Doc," said Harold Hermann.

"Thanks, Harold. I've eaten already," he nearly whispered.

"Why the long face, Doc? You feeling poorly?"

"Poorly? Yeah, guess I am." He paused for a moment and then continued with apparent difficulty. "It's on account of Mrs. Crabtree."

"How she taking it, Doc?" the sheriff asked.

Doc hesitated again, sighed, and then in a voice cracking with grief told the assembled men, "She's dead."

"Dead—what happened, Doc?" the sheriff questioned.

Doc shook his head as if he was trying to deny the facts. "I guess she just died of grief, Tom. I've been treating her for heart palpitations for a number of years now and because of that I've been sitting with her most of the day, 'cause I was afraid of what this might do to her. All this afternoon, she couldn't stop crying and going back over her memories. I gave her medicine to soothe her, but it turned out that it wasn't going to help her none. She just didn't want to live without her husband. Married him when she was just turned sixteen, she said, more 'n 66 years ago.

"This evening, before sundown, she got quieted down and was sleeping in the big chair right by his coffin, so I went out and got my supper. When I come back, she was just like I left her, only," Doc appeared to force the words out, "she'd stopped breathing. I guess Mason came for her while I was gone. She didn't look like she struggled against it. Real peaceful looking when I found her. Reckon that's one we can't lay directly on Browning, but he sure as hell is responsible."

Everett retired a little late and just a little drunk. Can't hold liquor like in my youth, he thought. The death of Mason and Lottie Crabtree troubled Everett more than he would have expected because he didn't know them except for what their friends said about them.

He lay on his back staring at the ceiling, thinking about Jacob's mother and the hard life she must have had, married to old Jess Mead. He compared it to the gentleness of the Crabtree marriage.

Wish I had the wherewithal to see her into her old age in comfort, he thought. Nonsense. What'd she want with a poor, old, wore-out bastard of a prairie hound like me. Nothin,' that's what. Tomorrow I'll go back to the ranch and be just what I been for the last five months, a dollar a day hired hand. No better'n one a the work horses out there. Could be let go anytime they've a mind to.

Everett knew he was feeling the effect of what he had been drinking and the sorrowful mood of the town. Tomorrow, maybe the world would look a little brighter.

Sheriff Carpinelli's posse was assembled and on its way before the first streaks of light tore open the fabric of the night sky. By mid-morning they were trying to decipher the meaning of the tracks around Christian Moss' abandoned vehicle. It appeared Browning had slipped back and used the vehicle for shelter during the night. As cold as it was, one would have expected him to seek shelter somewhere, and within the area, there was no other.

Moss had mentioned that he had loaded some food, and that they also took three heavy blankets by which to conceal the escaped prisoner. Moss had come into the Primrose wrapped in one. If he had left two, they were nowhere to be found.

During the previous day and well into the night, it appeared the man they sought had wandered up and down the road in opposite directions several times, for his tracks were on top of prints left by Christian Moss, Officer Leigh, and Marshal Quinabe. The footprints revealed that he had also wandered out onto the prairie on either side of the road. Was he attempting to confuse the tracker, or was it a wounded animal's instinct to keep moving, because moving meant life. In either case, it became impossible to discern his final direction of travel. Neil Browning's instincts to escape served him well. Continued searching revealed one of Moss' blankets a quarter mile north of the road in the scrub brush. It failed to be of help in locating the outlaw.

"He's probably dead, curled up under one of them sage bushes, or down in a gully within three feet of us. Either way we'd miss 'em," the sheriff finally was forced to conclude after hours of fruitless searching.

All agreed.

With the coming of late fall, the buzzards that normally circled the weak and the dead had already left for their respective wintering grounds, leaving the locals to speculate.

"He'll keep till spring; then we'll have the buzzards help us locate his carcass," Ike stated flatly.

The morning following the futile search, Sheriff Carpinelli, accompanied by the two lawmen from Emmett and Boise, headed east out of town. At the turn off to Emmett, they bade goodbye to Marshal Quinabe and continued on toward Boise.

"Might's well stop in on the Meads with me, Leigh. Meet Miz Mead and her boy. He's the one's had all the run-ins with Browning."

"Not a bad idea," the stocky policeman said, "but I got a long ride back."

"Well then, ya need something in your stomach to travel with, and Miz Mead's cooking is better'n fair, I kin tell ya that fer sure."

"They into taking in strays?" the policeman asked with raised eyebrows.

"You're with me. They'll take ya."

Wade Leigh squinted at the sun to determine the time of day. "Good cook, eh?"

"The best."

"Then lead the way, Sheriff. I think we should investigate this woman."

Sheriff Carpinelli grinned broadly. "I've been investigating her for over fifteen years, son. She's guilty."

As the two riders rode across the wooden bridge, the clatter of their horses' hooves caused Ma to stand up from where she had been napping in an easy chair on her front porch. "Why, it's Tom again," she said half aloud to herself. She waved her right hand, her left still carried in a sling. As the two men rode closer, she studied the sheriff's companion. A momentary sense of familiarity flashed through her consciousness and faded just as quickly.

"Howdy, Sheriff, who's that ya got there with ya?" but before he could answer, she smiled brightly and said, "Light down 'n sit a spell. I was just fixin to go inside and fix something for Jacob and Everett's midday. They'll be up from plowing directly. Won't take but a minute to set two more places."

Sheriff Carpinelli tipped his hat to her. "Why, thank you Evangeline, that there's a fine offer. I'd like to introduce you to this here policeman from over ta' Boise. This here's Officer Leigh. He's come by to help us round up Browning. Arrested him a few times over there back when Browning was a pup."

"Morning, ma'am," the young policeman said, with a polite nod. "Sheriff Tom's been saying so many complimentary things about you and your cooking, I just had to come off the road and meet ya'. Hope we ain't imposing."

"Imposing. My gracious no, Officer. Tom's welcome here anytime he takes a notion, an' that goes fer his friends, too. "Ya'll light down and sit a spell. Make yer'self ta home."

The riders dismounted, tied their horses to the hitching rail, and joined Mrs. Mead.

Farms and ranches often kept three or four comfortable chairs out on the front porch for weary riders, or for their own comfort at the end of a long day. Several hours in the saddle wouldn't kill a seasoned traveler, but dismounting and settling into one of the big wicker chairs was one of the greatest comforts in the world, as many a saddle-sore wayfarer would attest.

"Ya caught that bugger then?" Ma questioned after a moment.

"No, ma'am, we didn't," the sheriff answered with a weary sigh. "I'm sorry to say we didn't catch him, but as cold as it was the last two nights, we're pretty sure he's dead out there on the desert someplace. Come spring, no question we'll turn 'em up, or at least what's left of 'em time the coyotes finish wintering on 'em."

"Don't that beat all. Ya do reckon for sure that he's dead though, don't ya?"

"We cain't say for absolute sure. We didn't find his body. He might of got out if he was strong. But damn!" The sheriff paused and reddened slightly at the unintended cuss word. "Pardon me, ma'am," he apologized, "I mean he was sick and hurt. Don't seem likely he made it through the first night, and, like I said, it ain't been much more'n 20 above the last two nights."

Ma said sternly, "Well, we ain't relaxing 'round here till his bones is found or he's caught and I kin see the bottom of both his feet twixt him 'n the ground. He come 'round here, and you ain't gonna get a chance to lose 'em again or hang 'em, neither one."

Ma turned to the policeman. "Long ride fer nothin then, wasn't it, young man?"

"No ma'am, not a'tall. I been an admirer of Sheriff Carpinelli a long time and I've been wanting to meet 'em ever since I started policing six years ago and commenced hearing stories about 'em. This is the first real excuse I had to give to my boss to get 'em to let me come here. I'd like to talk to your boy, too, seeing as how Browning 'n him has locked horns a couple of times."

"Well sir, here comes yer wish."

Jacob and Everett, hearing voices out front, came around from the backside of the house.

"Afternoon, Sheriff, howdy, Officer," said Everett. "Off the beaten track, ain't ya, Tom. You wouldn't be looking for some of Ma's good grub, would ya?" He turned to Ma, forcing a straight face. "Ain't we near out of victuals, ma'am?"

"Everett, how you do go on," she said with an affectionate smile. "Officer Leigh, this is my son Jacob. Officer Leigh is from over to Boise, Jacob." She turned and beckoned to Everett.

"Yes, ma'am?"

"Come help me fix Tom and the officer something special."

She looked at the sheriff and winked, while Everett grimaced, then smiled at the sheriff and his friend. He liked being in the kitchen with Ma Mead.

CHAPTER 8

The trial of Danny Davenport and Ed Frey had been delayed by rumors that Neil Browning had been sighted, first in Oregon, then California. Investigators had been dispatched but found no evidence of him to support the rumors.

In early December, Danny was found guilty of the murder of Earl VanDiver, the cowboy at the Double Bar X ranch, and was sentenced to hang, a task which was quickly accomplished at the state penitentiary. Ed Frey was found guilty of aiding in a murder and of attempted murder in the attack on the Mead ranch and was sentenced to twenty-five years in the same state penitentiary at Boise.

Jacob felt real sorrow for Ed Frey during the trial. He had seen the look of absolute grief on his face when Frey looked up at Jacob in the haymow, cradling his dead brother in his arms. That brief glimpse was burned into Jacob's brain as clearly as one of those pictures he saw on some of the magazines left in the railroad cars when he finally traveled east.

He also remembered considerably more of his encounter with Danny Davenport and felt no twinge of sympathy toward the doomed outlaw, for such fate was earned by his reckless acts of violence.

Traveling by train from Boomerang, Idaho, to Syracuse, New York, had taken the better part of two weeks. The first few days of the journey took Jacob south to the Great Salt Lake in Utah, then east through

Wyoming, and south again down into Denver, Colorado. During the day, the landscape changed with every curve in the track. Interesting passengers, strangers only temporarily, engaged him in conversations, and the travel was as exciting as anything Jacob had ever experienced.

During the night of the fourth day of travel, the train descended the last of the Rockies and made a lengthy stop in the busy city of Denver. Jacob had some time to explore the city before reboarding. At 8:00 o'clock in the evening, his train pulled out onto the flat prairie that stretched from eastern Colorado to the mighty Mississippi. It seemed to Jacob looking out the window at the flat, featureless landscape that there was never to be an end to it. It also gave him time to reflect on the last couple of months, during which he, Ma, and Everett had become a real family.

Reaching into his possible sack, a canvas traveling bag that contained everything he could possibly think of that would be of use to him in the East, Jacob pulled the packet of papers entrusted to him by Ma as he boarded the train in Boomerang. He carefully unwrapped the package. There was the letter of introduction penned by Doc Highsmith, a letter authorizing cash transfers to a bank in Ithaca, and the little book that Ma had saved, hidden away since he was taken up from the Orphan Train. Jacob had read it before, but it still made no sense to him. The names were strange, and he was unable to decipher their meaning.

That his name was Jacob, there seemed to be no doubt. Ma had assured him that his name was tagged to his jacket when she first saw him. That his last name might be Hagemeister, Brindelli, Wadleigh, or Lund was as foreign a thought as finding out so late that his first name was Jacob. He was still getting used to that name, having for so many years been called just "Boy." Those strange looking, nearly unpronounceable names all appeared in the ledger, each with both Syracuse and Binghamton, New York, associated with them. Little else in the way of helpful clues was usable to Jacob if he was to seek and find his kin.

Ma had insisted he try. "Ain't nothin' more important than yer own kin, Jacob. You owe it to yourself ta see if you can find 'em," Ma had said as she, Everett and Jacob traveled to Boise to deposit Jacob on the train heading east.

"I don't need no other kin, Ma," Jacob protested. "With Jess dead, the ranch ain't so bad, and you're all the kin in the world I need."

"It makes my heart swell about to bust to hear you say that, son. But facts is facts, and somewhere back East I'm feeling that there's folks that might like to know you come out all right. Just like my own tribe kept tabs on me when I ran off with Jess. They was worried to death about me. And they was right to worry, too, being as how Jess turned so mean. So ya see son, somewhere there's some folks, yer own flesh and blood kin who'd be mighty pleased if ya was to show up all growed up and healthy."

"I cain't help it Ma," Jacob said. "I don't see no need to stir old dust just to see if there's paint under it. What if I was to find kin and they turn out to be outlaws or worse 'n that, like lawyers or such that wouldn't even talk to me. I ain't nothing but a no account farm boy from a scrub ranch out by the tail end of a one-horse town. What'd folks want with a pup like that?"

Ma grabbed his arm tightly looked at him with tears in her eyes, and in a firm voice said. "Jacob, you ain't none a that, and folks, especially kin folks, is gonna be proud of you wherever you go. Trust yer old ma, and do it. Look up yer kin. I promise you, you ain't gonna be sorry, and neither will I, 'cause I know in my heart, when you come back in two years' time, sure as birds fly south, you'll make us all proud of you."

There was no use in arguing with his mother, so Jacob agreed to commence his search as soon as he got to his destination. Looking out the window at his own reflection as the train chugged with endless monotony through the night, Jacob wrestled with the promise he had made to his mother. He was happy now with the kin and friends he had.

Going east for schooling at Doc's old university was an adventure he had looked forward to for months. The first order of business, though, would be some extensive private tutoring in preparation for the university. Doc had arranged that through a cousin Jacob was to live with.

For the next several days, time, stops, towns, and people all melded into a series of fascinating events that were forgotten almost as soon as they happened, as other events replaced the ones just concluded. Thus, did Jacob wend his way to upstate New York during first new days of 1907.

At the insistence of his friend Doc Highsmith, Jacob was to take a room in the home of Walter Highsmith, a first cousin to Doc. Mr. Highsmith and his wife Marta had awaited Jacob's arrival with anxious cheer.

Their own children, Benjamin and Dorothy had both studied at Cornell University and were now traipsing all over the world. Benjamin was in Japan to further his studies in agriculture, and was teaching the Japanese the American cultivation system. Dorothy, upon graduation from college, an unusual accomplishment for a gracious lady, had married a young officer recently graduated from West Point. He received a commission of second lieutenant in the United States Army, and soon after they were assigned to a duty station near the border of Mexico in the state of Texas.

Upon Jacob's arrival in Syracuse, the Highsmiths nearly swept him from the train station into their automobile, and into their lives.

Walter Highsmith appeared to Jacob to be about 60 years old. He was a portly man with bushy lamb-chop sideburns, red face, and an affable smile that he flashed often. Jacob felt that Mr. Highsmith must have been engaged in his business before their meeting at the railroad depot because he was dressed in an expensive-looking gray suit highlighted by a gold chain that spanned his enormous belly.

Marta was dressed for the cold of a New York winter in a full-length mink coat. She was a pretty woman with a bright smile and lovely silver hair piled and sculpted in graceful swirls. Perched upon her elegant nose were rimless glasses that looked more like fine jewelry than a vision aid.

Jacob felt uncomfortable in his western outfit of blue casual pants, home-made shirt, large-brimmed hat, and leather vest. He pulled his coat closed and buttoned it, embarrassed by the elegance of his hosts.

Walter Highsmith had received a great deal of correspondence from his cousin, the famous western doctor, praising the virtues of his protégé and begging his help in polishing and educating him. Marta insisted that not only would they mentor the young man, but that their home would be his home, their children would be his brother and sister henceforth, and he would receive no less than their own children in support, love, and education. Jacob, even before arriving in the snow-covered village of Ithaca, New York, was burdened with the responsibility of succeeding.

It was still pitch dark outside as Jacob walked cautiously into a brightly lighted dining room with its gaslights ablaze. The polished walnut table was already being prepared for breakfast. Jacob stood admiring the paintings hanging on the walls, the crystal clearness of the glass mantles on the gaslights, and the fancy furniture. Even the windows, framed with ceiling-to-floor curtains, were without blemish.

Jacob made a quick mental comparison to the worn curtains covering dusty windows, the soot-covered mantles on Ma's oil lamps, and the bare wood floors back home. He already missed them. "I never knew folks lived like this," he said quietly.

The house was humming with activity, fires being built, water heating, and the rattling of pots and pans. Rosalie Salinto, the cook who lived in Little Italy, a collection of small shacks down by the river, was bustling about, warming the house and preparing breakfast.

"You come'a sit," she commanded, in a heavy accent brightened by a brilliant toothy smile, as she swept through the dinning room with a steaming pot of coffee. She said not another word to Jacob.

As Walter and Marta appeared ready for breakfast and the activities of the day, Rosalie repeated the command, "You come'a sit." Jacob realized that the happy little Italian cook had used almost her entire English vocabulary in that short phrase.

A pleasant-looking woman appeared at the door of the Highsmith house at about the same time as the ice wagon with its cargo of frozen crystal, making one of its twice-weekly deliveries. The guest was introduced to Jacob as Mrs. Symanski, a teacher widowed in the Spanish American War and a great friend of the Highsmith family. Rosalie intercepted her and took her coat.

Mrs. Symanski stood for a moment until Rosalie commanded once again, "You come'a sit."

Walter was up on his feet quickly and ushered Mrs. Symanski to her chair while Marta introduced her to Jacob.

Jacob stood as Mrs. Symanski removed her gloves and offered a tiny hand, which he took lightly, fearing to hurt her. Mrs. Symanski was only five feet tall, with tiny waist and tiny hands. Her dark, almost-black hair was cut exceedingly short for the style of the day, and was sprinkled with a few strands of gray, adding charm to the prettiness of her face. Her dress of pale blue was full length and was closed tightly around her neck. She wore a small gold locket as her only adornment.

"Jacob, it is then. Well, my full name is Mrs. Greta Symanski, but I would appreciate it if you would simply call me Greta."

"Pleasure ta meet ya, ma'am," Jacob whispered, awed by the beauty of such a dainty creature.

"Uh, yes. Pleasure ta meet ya too," Greta mimicked. "My, we will have to work on your accent, Jacob."

"Yes, ma'am. Mr. Highsmith said you was gonna make a city boy out a ol' coonhound. I ain't against it, but is folks still gonna understand me when I git back home?" Jacob grinned as he spoke.

"I'm sure we can leave enough country in you that you will still be able to communicate with your friends, of which I am sure you have many. The nice thing about speech is that often the people some consider common are the very ones able to speak in such colorful phrases. They create wonderful visual images. Now, those very same people who look down their noses and claim to speak the king's English are often frightfully boring, having not a whit of color in their narration. We shall strive to retain your colorful speech patterns. In themselves they will be assets. In the interim we will add and reassign meanings, words, and phrases that will enhance your charm. There will very little subtracting, I feel. I love your description of yourself as an ol' coonhound. That is truly precious."

Mrs. Symanski continued, "Walter's told me the circumstances of your birth and your desire to search for relatives you were separated from nearly twenty years ago."

"Yes'm."

"Oh, Marta, don't you just love that western twang?" Greta exclaimed.

Marta Highsmith had been sitting quietly, absorbed in the exchange between Jacob and Greta Symanski. She responded, "Walter's cousin assured us we would be charmed. He was absolutely right."

Greta turned back to Jacob and said, "Let's assume now, that we have two tasks ahead of us to complete this winter. Our number one task is to see to your grammar and give you a foundation in mathematics. Agreed?"

"Yes'm."

"The first step in that direction will begin with your answering my questions with a simple yes, or something like 'Sure, Greta,' or 'All right, Greta.'"

"Yes'm. I mean, *yes*, Greta," he said with great effort.

"Good," she said patting his hand gently. "You're progressing already. Our second task then, if you will allow me to help, is to locate your relatives."

"I'd appreciate that a whole lot," Jacob said, raising his head and looking her in the eye. "I ain't got no idea where to even begin looking. I got a little book my ma give me with funny names I cain't even say. Then there's towns, too, which I don't know where they is."

"Are, Jacob. You don't know where they *are*, not is." Greta interjected.

"That there's right, I *don't* know where they are."

Teacher, instructor, and friend, Greta Symanski was soon Jacob's inseparable companion. Together they explored the libraries in the village and at the university. There was quite a lot of information regarding the Orphan Trains. The first name they eliminated was Lund of Syracuse. Mr. Lund, it turned out, was the name of the man assigned to meet and ride the train with the orphans to Buffalo, Chicago, and points west. The *Syracuse Herald*, a copy of which they located at the library, reported a story that read "Train Orphans Go West," on May 17, 1890.

Dr. Harold Lund, of Albany, New York, an officer of the Welfare Department of the State of New York, and his assistant, Dr. Franklin D. Foster, along with three nurses, Tuesday boarded an Orphan Train out of New York City. Dr. Lund, and Dr. Foster, took 79 children from Binghamton and communities of the Southern Tier to join

226 homeless children from New York City and Newark, New Jersey.

The 305 orphans are destined for distribution to families in the West who will pledge a Christian upbringing and a loving home. The orphans' range in age from one to 14 years old, and all are free of physical or mental defects.

No children 15 years old or older are included or considered, as they are quite capable of working and earning their keep.

The story highlighted the blight that took so many parents of these unfortunate orphans to early graves, leaving behind the burden of their children. A burden the state was not prepared financially to handle. The flu, typhus, or some other dread disease caused, some were sure, by waves of immigrants recently landed from Europe had left thousands of youngsters orphaned. The newspaper said the worst offenders were from Poland, Ireland, and Italy. These foreigners were poor, uneducated, and, except for the Irish, unable even to speak English. And because they were filthy there was no doubt that, "It was they who brought the diseases that killed our citizens, leaving the State of New York the responsibility of finding homes willing to accept the unfortunates."

In addition, many of this unwelcome populace were considered no better than common thieves, stealing jobs by accepting positions at ridiculously low wages, thereby putting good God-fearing Americans out of work. Jacob's investigation was going in directions he could never have imagined, as he read the old newspaper articles. He questioned his mother's decision about finding relatives if it turned out they were so dreadfully undesirable.

A series of telephone calls to Binghamton and the New York State Office of Public Welfare also eventually eliminated the names of

Hagemeister and Brindelli as possible relatives. Otto Hagemeister had been the director of the Broome County Relief and Orphan Home from 1883 until his death in 1899. John A. Brindelli was the assistant administrator of the home at the time, and the chief organizer of the Orphan Train's association with the orphanage in Binghamton, New York. He became the director at the death of Otto Hagemeister and served as director up until his sudden resignation in 1904.

The name Wadleigh, despite a careful search, did not appear on any rolls, either as an orphan or an employee.

All the names in Jacob's little book led to dead ends with the exception of Wadleigh. The investigation seemed to be coming to an end as Jacob and Greta were unable to locate any record of a person with the name Wadleigh in Broome County or the surrounding area.

"You may have to go to Binghamton and simply search through cemetery records, Jacob, if you are to locate any further references to the mysterious Mr. Wadleigh," said Greta one evening as they were finishing the day's mathematical lesson.

"I reckoned it'd come to that eventually. How big a town is Binghamton, anyway?"

"It's a lot bigger than Ithaca. And it's more of a workingman's town, with shoe factories, tanners, and iron mills. It can be quite frightening if you're not used to large cities. I believe there are over thirty thousand people living there now."

"How can so many folks gather in one place so thick?" he asked with awe in his voice. "When I came through Chicago the conductor said it was bigger 'n that even. That true?"

Greta answered, "Yes, Chicago is much bigger indeed. However, if you didn't wander far from your train, you didn't really get into Chicago. Therefore, I would say it would be hard to make a fair comparison."

"Well, I seen enough, and I don't think I'd be scared of it."

"Then you may want to try doing a little investigating on your own. Do you think you can handle the big city?"

Jacob grinned and said, "I kin handle anything if I go slow and think about it. When are we going?"

"I can't go, Jacob. I'd love to, but I need to go visit my parents in Syracuse for a few days. They're very elderly and I haven't been to see them for some time. While I'm in Syracuse, I'll try to unearth additional information for you."

One week later, Jacob Mead looked around at the frozen city landscape of Binghamton, New York. It was a winter wonderland of sun sparkling through fat crystal icicles, roofs piled high with a new blanket of snow, and deep impressions in the snowy sidewalks made by early morning pedestrians.

Winters in Boomerang had always been bitterly cold, windy, and dry with very little snow. When it warmed up, what little snow actually fell to the ground seldom melted in running streams; it simply evaporated into the dry country air, leaving nothing in the ditches and creek beds for the earth's thirsty plants and animals.

In contrast, the soft hills surrounding the bustling city of Binghamton were covered with a thick carpet of glistening snow that seemed to appear magically during the night as folks slept, its only purpose being to hide the promise of the coming of spring.

The previous day, the sun had warmed the air and ample streams of water had gushed from every direction in a mad dash to reach the Chenango River where it entered the Susquehanna. The night's quiet storm and freezing temperatures had temporarily stilled the hundreds of little streams, but the bright morning sun promised their return.

Maple trees, a source of amazement to Jacob, were all sporting sugar icicles where twigs had broken and released their sap, which had frozen into little stalactites during the night. The tree trunks were adorned with aprons of steel buckets to catch the thin, sweet sap that would be converted into that delicious maple syrup and sugar he had come to relish.

Smoke filled the air, thrown high by the belching fires of commerce. Within hours, the brightness of the fresh snow would be dulled by the soot emanating from those fires. But while soiling the snow, those fires meant life to this bustling hub of a community in the southern part of New York State.

Jacob had risen early. The long day on the train yesterday had allowed him ample time to think of his first course of action upon arriving in Binghamton. His plan was simple. He would search every cemetery in the surrounding area for a headstone bearing the name of Wadleigh. If it took more than a day, for there could be no more than a few, he was prepared to give up the search and abandon further effort to locate any long lost kin.

Jacob, carrying a small satchel containing his traveling supplies, walked briskly along Prospect Street around the old pioneer cemetery until he came to the main entrance. A massive ornate steel arch reached over his head and down to the sturdy brick columns that attached to the walls surrounding the vast snow-covered park. Beautifully scrolled wrought iron decorations with floating, robed angles smiling down, proclaiming this hallowed ground to be "Saint Mary's Memorial Gardens."

A shoveled path attested to an industrious employee and an early riser, for it was just now five minutes to eight o'clock in the morning. A cozy looking office building of red brick lay at the end of the path. There Jacob found the industrious man, heavily clothed in cap, gloves, scarf, heavy jacket, and thick pants which were tucked into tall rubber boots, who had cleared the path for him and those who would follow this day.

"Good morning, young man. Can I be of help?" the man asked as he straightened and pulled off his cap.

"Howdy, sir. You head man 'round here?" Jacob asked.

"Gracious no. In the winter, I sweep the paths, and when necessary inter bodies in the mausoleum until the ground is no longer frozen. In the summer, after the ground thaws, I dig the graves. I have help, of course, but I'm most certainly not the head man. He paused momentarily and studied Jacob in his fleece-lined coat, western boots, and cowboy hat. "Mr. Parks is the man I believe you'll want to see to make your arrangements. May I inquire if the deceased was a parent or perhaps a sibling?"

"Sibling. What's that?" Jacob asked.

"A brother or sister. Did you lose a brother or a sister?" the man asked gently.

"Reckon I did. I think I lost two brothers and a sister."

"Oh my goodness. Poor young man. Terrible, just terrible," he said with a sad shake of his head. "Would you like to talk about it. Can you tell me if tragedy was the result of a house fire or was it something like the flu that caused your siblings to go so suddenly?"

"I ain't quite sure what caused 'em to go so quick. That's the reason I want to see the head fella, to see if he can help me find out."

The man stepped back and eyed Jacob suspiciously. "Now see here, young man, if you don't know what killed your brothers and sister, how in heaven's name do you expect our Mr. Parks to know?"

"I ain't sure they's kilt. That Mr. Parks is maybe the only one that can help me. Is he in?"

"I must confess you've got me a little confused, but if you think Mr. Parks can help you, he will be in his office promptly at nine o'clock. If you wish, I can admit you to his office and you can wait for him inside. I've started a nice fire, which I do nearly every day of the year, even in the summer, just to take off the night chill."

"Thanks, pardner, but I'll mosey on down to a little café I saw and get some victuals."

The man grinned and said, "You're not from Binghamton, not from what I can tell from your accent, even if I didn't notice your manner of dress. Where are you from, sir?"

"Reckon I might be from here—maybe. That's what I'm a-hoping to find out from your Mr. Parks. But I was raised from kitten size out in Boomerang, Idaho. Ever hear of it?"

"No," the man said, his eyes sparkling with interest.

"Well, I never heard of Binghamton, New York, neither, till last summer. Jacob waved a salute to the caretaker as he turned to leave and called over his shoulder, "I'll be back in about an hour to see Mr. Parks. Meantime, I'll get my breakfast took care of."

The walk back to the restaurant was a walk through wonderland for Jacob Mead. He had been in New York for three months and the weather still amazed him. Snow crunched under his feet, threatening to set him on his arse if a misstep was made.

Wanting the best shoes he could find to travel and live in, he had visited the Falk Mercantile store just before the trial of Danny Davenport and Ed Frey and bought the finest pair of cowboy boots Harold had to offer in his size. And good ones they were, costing over forty dollars and made of two leathers. The bottoms, smooth and shiny were made of the toughest of cowhide, tanned, then beaten soft and dyed to a rich dark brown. They fit Jacob's feet as if they had grown on him.

The tops of the boots were of calves' leather carved in intricate designs and scrolls as befitted an expensive pair of boots for a rich range rider. Here in the slippery environment of a late winter snow in upstate New York, they were comfortable, but the range they were designed for was two thousand miles away. Walking took concentration.

A bell attached above the door of Molly's Cafe signaled to everyone inside that a newcomer had arrived for breakfast. Conversation quieted a little as heads turned to look at the strangely dressed young man, then rose to an even slightly higher level as the western style hat, slim line blue trousers, and cowboy boots were examined and discussed.

Jacob, immersed for the first time in a totally working man's world, wondered himself at the strange low brimmed caps, great gray jackets, and wide-legged ragged pants. These were the workmen of the steel mills and shoe factories. A gray, tired looking bunch trying to recover from their all-night shift with the help of Molly's strong, bitter coffee, thick-sliced buttered toast, and eggs fried deep in bacon grease. Piles of the maple-sugar-cured bacon were set in porcelain trays at strategic positions along the counter. The grease in the air, the cigar smoke, and the murmur of voices humming in a nonsensical rhythm betokened a close-knit group in their own lair, perhaps not taking kindly to strangers.

"Have a seat. What'll it be, cowboy?" the roly-poly woman behind the counter asked.

"A bunch a what he's chawing on." The grizzled-looking man to whose plate Jacob referred looked up and ignored the fact that the seat beside him contained his coat and cap.

"Move yer stuff, Plover. Man wants to sit down and eat," the woman ordered.

Plover hunched his broad shoulders, ignored the command and turned back to his breakfast.

"Phil, reach over and clear that stool for my customer, will ya. Seems Plover's gone deaf. Ain't 'cha, Plover?"

Plover, a gray faced, powerfully built brute of a man sneered as the man Jacob assumed to be Phil reached over, gathered and folded the coat, laid the cap on top and stored it under the sullen Plover's stool.

"Have a seat," said the man. He was as tired-looking as the other patrons, his bushy black eyebrows were gray with dust from the night's labor, his chin covered with black stubble. His smile, though, was warm and welcoming.

"Thanks, partner," Jacob smiled back. He set his satchel beside the stool.

"Partner, huh. Western talk. You from out west?" Plover asked, turning from his breakfast.

"Boomerang Idaho, over near the Snake," Jacob replied as he plopped onto the stool.

"Over near the Snake. Does that mean you only got one snake out west. Hell, we got hundreds of 'em right here in the county. Imagine that, just one snake in the whole out-West." The man guffawed at his own joke.

Jacob smiled back at him. "The Snake's a river, a big 'un. I seen your river yonder where I got off the train. The Snake's got little bitty creeks run into it bigger 'n that."

"You don't say. Bigger than that ol' Susquehanna River? I suppose everything's bigger out west." The man appeared irritated at Jacob.

Jacob smiled wanly and nodded.

"Well damnit, is it?" Plover suddenly demanded.

"Is it what?" Jacob asked, confused at the man's tone.

"Is everything bigger out West?"

"No. I don't suppose so."

"He don't suppose so," Plover mocked. "Well, me, I don't suppose so, neither. Fact is I'm so big I need two stools. One fer me 'n one fer my cap 'n coat, and I'm from right here in New York State. So if you get off my stool, I can get my gear off the dirty floor."

He turned to the woman behind the counter. "Why in hell don't you mop this place once in a while, Molly. Man can't put his cap an coat on the floor without it coming up filthy." He looked at Jacob, his eyes narrow slits of anger. "Move it out, Mister!"

"Clay Plover, you start trouble in here again and you'll spend the night in jail," Molly threatened, wagging a finger at him. "You want to drink on the job all night, that's your business. But don't come in here in the morning all hung-over and think you own my place. Cause you don't. As a matter of fact, I don't even want your business. Get your things and get out."

"Cowboy," Plover ignored Molly and concentrated on Jacob with venom in his voice. "you come in here looking for trouble, and I guess you found it. Molly and me, we ain't never had no words before until you showed up. Maybe I'd better stay and you better get."

"I came in here looking for breakfast, mister, nothing else." Seeking to avoid trouble, Jacob rose and headed for the door.

Jacob realized that bullies and cowards dot the landscape like trees and bushes. Not confined to the West, they flourished wherever there were people who looked weaker than they did. To Clay Plover, Jacob appeared no more than a slip of a boy.

The sinew-like muscles hidden beneath the warmth of his clothing would not have impressed the bully in front of him. Nothing of the power of Jacob's ranch-toughened prowess was revealed as he strolled toward the door. Nothing of the quiet, slender cowboy impressed Clay Plover, especially because of Jacob's reluctance to assert himself when challenged.

"Little man," Plover sneered, pressing his advantage, "don't come back in here."

Jacob, satchel in hand, took the last step to the door.

"You listening to me, little man?" Plover shouted, seemingly enraged.

Jacob stopped with his hand on the doorknob; the whole café was suddenly as still as a church, every eye turned his way. A trembling of excitement coursed through his body. Jacob turned slowly. His eyes swept the faces staring at him through the thin haze of smoke and cooking grease. The man was trouble, no doubt, but pride demanded a reply.

His gaze settled on the offensive man. "You know, partner, we don't have the biggest of everything out West." He hesitated, his eyes narrowed. "The biggest mouth seems to be in the East."

Raucous laughter erupted as Jacob exited into the blinding whiteness of the fresh snow. Pulling his turnip watch from his pocket, a gift from

Tom Carpinelli and identical to the one the sheriff carried, Jacob noted that he still had more than 40 minutes to wait for Mr. Parks. Hunger, not overpowering but gnawing none the less, caused him to stop in front of the unfriendly diner and consider other options for breakfast.

A tinkle from the bell above the door at his back alerted him that someone was leaving. He stepped aside. There was the slam of something heavy, a shout, and Clay Plover came stumbling out of the open door, across the icy sidewalk, and landed on his stomach in the soft snow bank on the opposite side.

Jacob walked gingerly over to the fallen man and reached to help him to his feet. Arising with a string of curses pouring from his lips, Plover ripped at Jacob's head with something he had pulled from his pocket.

Had Plover acted silently instead of advertising his bad feelings with his curses, he probably would have wounded Jacob grievously. However, sufficiently warned, Jacob stepped back in the nick of time, causing the still inebriated and wholly infuriated Clay Plover to whirl in a complete circle on the slippery ice, falling this time not into a soft snowbank, but onto the hard surface of the frozen sidewalk. A scream pierced the air from the fallen man as if he were mortally wounded.

Jacob stood with his back against the diner, from which two dozen pair of eyes peered at the fallen man. A second scream melting down into a groan escaped from Clay Plover's lips, as he flopped to his back and then returned to a rolled up position on his side. A fair amount of rich, red blood, its color enhanced by the whiteness of the fresh snow, oozed from beneath him.

"What's going on here now?" a gruff voice asked.

Jacob was startled to be looking at a city policeman. He was short, with pale skin and a shock of red hair sticking out from under his policeman's hat.

Patrons filed out of the diner talking excitedly temporarily abandoning their hot breakfasts, wanting to get close to some action in their otherwise dull lives.

The policeman, hearing no reply to his question asked louder in a rich Irish brogue, "Well, is someone going to tell me what's going on here or not?"

Phil, the man who had removed Clay Plover's coat from the stool for Jacob earlier, answered, "Clay there fell, Paddy. He had something in his hand, and he must'a fallen on it."

"Help me turn him over and get a look, will you?" asked the burley cop.

Phil pulled the protesting man back over onto his back. "Tis you again, is it Plover?" the policeman said. "On me mother's grave I swear, never I want anything bad to happen to you, lad, but should misfortune continue to befall ye, can't ye be more considerate and do your trouble on the other side of Clinton Street and out of my jurisdiction?"

Clay Plover winced in pain as the officer, ignoring his moans, examined the brass knuckles-knife combination protruding from his thigh.

"Hush now, you. That little pig sticker's not going to kill a stout fella like yourself. Get yourself up and off to visit Dr. Solonika. He'll stitch a fine thread to ya, and ye'll be good as new."

"That cowboy there, Paddy. He's the one what stuck me. Pulled this from his pocket." Plover gently touched the protruding weapon. Knifed me just as I walked peacefully out of Molly's."

"Well now, ya don't say. A cowboy eh?" Paddy reached for the weapon and deftly plucked it from the stricken man's leg, completely ignoring both his belabored whining and his statement. He turned to Jacob, "Which part of the grand frontier country are you missing from, laddie?"

"Idaho."

"Hummm, Idaho, is it? Here's you knife back." He folded in the stubby blade and handed the remarkable tool to Jacob. "And what part of Idaho is that, lad?"

Startled, Jacob examined the knife with a quick glance and said, "Western. Town called Boomerang, near the Snake River." Jacob looked at the officer and back at the brass knuckles. He had never seen anything like them. "Officer, that there mule skinner knifed himself."

"I know that, lad. A word of truth would have a hard life living in Clay Plover's mouth." The policeman turned his attention to the stricken man. "Get along now Clay, and get yourself fixed and sobered up. When ye've slept the night shift out of your system, ye're to report to me at the station house this afternoon. We'll be needing your statement regarding this incident."

"Go to hell, Paddy. I told you what he done to me." Plover turned to Jacob with clenched fists. "Gimmie my knucks back, you. Paddy, you gonna arrest him or not. If you ain't, I'm gonna be looking for him myself. He owes me."

"Ah Clay, Clay, Clay," the policeman sighed in exasperation. "Whatever are we to do with ya, lad. Can ya no see, man, ye've mixed your whisky with your muscle, thereby passing your brains altogether. This lad has harmed you not at all. To that I'm sure the entire assembled body will testify. Secondly, sotted as ye are, you'd be better advised to go start a ruckus with me own wife, Mrs. O'Brian. And I'm here to tell ya that'd be a picnic full of ants.

"Be a wise fellow and retire from the field this day. And be thankful to the Virgin Mary, ye've another day to draw breath, for sure as there are Saints in Ireland, with your nasty temper, ye've not got that many days ahead of ya. Now begone with ya." At that the glib-tongued cop turned to Jacob and offered his hand.

"Walter Erin O'Brian at your service. Everyone hereabouts refers to me as Paddy, as if I was as Irish as Paddy's pig. And to state the truth of the matter, lad, since I was indeed whelped on the old sod, even Paddy's own pig envies me."

"Jacob Mead, sir."

"Well then, Jacob Mead, where were we?" he mused. "Ah yes, we were discussing the great state of Idaho. Let's retire to a warm seat inside Molly's. I'd appreciate the time of ya, if ye'd be telling me more of the

West. 'Tis me dream to retire there one day and become, like yourself, a cowboy of sorts."

"Mr. O'Brian, this gadget ya give me belongs to the other fella," Jacob said uneasily.

"Clearly, the very fact that donny Mr. Plover accused you unjustly of accosting him transfers ownership of it to yourself. And, didn't I hear him say as plain as day that 'twas your knife. Now stick it in your pocket. It might come in handy to you in the future. Trust too, the nasty thing should be kept from sight, for just the owning of such a piece is against the law. Binghamton is a peaceful city, mind ye, but we do have our scoundrels and scalawags, and ye can be certain they'd like nothing better than to have a go with a nice country lad such as yourself. Stay alert, laddie, and may peace follow at your heels like a faithful hound. Now then, let's have a bite, shall we?"

They entered the diner behind a dozen or so others anxious to finish their meals and retire for the day's rest. A twelve-hour night, six nights a week at the furnaces, dye vats, or shoe machines wore a man to a frazzle. A good breakfast and long nap restored him just enough to repeat the cycle for another day until years spent, shop-worn and bent, he could work no more.

A man was fortunate to reach the ripe old age of forty-five or forty-eight. Such was the fate of the men dining in Molly's that morning, as it was for those now gone, and those yet to come. Heavy industry was a cruel master to the free working man, but it allowed him to eat and raise his family. This morning, as on all other mornings, except Sunday, they laid their coin on the counter and enjoyed Molly's hot, spicy offerings.

Jacob devoured a hearty breakfast while the uniformed man talked on and on about his extended family: brothers, cousin, nephews, Jacob lost track of who was related to whom in the long narrative.

"Help yourself to more bacon there, cowboy," called Molly, her good humor restored with the absence of Clay Plover.

"Yes, ma'am. Best bacon I ever tasted." Jacob reached for the platter two seats down. Clay's seat was now vacant, causing Jacob to stretch for the plate.

"Pardon me boarding house reach, laddie. At me sainted mother's table, you learned to reach or go without." Paddy, at his left, stretched around Jacob's back for the cup containing sugar, which another patron handed him. Coffee, to Paddy O'Brian, was no good if you could still taste the bean. Half of the cup of sugar would be barely enough sweetness for the officer.

They were each engaged in reaching for bacon and sugar simultaneously, to the good luck of one and the bad luck of the other.

A deafening roar and the shattering of splintered glass destroyed the tranquillity of the morning atmosphere. The buckshot hit Paddy's right shoulder at the spot Jacob's head would have been had he not reached to his left. The force spun O'Brian completely around, lifting him from his stool and over the counter in a heap at Molly's feet. Before the echo of the blast faded, everyone was on the floor amid the shattered glass, seeking cover from the crazy, waking nightmare that without warning had engulfed the smoke filled establishment. Yells of panic and the terrifying thunder of a second round filled the air.

Jacob, thinking that his new friend had leaped over the counter to seek cover, could see the wisdom of the move and also scrambled over and onto the floor next to O'Brian. It took only a glance to see the damage to the policeman, and the shock of it recalled the horror of the past with Neil Browning's gang.

To surmise that once under fire one matures and no longer fears the danger is one of the oldest and most useless myths passed from man to man. Jacob had no more desire to die that day than he had the previous summer, nor was his fear any less.

The next blast from the shotgun shattered the counter, passing through the thin supporting boards and into the wall behind Jacob, Molly, and Paddy, the shot barely missing Molly. With the policeman unconscious and bleeding, the shooter, who Jacob assumed was Plover, would have no opposition should he decide to enter Molly's and finish his task, which obviously was to kill Jacob and perhaps Walter Erin O'Brian as a bonus.

Paddy's service pistol was secured in its holster by a short leather tab fastened with a brass snap device. Jacob unfastened the tab, covering it with a handy rag to quell the noise of its unfastening, and pulled the stubby gun from its nesting place. It was heavy for such a small weapon. The gleaming tips of the bullets in their chambers assured Jacob that he had at least five or six rounds at his disposal. The tinkling of the bell above the door sounded like a roaring freight train's screeching whistle to Jacob. The gunman was stalking into the café to finish his business.

Jacob grasped the empty sugar cup lying near O'Brian that had been knocked behind the counter when O'Brian was hit by the first blast. As silently as possible, Jacob picked it up, looked to the far end of the working space they were ensconced in, and tossed the cup as carefully as if he were tossing another sharp stone on old Jess Mead's casket. It hit with a clatter, drawing the fourth deafening roar from Plover's double barrel shotgun.

Jacob lay still for a second, then heard the distinctive 'thunk' of the gun being broken for reloading. He cocked the little pistol and stood hands at his sides, facing Clay Plover. Clay wasn't looking at Jacob, he was fumbling with nervous fingers pulling spent shells from their chambers.

"Drop it," Jacob said in a shaky voice.

"Like hell I'll drop it. You're gonna die today, boy." Plover's face was contorted with wrath, his right leg red with blood, as he reached into his coat pocket for two more shells.

"Please mister, don't load. Just drop it."

Wordlessly, the insane Clay Plover, his hands shaking in his fury, slipped two shells into the barrel chambers. The shotgun snapped shut with a resounding click. Clay raised the double-barreled gun, preparing to fire again.

The world seemed to slow to a half or quarter pace for Jacob. He watched with fascination as Clay snapped the gun closed and raised the barrel directly at him. Time, running in a different rut for Jacob than for the rest of the diner's occupants, allowed him the luxury of observing the action coolly, as if he had all the time in the world. Seeing that Clay had every intention of harming him, and perhaps others, Jacob made the decision, almost causally, to defend himself. Effortlessly he raised his weapon, aimed carefully, and squeezed the trigger an instant before Plover's own gun roared harmlessly into the ceiling. A blink. That was the amount of time that had actually passed.

The bullet from Jacob's shot took the anger out of Clay's eyes, replacing it for an instant with a peaceful, rational look. He slumped dead to the floor. The stillness of the room hung like heavy dew in the air until someone finally realized the danger was over. Suddenly, the place erupted. Men, their weariness wiped away in the heat of terror, scrambled for the front door.

Most of the men who had been in the diner during the shooting had disappeared by the time additional police came on the scene. The few remaining witnesses were being interviewed by seemingly dozens of policemen, detectives, and curious onlookers. Jacob was not spared the harassing questions any more than the other patrons, though it was clear he was being regarded as a hero.

Chaos reigned for hours after the shooting. Officer O'Brian, grievously wounded, was rushed to Memorial Hospital. Jacob, shaken and confused, was transported in an official police car to the station with two other witnesses: the man named Phil, who had moved Clay Plover's coat, and Molly, the owner of the diner. It was growing dark before someone remarked that it was time to call it a day and go home.

At the end of the grueling day, Molly and Phil bid Jacob goodbye on the massive sandstone steps of city hall and left for their respective homes. Jacob stood looking down at the street below and pondered his next move. "Ought ta head back to the rooming house, I 'spect," he whispered.

In the gloom as Jake started his trek back to the rooming house, a pleasant, though tired-looking, man detached himself from the pillar against which he had been leaning and sidled up to Jacob.

He asked, "How are you fixed for the night, cowboy?"

Jacob looked at the man in the gray suit walking beside him. He was stocky and clean-shaven, with dark gleaming eyes. He wore a fedora hat that covered most of his black hair except for a tuft that protruded at his forehead. His tie was askew but otherwise he was dressed very neatly.

"I was aiming to finish my business looking up lost kin folks and heading back to Ithaca on this evening's train. 'Pears I'm forced to a change of trails." He hefted his single piece of luggage, which he'd been carrying all day. "I expect I'll just head back to the rooming house I stayed at last night."

"Why don't you tag along with me for a while?" The man paused and introduced himself. "I'm Danny Toronto, reporter for the *Binghamton Press*." He handed Jacob his calling card, saying, "It's the biggest newspaper in Broome County, as far as that goes, the biggest paper between New York City and Buffalo. I've got to get back to the office and turn in your story for the morning edition. That won't take long, and I'd appreciate it if you'd stick around and answer some more questions."

Jacob stopped walking and exclaimed, "Are you joshing me. I ain't done nothing all day but answer questions!"

Toronto smiled disarmingly, "No, I'm not joshing you, Mr. Mead. You're big news. People don't get to see a hero every day, and when the hero turns out to be a bon fide cowboy, people naturally want to read more about you."

"Well mister, you sure treed the wrong coon if ya think ya found a hero under this hat. I was scared as hell when that fella come a shooting. Liked to messed ma pants, and that there's the truth."

Danny's smiled disappeared and in a serious voice he said, "Let me see if I can change your mind. The men in the diner having breakfast when you came in, what was the first thing you thought when you looked at them?"

"I didn't think nothing, I was just looking to get something to eat, which, by the way, I'm needing to do again. I didn't get no midday, what with all them police running around and all their questions." Jacob took a breath and replayed his entrance into the diner in his head and considered Toronto's question.

"They was all looking, well, sorta tired-like. Like they was just done plowing forty acres behind a pair of good-for-nothing horses that didn't know their jobs, and there was still a barn to clean."

"Exactly right. They are tired," said Danny. "They're always tired. Right up until the day they die, they'll be tired. What you did today, saving those people in the diner, not to mention saving O'Brian, is stuff they'll thrive on. A year from now, every factory worker in this town will swear on his mother's grave he was in Molly's Café and he was the one that tossed you the gun that saved everyone's lives. It'll give them something to live for and a bright spot in their lives they can pass down to their grandchildren."

"Aw, dang it, Mr. Toronto, I can't let you go putting nothin' in the paper 'bout me being no hero. 'Tain't right."

Danny ignored the interruption. "Let me tell you what my readers will see when they look at you tomorrow through the lens of the newspaper. You see, I'm their eyes and ears in this town. I'm just like a magnifying glass, and what I see, I pass on to them. Right now, I see a six-foot tall or better young man with the weathered face of a range rider. I see, umm," he mused as he composed his story in his head, "about one hundred and, say sixty, sixty-five pounds of solid muscle, developed by hard work out on a ranch in the West. There's the obvious cowboy boots and that marvelous hat.

"Then I look at the whole package, and you know what I see, Mr. Mead?" He paused, not really expecting an answer. "I see potential, that's what. What kind of potential, I don't quite know yet, but as soon as I figure it out, I'll let you know. In the meantime, I've got a couple of chores to finish downtown. Stick with me and as soon as we're done down at the *Press*, I'll buy you the best steak in Binghamton and put you up in the best hotel in the city, courtesy of the paper."

Jacob was too tired to argue further with Danny Toronto. The offer of a meal and a place to get some rest was accepted gratefully. Jacob had plenty of money and later tried to pay for his own meal and room at the Chenango Hotel.

Danny would have none of it. "It's on the expense account, Cowboy."

During dinner, Jacob twice sent his steak back to get it "burned right," while Toronto continually pressed Jacob for details of the shooting, all the while taking notes and looking at the clock. "I've got to get the rest of this in before eight o'clock." Danny kept apologizing for the interruptions of Jacob's dinner, but he continued questioning never the less.

At five minutes to eight, Danny asked the waiter for directions to the hotel's telephone and excused himself to call in his story. When he returned, he was smiling from ear to ear. "Cowboy, you wait until the paper hits in the morning. You're the biggest thing that's happened in this town since Teddy Roosevelt came through. Oh, by the way, I called the hospital. O'Brian's awake and babbling about you as if you were his personal guardian angel. This is perfect. They said I can interview him in a couple of days if he continues to improve."

"Mr. Toronto," Jacob implored.

"Call me Danny,"

"Yes, sir, Danny" He scowled at the reporter. "But see here, Mr. Toronto, you got to stop this here nonsense. I ain't no hero, I just come to this town to see if I could locate some folks that might be kin to me.

Back home, folks'll laugh at me fer putting on airs like I done something, when I ain't done nothin."

"Oh, modest, too!" Danny said, clapping his hands gleefully. "Cowboy, I'll make you a deal, I won't ask you any more questions tonight if you promise to meet me in the morning. Fair?"

"Don't know if it's a fair or not, but I got a question fer you."

"Shoot."

"Could you help me get a holt of the Highsmiths up in Ithaca, so's they ain't worried when I don't show up on the train in the morning?"

"Sure. I've got friends on the paper up there. I'll call them, and they'll meet your folks at the station and tell them what's going on. In the meantime, is there anything else you want? Just name it."

"Nope. Not a thing, 'cept some sleep. Back home, we'd usually be a-bed by this time. Sun's up early, and with it chores. I got a heap of chores my ownself tomorrow."

Thus ended Jacob Mead's first day's search in Binghamton, New York, for his long-lost kin. In fact, it was the end of a part of Jacob, for with the rising sun came the headlines of the **Binghamton Press,** transforming Jacob into an entirely new person.

WESTERN STYLE SHOOTOUT IN LOCAL DINER
VISITING COWBOY RESCUES POLICEMAN

The story credited a visiting cowboy, Jake Mead, late of Boomerang, Idaho, with saving the lives of a score of patrons and police officer Walter O'Brian during an attack at Molly's Café on Prospect Street. The early-morning shooting caused the death of one Clay Plover, a man well known to local police. It told of the coolness of Jake Mead, standing calmly, facing a loaded double-barreled shotgun and, with the service revolver of the grievously wounded police officer, bringing an end to the terror. The article ran to several inches of news type on pages one and two. Jacob's life was about to change its course. The boy from Idaho was now a hero from out West.

Jacob was an early riser and was already dressed when he opened his hotel room door in answer to an insistent knocking at first light. There stood Danny Toronto.

Before Jacob could speak, Danny grabbed his arm, "Come on, Jake, let's get outta here. Have you eaten yet?"

"No, sir. I could use a bite."

"Do you mind if I call you Jake? Because that's what you're going to be known as, as long as you hang around this town."

"I guess I can handle it. Who changed my name and why?"

"I did that. It was almost an accident, but the fact is when I first heard your name, I thought it was Jake and it sounded so good in the report, you know, western he-man and all, then when I heard your real name later, it didn't fit. Jacob is a good name, don't misunderstand me. It's just that Jake makes you sound about three inches taller."

"Well then, I guess I'll be Jake for a while. Don't matter to me."

"Good. Now then, Jake, you said something last night that I almost missed. That's why I'm here so early this morning"

"What might that be? I talked to so many folks, I kinda forgot what I said."

"You said something about looking for some kin around Binghamton. I thought you were from the west. Did you emigrate or something?"

Jacob narrowed his eyebrows in question, "I ain't rightly sure what emigrate is."

"That means, did you move from here and go out west?"

"You could call it that, but I didn't move of my own free will. I ain't quite sure how it happened. Doc, that is, Doc Highsmith, and my ma told me that back in the 80's and 90's there was a terrible sickness that left a lot of young'uns with no folks. They was so many of 'em they had to figure a way to parcel 'em all out to folks to raise 'cause they was too many of 'em in the orphanages. Doc said they loaded a whole bunch of orphans on trains and sent 'em out West. Well, I guess I was one a them young'uns."

Damn, that's it!" Danny stopped abruptly on the stairs and grabbed Jacob's shoulder, turning him. "That's the potential I saw when I looked at you yesterday. What an incredible story. Orphan returns to look for relatives." Danny held his arms up as if he were reading the newspapers headlines.

"Jake, my boy, you and I are going to locate your family or find where they're buried, and the *Binghamton Press* is going to run the biggest lost and found story this paper has ever had. We'll sell a million copies of your story, first in the paper, then as a book."

Danny continued as Jacob, in wide-eyed wonder, followed him down the stairs.

"Let's start with yesterday, Jake. You weren't in Molly's Café by accident, were you?"

"Well, yeah I was. It was close to the cemetery, so I moseyed in fer breakfast. I stayed the night before at a rooming house over near the railroad where I come in. They didn't serve breakfast, but the lady, she was Polish, I think, she was real nice, and we talked after I got my room. She sent me out there to Prospect Street and I went up to the cemetery, Saint Mary's, like she told me. The fella there was telling me they could maybe help, only they don't open till nine o'clock, so I went back to Molly's for breakfast."

"But why the cemetery?"

"Me 'n Greta Symanski, she's my teacher up in Ithaca, we called all over 'n writ letters asking about the names I got out of the book Ma gave me. None of 'em was any good, 'cept for one. Well, I ain't saying even that one was any good. Fact is we couldn't find no one with the last name 'a Wadleigh, so I come to Binghamton to look at every cemetery hereabouts. If my folks was named Wadleigh, they got to be buried someplace. The other fellas in the book was the ones that took the orphans out West to give away, and we identified all of 'em."

"Wadleigh, eh. How'd you spell that, Jake?" Danny asked, pulling out pad and pencil.

Jacob fished in his pocket for his own little book. "W-a-d-l-e-i-g-h," Jacob spelled the name out. "Here," Jacob handed the book to Danny, " you can see for yourself."

Danny thumbed through the pages. Most were blank. Binghamton, New York, was stamped prominently on the inside front cover. The name Wadleigh appeared on the front page, just Wadleigh, no Mr. Wadleigh, no John Wadleigh, and no Mary Wadleigh.

"Doesn't tell you much, does it?" Danny looked at the other names, Lund, Hagemeister, and Brindelli. "Here's a name I recognize, Brindelli. I think this is Frederic Brindelli. If it's the same man, I did a story on him a couple of years ago. Well, not just on him really, on our local orphans' home and the whole damn mess they got themselves into.

"They lost seven or eight children in a three-week period to food poisoning in 1904. I went out there after a funeral director, who had buried three of those children in one week, called me and asked me to investigate. The place was a mess. The kitchen was filthy, and there must have been forty or fifty sick kids lying all around. There was garbage piled on the floor, dirty clothes, the beds looked like the sheets hadn't been changed in a year, and there they were, poor, sick little things lying in those filthy beds. It was awful. Brindelli was thrown out within a few days of the story breaking. He left town, not to be heard from again. I guess he took a lot of the state's money with him and went to South America. Anyhow, for your search, he's definitely a dead end."

"That's why I gotta go to all the cemeteries," Jacob said. "I promised my Ma I'd try and look up my kin. I cain't think of nowhere else to look. If I can find a headstone with Wadleigh on it, she'll be satisfied, and so will I. I went and told her she was all the family I needed. So, it don't make no difference if I find 'em or not."

"Jake!" Danny was wildly excited at smelling a great story. "We're going to find your family. You understand me. If there's anybody in this town who can find your relatives, it's me. I've got strings I can pull to get information that's buried so deep, only the coal miners in Pennsylvania get to see it normally."

Their plans for breakfast at Molly's were not to be realized. The café was closed for repairs. Back at the Chenango Hotel, the restaurant was open for business and full of well wishers when Jacob and Danny walked in. Contrasting with the tired and dingy-looking workers at Molly's café, the patrons of the Chenango Hotel were mostly suited businessmen and elegantly dressed ladies. Several men and women appeared eager to get a glimpse of the famous cowboy and they confused Jacob by the demand for his signature on anything from a hotel napkin to a man's shirttail. Danny advised Jacob that that was a way of sharing his glory and then letting other people know that the recipient of the signature had indeed been in the presence of the great Western hero.

When the initial hubbub had subsided, Danny and Jake enjoyed a sumptuous steak-and-eggs breakfast, courtesy of the hotel management. Jake was most pleased and embarrassed at the attention.

Their waiter asked Jake if there was anything else he could do for the famous personage.

Jake stammered, "Could I get ma' meat burnt a little more?"

They finished breakfast, and Danny Toronto excused himself. "Gotta run, Jake. Don't leave town. Your room is paid for for as long as you're here. Oh, by the way, the Highsmiths have your message. They said for you to stick with me as long as you think I can help you." Danny offered his hand to Jake. "Whatta say, Partners?"

Jacob took Danny's hand and said, "Partners."

"Got any plans to kill the day until I get back. I want to check out something I remembered just now."

"I got to start looking for my kin again in the cemeteries. I'm going back and talk to that there Mr. Parks up at St. Mary's."

"Good. I'll see you later then. If you need anything, anything at all, tell the clerk at the hotel desk. They'll take care of it for you. Don't worry, it's on the *Press*. Oh, I forgot to tell you. I hired a fella to take you around. He'll meet you out front whenever you're ready to go." With that, Danny shook Jacob's hand and left.

Jacob went to the cashier to pay for his breakfast. "It's all taken care of, son. You come back, we're having a great special for lunch. And may I say it's an honor to serve you, sir."

Embarrassed, Jacob thanked the man and stepped out of doors. Once his eyes had gotten used to the brilliant sun, he noticed everything was completely different from yesterday's pristine winter show. The snow, now gray with soot, had melted considerably in the preceding twenty-four hours. Icy sidewalks had bare stone down the center, making walking easier, though caution was still to be practiced. Additionally, all the icicles that were clinging to the eaves of the houses and buildings yesterday morning lay shattered in crumpled heaps around their hosts.

As he stood on the sidewalk in front of the hotel, a carriage drawn by a single horse pulled up in front of him. The driver leaned out and asked, "Where to, Mr. Mead?"

Jacob stared up at the friendly, wrinkled face looking down at him. "You must be the fella Danny hired to take me around."

"Yes, sir. I'm Bill Kosalek, and I'm instructed to take you wherever you want to go. I understand you want to explore all the cemeteries in the area."

"Yes, sir, I do." he said as he climbed into the seat. For the rest of the day he explored cemeteries.

CHAPTER 9

Danny stood in the office of Miss Bess Adderman, Director of Records for the Broome County Relief and Orphan Home of the State of New York. Almost an hour had passed since he had presented his card to the pretty receptionist banging away at an awkward writing machine near the drafty front door. Each time someone entered or left the building, the cold breeze disturbed her papers and left her shivering and distracted. Danny smiled at the cumbersome machine she was fighting with, trying to complete her task. The *Press* had more modern mechanical writing machines and, in fact, he hadn't seen a writer such as hers since he was in college nearly twenty years ago.

Danny wasn't the least disturbed at being made to wait. Two thoughts occupied him while he waited patiently. One, he was there unannounced on what appeared to be a busy day. Second, waiting wasn't wasted time at all. It was thinking time. When Miss Adderman did appear, she would know she had kept him waiting, therefore, she would be slightly on the defensive. Danny intended to keep her on the defensive and push her even further to defend herself. An unpleasant memory stuck in his mind. Miss Adderman and he had nearly tangled before. He wondered if she would remember him.

"Mr. Toronto?" An extremely tall, thin woman stood at his side.

Danny looked her over. She was dressed fashionably in a long black dress and with what Danny thought to be sensible shoes. Her once-red hair had gone nearly all gray and was pulled back in a tight bun. That's sensible, Danny thought, she spends very little time fussing with her hair, an altogether sensible, no-nonsense woman. Nothing had changed in the almost three years since he had last seen her.

"Miss Adderman, thank you for seeing me on such short notice." He stood and offered his hand.

She ignored the gesture and in an icy voice announced, "Mr. Toronto, state your business. I am in a great hurry to return to my work, and I really don't have time to chit chat."

"Hold on, Miss Adderman. I don't want you to get off on the wrong foot with me. I came here to help a man locate his family, and I think you can help me."

"However can I help you?"

"Do you remember back about twenty years or so, an event now referred to as The Orphan Train?"

"Yes, of course. An unusual influx of parentless children caused the train from New York City to re-route through our area and pick up several orphans. Many of the children who boarded that train were processed through this orphanage. Incidentally, those records are sealed."

"Sealed?" His question and his expression revealed his doubt.

"Young man, I've told you the records are sealed. Your investigation is done here. Now if you will excuse me." She turned abruptly to leave.

"Would you mind if I went to Albany and talked to Donald Peck?" Danny threw the question to the departing figure.

She stopped in her tracks, whirled, and faced him. Why would you involve Mr. Peck in your investigation?"

"Because, as you know, Mr. Peck is in charge of funds allocated to this and all orphanages in New York State. It happened that he and I became great personal friends back during my investigation three years ago, and he would still like to shut this hell hole down and throw the whole bunch of you in jail. When Brindelli left the country, that satisfied the people of New York State as far as the Governor was concerned, but it didn't satisfy me. My research," Danny leaned forward to emphasize his next statement, "revealed that every one of the employees, from the janitor to the top administrators, were stealing from this home. Included in that list of names was yours."

"That's preposterous," she stammered, her pale cheeks turning color as she spoke "Please leave here at once, or I shall have to call security."

"Call them if you feel you can stand the heat, Miss Adderman. While we're waiting, suppose we talk a little about that investigation. It appears you've forgotten it.

"I had a lot of damaging information about this place, solid facts. I still have the records in my file. Financial, purchasing, adoption, banking, any kind of record this institution kept, I have. I have accounts on you, Brindelli, Widgeons, Barnhart, and several others. I may not have enough to hang you, but I certainly have more than enough to force you to resign.

"My mistake was to share the story with Mr. Peck during the conclusion of my investigation. He was so horrified that he called the Governor. Governor Hughes, mind you, is aware of Brindelli, and everyone else. He's the one who stopped the investigation and killed the newspaper story. He felt the resignation of Brindelli was enough publicity for the orphanage, and he wanted no more punishment heaped on this institution and its children."

She held her hands to her heaving chest for a moment and then finally seemed to compose herself. "Mr. Toronto, come to my office please."

"Why, thank you, Miss Adderman. I appreciate your time." There was the hint of sarcasm in his voice, but it was softened by his broad smile.

In her office, Miss Adderman sat behind her desk and motioned Danny to one of the two chairs in front of her.

"How can I help?" she asked, her tone softening.

"Let me look at the records of the children and parents of the children who were sent west aboard The Orphan Train."

"I'm sorry, Mr. Toronto, that really is impossible. As I told you, the records are sealed to protect the children and any surviving parents who don't wish to be contacted. It has always been thus, you understand. It would take an order from the Governor himself to open any records."

"Fine. That gives us a place to start." Danny leaned forward smiling, "May I use your telephone? I need to call the *Press*."

"Certainly. I hope you're not going to turn us in. We've been quite honest and above-board since the scandal. I assure you amends have been made and training in the proper handling of funds and foundlings has been instituted."

"No fear, Miss Adderman." Danny cranked the phone, activating a line to the central operator. "Hello, Central. Connect me to the **Binghamton Press,** please. The number is 2-7-F-2-2. That's two longs and two shorts. Thank you."

He waited while the central operator made his connection. "Hi, John. Listen, it's Danny. Get someone to call Governor Hughes for me, will you?" He paused and listened. "Yes, I said the Governor. I need immediate access to the records here at the Broome County Orphanage during a period around 1889, the Children's Aid Society out of New York City, and the records of the Orphan Trains during that period. It looks like our cowboy may have been one of the orphans we sent out of here back then. Tell the governor the story about yesterday's shooting and why we want the records. And listen, tell him I'm not interested in anything else, just whatever I can find out about Jake Mead and some folks named Wadleigh. That's it. I'll wait here with Miss Adderman in her office."

Danny paused and looked directly at Miss Adderman. "I don't care what you heard about her, John. Fact is we're getting along fine. Now hurry it up, will you?" He hung the ear piece back on its hook. "He should get back to us in less than an hour, Bess."

"Please, Mr. Toronto." she said, averting her eyes from his smile.

"Call me Danny. Mr. Toronto makes me feel like you're talking to my father."

"All right, Danny, if you insist. Please don't humiliate my staff if you feel you must prosecute me. I have suffered for my sins of greed more than you can ever imagine. Every penny, every dime I misspent has been returned. When you were close to exposing us with your investigation, I thought seriously of ending my life. I promise you, my shame is endless. I have spent two and a half years trying to make up for it, and if I live long enough, I may some day be able to forgive myself. Won't you please give my staff and me the benefit of a doubt? If you wish, while you wait for your call I'll open the orphanages books to you."

"It's just like I told John," Danny said smugly. "I think we're getting along just fine. Instead of looking at old financial records, why don't you introduce me to some of the children."

She smiled a thin smile signifying her relief and said, "I'll notify Delores that we'll be touring the facility so she'll be able to find us when your call comes in. Can you really call the Governor just like that?"

"I think so. We'll know in an hour or less."

Near ten o'clock, Delores approached Miss Adderman and Danny as they stood in the back of a classroom listening to a student struggling with a Latin lesson. "Miss Adderman, there's an urgent telephone call for Mr. Toronto. I believe it's from Albany." she whispered.

Bess raised her eyebrows and looked at Danny with new esteem. As they hurried back to the office, Bess said, "It appears you do indeed have the Governor's ear. Shall we see if he can help you?"

Back in the office, an aide was in a conversation with the person on the other end. He stopped his chatter abruptly as Danny and Bess entered. "Thank you, sir. Mr. Toronto is with us now." He turned and handed the earpiece to Danny. "The Governor will be on directly, sir."

Danny held the device to his ear and listened with a broad smile plastered from one ear to the other. He liked to smile on the telephone. He felt his good humor came across to the person on the other end, and he had some important selling to do.

The Governor's voice came across the wire crystal clear. "Mr. Danny Toronto, it's been a long time, son."

"Yes sir, good morning to you, Governor Hughes. Kind of you to take my call on such short notice."

"Nonsense, Danny. As I told you after the election, your support in the Southern Tier is what got me elected. I believe a favor deserves a favor."

"Thank you, sir." Danny paused, then plunged into his task. "Governor Hughes, did John Dagenhart, my editor, explain the reason for my call?"

"Pretty well, I believe. You're investigating a former orphan who may or may not have been a ward of the Broome County Orphanage and the Children's Aid Society. And that orphan, now a grown man, proved himself a hero right out of the Wild West. Right?"

"Yes, sir. I'm convinced Jake Mead originated out of this orphanage. After his heroics yesterday, I promised him I'd help him identify his family."

"What have you got to go on?"

"Damn little, sir. But I've got a strong hunch about this. Something's nagging at me. Maybe it's something I turned up in that investigation a couple of years ago, I don't know. I just can't put my finger on it. And believe me, sir, I've got plenty to do without this, but I think it's important enough to ask you to lift the seal so that I can dig into it."

The Governor chuckled into the telephone. "I'll probably catch hell for this, Danny, but I love a good mystery. Whom do I need to talk to there?"

"Miss Bess Adderman," Danny replied, his smile broadening.

"That the same Adderman you found under a rock during your previous investigation?"

Smiling as if he just heard a good joke, Danny answered, "Yes, sir. You want to talk to her?"

"Put her on, son. And by the way, if anything interesting comes of this, I'm to know immediately. Got that?"

"Yes, sir."

"And Danny."

"Sir?"

"Good hunting."

"Yes, sir, Governor. Good to talk to you. Here's Miss Adderman."

Bess took the earpiece and leaned over the speaker. "Governor Hughes, Bess Adderman, sir."

She stood listening intently. "Yes, Governor."

Danny watched her closely as she nodded continually, her eyes glued to the mouthpiece of the telephone.

"Yes, Governor," she said again. "Thank you, sir, we will," and with that she replaced the ear phone in its cradle".

She turned to Danny. "Where do you want to start. He said to give you free rein."

"Let's go look at some old records, shall we?"

Hours later, the light filtering through the basement window was fading to a point that strained Danny's eyes. He sat at a monstrously large wooden table upon which lay strewn ledgers, files, and scrapbooks. The smell of dusty, decaying paper permeated the air adding to the fatigue that was overtaking him. Bess sat nearby, ready to fetch anything he needed. Together they had looked at nearly thirty years of musty records and in not one entry was the name Wadleigh mentioned.

"We've got to get more light in here," Danny said, rubbing his dry eyes.

"Sorry. They disconnected the gaslights from the entire institution when electric lights were put in. Unfortunately, this part of the basement has never been wired for electric lights. However, there must be a lantern nearby. I'll find one and be right back."

Danny waited in the fading light. He struggled to remain awake, but his eyelids were not cooperating. He rubbed his face, trying to wipe the fatigue from his eyes to no avail. He slipped gently into a light nap with thoughts of Jake, the governor, and Bess Adderman swirling through his mind. Intertwined in his thoughts, was the name Wadleigh, floating through his musings like a string, a spider web perhaps, stretching longer and longer until it threatened to snap. He mumbled quietly, "Wadleigh, Wadleigh, Wad-leigh, Wad—leigh, Wad—leigh. Leigh, I've seen that name!"

With a start, he snapped fully alert in his chair as if a clap of thunder had exploded in the room. "Bess!" he shouted. He jumped to his feet in excitement. "Come quick. I've found Jake's family. By damn, I've found them!" Danny's voice was hoarse from fatigue, but his eyes were suddenly as bright as fireflies. He began hastily shuffling the old scrapbooks sprawled in front of him.

"We didn't need a light, Bess!" he exclaimed excitedly, as she entered the room. "What we needed was enlightenment."

With an unlighted lantern in her hand, Bess hurried to the table with a look of apprehension on her face. "I thought I heard you say you found Jake's family.

"I have. That is, I think I have."

"But how could you? We've searched every record from 1899 back to 1850. There's never been a Wadleigh living in Broome County."

"Right you are, old girl. We can go all the way back to King George's original land grant and we won't find Mr. Wadleigh." Then, in a conspiratorial whisper with raised eyebrows, he asked, "And do you know why we will never find Mr. Wadleigh?"

Danny was delighted at her reaction to his question. Even in the dim light he could see her shiver.

"Mr. Toronto, have you gone mad?"

"Humor me a little, Bess." Danny was exhilarated with his discovery and he wanted the thrill to last.

"I confess I'm lost. You haven't moved since I left for the lantern. I've been gone for no more than ten minutes, and all at once you're telling me you've solved a mystery we've researched for nearly nine hours."

"All right, I admit I'm not being fair. The fact is, Jake Mead was not Jacob Wadleigh when he was born."

"Whatever do you mean. Is the name Wadleigh useless to us then?".

"Nearly." Danny pushed a book her way, smiling, "Help me look through some of this stuff from '88 and '89. I'm looking for a newspaper article I ran into early this afternoon. I just glanced at it. Oh, by the way, we're not looking for anyone named Wadleigh." Danny paused, enjoying Bess' lingering look of confusion.

"Jake's last name was Leigh." Danny spelled the name. "L-E-I-G-H, not Wadleigh. His father's name was Wayne or Wade, or something like that. Help me find it."

They delved into the pile of old documents with renewed energy.

Bess took time to light the lantern. "Enlightenment may be fine for you, Danny Toronto, but I need light."

In a few minutes, Bess gave a startled, "Oh!" and continued reading the yellowed copy pasted in the scrapbook in front of her.

"Whatta ya got, Bess?"

"Look Danny. Oh my heavens. How awful. Oh those poor children."

Danny looked over her shoulder at the news clipping. It was dated March 3, 1888.

NANTICOKE CREEK CLAIMS 2 LIVES

In an event of sorry misfortune, two lives were lost Saturday eve when the bridge over Nanticoke Creek near Main, New York, collapsed due to the warm spring rain, ice break-up, and high water.

Mr. Wade Leigh and his wife Helen were crossing the bridge at the instant it collapsed, sending them nearly a quarter of a mile downstream entangled in the wagon, harness, and debris from the bridge.

The leaving of seven children who will become wards of the State of New York compounds the tragedy. They are Phillip, age 17; twin girls Esther and Elaine, age 15; Myra, age 9; Hiram 7; Wade Jr., 5; and an infant, Jacob, three months.

The article went on to report that the two townships of Union Center, and Main, N.Y. were shocked at the loss of such fine citizens. There were no known adult survivors. Mr. Leigh was a farmer by trade and had been leasing the old Phetteplace farm near the township of Main.

"Oh, Danny, those poor babies. What have we done?" Bess asked in a voice verging on tears.

"Good question. Let's keep looking and see what we find. Any question as to whether or not this is our Jake?"

"I can hardly imagine that it could be anyone else, except..."

"Except what?" Danny asked.

"Except there are seven children. Didn't you say Jake thought he had only two brothers and a sister?"

It was midnight before the rest of the trail was uncovered. Records, incomplete, smudged, missing, and just plain not posted attested to the poor state of the orphanage and the corrupt and sloppy management running it at the time, and in the many years following.

The older children of Wade and Helen Leigh were placed in various jobs in Broome County. Esther was placed in a shoe factory in Binghamton, Elaine was sent to Lestershire, New York, as an aide at Memorial Hospital, and Phillip was hired out as a farm hand on a dairy farm near the village of Main, New York.

In the late 90's, these three people were considered troublemakers for their numerous endeavors to open the records in futile attempts to locate their missing brothers and sister. The records were sealed and were to remain sealed. That was the law.

"Well, that explains why Jake thinks he's got only two brothers and one sister, Danny said with a sigh. "His step-mother never knew anything about those who didn't make it onto the Orphan Train."

More heartbreaking yet was the fate of the younger children. In 1890, they were shipped west aboard an Orphan Train to be adopted by Christian families in order to alleviate the severe crowding at the orphanage. A single notation revealed that a family in Cedar Rapids, Iowa took Myra Leigh; however, the name of the family was not mentioned. There was no mention whatsoever of the placement of the other three children, Jacob, Hiram, and Wade Jr. It was as if no one really cared what happened to the children of the Broome County Relief and Orphan Home of that day.

Danny stood, stretched, and yawned. "I'm tired. Let's quit for tonight." He looked down at Bess and said, "Don't breathe a word of this to anyone just yet, please. I'm going to check around tomorrow and see if I can find Jake's brother and sisters. You all right?" he asked, seeing her teary eyes as she held the records tightly.

"I'm just tired, but not sleepy tired. I suppose I'm just emotionally exhausted because of what we've found. I pray that you find Phillip and his sisters for Jake."

"Count on it, Bess. Count on it."

At seven o'clock A.M., Danny was in his office at the *Press* talking to John Dagenhart, the *Press'* editor. No one ever beat John Dagenhart into the office. He'd been in since before 6:00 A.M., and he already looked as though he had put in a full day. His hair looked as if it hadn't seen a comb, his shirttail was out, his collar was askew, and his bow tie hung unknotted. Danny smiled at the rumpled skinny man.

"I need everything we've got regarding the Orphan Trains that went through Binghamton in that time period, John. See if you can get a line on any of the Leigh family while you're at it. That Phillip Leigh may still be around here. The last time he inquired after his brothers and sister, according to the orphanage records, was 1899. They haven't heard from him or his sisters now in seven or eight years."

"Got'cha, Danny. Want me to polish your shoes and press your pants while I'm at it?" Dagenhart snapped. "Just in case you haven't noticed, pal, I'm trying to run a newspaper here while you're out chasing ghosts and myths."

"Thanks, John. I'm heading for the Chenango. My boy ought to be up and having his breakfast about now. See you later."

"Okay, I'll call you there if I find anything."

Jacob was famished in spite of eating late the night before. He stood in the entryway of the dining room, deciding whether he should wait for someone to seat him or just grab the first available table.

"Morning, Jake. You still got room to eat after what you ate last night?" Danny asked, as he grabbed Jacob's arm and led him to the dining room.

"Oh, g'morning, Mr. Toronto. I was just fixin' to take a bite."

"Jake, my boy, I don't want to have to re-train you every day. If you don't stop calling me Mr. Toronto, I'm going to start calling you Mr. Mead, and I'll buy a cane to help you walk in your old age."

Jacob smiled at the obvious try at humor. "Plum forgot yer first name fer a minute. What say I buy you breakfast this morning, Danny. I got to use up some of this jingle I'm carrying. My money ain't been no good ever since I hit this town."

"Can't let you do that, pardner, that's Western money and it doesn't spend around here while I'm around. Let's get serious for a minute. You didn't have any luck finding a Wadleigh in any of the cemeteries you visited yesterday."

"No, sir, I didn't. Fact is we didn't get to very many. They got 'em pretty spread out. I was planning on hitting a few more today, then if you and me ain't found nothing, I think I'll head back up to Ithaca. Them cemetery records is missing a lot, so I was having to do a lot of walking around looking at stones. You sure got a lot a dead folks 'round here."

Danny's face turned serious as he said, "I wasn't asking you a question, I was telling you, you didn't find the Wadleigh name. I already knew."

"You talk to Bill Kosalek. He drove me. By the way, thanks for the buggy ride, we got along fine."

"No, I didn't talk to Kosalek, I found out at the orphanage." Danny paused and grabbed Jacob's arm. "Let's sit down. I've got just a few more facts I need to get straight, then I've got a story to tell you."

They ordered breakfast while Danny was organizing his thoughts.

"Jake, do you know anything at all about your past before you were in Idaho?"

"Not much, I don't. Well, wait a minute. I remember Doc saying they was two orphan boys with me. They told Ma I had some kin when we all started out. But they was took before me. I was the youngest on that there train. Ma said I was the last one took up out of the whole bunch. Ol' Doc said folks just naturally didn't want no babies, 'cause they usually died. So, I was left till last."

"So, you had some relatives, what kind of relatives. This is important, Jake. Can you remember what your friend Doc or your mother told you?"

Jacob squinted and cocked his head in thought. "Near as I can recall, they said there was two boys and a girl, brothers and sister to me. That's part of the reason I'm here. Ma, and I guess me, was hoping somehow they got back and left word. Ma puts a lot of store in family. Ya see, Jess wouldn't let her have her own, so she wants me to have mine."

"All right. Now listen carefully. You said you had two brothers and a sister on that train when you started, right?"

"Yes sir."

"And your given name, was it written on a tag or something attached to your clothes. I mean, how do you know your name is Jacob?"

"Just exactly like you said. Ma found a tag on me. Guess she and Jess had a big row about the name Jacob. He didn't like it. Liked to name his own stock he said. I didn't even hear the name Jacob till after he was dead. But it's Jacob all right."

Their waiter came and they paused while he poured them each steaming hot coffee. Danny sipped his carefully, then watched in amazement as Jacob picked up his coffee and drank it as if it were ice water.

"Where's that tag now?" Danny asked, wondering if Jacob would even be able to talk.

"Don't rightly know," Jacob answered, oblivious to Danny's awe. "I ain't never seen it."

"Damn. Wish you had that tag."

"Why's that?" Jacob asked, as he held his cup up for a refill.

"Because that would prove for sure who you are, and who your folks were."

"Good morning, Danny. Having a little pow-wow with our hero?"

"Mike, Bill, how you doing. Jake, meet Mike Stanlowski of the *Albany Herald* and this character is Bill Doans. Bill, you still working for that rag up in Buffalo?"

Jacob nodded to the well-dressed men and shook Mike's extended hand. It was unexpectedly soft and warm. Ain't no working man's hand, Jacob thought.

"Danny," decried Bill, "you know it's not polite to tell you what part of my anatomy to kiss right here in public. That rag, as he calls it, Jake, is the *Buffalo Evening Times*, the finest newspaper in the entire United States of America." He turned back to Danny. "We could use you, Danny. Why don't you come to work for a good paper?"

"Thanks Bill, I'll consider it, when people ice skate on the Nile." Grinning broadly at his own joke, Danny continued, "Jake and I were just getting ready to leave. He's got a lot of places he wants to visit before he heads back to Ithaca. I told him I'd show him around."

"You wouldn't be trying to brush us off, would ya? What you got going' anyhow? I was hoping to talk to you last night. I waited in your office until after eight o'clock. You usually call or get in with the tail of your story. You run into something or somebody?" Bill asked as if he were in on a secret.

Danny sighed and said, "Ah, you got me there, Bill."

"Come on, Danny, spill a little," Mike Stanlowski cajoled, as he placed his hand on Danny's shoulder in a friendly manner.

"What do you want me to say, Mike, that I'm sitting on the greatest story in the world? Okay, I'm sitting on the greatest story in the world."

"Sure ya are, Danny, and she's keeping you out late."

Danny turned to Jacob and said out of the side of his mouth, "You just can't hide anything from these guys." He turned back to the two men standing next to him and said, "Fact is, fellas, I was out past midnight teaching a lady some manners, and that's the truth. That satisfy you?"

"Danny Toronto with a woman!" exclaimed Bill. "Now that's a real story. We were getting worried about you. It's been a long time." Mike extended his hand again to Jacob and turned to Danny. "You take care, Danny boy, and good luck. We'll be seeing you." The reporters left them alone again.

"What's been a long time?" Jake asked.

Danny shook his head, saying, "Nothing, Jake. Nothing."

"Well, now ain't that a patch a weeds. You ask me near everything about me, and I can't even get one little question answered about you."

"Sorry, Jake, some other time, maybe. Here's breakfast; let's eat."

Jake was perplexed at Danny's sudden moodiness. They ate in silence.

After several minutes during which neither spoke, Jacob, concern in his voice, finally asked, "Are you all right?"

"Sure, kid. I'm just fine. You about done?"

Jacob noticed Danny's tight expression and merely nodded.

"Finish up, and let's get going. We've got a lot of ground to cover today if you're planning on going back to Ithaca tonight."

"Mr. Toronto," a waiter said as he leaned over Danny's shoulder. "We're holding a telephone call for you at the lobby desk."

"Thanks, Pete. I'll be right back, cowboy. Have another cup of coffee."

Danny put the earpiece of the telephone to his ear and leaned toward the mouth horn. "That you, John?"

"Hey, Danny," it was John Dagenhart's familiar voice.

"You find anything?"

"You're not going to believe this. I got the full police report about a half an hour ago. You sitting down?"

"I'm leaning, John. What'cha got?"

"The cowboy's brother. I've got that kid's brother right here in the police report. At least he could be."

"What?" Danny shouted, startling the people around him. He nodded at them in an apologetic manner and returned his concentration to the telephone.

"He was in the diner during the shooting. Remember a witness named Phil?"

"Phil, like in Phillip?"

"Yep. Like in Phillip Leigh, born January 20, 1872, now age 35. He married Agnes Tyler, October first, 1899. In attendance at the wedding were twin sisters, Miss Esther Leigh and Miss Elaine Leigh of Binghamton, New York. We ran the wedding in the *Press* on October 6, 1899. Looks like a small, close-knit family. There were no other relatives or guests mentioned."

"Geeze, now that you mention it, I got a glimpse of Phil Leigh at the police station. You know, there is a family resemblance between Jake and him. Johnny baby, I could kiss you!"

"Try it and your fired," Dagenhart chuckled.

"Call Governor Hughs for me, will you, John, and tell him what we've found. But keep it quiet. What are you hearing about O'Brian. He gonna be all right?"

"He's up and walking and chasing nurses. Least that's what I heard. He's gonna be released Monday or Tuesday."

"Good news. Thanks, John. I'll get back to you in a couple of hours. I've got to figure out how I'm going to tell Jake he saved his own brother's life. He still wants to go searching the graveyards around town."

Later, as they walked down Hamilton Street toward the Susquehanna, Danny dodged a large puddle and said, "Jake, how bad do you want to find your family?"

"To tell the truth, I never figured on finding 'em a'tall. I'm doing this mostly for my ma. If they're dead, what difference do ya think it makes to me if I find 'em or not. Far as my— what'd that fella call 'em, siblings— goes, if they ain't left word 'round here somewhere, I might as well hollar down a well for all the good it'd do looking fer 'em."

"But if it was possible, you would like to find them, wouldn't you?"

"Who, my real folks? I suppose. It'd satisfy Ma pretty much. That there'd be good enough reason to find 'em."

"What about your siblings?"

"Yeah, I'd like to find 'em, if they's still alive."

"Okay, cowboy, tell you what, sit down. I've got some news for you."

Jacob sat on a park bench and looked up quizzically at Danny, suddenly anticipating nervously where the conversation was heading.

"Jake," Danny said and paused.

Jacob stared unblinking back at Danny. Only a few seconds had passed, but for Jacob it seemed as if hours were furiously flowing by, as he waited for the newspaper reporter's next words. Jacob's mind whirled with the sure knowledge of what Danny was going to tell him. His parents' records had been found, and perhaps even some record of his brothers and his sister who had accompanied him west on the Orphan Train.

Danny, as if overcome by the shear enormity of his news, suddenly blurted, " Jake, I found your family. Or rather, you found your family, your brother, even before you had breakfast on your first day in Binghamton."

"That ain't true," Jacob stammered. "If what you're saying is my folks is buried up on that cemetery on Prospect Street, well I must of missed their stone, 'cause I didn't see no Wadleigh headstone, and Mr. Parks, his records didn't help none."

Danny shook his head and said, "There is no Wadleigh headstone."

"There, see, I been wasting my time on a wild goose chase." Belatedly, his mind finally grasped what Danny had said. "Wait a minute. What'd you just say, about a brother or something?"

"Let me back up a little," Danny said as he placed his hand gently on Jacob's shoulder.

"What about my brother?" Jake was surprised at his own sudden emotions.

"All right, here's the story." Danny sat down beside Jacob and took a deep breath. "Late last night, we, that is the head mistress of the orphanage and I, found reference to your parents and a tragic accident that took their lives. Only, their name wasn't Wadleigh, Jacob. Your father's given name was Wade. His last name was L-e-i-g-h, Leigh. Get it. Your mother's name was Helen. Who ever wrote it down in that little book of yours either copied it wrong from something else, or he was just a lousy speller. Helen and Wade Leigh are probably buried out in West Chenango, near the little town of Union Center. That's where they lived—you lived, with your six brothers and sisters."

Danny pulled a notebook from his pocket. "When your parents died, they left, let's see," Danny thumbed through his notes, "Jacob, infant son, age three months, that would be you, Jake, Wade Jr., age 5, Hiram, age 7, and Myra, age 9. Then there are your twin sisters, Esther and Elaine, they were fifteen and your oldest brother Philip, he was seventeen in 1889. That makes it seven brothers and sisters, counting you."

"Seven." Jake blurted in astonishment. "Ma was told only four, counting me."

"If they're all still alive, you've got three sisters, and three brothers."

"You sure it's seven? How come Ma only told me three and me? Seven, my gosh, can we find any of 'em? Did it say where they was took up off the Orphan Train? Imagine that, seven." Jacob murmured quietly in awe.

"They didn't all go on the Orphan Train, so your mother doesn't know about them. Some of them were old enough to go to work and support themselves, which is exactly what the State of New York had them do. They worked right around here. Some of them still do."

"Here, you mean in New York some place?"

"I mean right here in Binghamton." Danny pointed to smokestacks belching black soot a little way down the river. "Likely in one those factories you see over there.

"Your brother works in one of those buildings, Jake. And when he's done working night shift, he likes to go into Molly's for breakfast once in a while."

Jacob was stunned to silence.

Danny, sensing Jacob's questioning hesitation, continued. "What you're thinking is absolutely right. He was one of the customers having breakfast in Molly's the day before yesterday. Likely, you remember him, because he went with you and Molly to the police station as a witness. His name is Phil, Philip Leigh."

Emotions hadn't often visited Jacob Mead. When his Pa died, he had felt relief or anger, depending on the moment. When the outlaw, Willie Frey, hurt Ma, fear and again anger welled up inside his guts. But usually, in the everyday lonely solitude of fixing fence, stacking hay, or other ranching chores, emotions were just plain unnecessary to survival.

An indescribable and uncontrollable feeling engulfed Jacob. His face became suddenly drawn and pale as he sat looking at Danny. He was trying to accept and digest the incredible revelation, when unexpectedly the terror of the conflict in Molly's two days ago suddenly played itself before his mind's eye. He saw the drably dressed workers, one among them his own flesh and blood, trying to melt into the tiled, muddied floor to escape the killing rounds of Clay Plover's shotgun. He clearly heard the shouts of panic the crashing roar of the exploding shots slamming into the walls and he smelt the acrid odor of spent gunpowder. His mind spinning, Jacob lowered his face into his hands and wept softly.

Late in the afternoon, Jacob and Danny were standing in front of a modest wooden house at number 14 High Street in Lestershire, a village on the north side of Binghamton. The sidewalk was neatly shoveled and the snow had melted from most of the south-facing front yard, revealing the promise of spring in the rich green grass.

Danny and Jacob had spent the better part of the morning and all afternoon cajoling the city police department into releasing information about Philip Leigh. A frantic late call to Mayor Williamson an hour ago finally had gotten the information released. And so there they stood, at ten minutes after four, at Philip Leigh's front door. Jacob's heart was pounding in his chest so fiercely that he felt Danny could see the rise and fall of it.

"Go ahead, Jake, he's your brother; knock."

Jacob raised his hand haltingly and tapped lightly on the door.

"Here, let me do it."

Danny was about to rap on the door when it opened. There stood a pleasant looking, plump woman with strands of hair falling loose and with wet, steaming hands holding a towel.

"Yes, can I help you?" she asked softly, looking at him with curiosity.

"Mrs. Agnes Leigh?" Danny asked.

"Yes?"

"Uh, is Mr. Leigh home?" Jacob asked cautiously.

"Why, yes. He's sleeping, but I'll have to get him up in about an hour. Can I help you?"

"Mrs. Leigh, I'm Jacob Mead. I come to see your husband," he drawled. "Won't you please get 'em up fer me?"

"Jacob Mead. Oh my, you're the cowboy from Molly's, aren't you?"

"Yes ma'am, I expect I am."

"You're all Phil has been talking about since the day before yesterday." Mrs. Leigh opened the door wide and gestured them in. "Yes of course, come in. Phil will be thrilled to pieces to have you in our home. My goodness, he's so proud of you and what you did. And I'm eternally grateful to you also, Mr. Mead, for saving my husband's life," she took his hand and looked thankfully into his eyes. "I'll never be able thank you enough. Come in, please." She ushered them into the sitting room and offered them each an easy chair. Jacob chose instead a firm wooden rocking chair and eased himself into it.

"Phil, wake up honey, you've got company," she called. Turning to her guests, she said, "Our bedroom is just down the hall. He'll be absolutely stunned to see you."

"We're sure of that, Mrs. Leigh. In fact, I can I guarantee it." Danny smiled, flashing white teeth that drew the attention of the frumpish Mrs. Leigh.

"Excuse me a minute, I've got my hands in hot water, cleaning the cream separator. I don't want my water to get cool. I'll not be a minute."

Danny looked at Jacob and winked. Jacob, sitting stiffly, his hat in his lap, paled as the time neared for him to confront his brother.

"What if we're wrong, Danny?" he whispered across the room.

"So what, cowboy. We'll have a nice visit. But don't you worry, partner, we aren't wrong."

"Phil," Agnes called again to her husband.

"I'm coming, damnit, gimme a minute." Heavy footsteps, shod in slippers or socks, drew Jacob and Danny's eyes toward the hall. Jacob could feel his heart skipping about every other beat as Phil approached.

Then, there he stood, a tall, muscular-looking man, with graying hair, and thick mustache, wearing working trousers with suspenders over his long-john underwear. Sleep still clung to his face while his eyes adjusted to being awake. Looking toward the kitchen without focusing on his guests, he called to Agnes.

"Got my coffee ready, sweetheart. What time is it?" He glanced at the clock on the mantel. "Who're these folks here?"

Agnes entered with a mug of steaming liquid and handed it to Phil. "Can I get you boys a cup. Phil, this is Mr. Mead from the café, and what did you say your name was, sir?" she asked, turning to Danny.

"I'm Danny, Mr. Leigh, Danny Toronto, with the *Binghamton Press.* I'm a reporter."

Ignoring Danny, he turned to Jacob and extended his hand as recognition brightened his face. "Mr. Mead. Damn, I'm glad you came by. I never got a real chance to shake your hand and say thanks for saving my life. Me and the boys over at E. J. Shoe, that's all we've talked about for two days now."

"Phil," Danny interrupted, "I'd like to ask you a few questions if you don't mind."

Phil turned to Danny and said, "Mr. Toronto, to tell the truth, I'm about questioned out. Plus, I can't remember anything else I ain't already told everybody twice or four times."

"Well, first off," Danny said, smiling, "I'm not Mr. Toronto. He's my dad. You know him? He runs Toronto's Produce over near Endwell. I'm just plain Danny. Okay?"

"Hey!" Phil replied, breaking into a wide grin, I do know your dad. Stefan Toronto, right?"

"That's Pop. Listen Phil, we, that is, Jake and I, came here because of an investigation we've done over the last couple of days. It's not anything that concerns the shooting at the café; in fact, it concerns you and your sisters Elaine and Esther."

Phil's grin disappeared. "Yeah," he scowled, "what about the girls. They all right?"

"Sure, far's I know. They still live around Binghamton?"

"Yeah. Esther lives across the street at number 17. Elaine lives two streets down on Myrtle, number 14, same's us. We stay pretty close together. Where's this leading? *The Press* put you two up to something you ain't telling us?"

"Of course not, but if you feel uncomfortable talking to me, do you feel you can trust Jake?"

Phil sat in his big chair, set his coffee on the side table, and rested his chin on his hands while he contemplated the situation. He looked squarely at Jacob, saying, "Well, I don't really know you either, young fella, but if you give me your word nothing's wrong, me and Agnes'll go along. That okay with you, honey?"

She nodded in assent, smiling warmly at Jacob.

"Your real name is Philip, isn't it?" asked Jacob.

"Well, sure. But nobody calls me Philip. Too formal for a factory worker."

Jacob was too nervous to continue. He looked pleadingly at Danny. "You gotta ask 'em. I can't."

"All right, let's try this, then. Instead of our asking questions, why don't I just tell you what I know, if I'm wrong, you can straighten me out. That suit you?"

Phil scowled at Danny, "I got shift at eleven o'clock, and I still need a couple of hours of sleep. The kids will be in any minute, so I get up to fuss with them awhile before I go back to bed. Can you keep it short?"

Danny cocked his head and looked thoughtfully at Phillip before continuing. "What I've got to say may come as a shock to you. If you had to, could you take the night off?"

"Hell no, man. I don't work all night because I want to, for gosh sakes. Get on with it, will you?"

"Okay," Danny relented. "Let's start back in 1888, March second. That was the day your parents died. You were seventeen and the oldest of seven children. Your sisters were fifteen. The reason you live so close together now is perhaps the fear of being separated like you were nineteen years ago. The three of you cling to each other because the State of

New York and the Children's Aid Society took so many in your family from you. Am I right so far?"

"Mostly, 'cept I ain't scared of nobody. They know that for sure down at the orphanage. I liked to rip that place down brick by damn brick a couple of times."

"Yeah, you're well known there," Danny said gently. "So are your sisters."

"We aren't in any trouble for something that happened seven or eight years ago, are we?"

"No, of course not. But back in the late 1890s, you and your sisters did create a stir trying to get information about your younger brothers, Wade Jr., Hiram, your little sister Myra, and the baby, Jacob. Finally, though, you had to give up the search because the State had sealed the records and they remain sealed to this day." He paused for dramatic effect, then said, "Unless you know Governor Charles Evans Hughes personally."

"Personally?" Phil asked quizzically.

"I talked to the Governor yesterday, Phil. One of your missing brothers has been found."

Phil looked confused. He turned to Agnes and Jacob, then back at Danny. Repeatedly his gaze swept rapidly over the three faces in front of him. He reached for Agnes and grasped her hand. "My brother is found? How? Where? For God's sake man, where is he?"

Danny looked at Agnes. "Mrs. Leigh, look at your husband."

She complied.

"Now take a good long look at Jake." Danny watched the mystified look on her face. "His real name, in case you didn't catch it earlier—is Jacob."

Agnes glanced at the two men. Then as she concentrated more deliberately on the two faces memory and features melded.

"Oh, my dear God in Heaven. Phil—he, he looks just like you, only ten years ago. Look at him, Phil. Just look at him. Wait here. I want to get our wedding picture from the bedroom." Totally flustered, she ran out of the room, tears streaming down her face.

Phil was unable to talk or even think. Shock more stunning than the recent terror at Molly's clasped him in its iron grip, rendering him mute.

No less emotionally paralyzed, Jacob sat staring back at his brother. Not until Agnas returned with the wedding picture was a word uttered in the sitting room as the two men stared at each other, and Danny, always the reporter, etched the emotional moment into his memory for later recall.

Within minutes, Lois and Wade, the Leigh's daughter and son, Jake's niece and nephew came home. After a hurried introduction but without explanation, they were sent to Aunt Elaine's and Aunt Esther's with orders not to return without them.

Phil missed his first shift in seven years.

CHAPTER 10

Ed Frey lay staring at the ceiling of his cell, thinking about the trial. Twenty-five years in this stinking cell. When Danny Davenport had been sentenced to hang, he had felt envy. The cowboy they had killed over near Emmett, the attack on the Mead ranch, Willie and Pat Bracket's deaths—how did he ever get into such a confounding quandary? He wanted to die.

His mother and father had visited him yesterday for Christmas, and what an unholy Christmas it had been. Had he been given a choice, he wouldn't have seen them. In fact, he had refused and had been subsequently dragged, handcuffed and shackled, to the visitors' room. Before his mother entered, he relented and asked the guard to remove his restraints with a promise to behave and act civil to his parents.

The meeting had gone as Ed expected. His father was sullen and resentful, his mother tearful and remorseful.

Yes, he was sorry Willie was killed. Yes, he was sorry he had run away. No, he didn't know why he did it. Yes, he was afraid of what the coming years would bring. Yes, they were treating him good. Well, good enough. He didn't expect much. "Yes-No-Yes-No," whatever his mother wanted to hear, he tried to accommodate her, all the while thinking, Damnit, Ma, go home and leave me be, and get Pa the hell out of here.

Ed played the scene over and over in his mind, the picture of his mother's tears tearing at his heart, the scowling glare of Ormond Frey's piercing eyes hurling accusations into his brain. Ed rubbed his eyes to try to remove the floating face of his father. "I'll go crazy in this place long before twenty-five years," he said in a raspy whisper. "I've got to get out of here."

He lay in his prison cell, top bunk, all day the day after Christmas and waited. He waited for the pain of his parents' visit to subside, he waited for his loneliness to grow and mature, and he waited for midnight. Midnight, Wednesday, December 26, 1906, Danny Davenport, the one true friend he had left in the world, would hang. Ed had to wait for Danny to go. He would hold onto his sanity until after Danny was dead. Then it wouldn't matter any more—he could go crazy.

As the sun broke the company of the night and cast its oblique rays along the wall of his cell, Ed lay still, staring, unblinking. Small imperfections on the brick and plaster walls cast tiny shadows that looked to him like hills and valleys beckoning to him.

"Come on Frey, Foote," barked the guard, "Git yer asses outta them racks!"

He blinked, and the cool valleys and sun drenched hills vanished from his mind, leaving a tedious dingy prison wall in their stead.

"Is it done?" he choked.

"Yeah, it's done," the burly guard dressed in black working clothes sniggered. "Your buddy's deader'n hell. Hauled him outta here less 'n an hour ago. Now git outta that friggin' bunk!"

He swung his legs over the side of his bunk. His cellmate, Pross Foote, growled unintelligibly as Ed hoisted himself to the floor, careful not to touch the lower bunk. The hulking brute had laid the ground rules within five minutes of Ed's unceremonious dumping into the cell with his meager supplies three weeks previously.

"This is *my* house, Piss-ant!" Foote had said forcefully. "Stay the hell out of my way. Is that clear? Don't never touch my bunk or my stash, and don't talk to me 'less I ast ya." Pross Foote was king in the cell, and he carried considerable weight out in the yard, as Ed was quick to learn. As time passed, Ed learned other facts about Foote. Surprisingly, he wasn't a killer. The fact was almost an accident. The three men he had shot had all lived.

Fifteen years ago, Pross had been the best ramrod foreman the Moss Brothers Mills had ever had and was consequently left pretty much alone. He carried a short fuse and could be difficult to manage, but the amount of work that came out of a mill meant money, to Christian and Willis Moss, a substantial amount of money.

Pross Foote would get raging mad at almost any infraction of his rules. Bump into him by accident, and you would find yourself looking up with a lump on your jaw. Touch any of his tools and it was trouble. If he was coming in your direction, you were advised to step aside, especially in the narrow catwalks around the huge, screaming saw blades. Fall behind in production, even as little as five railroad ties a day and he would erupt in a tantrum that scared the hell out of his employees. He ran the entire operation in an atmosphere of intimidation, but the work got out, and the owners were satisfied.

Pross was satisfied, too, until an unusual postal error fifteen years ago. That was when he accidentally found out how much the Moss Brothers Mill was making from their contract with the Union Pacific to produce railroad ties. Mail containing a copy of the coming year's contract and destined for the offices of the Moss Brothers Mills in Boomerang, Idaho, was misdirected to the mill in Grangeville, and into Pross' hand.

His mill was churning out ties at the rate of 200 a day. The railroad was paying a dollar and four bits for every tie, and he was being paid a mere two cents each, with a half cent bonus if they turned out over 5000 ties in a month.

The Moss brothers, Willis and Christian, were hauling in $7500 every month, and Pross barely earned $160 a month. The injustice of such unequal distribution of so much wealth gnawed at him for more than two years, until he decided it was time he was properly paid for his efforts.

He hadn't left the mill or missed work for more than three years, so when the request for time off for *vacation* arrived at the office of Christian and Willis Moss, they were only too happy to grant it. Complaints about Foote from the workers had always fallen on deaf ears. The mill was remarkably successful and Pross Foote got the work out, so he had earned a little time off.

Before taking the time off, Pross, through diligent investigation, learned that the Union Pacific shipped their cash payment to the Moss Bros. Mills office in Boomerang, Idaho, on the first day of each month for work completed two months previously. The payment came in the form of gold coin and was transferred from the railroad car to the office for the purpose of counting, and subsequently to the bank by armored wagon from the siding rail at the edge of Boomerang. One other fact that wove itself into Pross Foote's scheme was that the money car always arrived late in the day, and so the money and the car languished for the entire night on the railroad siding north of town, just waiting for him.

Boomerang being a backwater little town, Pross figured the chances were better than good that he could grab the whole payment and be a hundred miles away before they could get a posse organized to chase him and his accomplice.

His plan, though scrupulously fashioned, failed miserably. Two youngsters fishing after dark for catfish in a slough near the railroad siding had seen men with guns stalking the money train and had alerted the sheriff.

Inside the dimly lit interior of the car, two guards played cribbage while a third watched. When one of guards opened the armored coach door to relieve himself, he was gunned down, as were his companions, in a frenzied hail of bullets. In almost the same instant, Tom Carpinelli, the Sheriff of Canyon County shot and killed one of the bandits, and shot and wounded Pross Foote.

The three guards recovered from their wounds, as did Foote. After simmering in prison for thirteen years of his 25-year sentence, he was as wily as a caged wolf, and just as treacherous.

Months later, overcome with grief one night after lights out, Ed, in a quiet bitter voice to his cell mate, said, "Foote, I want ya to kill me,"

"Kill you, Piss-ant?" Foote whispered loudly from his lower bunk. "Now what the hell would I want to go and do that for? I'd just get myself hung killing you."

"Dying ain't so bad," said Ed. "It's a damn sight better 'n being penned up to the likes of some of them animals out there for 25 years and herded like a bunch a sheep waiting to die or get clipped. You kill me, then they hang you and we're both out of it. Think about it, Pross. If it ever gets to be too much, I'm willing to die if that's what it takes."

"Piss-ant, you ain't listening, are you? I ain't dying in here, and I ain't staying here. Come time to go, I'm going. And it's getting damn close. Fact is, I may need your help, but you gotta want to live, 'cause if you really want to die, I can't trust you. An' if I can't trust ya, I ain't gonna kill you, but you'll wished to hell I had, 'cause I'll break you into little chunks and cut you to within an inch of your damn useless life and leave you crippled. But you'll still be alive. They won't hang me for crippling you. Six months in the hole, and I'll be out working on my plan again."

Ed cocked his head in curiosity and questioned the hardened Pross Foote. "D'I hear you right?"

"You heard what you heard. You got till morning to make up your mind."

"Morning. I ain't gotta wait till morning. You want help, I'm your man. I ain't wanting to be no cripple neither. Never did like that sort of life." Ed was suddenly a little euphoric at the prospect of escape.

"All right, shut up. We ain't talking about it no more till I say so."

Ed didn't say another word that night, nor did he sleep.

By mid spring in 1908, it began to warm up every day into the eight-ies and nineties, and the prisoners were hustled off to various road proj-ects, most of them backbreaking labor, working as virtual slaves for the State of Idaho.

Sometime during the previous year, Ed Frey and Pross Foote had reached a sort of truce in their relationship. Ed was still required to remain strictly away from Foote's belongings, however; he could initiate conversations, and he could boost himself up to his own bunk by plac-ing his foot just so on the end of Pross' bunk without disturbing the hulking brute. The routine of prison life was still brutal, though.

Ed was unable to sleep nights, tormented by his memories and the insane screams of pathos from lights out until dawn ended the night-mares of his companions. His working hours, beginning at 4:00 a.m. and lasting until 7:00 p.m., produced the torture of merely trying to keep up his end in the hard labor of road building and staying awake. Any little break in the work routine would cause him to fall in his tracks and grab a few minutes of rest. Unsympathetic guards, hardened by years of forcing inmates to accomplish scheduled tasks, had developed highly effective, cruel methods of rousing the lethargic, exhausted pris-oners back to their work.

The break came when Ed least expected it. Pross Foote and he had been working in knee-deep freezing water for most of the morning, grubbing large rocks out of the channel of a nameless streambed under a half-completed bridge. Ed's legs had lost all feeling, causing him to watch his feet shuffle and move just to make sure they were behaving properly. He had just finished a short break, trying to warm his legs by rubbing them vigorously, when Pross handed him a long-handled shovel.

"There's three of 'em and eleven of us. Time to take our walk, Piss-ant."

"What the heck you talking about?" Ed hissed.

"Get your butt over behind Mack and wait till I yell to 'em to get his attention, then you wallop him as hard as you can on the head with that shovel. If I don't yell in the next five minutes, get back down here in the mud with me, and we'll try it another day."

"We gonna try escaping today? Why didn't you warn me?" Ed's legs suddenly felt as if they would crumble under him.

"Shut-up and get over there. Just walk casual like, like you was gonna take a piss or something."

Ed glanced at the other prisoners. They were all working as if nothing was going on. He strolled toward the guard.

"Hold it, Frey, where in the hell do you think you're going with that damn shovel?" the guard dressed in black uniform demanded. Mack stopped Ed in his tracks. Whip thin, Mack Keiver, in his mid forties, sported a thick black and gray walrus mustache that covered his mouth and which made up for the lack of hair on his head. The wiry prison guard doffed his hat, wiped his sweaty dome, and glared at his prisoner.

"Sorry, boss, gotta go. Just heading for the bushes. Gonna cover it when I'm done."

"Be quick about it." Mack turned and continued watching his other charges.

Ed slowed his pace as he passed Mack and glanced at Pete and Al, two convicts working the opposite side of the creek. Pete managed a small hand signal and a wink. The break was on.

Under the first strand of road trestle, Foote dug into the bank near a flat black rock about twice the size of a pie tin. As Mack glanced toward some of the other prisoners, Foote quickly tilted the rock, reached under it, and grabbed a small oil-cloth-wrapped object that he furtively shoved down into his pants.

He straightened and stretched his back, bending backward just as Pete crossed the creek. As Pete passed close to Pross Foote, he furtively snatched the concealed pistol from Pross and continued walking toward the water bucket where one of the other guards, Joe Goodrich, was sitting with a shotgun laying across his lap.

Pross bent and again lifted the black rock, revealing another gun. Pushing the rock aside, he pulled his bandanna from his pocket and wiped his brow, then he laid the bandanna across the depression containing the second six gun. He was ready.

"Hey, Boss!" yelled Pross Foote.

"Get the hell up off your ass, Foote, and get to work," Mack hollered back.

"Sorry Boss, leg cramps." Pross stood to force Mack's attention as Ed Frey whirled, took one step, and slammed his heavy shovel against Mack's skull, knocking him unconscious.

With the loud 'twang' of Ed's shovel smashing against his skull, Mack slumped in a disorderly heap to the muddy ground, at the same time as Pete pushed his pistol against Joe Goodrich's spine and pulled the trigger.

The third guard, panicked by the sudden mayhem of yelling inmates, whipped up his shotgun and with a scream of panic on his lips, fired a round of double ought buck into Pete that tore him nearly in half. Immediately, the guard was surrounded and wrestled to the ground by the other inmates.

It was over in less than ten seconds. One guard dead, one unconscious, one prison inmate dead, and ten convicts free.

"Hold on to 'em, Jackson," Foote commanded as he ambled over to the pinioned prison guard. He casually aimed at the frightened man.

"No. Please no." The guard's imploring words were wasted in the wind of the high prairie. The pistol in Pross' hand barked powerfully.

Life and spirit sped from the man's body as his blood seeped into the mud-trampled earth.

"Won't be no more whippings by that boy no more," an inmate said gleefully.

"Mack's still alive!" shouted another. "Let's do him 'fore he wakes up!"

Ed was aghast at the casual killing of the guard. Pross Foote had killed with no more thought than if he was lighting a cigar. Ed stood motionless over Mack, who had truly been the cruelest of the three men guarding the prisoners. He still didn't need to die, Ed thought.

"Okay, Piss-ant, Mack's turn. You want to do him?" Pross asked.

"Uh, no," Ed stammered, his eyes wide and watery. "Don't kill 'em, Pross. He ain't gonna hurt us. I wholloped 'em good enough, he'll sleep all day."

"Yeah, he'll sleep all day, all right," said Pross as he aimed at Mack's temple and fired. The body jumped into the air, then sagged as the remnants of life, scrambled by the exploding bullet, ceased to dwell in Mack Keiver.

"Shit, Pross. Ya didn't have to do that. What the hell'd ya have to kill 'em for?" wailed Ed, agitated, frightened, and near hysteria.

"Piss-ant," growled Pross Foote, "I hear one more word outta you like that and you're going down just like Mack 'n Joe. I got ya loose and that's that. Now, get the hell outta here 'fore I change my mind 'bout letting you live."

Ed Frey was free. He had been in the state prison 520 days, that amounted to 12,480 hours give or take a couple, and now, finally, he was free again.

He had no delusions that freedom would mean that he was able to move about as he pleased. He could never visit his family, he couldn't go into a town without the risk of capture, and he could never stop looking over his shoulder. He was wanted for murder and escape. The question was, not if, but when, they would catch up with him. The conclusion, that *that* day would be his last was certain. A day, a week, hopefully a year or better, would pass before he would have to face his final stand.

In the meantime, he had to put space between himself and the state of Idaho. Montana was less than eighty miles to the northeast from Lowell, where the convicts had been working for the last month. Washington was about twice that distance in the opposite direction, and Oregon was too close to Ed's original crimes and his family.

Twenty-two days later, just outside the small settlement of Two Dot in Montana, Ed found temporary work riding for an outfit that asked no questions. He was a city boy learning to cowboy.

The Rocking Pine Cattle Company was an empire consisting of two ranches in Montana of about 100,000 acres each. They found it profitable to hire anybody they could find who was willing to help in controlling cattle and squatters on surrounding open range land, thereby increasing their holdings to more than 500,000 acres. Your past or your name didn't matter much. If you could ride and were willing to shoot at a squatter, "Just to scare 'em off ya understand," you were qualified to work for a dollar a day and your keep.

Ed, using the name of his dead friend Pat Bracket, went to work learning an honest trade for the first time in his young life. As Pat Bracket, he kept to himself for most of the first month. Cowboy pranks and small talk went on around Ed constantly, but he ignored the activity, or snapped at his companions if they tried to get him involved. A year and a half ago he was a happy-go-lucky kid with a reputation of getting into mischief at every turn. The education he had since endured caused him to be sullen, aloof, and wary.

On a warm late-June morning, assignments were handed out. The foreman called each man with the day's tasks. "Pat, I need you to go up to Pioneer Meadow and clean out the spring, and fix the drain down to the watering trough. There's likely some fence needs mending, and watch fer any fresh cows and herd 'em closer in. Not much chance of it, but watch for squatters, too, an' if ya see any, get 'em out of there. Can you handle that by yourself?"

"Yes, sir, boss." Ed mumbled, his hat pulled low over his eyes.

Samuel Hanks, the foreman, well over six feet tall, lean, and Negro, looked closer at the young man in front of him. He stared at Ed so hard that Ed began to shift nervously where he stood until Hanks finally looked away.

Ed, sitting high on the wooden seat of the work wagon, slapped the reins against the horse's rump and the old horse responded with patience as they headed out to complete the assigned tasks. With the sun on his back and the slightest hint of a breeze out of the south, Ed savored the morning ride to his assignment. Half asleep, he reviewed his situation at the ranch. Good food, plenty of work, a place to sleep and relax evenings, and though he didn't feel comfortable mixing in, he had pretty good companionship. He could almost forget the circumstances that had forced him into his current situation. Almost.

"Willie," he said aloud to his brother, "you would have loved it here." Ed hadn't talked to his little brother's spirit since December 14th of 1906, more than a year and a half ago. As the judge handed down his sentence, following the guilty-on-all-counts verdict, Ed had silently spoken to the dead Willie, "Thank God, Willie, you ain't gonna have to be locked up like an animal."

Behind the plodding farm horse, Ed relished the deep blue of the heaven's dome, contrasting the whiteness of billowing clouds and the snowcapped mountains floating in the distance. Rich, dark green meadow grass and fluttering aspen trees of the flat high country stretched away from him in an endless display of spring growth. Willie's smiling, happy face played in Ed's imagination in the morning sun. "You would've been happy here forever, Willie."

With an unexpected crack, the wheel of the utility wagon slipped sideways off a rounded boulder and into a shallow dry rut. Spokes shattered and the wheel collapsed, throwing Ed to the ground in a bone-jarring heap. "Whoa, boy. Whoa, whoa," he shouted to the frightened horse entangled in the straps and harness. He jumped to his feet, ran to the horse's head, and grabbed the bridle to steady the animal. "Easy, boy. Easy, Charlie, 'tain't nothing but a broke wheel."

A half-hour later, Ed and the horse were back at the ranch looking for help.

"Nope, cain't help ya, Pat. Ain't nobody left 'round here that I know of," said Cookie, the fat hairy old man who prepared grub for the ranch hands. "Fixed ever' one of 'em a sack and they's gone. Cain't help ya a'tall. Might check the bunkhouse though, see if any of 'em's laid in sick or hurt that can give ya a hand."

Ed headed for the barn to look for a spare wheel or another wagon, when he happened past the bunkhouse and out of the corner of his eye saw a head ducking out of sight below the window. Thinking that there would be help, he turned into the bunkhouse and caught a glimpse of Bruce Shotwell ducking out the back door.

"Hey, Shotwell, hold up!" he called. He suddenly noticed his bunk. It was covered with everything he owned. His bedroll had been opened, and though his possessions were meager at best, everything was strewn about. "What the hell?" he shouted.

Ed dashed out after the fleeing figure and caught him just inside the hay barn. "What the hell you doing going through my stuff?" Ed grabbed and slapped the cowering Shotwell.

"Nothin, Pat. I wasn't lookin' fer nothin," he whined.

"Then why'd ya get into my stuff?"

"I was worried about ya. I was afraid ya might be in trouble 'n maybe I could help ya."

"Well, forget it. I catch you near my stuff again, I'll kill ya. You understand, you sorry son of a bitch?"

"I'm sorry, Pat." Bruce stuttered. "Thought I could help ya, was all." Shotwell flinched as Ed towered threateningly over him.

"What the hell you talking about, helping me. What'd make you think I'd need or even want your damn help?"

Bruce raised his head cautiously. "I seen yer picture. Least it looked a lot like you over in Butte. Said you was wanted in Idaho for murder and escaping from prison, and your name is Ed something. I looked through yer stuff so's I could find out if it was you or not." Shotwell's tone changed, his eyes narrowed. "Listen, I can help ya if ya was to get found out by the law. I got friends."

Ed snorted in disgust. "I 'spect you'd help me all right. Help me get hung so's you'd get a reward. How much reward was on the picture anyway?"

"I don't remember, maybe a couple 'a thousand dollars. Hell, I wouldn't turn nobody in, especially a friend, for no measly thousand dollars 'er two." Bruce started to move out of arm's reach. "And I know somebody else who'd help ya."

"I don't need no help, Shotwell. I'll just do my job and get by." Ed's voice became harder and his words sharper. "You stay out of my way, you little pip-squeak, and I might let you live. Cross me, and you'll be dead 'fore you hit the ground."

"Can ya tell me something then?" Bruce asked as he stood cautiously and brushed off the straw. "I mean, just in case things ever get too hot for ya."

"What?" Ed said tightly.

"If ya get into trouble 'round here, ya got a plan?"

"Yeah, I got a plan. I got a damn good plan. First, I'm gonna shoot you right between the horns, then I'm gonna ride like hell across the closest border. That good enough for ya. See, I even included you in my plan."

"You know a fella name a Neil Browning, don't 'cha?" Bruce's eyes narrowed in a wicked gleam.

Ed was startled at hearing the familiar name. He couldn't speak for a moment, then he whispered, "Browning. Never heard of 'em."

"Yeah, you know him. He knows you."

Ed looked closely at the pocked, weasely face of Bruce Shotwell. "What about 'em?"

"Oh, nothing, only me and him's friends. He told me he was with Pat Bracket the day he died. Now here you are claiming to be Pat Bracket."

"So Browning didn't die back in Idaho?" Ed said almost to himself.

"Die, hell no. Almost did. I found him in the railroad yards in Butte. He was stiff as a board and as near dead as ya can get and still breathe a laying in a boxcar in the switching yard. I was just looking in open cars for some stuff that I could turn into a little cash. Well, I seen this body lying over in a corner and figured some tramp probably froze to death coming off the Divide.

"I was just about to check his pockets to see if he had any money or anything, and I was gonna leave him. But damn, he come alive on me. Scared me to death, he did, and then he pulled a gun on me and made me take him over to where I was living with my cousin at the time. He lived through it somehow, being sick and all and we got to be pretty good friends. He's growed a mustache and beard, 'n he's put on considerable weight, so if you knowed him back a little, you wouldn't know him no more."

"Where's he at now?" queried Ed.

"Working for this same outfit we're working for, the Rocking Pine Cattle Company. They got another spread up by Sweet Grass. It's still in Montana, almost into Canada. Says he wants to stay near the border till things cool down."

"I'll be damned, he made it," Ed exclaimed, smiling at the thought of Neil, not only surviving but being in Montana. "Listen, Shotwell. Don't say a word to anyone 'bout this conversation. And if I ever hear you spilled the beans to Neil Browning 'bout me being here, you can just figure you're another day closer to meeting your maker. Any questions?"

"Ya don't have to worry none 'bout me, Pat," Bruce emphasized. "I figure there can easy be two Pat Brackets in the world. Probably it was some other guy he was talking 'bout all the time. But I ain't saying nothin' all the same, that's fer sure!"

For the rest of the summer, Ed Frey worked closely with the repugnant Bruce Shotwell. Bruce's desire to belong, and Ed's distrust of letting Shotwell out of his sight forced their companionship. As was the case in prison when he was forced to live with Pross Foote, Ed managed to work out an arrangement with Bruce Shotwell that allowed them both the satisfaction of surviving and working without getting on each other's nerves too much.

For the next two years, Ed Frey was content with his work on the Rocking Pine. When he was alone, he talked often with his little brother, whose ghost was his constant companion.

"Willie, Neil Browning is gonna have to pay for what he done to you and me. Ain't no place but here that's safe, thanks to him, and he kilt you. He's got some mighty big payments to make."

But Ed refused to harden. He worked hard on the ranch and made friends sooner or later with all he met. Revenge was his constant companion, but it didn't consume him. In fact, he didn't really even hate Neil Browning. He and Neil had run together for years before the Mead Ranch disaster. In thinking back, Ed had to admit that Willie's death was his fault too. Neither he nor Willie was forced to go with Neil. The real reason Willie was dead was because Willie was there.

Ed Frey went to sleep every night with the tragic events of the fall of 1906 coursing through his mind. Danny Davenport hanged, Pat Bracket shot through with a buffalo gun, Willie killed by a wild shot, and Neil run through with a pitchfork.

Yes, sir, Neil's gang was some bunch, Ed thought one night while lying on his bunk. And here I am hiding out and on the run till the day I look over my shoulder and some lawman's rifle will be pointed between my shoulder blades. The three massacred prison guards left sprawled beside a remote mountain road back in Lowell, Idaho, were the guarantee of that, all thanks to following the lead of Neil Browning.

"Neil, old buddy, someday you're gonna have to pay the debts you owe Willie, Danny, Pat, and me," Ed Frey vowed.

Chapter II

Pross Foote sat patiently in the saddle and looked back at Neil Browning. "Fat lazy bastard," he said to himself as he watched Neil struggling to stay in the saddle while horse and man climbed the last few feet of the canyon ridge.

Neil's body had changed since his accident. No longer was he firm and lean. A welt of fat had added inches to his girth. Prior to being gravely wounded by Jacob Mead two years earlier, Neil Browning had been smoothly handsome. But during his convalescence he had gained an enormous amount of weight that he found impossible to shed. At only 22 years of age, the ravages of fever and infection had forced a great deal of gray into his hair and beard. Except for the lack of wrinkles around his wickedly slitted eyes, one would have easily mistaken Neil Browning for a man nearing 50 years, instead of a young man of an age when he should have been entering his prime.

The Rocking Pine Cattle Company, Northern Division, had sent Foote and Browning on a mission to remove some squatters who had settled on the old deserted Whitmere place two and a half a years ago in the Cut Back Creek Canyon country, and to put the fear of God into them. The expectation of the cruel winters driving them off the forlorn farm had not materialized and action was expected to be taken. The selection of these two cowboys was not an accident, as both men had, over a period of months, proved themselves capable of bullying those around them in order to effect their own desires.

Neil had shown his colors by intimidating Nat Chalmers, one of the oldest cowboys on the ranch. Shortly after arriving at the ranch, Neil had evicted Nat from his choice spot in the bunkhouse. The bunks were pretty much the same, except Nat's happened to be closest to the door and in the northeast corner, so that it caught the first cool breezes of the evening, making it the coolest possible spot in the room on torrid summer nights.

Nat Chalmers awoke one night, and in the bright moonlight found himself staring at the point of Neil Browning's knife, less than half an inch from his eye.

"Morning to ya, Nat. Having a hard time sleeping?" Neil whispered hoarsely. "Take my bunk 'cross the room."

"What the hell you doing, Browning?" Nat asked, his voice thick with sleep.

"I'm a sick man, Nat. I need a cooler place to sleep."

"Get the hell away from me, and get the hell out of here."

"Sorry you feel that way. We'll talk in the morning." With that, Neil slowly lowered his knife against Nat's left eye, and held the old man's eyelid open with the point of the blade. "Go to sleep, Nat," Neil said in an almost kindly, sarcastic whisper.

Neil continued holding his knife against Nat's eye for several seconds, until Nat was forced to blink, and could not.

"Browning, get that damn knife the hell away from me. You can have the friggin' bunk," Nat rasped in panic.

"Thank you, Nat," Said Neil, his teeth shinning in the dim light. "You're helping a sick man."

Released by his captor, Nat, overcome by excitement and the terror of his close encounter, jumped up, grabbed his gun, and pointed it directly at Neil's grinning face. He screamed, "You son of a bitch!" He pulled the trigger, one, two, three, four times. The fury of his words, babbled and sobbed in panic, awoke the rest of the lightly slumbering cowboys. There were plenty of witnesses to the attempted murder of Neil Browning, who defended himself against a gun-waving madman with a simple skinning knife. Nat let out a belly deep groan as Neil sank his knife fully to the hilt into and through Nat's skinny forearm.

Neil grabbed Nat, pulled him close, and whispered in his ear, "I took the time and trouble to see to your piece, Nat. You ain't got no bullets in it." He shoved Nat away violently and said out loud so the others could hear him, "Better go see Cookie and have him fix up that arm of yours."

Nat, at 71 years of age, didn't need to be working with a damn crazy man, and he quit the Rocking Pine Cattle Company later that afternoon. He told Ray Segura, the foreman, why he was quitting, and that he should be wary of that crazy Browning. But Nat knew that the likes of Neil Browning would to be considered an asset to an outfit like the Rocking Pine, to be tolerated and fed until he was needed.

As Neil and his horse cleared the top of the ridge Pross dismounted and motioned him over and pointed at smoke drifting above the trees a mile or more to the south.

"That'd be them pilgrims," said Pross. "Firing slash to clear fields for planting. It's too late to jump 'em today; let's hole up here till morning and catch 'em 'fore they get the sleep out'n their eyes."

Neil climbed off his horse with a sigh of relief and grunted in agreement. He tolerated Pross Foote as an equal, but there wasn't any illusion of friendship between them. Neil's fatigue left him no energy to make camp. "I'll grain the horses, you start camp."

Pross reached over and grabbed Browning roughly by the shoulder of his coat and glowered at the fat rider. "Listen Browning, you start giving orders to me and you're gonna find life tough going. Get out there and you get some wood together."

Neil jerked his shoulder free and lowered his voice until he was barely audible. "What'd you say Foote? You gonna give me trouble?" Neil's pistol was in his hand and pointing at Foot's belly faster than Pross Foote's eyes could follow. Months spent mending his body had not been wasted. Neil had been a fervent devotee in practicing the fine art of the fast draw.

The distinctive click of the hammer being cocked over a live round sent an involuntary shudder through Foote. "All right, all right, take it easy Browning. Put that damn thing away," he said, raising his hands in front of his chest defensively.

"Not until we reach some kind of understanding." Neil's voice was as cold and hard as the pistol he pointed at Pross Foote's gut. "I ain't taking no orders from the likes of you. Not today, not tomorrow, not never."

"Looks like we got ourselves a stand-off here, Browning. You can't shoot for fear of alerting the nesters, and I ain't about to challenge a man with a gun in his hand. So I'll tell ya what: you put that thing back in your holster, and from now on, you don't give me no orders, and I don't give you no orders. I'll fix my own camp, you can do whatever you want about a fire 'n coffee and such. Come morning, if we can't work out how ta' handle the nesters, you can handle 'em yourself any way you want. No bosses in camp."

Neil slowly lowered and uncocked his weapon, warily watching his companion for any aggressive movement. Pross Foote turned; ignoring Neil's threat, he commenced to prepare his camp in a rock-surrounded depression at the edge of a stand of tall firtrees.

Neil was a city boy, born and bred. He had camped out with his cohorts from Boise on their forays often enough, but he had failed to pick up any of the finer points of out-dooring, simply because he had always seen to it that others did the work. His business in camp had been to eat and sleep. His lack of outdoor skills, and being less than fifty miles from the Continental Divide where night temperatures dropped to barely above freezing, were brutally working against him now.

Several attempts at building a fire were ruined by the slight evening breeze that wafted Neil's few matches before he could get so much as a twig burning. His resentment of Foote's cozy fire, along with the smell of boiling coffee and sizzling bacon, were beginning to drive Neil to considering a truce with Pross.

"How ya doing, Browning?" Foote asked with a sarcastic chortle. "I'd build a fire if I was you. It's gonna get close to freezing tonight this high up." Pross chuckled in exaggeration.

Neil sighed and reluctantly said, "I run clear out of matches. You got any?"

"Sure, I got matches. How many you want?"

"Three or four should be enough."

"How many'd you waste already?"

"Quit funning, Foote. You gonna gimme some matches or not?" Neil demanded.

"Give you some matches. Nobody said nothing about giving nobody no matches. They're five bucks a piece."

"Shit!" Neil fell silent as the last of the daylight slipped away. He had had nothing to eat and only plain water to drink since midday. His mood was not pleasant as he hauled his saddle off his horse and wrapped himself in his blanket. An hour later, he was still awake, entertaining a fantasy of Pross Foote lying in a pool of blood.

"Browning" Pross called softly into the darkness.

"What the hell you want, Foote?" Neil snapped.

"I want you alive in the morning. Get on in here by my fire, and no nonsense with that friggin' gun of yours."

Without a word Neil rose and walked into the lighted camp. Pross had built his fire right at the base of a tall, flat granite outcropping that tilted slightly downward. The small fire reflected off the granite face, providing a circle of comfort that easily accommodated the two men.

"Thanks, Pross."

"Hey, ain't no reason for us to quarrel, now is there? Hell, we're both of us here to do a job for the Rocking Pine. Help yourself to coffee. It's still hot."

"Guess I figured you all wrong," Neil said, giving Pross a tight smile. "Thanks again."

"No, you ain't figured me wrong a'tall. It was me that figured you wrong. I thought you'd be whining out there in the cold, 'stead you just settled down without no complaints. Ya kinda took me by surprise."

Neil poured a cup of coffee into a tin cup and sat close to the fire. "Well, I been out in the cold before. Spent three or four days, I don't remember how long, maybe a week, in a boxcar and it was a lot colder 'n tonight, 'n I was gut stabbed to boot. I was so sick, I don't remember much about it. I'd a died, 'cept I ain't dying till I get that bastard that stuck me.

"Where'd that happen?" Pross asked, sitting up on his bedroll and staring at Neil across the fire.

"Boomerang."

"Boomerang. Over by Oregon?"

"Yeah, you know it?"

"Hell, yes, I know it. The sheriff there, he shot me and I got sent to prison for twenty-five years for trying to rob the Moss Brother's money train a few years ago."

"Moss Brothers. You tried to rob that outfit. How come."

"Something I learned when I was ramroding for 'em at their mill in Grangeville back in '85. The Union Pacific mailed their contract to me by mistake, telling how much they was making and how they was to be paid. Hell's fire, man, I couldn't believe how much they were robbing me, with me and the men doing all the work and them getting all the loot. Some damn kids turned me and Miles in whilst we was getting ready to clean the place out, and Miles got kilt. I spent thirteen years in prison on account'a that sheriff, and I ain't forgot him, but then again, I ain't in no hurry to go back to Idaho any time soon just to finish my sentence."

"I'll be hornswagled. You worked for Christian Moss?" asked Neil.

"Christian an' his brother Willis too. Willis died during the trial."

Neil looked at Pross Foote. He thought a minute and decided that Pross might be just the man he had been looking for to help him form a new gang. There was a great deal of money back in Idaho, and he was entitled to it. He had suffered for it, and he was damn well going to collect payment.

"Hey, did you know Moss personally?" Neil asked casually.

"Yeah, I knew him pretty good. He and that snotnosed brother of his would show up from time to time and snoop around, sticking their noses in. It was their mill an' all, but I run it for 'em. Hell, I even run 'em off their own place once. I was the boss, we got the work out, and I didn't need him or Willis, neither one, telling me and my men how to do our business."

"Let me tell *you* something about Moss," Neil interjected. "Me and my cousin we know'd Moss since we was little kids. Hell, old Moss bought me my first pair of cowboy boots. My cousin, Randy Alsman, was his nephew, and Moss always treated Randy and me like we was brothers, just the same as if I was kin of his."

"That a fact?" asked Pross, his eyebrows raised in interest.

"Fact," Neil said nodding slightly. And I been in his house lots of times too. He's gotta be rich. He's got more doo-dads in that place of his than you can shake a stick at. I'll bet he hides a lot of his money right there in the house."

Pross sat straighter and his eyes opened noticeably.

"'Nother fact, Pross, it was ol' Moss hisself that helped me get out of Boomerang couple years back, if you know what I mean."

"Meaning you was on the run, right?" Pross looked across the fire at the ungainly fat lump of a man reclining against his saddle. He smiled at Neil suddenly, his constant sneer gone.

"Meaning, in fact, that I escaped the hangman, Pross. I escaped the hangman with the help of *Mr.* Christian Moss."

"Ya don't say. Well, I'll be damned. Ya know, Browning, I ain't got no reason to doubt ya, but ya sure don't appear to look like a fella that's been through so much." Pross rolled a smoke, struck a match, and sucked a fire onto the tip of his cigarette.

Neil waited until he had Pross' full attention and said, "Foote, let's you and me bury the hatchet. I got a couple of ideas that might interest you."

"All right, let's just say for a minute we agree to not disagree, whatta you got up that sleeve of yours?"

"Mead money is what I call it. You ever hear of a family a name 'a Mead?"

"Nah, never heard of 'em," Pross answered, taking a deep drag on his cigarette.

"Ain't surprised. They live way out in the sticks, east of Boomerang. Heard tell that 'fore old man Mead died, he dealt stock to the army during the Indian wars in Washington and Oregon. Made a fortune, and never spent a penny of it 'cept to buy that place his widow and her kid live on. Well, he ain't exactly a kid no more, he's close to the same age as me."

Pross chuckled. "That sure would make a mighty old youngster if he's as old as you, Browning."

"Hell, Pross, I ain't but twenty-two. He's likely not more 'n two 'er three years younger 'n me."

Pross scowled and said, "Twenty-two. You ain't no twenty-two. A fool can see you ain't gonna see forty again."

"Getting gut-stuck ages ya, Pross," Neil said morosely. "What I been through, you wouldn't believe. Reason I look like I do is 'cause that damn Mead kid stuck me clear through with a pitchfork, 'n I got septic and it done something to me. I got through it, but I ain't never gonna be right again. You think I like being fat, or having all this gray in my hair and beard?"

Neil stroked his scraggly beard and continued, "Only good come of it is the law don't know what the hell I look like no more, but I don't never feel good. Can't hold food, can't sleep, riding hurts like a son of a bitch.

Hell, I can't even take a good shit I'm so tore up inside. That bastard is gonna come across my sights again someday, and he's gonna get paid for what he done to me. And by damn, I'm gonna kill his ma, too, for whelping that pup.

"I want ya to help me clean out that Mead bunch. There's plenty in it for both of us, and then I'll help you. Fer instance, ya'll got something coming from Moss, ain't 'cha?"

"After thirteen years in prison. I haven't even calculated what ol' Moss has put away since I got arrested, but whatever it is, he owes at least half to me. The way I got it figured, that'd be about thirteen years of my life and more'n a hundred grand."

A twig snapped out in the darkness. The two men froze, listening with intense concentration. A chill ran up Neil's spine. A stunning silence filled the night and then a soft rustle of dead fir needles being shuffled on the forest floor outside of the lighted circle.

"Don't move, you two," a voice boomed out of the darkness, amplified by the stillness.

"What 'cha want?" asked Neil.

"Ya'll from the ranch?" a second voice asked from another direction. It was difficult to locate the true direction of the voices coming out of the darkness.

"You them squatters?" asked Pross Foote.

"Don't matter none who we are. What 'er you doing up on this ridge?"

Pross was leaning to his left to clear his holster when the mysterious voice commanded, "Mister, you move so much as a whisker and you're gonna spring a terrible leak. For the last time, who sent you up here and fer what?"

Two shots rang out, shattering the night air. A shriek of terror tore from the throat of a forest animal panicked by the sudden roar. Before the echo returned from the opposite canyon wall, there came the dull thud of two bodies as they hit the cushioned forest floor.

In the time it took for the shots to roar out, Pross Foote, with cat like quickness, rolled from the lighted circle and into the protective blanket of total darkness. The echo of the crashing shots returned and faded back across the canyon.

Seconds passed until finally Neil called out. "Pross. Where the hell'd you go, man?"

Pross rolled onto his hands and knees. "Geeze, I thought I was dead," he mumbled from his dark hiding place. Shakily he called back louder, "Over here, Browning. What the hell happened?" He rose to his feet and walked unsteadily back into the light of the fire.

Neil Browning was still reclining against his saddle, his six-gun in his hand with the tiniest wisp of smoke curling from the barrel.

"Pretty careless, them buggers. With my back to the fire, and them looking at me outta the dark woods, I could see the fire shinning off their guns. Hell, I could see their teeth and the whites of their eyes. Seen there wasn't but two of 'em. Reckon the Rocking Pine is gonna owe us a little bonus, don't ya think?"

Neil paused, seeing Foote's pasty skin. "What the hell's wrong with you, Pross. You look like ya seen a ghost."

"Ya scared the shit out of me's all. I ain't never seen shooting like what you just done."

"Yeah, I had lots of practice. When I was laid up, I figured the law'd probably catch me in the bed a long time 'fore I got better enough to stand up and fight, so I practiced pulling my hog-leg every day while I was a-bed. Got pretty damn good at it 'fore too long. Sure paid off tonight."

"Shit, I guess!" Pross exclaimed, smiling broadly at Neil. He offered his hand, which Neil shook vigorously.

"Nice shooting, partner. Let's go see what ya shot," Pross suggested.

Pross Foote picked up a pine knot burning brightly at the end of a short piece of limb and walked gingerly out of the circle of the campfire's light. The first body was a man with a heavy beard in rough-look-ing clothes. He was perhaps thirty years old.

"Drag him over by the fire so we can get a look at him," Neil ordered.

Without so much as a glimmer of resentment at the order, Pross Foote bent and grabbed the dead man's coat collar and pulled him back into the circle of light.

"Here's the other'n. Gimmie a hand, will ya?" Neil tugged at the second body by the coat collar until Pross returned and took over the heavy burden.

"Weighs a ton," Pross grunted at the weight. "Ain't missed many meals, but he's sure gonna miss a few from now on."

"Check them pockets. Soon as it's light, we got to find their horses. They gotta be worth something." Pross was inspecting the bodies for any wealth. "What'cha find, anything?" Neil asked.

"Naw, hell, they's poorer'n you 'n me."

"Let's haul em back outta camp and get some sleep. We got us some work to do in the morning, and it's gonna be a damn sight easier with these two out'a the way."

Browning and Foote rode into the clearing in the morning, each leading one of the stolen ponies that had been the property of the men Neil had killed the night before. There was a small barn, a tool shed, a couple of other shanties, and a corral. They approached the cabin and could see it was constructed back against a rising hill, in the usual squat-ter manner of using handy materials, mostly sod, with a few logs for support and with a sod roof at least two feet thick. The back of the cabin was built into the hillside, giving added protection from the searing summer heat and bitter winter cold. The tin stovepipe on the roof emit-ted a thin column of smoke, proof that there were people inside.

"Yo. You squatters in the cabin, come on out so's we can get a look at ya," Foote shouted, but he received no answer. "Looks like we'll have to smoke em out," he called to Neil.

A shot fired from a small opening in the shuttered window broke the stillness and kicked up dust between the two riders, causing Neil Browning's mount to rise on his hind legs and whirl. Totally unprepared for such an abrupt move, Neil slid unceremoniously out of his saddle and was barely able to catch himself and land on his feet. Another booming shot struck the ground in nearly the same spot.

"Mister, I got the fat man dead in my sights. Don't neither of you move, or he's a dead fat man," a distinctly female voice commanded.

Neil reached for his horse to use as a shield. A cloud of dust spattered his ankles with the crash of another shot. "I told you don't move. Lift that gun out of your holster. Slowly," the nervous voice barked. "Where'd you get our horses?"

Neil stood unprotected in front of the cabin, adding up his chances of surviving the situation. He had been in worse situations. A damn woman getting him in her sights was not particularly frightening to him. His thoughts were interrupted by another command from the concealed voice.

"Fat man, I told you to let that gun down."

Neil's mind didn't tell his hand to draw and fire, it was a reflective instinct. Before the woman in the primitive house could blink, the shuttered window was shattered by the force of five closely placed slugs thudding into it with such force that she was driven across the room with splinters of wood embedded in her face, arms, and neck. From inside came the screams of terrified children, then sudden quiet.

Neil grabbed his horse's bridle, mounted, and cantered out of range. "Let's back off a little, Pross, and figure this out. We ain't gonna be able to dig 'em outta that fort, and ya can't burn them sod shacks no how."

For two hours, Pross and Neil waited for something or someone to move near the cabin. Growing tired of the stillness and lack of activity, Pross told Neil he was going to sneak up to the cabin for a close look.

"Careful Foote, don't get yourself snake-bit by a couple of women and a bunch of young'uns."

"Just keep me covered, I'll do the worrying about getting snake-bit." Pross cautiously approached the shack, using every bit of cover he could. He crouched at the heavy front door, listening for sounds of life inside. It was dead still. He slowly crossed the front of the house and crouched below the broken shuttered window, again, no sound of activity within the confines of the small cabin. Carefully, he peered into the darkness of the cabin.

"What the hell!" Pross shouted. "Hey, Browning, come here. They're gone. Ain't nobody in here." Pross stood looking into the empty interior of the deserted shack.

Hobbling as fast as his heavy body would allow, Neil, breathing heavily, approached the cabin as Pross tried to force open the front door.

"It won't budge. Try crawling through the window," Pross said, smiling wryly.

"Don't try being funny," Neil hissed at him.

"Just kidding, Browning. I couldn't even fit. It's too small. How the hell you 'spose they got out?" Pross asked, with a shrug of his massive shoulders.

"Around back, somehow. I thought this place was built into the hill. Let's take a look."

In back of the cabin they found a rising grassy knoll that sloped back down to the edge of Cut Bank Creek. The stream had been invisible from the front of the cabin. The rear entrance, a hand dug cave not much more than a small crawl space from the cabin to the creek, had been blocked by the fleeing squatters who released a large bolder that crushed the outside entrance. Foresight by the builder had provided protection for the cabin and escape for the occupants should they ever be threatened by entrapment.

"Let's get the horses. They ain't but a couple of hours or less ahead of us," said Neil.

"Let 'em go for awhile. We gotta make sure they ain't got nothing to come back for." Pross began gathering straw and piling it against the front door of the soddy. "Once they's burned out, they ain't coming back."

It took a couple more hours to burn through the heavy door. Neil was all for throwing a burning brand through the window he had destroyed earlier in the day, but he was stopped by Pross Foote's good sense. "There might be something inside worth keeping."

Neil amused himself by burning the rest of the outbuildings after rounding up all the tools he could find and putting them inside.

By midday, they were rummaging through the dark smoke-filled interior of the cabin. There was a cache of dried food, a few dried skins, rough-hewn furnishings, and some soot-blackened cooking utensils. The two side rooms were furnished equally as crudely, with two beds to each room, separated by a combination of cloth and animal skin curtains.

Pross was disappointed with the total lack of anything of value in the cabin and vented his frustration by throwing everything he could lay his hands on. "Just in case it don't burn," he told Neil. Though, in fact, the tinder dry interior would undoubtedly burn brightly for hours and smolder for days. As he grabbed bedding from one of the beds, something slipped from the straw bundle mattress and through a loop to the dirt floor under the flimsy rope bed. Pross flung the bedding aside and reached through the ropes and retrieved the object. "Whoh. Lookee here what I found, Browning!"

"What'cha got," Neil asked as he crossed the small room.

"A charm on a chain of some kind. Look at all them beads."

"That's a cross. Something to do with a church 'er something. Seen one once back in Boise. One of the kids I went to school with carried it. Told me it brought him luck. Well, today's your lucky day, 'cause I ain't found nothing to keep. Let's set fire to this friggin' place and go find them squatters 'fore they cause trouble."

Twenty minutes later, they rode away, leaving roaring flames to consume the labor of two years and the dreams of two murdered settlers and their families. Laughing and talking of things of no consequence, a second thought was never given to the heartbreak caused by their mission for the Rocking Pine Cattle Company.

Pross had, with some difficulty, slipped the Rosary over his head and rode with it thumping against his sweaty, dirty chest in the same rhythm as his horse's canter. A nice trinket, but no grand prize.

The hours squandered ransacking and burning the cabin eventually proved to have been a mistake to the two cattle company employees. The nesters had managed to follow the creek to its outlet in the swift waters of the Cut Bank River. A passing boat, or a hidden canoe, it mattered not which, had aided their escape.

Disappointed, but feeling that their mission had been successful, Pross Foote and Neil Browning returned to the headquarters of the Rocking Pine Cattle Company, Northern Division, to be fed, kept, and to await their next assignment.

CHAPTER 12

Myra Loder stood shaking in the charred ruins of her home, struggling to hold in her grief. She was a pretty woman, a little too thin, perhaps, with long light-red hair that hung to the middle of her back. Tiny crows' feet appeared at the corners of her hazel eyes as she glanced at the sun, wishing to wash the picture from her mind. She clutched a wide-brimmed old hat in her hand as she again inspected the results of another tragic chapter in her life.

Weeks had passed since the men had shot up Myra's cabin and forced her and Mrs. Loder to flee with her children. Finding Dusty and Frank's bodies would be impossible without Soft Step. Myra trailed behind the lank Indian as he led them toward the hills. She stopped her horse and looked back at the destruction; a few burned timbers and the twisted, rusting tools of a sod farmer were all that remained. She shook her head sadly and loped to catch up with Soft Step.

Myra's entire life seemed a tragedy, from the time of her parents' drowning, right up to the present. Within a few days of her parents' death, Myra and her three younger brothers had been separated from their older twin sisters and their big brother Phillip. She, along with the two small boys and the baby, had been placed in an orphanage some-place back east. Myra couldn't remember where the orphanage was located, except somewhere in the back of her mind she remembered that it was either in Pennsylvania or near Pennsylvania. Eventually, she and her brothers were consigned to The Orphan Train that took her to Iowa, where Tom and Julia Thorpe adopted her.

By now she had forgotten her sisters' and brothers, names and what they looked like, but the memory of her big brother Phillip endured. He remained in her mind, a vivid image of a mighty warrior who would come, someday, riding out of a shining sunrise and rescue her. She saw him as tall, handsome, and with a fierce determination to face any formidable task, even the impossible challenge of finding a lost sister.

Also dwelling within her memory was the faint image of a tiny baby. Her heart ached often, as she watched her own sons growing up, at the puzzling recollection of a baby being torn from her arms.

When Myra first saw her future husband, Dusty Loder, at a barn raising back in Cedar Rapids in 1901, she was 22 years old. Musings of Phillip as a great knight coming to rescue her had long given way to more practical thoughts. Dusty's resemblance to her memory of her brother gave her hope that even if Phillip was never to find her, Dusty, handsome and tall, was clearly sent by her guardian angel to marry her, protect her, and take her away from the resentment she felt in Cedar Rapids.

They married in the summer of 1902, and their first son Larry was born in 1903. Dusty was a hard worker, no question about that, but even with hard work, with so little education, luck, or ambition, at the end of their first year together their total income had only amounted to $87 and the food they had raised on the farm.

"We've each got to get new jobs, or we're going to starve," Myra had told him.

"Ain't no woman of mine working out," he said, "and that's final."

Myra never broached the subject of finding work again. As the months of poverty slipped by, however, she became extremely resourceful. She mended clothing for her neighbors for a few cents and made rag pot holders, which she sold for a nickel each, whenever she could get her hands on any cloth discards.

When Frank was born in 1905, Dusty shocked Myra with the announcement, "Ain't gonna be no more babies in this house. Got me two mouths extra to feed now. Be more'n five years 'fore these young'uns is big enough to work and earn their keep."

Dusty had appeared a guardian angel to Myra in the summer of 1901, but by the birth of their second son, the illusion had totally faded. After Frank was born, never again did Dusty get intimate with her. When he worked, he would come in from the fields sweaty, caked with field dirt, physically exhausted, and emotionally drained. At any other time he was usually off hunting or exploring. He would sometimes disappear for days at a time. Conversation between them nearly ceased, and, as far as the boys were concerned, Dusty showed no interest.

On rare occasions Mrs. Loder, Dusty's mother, visited Myra. Myra fairly bubbled with joy at having an adult to talk with. Mrs. Loder was such an enjoyable creature. Good natured, plumpish, and lovingly kind to the boys, she filled the room with conversation, bustle, and love. It was Mrs. Loder who first broached the subject to Myra of moving to Montana, lock, stock, and barrel. Dusty never did discuss their move until the day they had to start packing.

Myra's father-in-law, Frank Loder, became involved in 1907 with a land speculator who filled him with fantasies of owning his own land and getting out of Iowa. Frank was as much of a dreamer as his son Dusty. The old Whitmere ranch in northern Montana had been abandoned in 1904—never mind the reason—and was available for less than $3.00 an acre if a man was tough enough to homestead it. Frank and Dusty decided to take the whole 91 acres for the princely sum of $275.00, payable at $75.00 down and $100.00 a year plus a little interest, for the next two years.

The end result of months of planning and scrimping, three months of nearly impossibly hard travel, and over two years of the most back-breaking work any of them had ever experienced now lay behind Myra in ruins. Ahead lay the bodies of her men, poor honest men who planned and labored and finally sacrificed their lives for their dreams.

After escaping to Shelby, Montana, with her two children and Mrs. Loder, as she always referred to her mother-in-law, Myra settled her remaining family, hired a guide, and returned to the homestead she and Dusty Loder, along with his folks, had struggled for almost two years to build. There had been no doubt that Dusty and his father were dead. The men that showed up with Dusty and Frank Loder's stolen horses the morning she and Mrs. Loder had been driven from the cabin were a confirmation of that sad fact.

As she stood over the charred ruins, which represented months of ceaseless, backbreaking labor, her heart and spirit were crushed. The last flicker of hope, as cold as the black ashes lying before her, was gone. The cutthroats hadn't been content with just shooting up the homestead and scaring off the women and children, they had ransacked the contents and then gutted the place.

Myra looked frantically through the charred ruins for the only thing of value she possessed, the Rosary, passed on by her grandmother and finally given to her by her mother when the Loders left Iowa to homestead in Montana.

"Sweetheart, take care of this, and I promise you the Virgin will protect you from harm," her mother, eyes brimming with tears, had said. Myra had remained distant from her mother ever since she married Dusty, until they day before they were to depart for Montana. And now, Myra's only treasure, the precious icon her grandmother had passed to her, and which she had carefully tucked in the straw of her mattress, was gone.

Dusty Loder had been a hard-working, unromantic young farm boy, but he had never made as much as a hundred dollars in a single year in his life share cropping in Iowa. The lure of cheap land in western Montana appeared to be the answer to his dream for riches for himself and his family, but with the cutthroats crossing his path, he died as he had always lived, with unexpected bad luck and empty pockets.

For Myra, there remained nothing of value to recover. She turned to her Indian guide.

Soft Step appeared to Myra to be as old as the hills. His face, darkened from over seventy years in the outdoors, was lined with age and his hair was streaked with white. He had long ago adopted White Man's clothing, but he also decorated himself with some ancient Indian adornments. "Why did they have to burn and destroy everything, Soft Step?" she asked, suppressing tears.

Soft Step was a Nez Perce Indian. In 1877, at the advanced age of 47, he and two of his sons had survived the "Long March" with Chief Joseph through Oregon, Idaho, and up into Montana. His squaw and three of their children were forever part of the mountains, victims of the cruel winters, short rations, and relentless pursuit. Great sadness rested in his eyes as he viewed the sun-darkened woman sitting slumped and broken astride her horse, awaiting his answer.

"The White Man always burns out his enemies," he said. "A burned shelter breaks the will of the man and carries no invitation to return." Soft Step had empathy for Myra and added softly, "Come, let's leave this place and we will find your men. Your lodge of sorrow is not yet full, and your inner spirit cannot rest until we find your husband and his father and release their spirits to the forest and the mountains."

Soft Step sensed the presence of death before he came upon the appalling scene of scattered rags and bones. Gently, he tried without success to shield Myra from the sight of the decayed bodies, scattered about by woodland scavengers. But Myra was no shrinking violet in resolve or personality and she insisted on being involved in the internment of Dusty and his father.

"It is a sad day for you, Myra, to see your men so destroyed," Soft Step said in his deep gentle voice.

Myra nodded silently.

"The land and its people have taken your husband and his father to them," the pensive Indian said as he gestured with his hands. "For your men, such acceptance is joy for their spirits."

Startled by his remark, Myra looked puzzled at the Indian who spoke unexpectedly of the joy of the spirits amid such bodily destruction. "How can you even mention joy amid such carnage? Have you no compassion for the dead?" she demanded with sudden rancor in her voice.

"Yes, I have compassion, but for you only, Myra Loder, for my heart knows that now your lodge of sorrow is full. Look around you, Myra. What you see, you are seeing through the eyes of the White Man." He stepped in front of her and gently placed his hands over her eyes.

"Close your White Man's eyes and look at this place with my eyes, the eyes of an old Indian who has seen death many times and knows that death is not death. Where the flesh and bones of your men lay scattered is what the Great Spirit intended for all people of the land. The deer, the crow, the fox, and man are each people of the land. To each is given respect of the other, and to each the flesh of one is life to the other. It has always been and will always be.

"To die is to become part of the people who survive. Even these scattered bones will someday return to the earth to nourish the soil, the trees, and the creatures we cannot see. There is truly never any death. Your men will live forever." The old Indian paused, and his arms opened in gesture that swept the entire vista. "In these mountains, this forest, and there," He pointed skyward to an eagle soaring effortlessly above the canyon walls. "Even there, your men live."

As Soft Step prepared a burial platform for Dusty and Frank, Myra gathered what she could of the scattered remains with tears coursing down her cheeks. The tears were neither of grief nor of joy, for who could be joyful at such a task. Her tears were tears of release, the letting go of devastating anguish provoked by violent death. Soft Step had given her a simple, unrivaled view of death her Christian teachings of thirty years would never have allowed.

But isn't it possible that such an unadorned, clear view of life and death is exactly what is meant when we are taught that life is everlasting? Myra wondered. Dusty still lives in these hills, and if he has sinned, the sin has ceased to exist while he continues on forever. She said a silent prayer to her Savior.

Soft Step reverently arranged the bones and scraps of clothing on the burial platforms as Myra stood watching.

"Do you mind if I give them an Indian ceremonial prayer?" he asked in almost a whisper.

"That would please me greatly, Soft Step. Thank you."

The Indian took a leather pouch from his horse's saddle and spread the contents on a blanket. From among them he chose a small vial of liquid and, taking off his shirt, he smeared his torso with the oil. He reached for a nearby spot of bare ground and scooped up a handful of the forest dust, which he threw against his body. With deliberation, he scrawled a design on his chest and stomach in the dust. Next, he took up a fan of feathers with eagle claws at the end and, in his other hand, a gourd rattle. Sitting quietly, he began to hum and softly shake the rattle. Slowly, the pitch of his voice changed. When the chant reached deep into Myra's mind, he opened his eyes and stared through her, seeming not to see her as he arose. In time with ancient rhythms only he heard, he started a shuffling dance around the burial platforms.

Though hours passed, time appeared to cease its relentless passage for Myra. She stood transfixed, hypnotized by sights and sounds far older than the towering trees surrounding them, a ritual, perhaps as old as the cliffs and rocks themselves, performed by this native of the soil.

Soft Step stopped abruptly. Myra wasn't sure if it was the end of the ceremony, or if she had done something to distract him, in any case, she was surprised to notice that the sun had descended to the horizon. *Where has the time gone?* she thought.

"At the end of each day where the sun touches the mountains, that is the place the spirits can join it and travel to the other side. I have asked the Great Spirit to allow your husband and his father to climb upon the sun and join him in his journey. He has allowed it. Sometimes, if you look closely, you are able to see the spirits leap aboard for the ride to the night side of our mother earth. Usually, though, the sun hides the spirits behind his bright light. Today is such a day."

"Never again shall I fear death," Myra vowed with new strength in her tone.

"Tomorrow we will look for my friend McBride. He is a great tracker of the white man, and he will help you find who did this, if that is your wish."

"Yes, that *is* what I wish, but first, I must go and see my sons and tell them of the great adventure their father and their grandfather are on. Thank you, Soft Step, for helping me through this day."

Del McBride was pretty much all the law available in western Montana. Civilized folks were widly scattered in the northwest corner of the rugged Rocky Mountains and regular law enforcement was difficult outside of most town limits. A bounty hunter, by contrast, was able to cross county and state lines as if they didn't exist, because in fact to the bounty hunter and his quarry, they *were* only political figments. By the time Myra Loder located the elusive McBride, her husband and father-in-law had been dead two months.

McBride had built his house to match his own personality. It was a sturdy, spacious building decorated with animal and military trophies gathered over the years and beautifully displayed. He sat at a large, polished wooden table and leaned back comfortably in his chair. He was a big man, broad shouldered, thick chested, and brawny armed. His mustache was neatly trimmed, as was his soft brown hair. In his massive hands he held delicate rimless glasses, which he had been wearing when Soft Step and Myra came to see him. Soft Step stood silently back as Myra and the bounty hunter interviewed each other.

"Two hundred dollars?" Myra gasped in reply to McBride's price for services. "Mr. McBride, I have no money to hire you. I'm sorry I have taken your time. Good day, sir."

"Now hold on a minute, Mrs. Loder, you don't have to pay me now. Hell, I never get paid in advance. Do I, Soft Step?"

Soft Step remained stoic, with not a hint of acknowledgment.

"Well, do I?"

Soft Step shook his head.

"There, ya see," McBride said, nodding at Soft Step. "Yer credit's good enough. Here's a proposition I'm gonna offer ya. Ya can take it or leave it. Fair enough?"

Myra glanced at Soft Step. The old Indian winked and nodded as if to say, "Listen to my friend."

Myra's attention returned to McBride. "Please make your offer, sir."

"All right, then. These cutthroats, as you call 'em, are probably hidin' out at some ranch up in that country. Most of that ground ain't settled yet, and the cattle barons have claimed millions of acres of it as theirs, and, of course, they want everybody off the land they control. They'll hire anyone who can set a horse and shoot a gun. The worst of 'em usually has a reward on their heads." McBride paused to gather his thoughts

"Go on, Mr. McBride. What is your offer?"

"I'm getting there, I'm getting there. Give me a minute to think," he said, appearing irritated at her impatience. "As I was saying, a good part of them hired guns has their pictures down at the post office, sometime with a pretty good reward.

"So, here's the deal. I need your information to set me on the trail of a particular outlaw, or in this case two particular outlaws. What they looked like, where you saw 'em, anything you can identify that they stole from you, that kind of information. You and me need to go to the post office and see if we can get a picture of 'em. That not only helps a lot, but it'll tell me how hard I want to work tracking 'em.

"When I got me some information, maybe a picture, and enough of a reward to make it worth my time, I'll go a looking for 'em. All from your helping me. So you're entitled to part of the reward. What would you say is fair?"

"Fair?" Myra asked with raised eyebrows.

"Yeah, 'cause it could go the other way, too. Maybe I don't catch 'em, or maybe they catch me and I get killed. I'm gonna have to make arrangement to charge you, so's me or mine don't end up with nothing."

"I guess I just don't understand you, sir." Myra cocked her head in question, "If the killers are worth a substantial reward, and you catch them, you'll pay me, and if you get nothing, I'm to pay you?"

"Mrs. Loder, you are a very bright young lady," McBride said with a deep chuckle. "Would half of the reward money be fair?"

"Indeed it would not!" Myra exclaimed, putting her hands on her hips in defiance.

"What?" he asked incredulously.

"Mr. McBride, I have no prospects of ever paying you or your estate if you fail; therefore, I will forfeit any and all reward money if you succeed. I will help you in any way I can to catch my husband's and father-in-law's killers; however, I cannot burden myself and my sons with a debt I cannot foresee a way of paying."

"Well said, Mrs. Loder!" McBride nearly shouted with enthusiasm. "Well said." He jumped up and offered Myra his hand. "Did you hear that, Soft Step? This lady is a real lady. Mrs. Loder, I accept your offer. Shall we retire to the post office while we continue our conversation?"

They walked along the dusty wooden sidewalk in silence for a short while. McBride questioned, "Mrs. Loder, what can you tell me. Did you get a look at either of 'em?"

"I did. In fact, I shot at the fat one and knocked him off his horse. The next instant, he drew his gun and fired five or six shots so rapidly into the shutter of the window that it splintered and the shock sent me flying across the room. I could hardly believe anyone could draw and shoot so fast. I had a rifle trained on him and still didn't have enough time to pull the trigger before he drew and fired. I'm afraid for you, Mr. McBride, when I recall that awful morning."

McBride pushed his hat back and wiped his brow. "How did you manage to escape?"

"When Dusty and Frank built the cabin, they carved a root cellar into the back of the house which was built into a small hill. The cellar was for storage of potatoes and such. During last winter, when the snow got too deep to go out, we decided that since it was soft digging, a rear entrance would be handy to get to the creek for whatever reason. Mr. Loder, my husband's father, suggested that they make a trap door, a kind of a dead fall in case we were ever attacked from behind. We slipped out the back, crashed the dead fall, and made it to the river and safety."

"Did you see the other one?" McBride inquired.

"Actually, I saw him better than the fat one. He rode up first, leading one of our horses. That's when I fired a warning shot."

"What'd he look like?"

The pictures of both men were burned into Myra's brain as plain as a painting hanging on a wall. "He probably wasn't very tall, though I never saw him standing. He was heavy of body, not fat, but solid looking. His face was round, not long, with a heavy black mustache that matched his eyebrows in color and texture. His hat was more of a sombrero rather than the usual western hat, gray with a rattlesnake band. Even from a distance, I could see that his arms and the open neck of his shirt were covered with thick black hair. His horse had one white stocking, otherwise it was all sorrel."

"Very good, Mrs. Loder." McBride rubbed his chin a moment, then said, "I know half a dozen men who would fit that description.

However, that eliminates another hundred who don't. Now what about the fat one?"

"A remarkable man, I think," Myra said. "When I fired at them, his horse reared and nearly fell on top of him, but he dismounted and stepped clear of the animal as gracefully as you please. I kept him under my sights, for I surely knew they had murdered my husband and stolen his horse as well. Their intentions were clear from the minute they showed up. They were clearing out nesters, and they intended murdering us, I'm sure. I'd hoped to disarm them somehow and bring them to justice, even if it meant shooting one of them. However, in the time it takes to blink, a gun appeared in his hand and I was slightly wounded."

Myra looked up at the big man with a wan smile and said, "But, of course, you asked what he looked like. He wasn't as unpleasant looking as the other one, but he was horrid enough in his own way. How his horse managed such a burden is beyond me. You'll be looking for a man who weighs at least three hundred and fifty pounds, if I were to guess. He looked rather out of sorts. No muscle tone—as if he'd been sick. He wheezed with exertion and his shirt was wet with perspiration. He too wore a hat, of course, brown and discolored with sweat. The brightness of the sun darkened his face, which seemed totally covered by a white beard and mustache. I would guess him to be near fifty years old. Far too old to be engaged in such a business, but one never knows."

"A pair like that is bound to stick out like a sore thumb," McBride said, seeming to anticipate the hunt. "Let's see what the postmaster of this here berg has up on his walls."

The general store in Shelby resembled hundreds of other small town stores. What wasn't readily available in the store could be bought and shipped up from Great Falls. If it wasn't available in Great Falls, then the Sears and Roebuck catalog lay on the counter, and Paige Martindale could order it for you, direct from Chicago. Being remote didn't mean uncivilized. Mr. Martindale could and would bring the entire world of goods to Shelby if you desired and if you could pay for it. Only trouble was, most people living within fifty miles of Shelby were poor. So poor, that the Sears and Roebuck catalogs they had at home were left mostly in the outhouse where they were put to more practical use. Consequently, Mr. Martindale had the only complete catalog available.

"Morning, Martindale," McBride hollered as he entered the store.

"Morning, Del. What can I do for you?" the kind-looking old man asked.

"Need to look at a few pictures in the post office section."

"Sure, come on in. Morning, ma'am," he said, smiling at Myra.

"Oh, 'scuse me, Paige. This here's Mrs. Myra Loder, lately widowed. We're fixin' to see if we can find out who done it," McBride said.

"Good morning, sir," said Myra firmly.

"Pleasure to make your acquaintance, ma'am. My sympathies on your loss." Martindale turned his attention to the bounty hunter. "Del, most of the new ones are tacked up on the front of the door, next to where folks can see 'em. I got a box of old ones, two years old and older, in the back. You want to look at 'em, just give me a hollar, 'n I'll get 'em for ya."

"Right. Mrs. Loder, let's take a look."

Twenty or so posters decorated the wall, some pinned five or six deep. Myra studied them all carefully. She found nothing.

"I'm sorry to disappoint you," she said, turning to McBride.

"Now, don't give up so easy. We got a box stashed in back to look at. I'll find Martindale and get 'em."

Del returned in a few minutes with the postmaster, who dug out a wooden shipping crate nearly full of old "wanted" posters.

"Help yourself, folks. Some of 'em ain't wanted in Montana, so I don't post 'em. But ya never know. I been saving 'em 'cause I figured someone might be interested in 'em someday." He dropped the crate to the floor, causing a cloud of dust to billow up. "I better get Rosey in and sweep this place out a little more often, eh, Del?"

"Wouldn't hurt. Thanks," McBride said, with an affable grin.

"Mr. McBride, look!" exclaimed Myra as she grabbed the very top poster from the box.

"That him?" asked McBride.

"Yes, I'm sure it's him," Myra said, as she studied the picture.

"Hey. He's a good one that's for sure. He's worth some real money from the State of Idaho," Del asserted.

The poster read: WANTED for Murder and Escape. There followed the picture of Pross Foote and pertinent information. Age 42, Height 5' 7", Weight 200 to 220 pounds, Dark hair and dark complexion. Extremely Dangerous. Pross Foote was serving a twenty-five year sentence for armed payroll robbery and attempted murder. He escaped from a work gang on April 6, 1908, during the 13th year of his sentence. He and his fellow inmates murdered three prison guards in cold blood, making good their escape. The State of Idaho offers a reward in the amount of $10,000, and the family of one of the slain guards offers an additional reward of $1000. Contact Warden Michael L. Lambert, Idaho State Penitentiary, Boise, Idaho.

"Well, well, Mrs. Myra Loder, you might want to change your mind on awarding me the entire reward. That's more money than I can use," Del declared.

"Once again, thank you," she replied curtly. "I won't bargain. In fact, from this record, I'm ready to implore you to simply forget my situation and drop the whole idea of hunting this horrid man down. I fear for your life, and consequently for your family."

"Mrs. Loder, for ten thousand dollars, I'm willing to take great risks, though in truth I don't need the money. Also, I'm disappointed in your lack of confidence in me. I thought Soft Step would have told you enough about me to eliminate your fears, and save me the embarrassment of having to brag on myself."

"Yes, he told me you are a great tracker of White Men, nothing else."

"Very well, let me add a little refinement to your knowledge about me. I graduated from West Point in 1868. I served in the Indian wars and had a couple of skirmishes with the Mexicans down in Texas and California in the 80's. Then in about 1895 I retired when they tried to stick a chair under my ass." He blushed slightly at his off-hand remark and said, "Excuse me, ma'am, what I meant to say is they tried to make a paper shuffler out of me. I served as US Marshal in Arizona and New Mexico for about seven years, then gave that up and retired again for the same reason.

"I work as a bounty hunter because I found I lacked excitement in my retirement, and because some of our laws are so restrictive and this country is so vast that many of our worst criminals can't be brought to justice. I do it for myself and for people like you. I'm very capable of protecting myself from the likes of this Press Foote character and any others even more dangerous than him. I operate from a platform of wit, patience, common sense, and a fair knowledge of tactics, while most criminals do not. I act like a backwater bumpkin because it suits me, and in fact I like to relax and be a little countrified. Satisfied now?"

Myra stared at McBride. She had suspected he wasn't what he appeared to be, but she had had no idea. Actually, as backwater bumpkins go, she considered herself the prize one and not just acting one either. Cedar Rapids wasn't exactly the hub of the world, and from there she had become even more isolated in the mountains of Montana.

"I'm sorry, Mr. McBride. Please, let's continue our search for the other fellow."

"Atta girl, dig in," he said, patting her shoulder gently.

An hour later, they had looked at every poster in the box at least twice and had even reviewed the flyers on the post office wall again.

"He doesn't travel alone, but he doesn't travel with any of this gang either. Interesting," Del mused. He grabbed the stacks of posters, put them in the box, and carried it back to the storekeeper. "Thanks Paige. We're done."

"Any luck?" Martindale asked.

"Damn good luck. The very top poster was one of the men I'll be looking for. Fella name a Foote. Real bad 'un. He's out of Idaho. No luck on who was with him, though. Maybe he's from Idaho, too, or from back East or something. Thanks for the help."

Walking back to McBride's house, Myra asked curiously, "Your family, Mr. McBride. You said you needed to take care of 'me and mine' a while ago. What did you mean?"

"Indian kids. That is, part Indian kids, a boy and a girl. "You see, I killed a lot of Indians as a soldier when we were at war with them. When the wars ended, I began to see what we'd done to the natives of this country. Some of it my doing, some of it settlers, the army, land grabbers, fortune hunters, buffalo hunters, you name it, we've all had our hand in killing 'em off. I can't undo what's been done, but I can do a little to make amends for my part of it.

"The 'mine', refers to two half-breeds I pulled out of a back alley down in Butte, where their mama dumped 'em. I caught 'em eating out of the garbage in back of the Board of Trade. That's a kinda fancy gambling institution there in Butte. Their daddy was a soldier from Pennsylvania or New York, I forget which, and when he returned to polite civilization, he had no more use fer her or her papooses. I gathered up them two little tikes—they weren't but three or four years old—'n we started looking for their ma. By the time we found her, she was near dead. She did die within a few days, so I just took 'em home, fed 'em, and I ain't been able to get rid of 'em since. They're my kids."

"You make them sound like pets, Mr. McBride. Do they come when you call?" Myra asked with a charming grin.

"Of course they come when I call, Mrs. Loder, don't your children?" He laughed and said, "Most days, though, I don't call 'em any more 'cause they're in school. Dorothy's in college and soon to become a schoolteacher. She's just about the prettiest girl west of the Mississippi, and the smartest too." McBride beamed with pride. "John is about to graduate from high school and has his sights on becoming a West Pointer like his dad."

"His dad?"

"Yep. I adopted 'em."

"What a remarkable story. Is there no end to your surprises?" Myra felt a welling of respect for the rugged soldier.

"I don't think so, ma'am." He smiled at his little joke. "Now then, is there anything else you can remember about the outlaw that I might look for?"

Myra thought for a few seconds. "My mother gave me a rosary as a going away gift when we left Cedar Rapids. I searched for it in our burned-out cabin, but I could find no trace of it. I took it for granted that it burned up along with everything else, but, as I think of it, the beads were made of stone, and stone doesn't burn, does it?"

"No ma'am, it doesn't."

"See if you can find my rosary, Mr. McBride. That will do for my share of the reward."

Chapter 13

Jacob Mead and Danny Toronto stood on the high wooden platform amid bustling passengers arriving and departing, and a harried freight handler anxious to complete his chores of loading or unloading freight and baggage, depending on their destinations. Smoke, steam, and the alarm of frightened cattle being loaded on an eastbound train down the track added to the din. Jacob looked up at the ornate lettering over the station entrance.

Welcome To CEDAR RAPIDS IOWA
Gateway to the West, Pop. 4476, Elev. 864

"Well, Danny, what's our next step?" Time had changed Jacob from a skinny, lanky lad to a man to be looked up to. He had grown a few inches and added twenty pounds, due no doubt to his sisters' lavish meals. After he had found his brother Phil, and his sisters Esther and Elaine, there was never any discussion of returning to Ithaca to live. Jacob had settled in and completed his education in Binghamton, with occasional trips to Ithaca that allowed him to keep in touch with the Highsmiths and Greta Symanski. Three years had passed quickly.

Jacob's decision to return to Boomerang, Idaho, came abruptly with the receipt of a letter from Ma in June 1910. It was only the second letter he had received since he left home, but he hadn't been concerned since there was seldom anything to write about in a sleepy little western town like Boomerang. Ma's letter this time, though, carried startling news. Jacob was shocked by the sad news that his old friend, Sheriff Tom Carpinelli, was dead.

The second shocking bit of information was that a policeman from Boise, Idaho had been elected Sheriff of Canyon County; his name— Wade Leigh. Jacob was stunned. That had been his father's name and, if the records at the orphanage were correct, he had a brother by the same name. Jacob had immediately contacted Danny Toronto and began plans to return home.

It was Phil Leigh who suggested that Danny go with Jacob and finish writing the Leigh story. Danny's report in the *Binghamton Press* had twisted more than a few tails, and had caused the New York State Legislature to change or rescind several laws regarding the separation of orphans in that state. Circulation had gone up more than 15 percent with the story of Jake Mead the hero in Molly's Diner, and the subsequent story of Jake Mead, the orphan hero from Binghamton, New York.

Danny agreed with Phillip Leigh about the importance of the story, and asked Jacob to accompany him to the office to strengthen his argument that he and Jake should both go west and finish the job.

"Go back to the desert with that cowboy. Are you out of your mind, Toronto? You've got a job here, a responsibility to the paper. How in hell can you even think of taking six months off to chase some cockamamie story out in the middle of nowhere?" John Dagenhart's arms were flailing the air like windmill blades in his agitation. "What the hell are you trying to do, make an old man out of me. Get back to work. And take your cowboy with you." Dagenhart pointed to the door, glaring at Jacob. Danny Toronto's boss was not pleased to be losing his best reporter for six months.

Danny simply reminded his editor, "Fifteen percent, boss, remember. And this story isn't finished unless we find the rest of the family."

A week and a half later, armed with some facts regarding Jacob's sister, Myra Leigh, Jacob and Danny were on a train pulling into Cedar

Rapids, Iowa. They knew Myra Leigh had been adopted, or at least taken, in Cedar Rapids, Iowa, in 1890. At that time, she was ten years old, so she would be thirty now. Leigh was a common enough name, but Myra wasn't, and chances were that someone in Cedar Rapids would remember the Orphan Trains of the late eighteen hundreds and the little girl named Myra who got off the train and stayed. In a small village, that would be an eventful occasion. Cedar Rapids in 1890 had a population of only about 1250, a town small enough so that everybody knew everybody else.

"Let's start where I'm most comfortable, the newspaper." Danny picked up a discarded newspaper from the worn bench on the station platform. "*Cedar Rapids Gazette*, a solid enough sounding name, founded 1850. Good, it's been around long enough. Let's go see if they had any reporters back then." Danny was in his element.

Inside the dusty old newspaper office, Danny stood in front of the desk marked "Editor," frowning at the old leather chair with its horse-hair filling poking through. "Damn poor excuse for a newspaper office if you ask me," he mumbled to Jacob.

"Yeah, just what the hell's wrong with it, young fella?" a voiced boomed out from the darkness of a back room.

"Sorry, mister," Danny called back. "We were looking for the editor. He around?"

A man, soiled with ink, wearing a printer's apron, a pencil stuck behind his ear and shirtsleeves rolled up, came glowering into the front office. In his hands he held an incredibly ink-stained rag with which he appeared to be trying to clean his hands, "You've found 'em; Thomas J. Pruitt, owner and editor of the *Cedar Rapids Gazette*. What'cha you find wrong with my paper?"

"Absolutely nothing. I'm just adjusting to your western ways."

"Damn right, there ain't' nothing wrong with it. What can I do for you fellas?" The insult, unintended, was quickly forgotten.

Danny introduced himself and Jacob Mead. "Mr. Pruitt, Jake and I are looking for his sister, a young lady who came to Cedar Rapids back in 1890 aboard an Orphan Train. Do you recall the incident, and have you got the back issues of your newspaper from that time that we can look at?"

"Well, yes and no, Mr. Toronto," Pruitt mused. "Yes, I remember the occasion of the Orphan Trains; we've had two of 'em come through Cedar Rapids; one in '90, and another a few years later. Let's see," the printer looked at the stained rag in his hands, shook his head in surrender and threw the rag on his desk, "probably '95 or '97.

"Got to disappoint you, though, if you you're looking for records of the earlier train. We were wiped out in the flood back in '18 and '91." Mr. Pruitt leaned against his chair. "You boys want to have a seat?"

Danny shifted his feet. "No thanks. We've been sitting for five days."

Pruitt nodded and sat. "As I was saying, we got hit bad in that flood. Indian Creek from the east and the Cedar River coming out of the north joined up and they went wild that year. Took damn near the whole town, including my newspaper, the courthouse, and twenty-three of our citizens. Lots of folks moved away after that. Hell, even after an average winter like last winter, folks are still moving out. Ain't much to keep 'em here, 'specially the youngsters. St. Louis, Chicago, Des Moine, any place to get away from Cedar Rapids. Too bad, too, 'cause if you give it a chance, it's a great little town.

He shook his head. "Well, that's the way it goes 'round here. Let's see if I can think of some old timers that I can steer you to who can help. There's a family that lives over on Turner Hill just off Fourth Street, name of Thorpe. Toms dead, but his widow still lives there. They've owned the place since back in the '60s, I think."

Jacob repeated the name Thorpe, while Danny wrote the information in a little notebook.

Pruitt continued, " You might try Mrs. Turner down at the library. Turner Hill is named after her grandfather. He was killed in the Civil

War. Rachel used to teach in the high school. She'd be a good source, then so would her sister, Phoebe Blum. Phoebe lives in a cottage over near the school. If them leads don't work out, come on back and we'll try something else." Pruitt got up and went over and pointed out the dusty front window to an imposing two-story clapboard house looking down on the city. "Thorpes' live the closest; that's their house, up on the knoll. Let me know how you make out, will you. Sounds like a pretty interesting story."

"Mr. Pruitt, if it works out, I'll write the story for ya, free of charge," Danny said, with his habitual grin.

"Mr. Toronto," Pruitt said, scowling, "I'd like to point out that to write a newspaper story you need years of apprenticeship. You don't just write a story without training."

Danny winked at Jacob. "Thanks for the help, Mr. Pruitt. Oh, by the way, call me Danny, that way I don't sound so old. Come on Jake, my boy. We're gonna find your sister."

Jacob was feeling that same excitement he had felt when Danny first found Phil, Esther, and Elaine. Could it be possible that his sister was still living right here in this little town? he wondered. Would today be the day he found more of his family. His mind reviewed the letter from Ma. Wade Leigh was elected Sheriff of Canyon County after the death of Tom Carpinelli. Was that Wade Leigh his brother? Most likely. Jake's heart raced with anticipation as he and Danny turned left on Fourth Street and headed up Turner Hill.

Early summer's building heat and a brisk walk up the dusty road, were enough to sap their breath, but the excitement of the coming encounter forced them to walk even faster as the Thorpe house came into view. A curved, stony driveway, which was quite steep, had a little trickle of water from a nearby spring that gurgled down one wheel track only to disappear into tall, lush reeds filling a ditch beside the road. Looking up, they beheld an imposing two-story structure that, while not tumbling down, had definitely seen better days.

"Well Jake, how you feeling? Here's the Thorpe place."

"If I wasn't out of breath from the climb, I—." He couldn't finish the thought.

"Come on, old pal, let's go talk to 'em."

A pretty lady, obviously too young to be Myra Leigh, answered Jake's knock. "Good morning, may I help you?"

"Morning, ma'am. I'm Jacob Mead from Idaho, and this here is Danny Toronto from New York. We're looking for my sister." He struggled for his next thought as he searched her face for a glimmer of recognition.

"We've seen no strangers in the neighborhood, Mr. Mead."

Jake stammered "I, that is my—."

Danny took over. "Are you Mrs. Thorpe. Mrs. Tom Thorpe?"

"No, sir, that would be my mother, Julia Thorpe. I'm *Miss* Lucille Thorpe. I hope you don't want to speak to Mother. She's not well, and I'm sure she wouldn't be able to help you. She's not left her bed in nearly three months, so I'm sure she's seen no one.

"You see, my father died in March, and it hit her awfully hard on top of the news about Myra last year. I'm afraid she's just lost the will to live."

Both men standing at the door gasped. Jacob whispered, "Myra?"

"Yes, I have a sister, Myra. She and Dusty and his folks and the boys left for Montana more than three years ago. We got word last summer from some of Mrs. Loder's family— they're Myra's in-laws— that there was a death in the family, but we haven't been able to find out any more, and it's just killing mother."

Jacob grasped Lucille's hand. "Miss Thorpe, was Myra always your sister? I mean, was she your natural sister, or could she have been adopted?" His excitement was heightening.

Lucille pulled her hand back quickly looking alarmed and bewildered. "Myra and I are both adopted. Mother and Daddy adopted me in

1895 from the Orphan Train. Myra came earlier, the same way. Mother knows when. How on earth could you have known?"

Jake suddenly realized what Lucille had said. "You said there was a death in Montana. Myra?"

"I don't know, Mr. Mead. None of us know. Why do you inquire about Myra? Do you have news?"

"I was one of a family of four orphans who left New York in 1890 on an Orphan Train bound for the West. With me were my brothers Wade and Hiram Leigh and my sister, ten years old at the time, Myra Leigh. Danny and I have traced Myra to Cedar Rapids, where it was reported she was adopted. Myra Thorpe, I believe, is my sister; our sister, yours and mine. May I please speak to your mother?"

Lucille led Jacob and Danny into Mrs. Thorpe's bedroom. There, with curtains tightly drawn, they found a frail old woman with scraggly, unkempt gray hair, lying covered with a number of heavy quilts. Her skin was pasty, her eyes listless, and her few remaining teeth were stained yellow.

After introductions, Julia Thorpe, Lucille, and Jacob sat and listened attentively while Danny, the expert storyteller, unraveled the tangled string of Jacob's life, from the time his parents died up to the present. When he began connecting Jacob and Myra Thorpe, there was a visible heightened interest taken by Mrs. Thorpe. At the end of the story, she beckoned Danny to sit down while she filled in the other side of the tale.

"Myra was a beautiful young girl. Good in school, attended church regularly, and she was a dutiful, if somewhat distant, daughter, until the day she started mooning over that ner'do well, Dusty Loder. Dusty was from a family that, for long as I can remember, was on the county dole, that is to say, on welfare.

"Frank Loder and Mrs. Loder had four boys to begin with. Two of them died at about eight or nine years of age, swept away in the flood-waters in 1891. One, the oldest, joined the army and went off to war—maybe. Anyway, he was never heard from again. Dusty was just like his father. He worked odd jobs, stayed away from school, and while he did-n't seem ever to get into trouble with the law, the law kept pretty close tabs on him and his family."

Danny was writing furiously in his notebook as Mrs. Thorpe talked.

She paused, pulled herself into a sitting position and continued. "No amount of persuasion would convince Myra that Dusty was heading for no good. He was a tall, very handsome boy, and a hard worker, it seemed, but he never stuck with anything long enough to learn a trade. He'd work a day or two, then take off fishing, or hunting, or just traips-ing off into the woods. His future looked bleak indeed." A tear escaped from Julia's eye, which she wiped quickly.

"Then suddenly they were married. She never consulted us or even invited us to the wedding. Right out of the blue, Myra came home one day, packed up, and moved out. Four years and two babies later, her daddy and I found out that they were moving to Montana.

"My heart just about broke right then. She never came by to visit even after the babies came. And I know they were terribly poor, but Myra never asked for help; not once.

"Dusty just couldn't earn them a living, and it seems like he was becoming cruel, too. I don't know for sure that he hurt her, but when I'd see her, she'd act like she was afraid to even talk to me.

"Then, the last day before she left for Montana she came home, just like that, and we cried together, and she told me they was going out West. She said to me, 'Oh mother, how did I get into this?' That broke my heart.

"I held her and told her I loved her and gave her a hundred dollars that her grandfather had left for each of my girls for their education. Finally, for luck, I gave her the rosary that Grandma Thorpe left me when she passed. Myra always admired it; it reminded her of her grand-mother whom she loved dearly. That was the last time I saw her, Mr. Mead. She's never even written me.

"Lucille," Julia said as she turned and looked at her daughter, "when was it that Hattie Slater said she got that letter from Mrs. Loder? Hattie is Mrs. Loder's sister, from over in Newhall," she explained to Jacob.

Lucille answered, "Some time last summer."

"Hattie was saying someone died." Julia squeezed her eyes shut tightly and held a handkerchief to her mouth, as if to keep a punishing notion out of her head.

"But don't you know who died?" asked Danny. "Was it Myra or Dusty? How about Frank Loder, could it have it been him? Where did they go? Montana's a big state." He looked toward Jacob.

Julia Thorpe ignored Danny's insistent questions. "Jacob, come sit here on the edge of the bed. I've something very personal to say to you." Julia's eyes began to fill with tears. "Jacob, you've got find Myra. She has held a terrible hurt in her heart, and I'm afraid you and I are the cause of it." She thought a second, then exclaimed, "No, not you. I don't mean that a'tall. I am so sorry." Julia was barely holding on to her self-control.

Jacob leaned toward the old woman with a quizzical look on his face.

Julia began speaking again slowly, carefully choosing her words, while fighting with herself to force them out and tell of her regret and shame.

"Jacob, this isn't the first time we've met, you know." She couldn't look into his eyes. The patterns of her patch work quilt shimmered in her tears as she gathered her thoughts, the stillness suddenly as thick as cotton.

Jacob and Danny looked at each other. Absolutely perplexed at her last statement, they were utterly unprepared for her next.

"When Tom and I took Myra from the Orphan Train, we made her put down a baby she was holding in her arms. And, oh my dear, how our sweet daughter behaved. She put up such an awful fuss about taking her little baby with her, but we selfishly ignored her pleadings and later did everything we could to make her forget." Julia paused, her words sticking her throat. "Jacob, you were that baby," she whispered hoarsely through a sob. She lowered her head in shame and cried uncontrollably into her handkerchief for several minutes.

Finally regaining control, her face contorted by her painful memories, she continued. "Over the years, Myra talked about an older brother. I believe his name was Phillip, and there might have been sisters. It's been nearly twenty years, and I've forgotten some of what she used to claim about her family. We wanted her to forget. We forced her to forget. We wouldn't even let her talk about the time before the Orphan Train, because she was our little girl. We were her family.

"But, oh, she never forgot Philip. Every time we would argue, Myra would threaten that Philip was going to come and rescue her from us one day. From us, her very own family, and he was going to take her away from Iowa. Myra always claimed she never liked Iowa.

"Phillip was a little girl's dream, but to Myra he was as real as you are now. Eventually, she quit talking about the baby, and the brothers and sisters, all except for Phillip. She recalled Phillip often, wondering when he was coming. She last mentioned him, though, just about the time she met Dusty Loder.

"I must say, Jacob, that if you look like your brother Phillip, you also resemble Dusty Loder around the eyes, and you have his mouth."

She began to cry once more and choked out her words. "How can you ever forgive me, Jacob. I've torn your family asunder for my own selfish reasons, and I can't even remember what they were. And now I finally understand for the first time that it was I who drove Myra off with Dusty. Damn it, it was all my fault." Julia sobbed uncontrollably, her face wet with tears of shame

Jacob, Lucille, and Danny sat stunned at the tragic story of the spurned baby and the broken hearted Myra.

Monday afternoon, the last day of June, 1910, Jacob Mead and Danny Toronto boarded the train headed west across flat prairie country that stretched for almost a thousand miles across Iowa, Nebraska, and into Wyoming. They were heading for Butte, Montana, on the strength of Hattie Slater's letter.

As the cornfields flashed by, they reviewed the information they had received from Julia and Lucille Thorpe and from Mrs. Loder's sister, Hattie Slater, whom they visited in Newhall, a small berg west of Cedar Rapids. Danny, on his expense account, had hired a local businessman to drive them over and back in his automobile to interview Mrs. Slater just yesterday.

Hattie Slater had been reluctant to talk to the two unusual looking men at first. She was reclusive, eccentric, and very distrustful of strangers, but the letter of introduction, penned by Julia Thorpe, and Jake's intriguing tale, narrated by Danny Toronto, convinced her to share what meager information she had. She handed her sister's letter to Danny and told him he could keep it if he could help the stranded woman.

June 12, 1908

Dear Hattie,

Myra has left me and the children and she has ran off with a wild Indian to look for them what's kilt. We kan't come home without no money. We are at Butte at the Copper City Hotel.

MILDRED

"That Mrs. Loder would have made a hell of a newspaper reporter," Danny chuckled. "I've never seen so much information left behind. At least we know Myra is still alive, if she's run off with a wild Indian.'"

"She ain't no worse than my ma," Jacob replied. "'Spose'n they're kin. I'm about to bust wondering about what happened to poor old Tom and how Wade Leigh got involved with Canyon County and all."

Jacob stared out of the coach window for several minutes, his mind idly sifting the events of the last few days. Danny had been invaluable, as usual, in tracking down facts about Jacob's family. Jacob felt sure that Myra and her two boys would be found in Butte. He felt equally sure that when he got back to Boomerang, he would meet the new sheriff, and that Sheriff Wade Leigh would turn out to be his brother. As the miles slipped beneath them, and the sun began to set, Jacob and Danny rose to go to the dinning car for their evening meal.

The meal finished, Danny leaned back, fondled a cigar, and remarked, "Jake, m'boy, let me see that picture of Myra again."

Jacob pulled the photograph from his pocket that Julia Thorpe had given him and glanced at it before he handed it to Danny. "You reckon she still looks the same, Danny? Mrs. Thorpe said the picture is more'n ten years old."

Danny studied the likeness intently, ignoring Jacob's question. Several minutes passed.

"You think we'll find her?"

Danny remained silent for two or three minutes more. Finally, he spoke. "Jake, twelve years ago, I lost my two beautiful ladies. My wife was about the same age as Myra looks in this picture. We had a daughter." He fell silent again, brooding, the picture now lying on the table in front of him.

The prairie slipped by windows now darkened by the night, which reflected like black mirrors, the images of the two men sitting across the table from each another. One was recalling a sorrowful memory that he had suppressed for many years, the other waiting patiently for an answer to a question he asked long ago, back in New York, and sensing that his friend was struggling with the memory. The noise of the steel wheels and the clinking of plates and silverware being gathered by the Negro porters filled the evening air.

Danny looked up at Jacob. "We'll find Myra and her children." He paused. "We'll find Wade and Hiram, too, all of 'em. I promise you."

The train bore them into the night, Jacob's question unanswered, Danny's memory unspoken.

CHAPTER 14

Pross Foote and Neil Browning had been riding since well before sun-up, with neither saying a word to the other. The previous evening, Ray Segura, manager of the Rocking Pine Cattle Company ranch's northern operation, had called them into the low ranch style log house for an intimate conference, with the windows covered and the door closed and latched.

"You boys is gonna have to move on just as fast as we can get ya outta here. 'Fore morning if possible. Trouble's brewin' and I got word to have ya'll off the ranch and outta the county damn double quick."

"What the hell's going on, boss?" Neil had asked the gnarled rough-hewn cowboy.

Segura turned to Neil, saying. "Might be you can stay, Browning. Ain't no one looking fer you near as we can tell, but Foote," Segura looked at the bulky Pross Foote, "someone's got you pegged for sure as being in on cleaning out them nesters."

Foote acknowledged the statement with a simple grunt of assent. He and Neil had been expecting something like this ever since they had reported back with word of the killing of the two squatters, the burning out of their cabin and barns, and the escape of the women and children the previous year.

"What about going down to the south spread, boss. Any chance they kin use a hand there?" Pross asked.

"Sorry, can't use ya a'tall right now. Ivan from down at the post office sent word this afternoon that there's a fella, name of McBride, I think he called him, poking around. Ivans pretty damn sure he's a bounty hunter. Said the man has a "wanted" poster with yer name and picture, n' he's showing it 'round town and asking fer you. I'm damn sorry now I ever sent ya down ta get the mail 'n supplies, 'cause sooner of later he's gonna pick up your trail 'n connect ya back to the ranch. We don't wan- t'a attract no kind a law up here, bounty or legal," he emphasized the word legal, "if'n we kin help it. Far as they know now, you two was just a couple of drifters robbing somebody. They find out you was working fer me, well, shit, you know where it'll go from there. I've been told to give you an extra month's pay and get you off the place."

"I might's well be going, too, boss," Neil offered. "I got a couple a ideas I been meaning to try out, that is, if you don't mind paying an extra month's pay to me, too, and Pross don't mind me trailing along with 'em." Neil's scraggly beard barely concealed a sinister smile, brought on by this sudden turn of events.

As the morning sun rose over their left shoulders, Neil shook off the night chill and tried to rearrange his position in the saddle to a more comfortable placement. After more than three hours of riding without saying or hearing a word, Neil twisted his fat torso and looked back at Pross Foote, riding a few yards behind him.

He called back, "Hey Pross, I been thinking about them plans we been making 'bout Moss and the Mead bunch.

"Yeah, me too. Got any ideas?" Pross called back.

Neil waited for Pross to catch up. "I am the idea man, Pross. Listen here, we got to get us some kind of grubstake. Sure can't go to Idaho 'less we can afford to hide out somewhere. That costs money. You can't get into no town in Idaho without somebody's gonna shoot yer head off at the first post office you pass. So, my first plan is to get on down and pick up a friend a mine working on the Rocking Pine down near Two Dot, name a Shotwell. He ain't never been in no real trouble, so he kin be our eyes and ears and help us get a line on what's going on in Boomerang. He used to live there. He come into Montana 'bout the same time I did, for his health, he says, least that's the most of it. He whacked a cowboy on the head, then got scared the fella was gonna catch 'em 'n beat him to death."

"And you trust him?" questioned Pross suspiciously.

"Hell no, I don't trust, him. But I can control him, 'cause he's scarder of me than he is of that cowboy. If he don't work out, we'll just knock him off. He knows I'll do it, too." Browning hitched himself up, trying again to relieve the pressure of the saddle against his flesh. "Then I figure the best place to pick up a stake is to go where there's a lot of excitement. I figure on Butte. Ever been there?"

"Once. Lot of action that's fer sure. Maybe we kin get inta a card game 'er something."

Neil smiled with satisfaction. Butte was his kind of town.

Four days later, Neil rode boldly up to the ranch headquarters of the central Montana branch of the Rocking Pine Cattle Company and dismounted. A modern truck, with the ranch brand painted in gold on its shiny black doors, was parked in front of the hitch rail, and Neil's horse objected to being tied next to it. Neil walked over and tied the animal to the bush growing at the other end of the long, low front porch. He had just put his foot on the front step, when a tall, handsome Negro man of indeterminate age opened the front door and stepped out.

"Yes'sa, what can we do for you, sa?" the black man said in a slow southern style of talking.

Neil had heard that the ramrod of this spread was Negro, tough, and not to be trifled with.

"Looking fer a fella I know, might'a throwed in with yer outfit a year or two ago name 'a Shotwell. He still around here?"

The foreman studied the overweight, gruff looking man in front of him for a couple of moments. "You ain't looking to get hired on, is ya?"

"Not today," Neil said with a slight grin.

"Eat yet?"

"Had a hardtack biscuit 'fore sun up."

"Get on over to the chuckhouse, and tell Cookie I said ta feed ya." The black man stared down at Browning. "Shotwell, he riding line ten er twelve mile south. He be back in after sundown. Ya'll welcome to wait."

"Well thank ya kindly, Mr.——." Neil had heard the ranch manager's name but had forgotten it.

"Hanks, Samuel Hanks. An who might ya'll be, sir?"

"Just a drifter, Sam. Fact is you can call me that, Drifter. I kind'a like the sound of it."

"Samuel, Mr. Drifter. I prefer to be called by my full given name, Samuel, or if you prefer, ya'll kin call me Mr. Hanks." He spoke with a deep, authoritative voice and a harsh glare, which caused visible discomfort to the man standing on the steps below. Samuel Hanks smiled humorlessly at the suddenly chastised cowboy.

Before Neil could react to Samuel Hanks' rebuke, the foreman instructed Neil, once again politely to, "Go ahead on down, suh, and get fed. Like I said, Bruce'll be 'long sometime 'bout dark." Samuel Hanks stood as if at attention and watched Browning leave.

As Browning disappeared from sight, Samuel caught the eye of Pat Bracket who was walking a horse towards the corral, and motioned to the young cowboy, one of his most trusted and hard-working hands, to come up to the house.

"Pat, I just sent a fella down to the chuckhouse fo' some grub. He looking fer Shotwell. I want ya'll to keep an eye on 'em, 'n see kin ya find what they's up to 'n report back to me.

Hanks told Pat that Ray Segura, foreman of the north spread, had written a letter late last week warning Samuel to watch for the men he had fired and, if possible, "Keep track of them just in case we need them again. But," Segura had admonished, "don't let them get involved directly with none of our operations. And fer sure, don't hire neither of them."

Ed Frey, still using the name of his dead pal, Pat Bracket, did as he was bid and sauntered down to the chuckhouse and entered through the back door. "Looking fer a good hot cup 'a coffee, Cookie. Got any?"

"Sure, Pat," the flour-covered man said. "Help yourself. How's that colt coming. You up on 'em yet?"

"Today, I 'spect. He's gentling down pretty good. Gonna make som'n a damn good cowpony." Ed peered into the eating area and observed the hulk of a man hunkered over a cup of steaming coffee.

Cookie sidled up next to Ed, looked at their guest in the other room, and whispered in his ear, "Boss sent 'em down ta have me feed 'em. He looks like trouble on the hoof if ya was ta ast me. Said his name was Drifter. Ain't that original?" Cookie said with a grunt. "Bet it don't say that on his pitcher down at the post office."

"He's probable trouble alright. Wonder why Hanks didn't tell 'em to just keep riding?" Ed lowered his voice saying, "He's waiting for Shotwell, ya know."

"Didn't say nothin 'bout want'n Shotwell, but it figgers. Always did figure that bum run with pigs. Say, you don't suppose he's gonna get Bruce to get him hired on here, do ya?"

"Naw," Ed said, shaking his head.

Cookie left Ed and took the visitor a steaming platter of eggs, bacon and potatoes, which he dove into hungrily.

Ed hung around the rest of the afternoon, staying out of the direct sight of Drifter, all the while keeping an eye on him, a vague feeling of familiarity nagging at the back of his mind. At one point, the man turned, giving Ed a full look at his whiskered face. There wasn't a glimmer of recognition, but still there persisted an indistinct uneasiness.

As the sun began one of its glorious shows of fire and light in the high clouds to the west, cowboys and ranch hands began drifting in and preparing for the evening. Tools were stowed, livestock and horses fed and groomed, friendly chatter of the day's events shared and finally, with hands and faces lightly watered if not really washed, the crew assembled in the chuckhouse for another of Cookie's meat and potato masterpieces. This was usually followed by gallons of coffee and huge slices pie of some sort or other, depending on what fruit was in season or brought up from the root cellar.

Ed Frey sat unobtrusively concealed in the shadows, away from the table by the door where this afternoon's guest had plunked himself.

As each hand entered the chuckhouse, Neil Browning studied his face, not sure when Shotwell entered if he would recognize him right away. It had been nearly three years since they rode together out of Boise and split up. Neil, grown fat during convalescence, had gained another thirty pounds since last seeing Shotwell and now had hair down to his shoulders. Hell, if'n I don't look the same as three years ago, he mightn't neither, he thought.

Neil needn't have fretted. In walked Bruce Shotwell, a little thinner, actually, but Neil couldn't miss the rounded shoulders and pock-marked, thin face. "Hey pardner. Shotwell, over here," he called.

Bruce looked at the fat man calling him. An obvious chill ran through his entire body.

"Neil, that you?" Bruce stuttered. "What the hell you doing down here? I thought you was up north!"

Neil motioned Bruce over, grabbed his shirt collar, and pulled him close. "Dammit, Shotwell, don't say my name no more 'round here, understand!"

"Sorry, uh—." He fell into a series of nervous stutters, but finally calmed down enough to say, "What're you doing here, anyway?"

"I come to fetch ya. I'll tell ya more 'bout it when we get outta here."

"Fetch me, fer what? I don't wanna go nowhere." Beads of sweat suddenly appeared on Bruce Shotwell's brow.

"Ya will, when we get a chance't ta talk. Now let's eat, and tomorrow you tell Samuel," Neil pronounced the name contemptuously, "ya wants yer pay, cause you and me's throwing in together."

Neil pushed him away and Shotwell, tail between his legs, walked dejectedly over to grab his dinner from the line of steaming food.

Ed watched the hushed intense conversation between the stranger and Bruce Shotwell. That they conspired to something was certain. Their mission, however, remained a mystery to Ed, so he felt obliged to slip out and give a strong warning to Samuel Hanks to watch the ranch and its valuables closely until the fat man left.

During Ed's absence, aided by darkened skies, a lone hungry rider tied up out at the corral and, in spite of his bulk, scurried gracefully, though furtively, to the chuckhouse and entered cautiously. He said the thing any lone, hungry cowboy would say to Cookie and was quickly invited to partake of victuals, such as they were, with no questions asked. Such an entrance and acceptance was a common occurrence at the sprawling ranch. Most drifters left immediately after eating, but once in a while one would stay for a short time to earn a few meals before moving on.

Pross Foote carefully avoided contact with Neil Browning and his eating companion, savoring his meal and enjoying the surroundings. He joined in small talk about cattle, weather, horses, and drifting with the cowboys near him, trying not to draw attention to himself. To the other men, Pross Foote, dirty, gnarled, and mean looking, appeared no worse than several other 'road rats,' as they were often called, who shared a meal and then disappeared. There was nothing remarkable about him until he suddenly lit up as Ed Frey re-entered the room.

Ed Frey, spotting Foote, immediately stopped and wheeled back out the door toward the ranch house at a rapid pace. Pross Foote sprang from his chair and bolted out the door after him. The men sitting near by were astonished to see someone so big move so fast. "Don't look like he's staying fer pie." remarked one. "More fer me," retorted another, and Foote was dismissed.

Outside, Pross pushed himself as fast as he could to catch up with Ed Frey. "Dammit, Frey, hold up. Quit or, by damn, I'll shoot." Pross's gun glinted in the moonlight.

Ed Frey felt the mental chill of a bullet sinking into his back and stopped running allowing Foote to catch up with him. "What the hell ya running from me fer, Frey. You forget who yer friends are and who it was that sprung ya, already?"

Ed Frey sank into the dark shadow of the tool shed and faced his old cellmate with a sigh of resignation. "Foote, what the hell you doing on the Rocking Pine? Ya ain't planning on robbing it, are ya? Cause if ya are, I ain't gonna let ya. They been mighty good to me, and I ain't turning my back on 'em."

"Get a holt of yer'self, Piss-ant. We ain't planning on robbing nobody in Montana, so don't go worrying yer'self 'bout nothin' like that."

"Who's we. Ain't you alone?" Ed felt a desperate need to get away from his old cellmate.

"Me and a fella I met up North come to get his pal and we're all gonna head back to Idaho and finish some business. You ought to throw in with us. They's gonna be a pile a loot to divide the way we got it all figured out."

"There ain't no going back to Idaho fer me, Foote. You know that. Never! They catch either one of us, they'll still hang what ever's left after shooting us all to hell. You sure got a short memory about them three prison guards lying dead up on that mountain. I been here three years now, and I just about got used to not having to look over my shoulder every minute, and now you got to show up. Tell ya what, you pretend ya never saw me, and let's let it go at that. Okay?"

"No, by damn, it ain't okay, Piss-ant, it ain't okay a'tall." Pross's voice suddenly sounded more like a wild animal's growl than a mere man's declaration. "Let's go get your shit, grab a horse, and git outta here." Pross pressed his gun against Ed Frey's chest.

The blood ran out of Ed's face. Thankfully, darkness hid his fear. With Pross Foote trailing only yards away, Ed Frey did as he was bid and hours later, with his meager belongings, they waited in a draw for first light and Foote's partner.

A couple of hours after sunup, two riders approached. Ed recognized Bruce Shotwell immediately; the other rider was the stranger he had been assigned to spy on the previous day.

"Hey, Browning," Foote called, "turns out I had a partner down here too."

Ed's eyes flashed wide with shock as he stared at the man Foote had called Browning.

When Neil pulled up next to Ed, Pross smiled and said, "Neil Browning, meet my old cellmate Eddie Frey."

Ed had a dropping feeling deep in his gut. I'll be dead in a month or less, he thought. He had stared death in the face once before with Neil Browning as his companion, and had somehow escaped its clutches. The job would now be soon completed. He remained tight-lipped, staring at the man who had killed his little brother, knowing with finality that there was no escaping his criminal past any longer.

Neil's reaction was totally opposite of Ed's. "Ed!" he exclaimed exuberantly. "Geeze, Eddie Frey. I can't believe it, boy. Is that really you? Man, I hate to say it, old buddy, but I thought you was dead.

Neil turned to Pross and said, "You know who this character is? This is my old pal Eddie Frey from Boise. We been running together since we was, what—four or five years old. He ain't one of the guys you broke jail with, is he?" When Pross grinned and nodded, Neil exclaimed, "Damn. Don't that beat all!"

Ed stood stoically, numb with the dread that he would be forced to leave with these men, and certain in the knowledge that leaving the Rocking Pine Cattle Company would seal his fate.

On April 22, 1910, at 3:10 A.M. Pross Foote picked up his cards and glanced furtively across the poker table and around the smoky noisy parlor.

The Board of Trade was a marvelous establishment. Opened in 1857, it catered to rich and poor, miners, cowboys, salesmen, drifters, gamblers, con men, and every other sort of high life and low life imaginable. The pungent odors of beer, whiskey, cigars, and sweaty miners and cowboys mingled with the sweet smell of freshly washed businessmen and perfumed working ladies of the evening who filled the ornate and famous establishment. The beautiful women were available for a price, and the food was both plentiful and inexpensive.

House games of roulette, 21, craps, and poker were ceaseless. In the southwest corner of the great room, where the sun created the most discomfort during stiflingly hot summer afternoons, was gathered a group of boisterous Chinese miners at a table that was never empty. They were totally engrossed in an incomprehensible game that seemed to consist of slapping down domino like tiles on the table, which sounded almost like pistol shots, and shouting at the results.

Pross Foote preferred good old-fashioned American poker; five card draw. He fingered his cards nervously and called the last bet. Twenty dollars was all that remained in front of him, the rest of his poke having been pushed into the center of the table over the last four or five hours. He and Neil had pooled their small hoard of cash with the idea of winning enough to finance their plan to rob the Mead ranch and the Moss payroll. There was, however, and the outside chance that he might lose, and so a second plan was concocted to cover such an unlikely event. Foote fancied himself an expert card player, having cleaned out nearly every prisoner in the Idaho State Prison over a period of thirteen years. He had no doubts he would get their stash.

Pross kept a pair of sixes and drew three. He deliberately hid his elation after the draw. He had hit and hit big. He drew another six and a pair of jacks. A full house; a big winner, he thought. A ten-dollar bet came from across the table. One player in front of him folded; it was Pross's turn.

"Call, and raise ya ten. I'm all in," he added and looked again carefully at his cards. He leaned back, thinking, Look at the size of that pot, must be more'n a hundred 'n eighty bucks in it!

The miner sitting next to him folded, as did the next man. "Thankyou, gentlemen," Pross said and started reaching for the pot.

"Whoh! Hold up there, pardner. I ain't folded." Fred Rosenberg, the cook from the Copper City Hotel, and the last player holding cards, casually tossed twenty dollars into the pot. "See you, and raise you twenty." His chips bounced into the center of the table.

Pross Foote stiffened and looked across the smoke filled room, over to where Bruce Shotwell was sitting with Neil Browning. Bruce shook his head, indicating that he had no more money.

"I ain't got no twenty dollars," Foote growled. "I said I'm all in, dammit. Pull it back."

Fred Rosenberg smiled sympathetically. "This ain't no table stakes game, my friend, this here is man's poker. You got twenty bucks ta back that hand, maybe you collect what's on that table. Short a that, you ain't got no claim on this pot."

"Now wait a minute, dammit!" A good hand and he couldn't call. "You willing to take something worth more'n twenty bucks? Maybe more'n a hundred even." Sweat began beading on Pross's forehead. He silently cursed the close, stifling hot room.

"Could be, could be not. What'cha got?"

Pross opened his shirt down a couple of buttons, exposing the rosary cross buried in his thick black hair. "This here was give to me by a whore down in Denver. She was mighty fond of me, 'n give it to me to remember her."

"Can't do it, pal. Even if it was worth two hundred, I couldn't take it. That there's a crucifix, a religious thing. It don't belong in no damn card game." Fred bore down on Pross, amplifying his embarrassment. "What the hell's wrong with you offering a thing like that in a poker game?"

The inevitable standees and watchers laughed at Fred Rosenberg's sarcastic question and Pross Foote's obvious discomfort.

Pross, turning red in the face, veins protruding from his neck and temples, calmly laid his cards face down, rose, and strode out of the Board of Trade. His investment was secure. Fred Rosenberg pulled the chips and organized them, adding to the numerous stacks already in front of him.

Bruce Shotwell and Neil Browning stayed behind watching the game until Rosenberg tired of the play and, conscious of the lateness of the hour remarked, "Sorry fellas, I'd like to give you a chance to get even, but I got to start breakfast over at the hotel." He gathered up his chips, cashed them at the bar, and left for his work.

Shotwell and Browning followed him.

Bruce Shotwell's nerves were still shaky as he huddled in the saddle. His teeth chattered from cold and anxiety as he tried to keep warm under his thin coat. He hadn't meant to hit the poker player so hard. Bruce could still feel the steel bar crushing deeply into the man's skull and the sudden rush of warm blood as it gushed over his hands.

Pross Foote had acted quickly, rifling the inert man's pockets, taking a pocketknife, his watch and fob, and a money-stuffed wallet.

With the body picked clean and finding nothing else of value, he had straightened, put his arm around Shotwell's shoulders, and gave him a firm hug. "Teach that son-of-a-bitch to try 'n make a fool outta me. Nice job, Shotwell. We got us the money now to get us to Boomerang in good shape."

"Is he dead?" Bruce asked in a shaky thin voice.

"Hell, yes, he's dead. If it wasn't so dark, ya'd be able t' see clean through the bastard's skull. Ya done fixed him good. Now we gotta get hell out 'a town 'fore some yahoo figures out who was in that card game."

"When, tonight?" Shotwell was shocked and confused at what he had done. He had whacked people on the back of the head before, but he had never killed anyone.

"Yeah, tonight. We gotta get, 'fore they realize someone from the game is missing."

The sun rising out of the eastern mist and coating the hills with its warming light did little to dispel the bone chilling apprehension gripping Bruce Shotwell as he hunkered over the pommel, immersed in self pity. Riding a few paces behind Shotwell, also appearing utterly depressed rode Ed Frey. Only Neil Browning and Pross Foote rode as if today or tomorrow would bring great fortune.

For a week after his mysterious departure, the disappearance of Pat Bracket was discussed on the ranch. He hadn't even bothered to pick up over a half-month's pay. Unusual, but it had happened before. Life continued its daily monotonous but harmonious rhythm on the ranch without the friendly young cowboy, and eventually he was nearly forgotten.

A few weeks later, a leathery, rugged-looking man holding a "wanted" poster stood on the front stoop of the Rocking Pine Cattle Company headquarters near Two Dot, Montana, talking to Samuel Hanks.

"No, sir, I ain't seen nobody look like him, but ya'll kin talk to my hired hands if you want."

"How far are we from Idaho, here?"

"'Bout eighty mile as the crow flies, but more'n three days ride by road and trails, and that's just to the border."

"Thank you, sir," McBride said, touching the brim of his hat in an informal salute. "I'll hang around a couple of days if you don't mind. Like to talk to a few of your boys and see if I can get a clearer picture of where I'm heading."

McBride walked to the chuckhouse and found the affable Cookie.

"There was a fella I vaguely recall," Cookie said, as he took a break from kneading a giant mound of bread dough. Seems he could'a been yer man. Come in here after dark, let's see now, four, maybe five weeks ago. I know t'were 'bout the time the kid disappeared, Pat Bracket. Hated to lose him. Good hand. That was a kinda funny thing, him running off the very day them two buggers showed up. Never thought about it before, but he must of left with one or the other of 'em fer some reason."

"Two strangers were around then?" McBride asked with heightened interest.

Cookie reached into the flour barrel and grabbed a handful of flour, sprinkled it generously on his dough and began kneading it again. "Yep. One come in the forenoon. Hung 'round all day, stayed the night, and took off soon as he got fed. That damn old polecat, Shotwell, left with 'em. That fella there," Cookie nodded at the "wanted" poster McBride had laid on the work table, "he come in later, after dark. He weren't here more'n a hour. In 'n out, 'n gone. Must been a'running 'n 'feared a stoppin.'"

That night Del McBride sat on a bunk, graciously provided by the ranch, and reviewed the notes gathered over the period of nearly nine months of investigation.

The Rocking Pine Cattle Company ranch hands up near Sweet Water, on the Canadian Border, had not been as cooperative as he had hoped, but eventually McBride had encountered a drunken cowboy in town who had worked at the ranch for a couple of weeks and then been fired. He told McBride, after a bribe of a couple of slugs of whiskey that he had worked with Pross Foote one day, and that after that day he never saw Foote again. Word was that Foote and another hand had left together hastily; destination, unknown.

McBride had followed a couple of false leads during the winter, two murders, actually, one up in Canada and one that took him as far south as Wyoming, only to come to a dead end on each. Nine months of wasted effort, but never mind; bounty hunting was its own reward, and if it took two more years, hell, if it took three, he had time. On his way through Butte, he visited a short time with Myra Loder at the Copper City Hotel, where he'd managed to get her employment through his friend John Masters. He had also passed through Shelby and checked on John and Dorothy McBride, his adopted children.

Returning to Sweet Water, the town nearest to the double murders of Dusty and Frank Loder, McBride recalled the urge Dan'l Boone was supposed to have harbored of having to move every time he could see smoke coming from a neighbor's chimney. He chuckled at the thought and said to himself, "I'm getting as bad as ol' Boone." McBride would hardly talk to a living soul for days or even weeks at a time while out on the trail.

After returning to Sweet Water for the second time, he again picked up information. Foote was reported to have been seen some time previously at the south ranch down near Two Dot. McBride had hurriedly gotten himself down to Two Dot and indeed, Foote had been there. So had another strange visitor—the same day. One of the hands, a man named Bruce Shotwell, had left the next morning after quitting unexpectedly and picking up his pay. He left with the man who identified himself only as Drifter.

McBride still wasn't sure who Pross Foote was traveling with, but the cook had been sure that Bruce Shotwell was originally from Idaho. Why would Shotwell leave a good, steady job so suddenly. He was an ordinary ranch hand of no particular skill, but he left with a killer, apparently voluntarily.

From the description of the second man, it was apparent that Dusty and Frank Loder's killers were still traveling together. The fat man was undoubtedly the same man who had shot up Myra Loder's cabin.

The big mystery to McBride was Pat Bracket, another hand who disappeared about the same time. Where did he fit in. He was remembered as a good worker, helpful and polite. Some of the hands thought he must have had considerable schooling, because he could read and cipher numbers with no trouble. He had even helped a couple of the hands write letters back to their families in Virginia and Maine.

McBride needed help figuring out where this gang might be headed. He made up his mind to spend some money and telephone the Idaho State Prison. Answers would lie there, he was sure.

CHAPTER 15

Myra Loder was weary. Her day had started at 5:00 A.M. and ended finally, when the last dinner guest had been fed, and the last pot washed and stored. Thankfully, tomorrow was her short day, and she had Sunday off altogether.

She felt inside her pocket. It was still there, the letter from Del McBride, delivered to her by the postmaster's runner sometime during the noon hour. She had been too busy to open and read it, and it now felt like a burning brand next to her thigh.

Myra stepped out of the back door of the Copper City Hotel into the fading twilight of the cluttered, dirty alley. She hated the feeling that came over her every evening as she exited the back door of the extravagant hotel.

Butte, Montana, was a rough-and-tumble mining town, and more than one body had been found in its back alleys, not to mention the many whom had been simply assaulted in the dark frightening back streets. She shivered involuntarily and scurried out onto the busy street. The Copper City Hotel boasted one of the richest and most inviting facades of the six hotels that dotted the city. Its back alley, on the other hand, resembled the back alley of every other hotel and store in town that needed to hide the necessary but often untidy side of its business.

Grit, dust, noxious odors, and raucous noise were present twenty-four hours a day in Butte, with its saloons, gambling houses, screaming trains loaded with ore, crashing hammers in blacksmith shops, and the tangle of horse-drawn wagons and chugging automobiles. In addition, there were the ever-consuming copper and silver mines threatening to eat right into the heart of the city. But Myra had learned to relish the chaos, for out of all of the confusion, noise, and clutter she was finally able to find a well paying job.

She had first worked at the hotel in exchange for a small set of rooms for herself, the boys, and Mrs. Loder. However, Myra quickly learned her way around the huge kitchen and was soon helping the cook, Fred Rosenberg, prepare meals for the guests. Starting with breakfast at the first hint of dawn through the last meal of the day, often long after the sun set in the west she was either, washing dishes, preparing meals, or cleaning rooms.

When the cook had failed to return from an all-night poker game several months ago, Myra had been drafted for the day to fill in for him. Two weeks later he was late again. This time Fred Rosenberg's body was found in the alley, behind the Board of Trade, a fancy gambling saloon across the street and down a few doors from the Copper City Hotel.

With an appalling head wound and his pockets turned inside out, there wasn't much speculation as to a motive for his murder. The police investigation discovered that Fred had won over five hundred dollars in a poker game the previous night at the Board of Trade and had left the game after 4:00A.M. Everyone convenient was questioned. One player reported to have been in the game had disappeared.

It was assumed the missing poker player had followed the victim, killed him for his winnings, and left Butte immediately. If it wasn't the missing player, then anyone in the room could have been the killer, and there was no way to tell who might be missing in a room of fifty or sixty strangers and drifters. It was not an uncommon crime, nor was a great deal of effort wasted looking for the missing poker player, described as a dark, heavily bearded man. That description matched almost a quarter of the male population of the mining community.

Myra, due to Fred Rosenberg's misfortune that April night three months ago, suddenly found herself earning thirty dollars a week as head cook, more money in a single month than she and Rusty had earned in a whole year.

She hurried home in the fading light. The holiday two days previous was now just a memory, but the boys were still talking excitedly about the fireworks, and she hoped to discuss it with them some more.

I hope Mrs. Loder has allowed the boys to tarry some, Myra thought as she walked briskly in the evening heat. Mr. Masters, owner of the Copper City Hotel had provided the neat little cottage she shared with her sons and Mrs. Loder, for the most fair sum of twenty-five dollars a month. As Myra stepped through the gate of the picket fence surrounding the house, she stopped to admire what she considered her castle, and to wonder again at her good fortune.

It was 9:15 P.M. Myra often arrived home too late to talk or read to the boys. Larry was going to be eight years old next Saturday, and next month Frank would turn six.

Mrs. Loder smiled brightly as Myra entered and the two tow-headed, darkly tanned boys came running from their bedroom.

"Honey," Mrs. Loder said, with a beaming smile, "Larry has a job, and I'm just as tickled 'bout it as he is. Larry, darling, tell your ma the good news." She turned to Myra. "He want's to tell you his ownself. He's so proud."

"Hi, Ma!" exclaimed Larry, hugging his mother. In one long, breathless sentence he blurted, "Me and a couple a other kids is gonna be sorting apples 'n pears over at Buswell's, 'n it ain't hard Ma, 'n we already tried it 'n we got to throw out the bad 'uns, 'n he give me two bits already just fer trying 'n told me to come back tomorrow, 'n he'll give me 'n Herm 'n Tommy each two bits every day we show up. That's a whole dollar just working four days!"

"Wonderful, son." Myra said as she handed her wrap to Mrs. Loder. Her eyes sparkled with pride at her little boy. His wide eyes and happy smile reminded her of Dusty when she first met him.

Frank stood behind his grandmother looking as if he was about to cry. "What's the matter Frank, honey?" Myra asked, walking over and leaning down to give him a hug.

"Tain't fair, Ma. I wanna work and get two bits, too."

Myra laughed, hugged Frank, and assured him his time would come soon.

After fussing with her sons for a while, Myra remembered the letter she had received during the afternoon. "Mrs. Loder," Myra called to the older lady, "a letter came today from Mr. McBride. I've not even had a chance to look at." She pulled the letter from her pocket and sat under the dim glow of the bare bulb hanging over their dining table and began to read.

June 7, 1910

Mrs. Myra Loder

Care of the Copper City Hotel

Butte, Montana

My Dear Mrs. Loder,

I am hopeful this letter finds you and yours in as good health as I am. I have news to report as follows.

I am in receipt of information through the Warden of Idaho State Prison and the sheriff of Canyon County in western Idaho. That information leads me to conclude that Foote is still traveling with the same man who was involved in the destruction of your homestead and the demise of your husband and his father.

As you may remember from the poster, Foote was involved in a bloody prison break from an Idaho road crew. All but two of the escaped prisoners have since been captured or killed. Foote and a prisoner by the name of Edward Frey remain at large. I do not believe Foote was with Frey at the time of your encounter, as the description of Edward Frey does not match the one you relayed to me

It further appears that Foote has formed a gang for the purpose of mischief, the nature of which I have yet to discover. Two other men have joined them within the last month, and one may very well be the missing Edward Frey, using another name. It appears that at least two of the gang members, Foote and a man named Shotwell, have common ties to a town by the name of Boomerang, on the western border of Idaho.

Edward Frey has family in Boise, Idaho, and therefore I am here in Boise, attempting to trace a couple of leads that may include a sighting of the outlaws. I will depart for Boomerang within a day or two for further investigation.

Your Servant,

Del R. McBride

Mrs. Loder watched as Myra read and re-read the letter from the bounty hunter. "What does he say, dear? Good news, I hope. Has he caught the cutthroats yet?"

Myra glanced up at the older woman and sighed. "He's in Boise, Idaho. There may have been a sighting of one or more of the outlaws. Otherwise, the news isn't very encouraging."

Myra noticed the lateness of the night. It would be 4:30 A.M. in a few short hours. "Good night, Mrs. Loder. I'll go tuck the boys in, then I must get to bed myself."

As Myra prepared for bed, she heard the rumble of the evening freight train returning from Chicago as it pulled into the switchyard behind the cottage. She wasn't aware, nor would she have cared, that it was made up of thirty-five empty ore gondolas, seventeen boxcars full of heavy mining equipment, five cattle cars, two refrigerated cars, three Pullman sleepers, three passenger cars, a dining car, and a caboose. She stood in front of her mirror in the faint light of her lantern. I'm beginning to look old, she thought, as she turned the light down slowly. Her image in the mirror faded in the gathering darkness. She sighed and climbed into bed.

Jacob Mead and Danny Toronto, having arrived on the late train from Chicago and Salt Lake City, stood at the reception desk of the Copper City Hotel at 11:45 P.M. They admired the beautiful copper sculptures and decorations that filled the lobby as the drowsy night clerk assigned them adjoining rooms on the second floor.

In response to a question by Danny he replied, "No, sir. I just started working here today so I'm not familiar with the name Loder, and unless there was something special about them—well sir, I just couldn't help you. Check with Meryl in the morning; he might be able to help. Just a minute, sir, I'll help you with them bags."

"What the hell, Jake, don't look so dejected," Danny said, slapping Jacob's back. "I never did expect to walk into Butte and just fall over her.

Come morning, we'll find someone who knows her. I haven't let you down so far, have I, partner?"

"I'm okay," Jacob replied quietly. "I was just hoping we'd hit the jackpot on the first pull."

Jake was already drinking hot coffee the next morning when Danny walked through the lobby and into the dining room. It was past 6:30 A.M.

"Morning to ya, partner. You got an argument going with the sun, beating it up like you always do?"

"Morning Danny," Jacob said, looking up from his breakfast. "Ma always said, 'Life's a race betwixt a man and the sun, and if'n ya let it beat ya, yer crop's 'll die, 'n so will you.' Pretty grim, huh? Well, that saying's got ahold of me, so I race 'em every day. Want some coffee?"

"Sure, thanks." Danny answered as he sat down. Jacob poured him coffee from the pot sitting on the table. "You check with the day clerk yet? What's his name, Myron, Mike, uh, Mary? No, that ain't it," Danny chuckled.

"Oh, Meryl? Yeah, he came on at 6:00 o'clock. I talked with him, but he's only worked here a month and don't remember no one name of Loder. Right unfriendly cuss. Doubt he'll last another month, no friendlier 'n he is. Anyway, he said the owner is coming in today 'round two o'clock to do the books, and he might let us look at some old records."

After breakfast, the pair wandered over to the imposing two-room school that rose high above dusty Ore Street. Its dirty windows looked down on patches of dead or dying grass that showed signs of the wear of forty or perhaps fifty students now scattered throughout the community on their summer adventures. The school was closed; however, two workmen were busy scraping and painting the dry, tired looking exterior.

"Excuse me, sir," Danny said to the nearest worker.

"Yes, sir. What kin I do fer ya?" The painter laid his brush aside and picked up a dirty paint rag and wiped his brow.

"My name is Danny Toronto. My friend, Jake Mead here, and I are looking for a couple of boys who might be going to school in Butte. Know how we can get any information on 'em?"

"Not fer sure, but I 'spect they's kept track of by somebody. Head of the school here now, he us'ta be around all the time, and he could'a helped ya, but he ain't gonna be no help now. Lived right over there he did," the man pointed with his rag, "in that brick house. Well sir, the bugger lit out fer parts unknown 'bout the time school let out." The painter pulled off his cap, scratched his head and chuckling, said, "He took the prettiest girl in the school with 'em too. He'll get shot, sure as hell, if he ever comes 'round here again and her daddy catches 'em." A grin spread across his face, revealing only three teeth.

""Let's see," he said, resettling his hat, thoughtfully. "Why don't 'cha try over ta the county clerk's office on Silver Street? They's the one what hired us'ns ta paint 'n clean up. Other 'n that I can't help ya, mister."

Myra glanced at two well-dressed men standing on the steps leading to the clerk's office and nodded a greeting. "They're not open on Saturdays, sir," she volunteered as she walked by and turned up Main Street toward home.

The younger of the two called, "Thank you ma'am," as she passed on and disappeared.

A chill caused Myra to shudder. That's curious, she thought. I hope I haven't caught the bug. An image of the young man lingered in her mind for a few seconds as if it were an insect trapped in a spider's web. She unconsciously examined the floating figure for a few seconds, and just as unconsciously allowed it to drift from her mind.

It was after 1:00 o'clock, and she had laundry, a bit of mending, mopping, and straightening up to do at home. Mrs. Loder was good with the boys, but she had severe shortcomings when it came to keeping a tidy home.

It was getting hot, so Danny told Jacob he wanted to go back to his room and remove his jacket, vest, and hat, and splash his face with water.

"You look a little better without all them clothes hanging on you on such a hot day," Jacob said with a grin, when Danny returned.

"Uh, yeah, right," Danny said distractedly. "The owner in yet?"

"Think so," Jake answered. "A fella just went in there with a tray." Jacob pointed to a room across the hall. "Maybe lunch. He left already, but I could see another man working on papers. I been waiting for ya to come downstairs."

They walked over to the room together and Danny knocked on the door. It was marked Office.

"Come on in," called a voice from inside.

As they entered, the stocky, clean-shaven man working at the desk, without looking up, said, "You got those freight bills, Hank?" When Jake and Danny didn't answer, he looked up. "Who the hell are you? I don't see salesmen on Saturday or Sunday."

"Danny Toronto, sir. This is my partner, Jake Mead. We'd like to ask you a few questions if you've got a minute."

"Come back Monday," he growled and looked back down to his papers.

Jacob stepped forward. "Sir," Jacob hesitated.

"John Masters," the man offered, looking back up at Jacob.

"Yes, sir, Mr. Masters," Jake continued, "we're guests here at your hotel, and we need your help with a personal matter. We'll be out of here in five minutes."

He looked up once more and sighed, "Five minutes. All right, shoot. But I'm damn busy, so state your business."

Jacob pulled the picture of Myra Loder from his pocket. "We're looking for her," he said as he handed the picture to Mr. Masters.

Masters studied the faded picture for several seconds. "Don't mean a thing to me. She got a name?" he asked, looking up at the two men. "You boys the law?"

"No sir, we're not the law. I'm looking for my sister, that's her, and Danny's writing a story about my family."

"Hmmm. Interesting." Masters studied the photo more closely. "So, why do you think I can help you?"

"We got a letter here from her, that is, from her mother-in-law, written a few month ago, saying they were in this hotel. Thought maybe you had guest books or could remember something that could put us back on her trail."

Danny added, "Your desk clerks weren't very helpful, nor too friendly."

"I'll have a word with them," Masters said sharply. He studied the photo more closely. "What'd you say her name was?"

"Myra Loder is the name we believe she uses, 'less she remarried," Jacob answered.

"You're looking for Myra Loder?" Masters said explosively. "Did you say she's your sister?" Masters stood and strode over to the window for better light in which to study the picture again.

"Yes sir!" Jacob said, anticipation in his voice. "You know her?"

"Hell yes, I know her. This picture doesn't resemble her at all. She works for me here at the hotel. Head cook; hell of a good worker, and a damn fine woman. Let's see." Masters cupped his chin thoughtfully.

"She's off this afternoon. Probably home doing chores right now. How in hell did you lose her in the first place?"

Danny spent the next twenty minutes telling John Masters as much as he could about Jacob Mead's life and his search for his family.

As the three men left the hotel, Masters left word at the front desk that he would be gone at least two hours. His appointment with a couple of friends, due shortly, was to be canceled or delayed.

A few minutes later the three of them, Masters, Toronto, and Jacob Mead were standing at the front door of Myra Loder's cottage.

A woman, her hair up in pins, looking generally rumpled and sweaty from working in the 90-degree heat, answered the knock at the front door.

Danny and Jacob looked at each other. This was the lady who had spoken to them while they were on steps at the county clerk's offices. Myra seemed to recognize the two men as well, and she looked quizzically at John Masters.

"Mr. Masters, is anything wrong?" she asked.

"Glad we caught you home, Myra. These men need to talk to you. This is Jake Mead, and this fellow is Danny Toronto. Mr. Mead has some important news for you."

"Oh dear!" Myra pushed a loose strand of hair away from her face and smoothed her dress, saying, "I'm such a mess for company. Come in, gentlemen. Please sit down. I'll need a few minutes to straighten myself up."

She ushered them into her bright sunny sitting room furnished with three overstuffed chairs an inviting davenport, and decorated with framed paintings and knickknacks. Jacob could see by its furnishings the pride Myra took in her home.

Danny stared at Myra. He couldn't take his eyes off her. "Never mind that, Mrs. Loder. You look fine just as you are. Please." He motioned for her to sit down.

"If you'll just give me a couple of minutes, Mr.—?"

"Toronto, Danny Toronto. And please just call me Danny."

"Mr. Toronto," she said firmly. Myra turned abruptly and walked briskly out of the parlor, leaving the three men standing sheepishly in the middle of the room. In a little over five minutes, she reappeared, face scrubbed, hair combed, and in a fresh dress.

Myra stood next to the chair near the fireplace that Mr. Masters had seated himself in and said; "Now, Mr. Masters, you've brought me two unexpected guests. I assume their intentions are for good, otherwise I know you would have not brought them to my home. What is going on here?" Her jaw was set, and she had pulled herself to her full height.

"Myra, I hardly know where to start," Masters said, looking up at her. "You're right, I wouldn't have brought them had I thought for a second they meant you harm. They have a most incredible tale for you. I suggest you sit and listen, please." Masters gestured her to one of the chairs and turned to Jacob.

Jacob looked reverently at the beautiful lady in front of him and thought of Phil, Esther, and Elaine, and of his last two-and-a-half years with them. "Myra," he said, his voice caught in his throat. "Your brother Phil…" There was a long pause, then he said, "and your sisters Esther and Elaine send you their love."

The room, stifling in the mid-afternoon heat, was as quiet as an empty church as Myra digested Jacob's stunning pronouncement.

"Phil?" "I had—," Myra stammered, the color rushing from her face. "I have a brother Phillip."

"Phillip Leigh," Jacob said, his voice raspy with emotion. "Do you still remember him?"

She leaned forward expectantly, her voice strained. "Yes. Yes, of course I remember him, what about him? Do you know something about my brother?" She paused to catch her breath. "We were separated as children twenty years ago. Oh, let me catch my breath!" Myra's chest was heaving in her excitement.

"Do you remember Esther and Elaine Leigh?" Jacob asked as gently as he could.

"My sisters, Mr. Mead," she cried. "Have you found my family? Have you? Are you a detective, and you, too, Mr. Toronto? Please?" Myra was confused and was beginning to cry just as a little boy walked into the room.

"What's a matter, Ma? Mr. Masters, them fellas come to scare my ma?"

"No, of course not, Frank," John Masters said as he picked up the little boy and carried him out of the house. "Sometimes women just cry when they're happy. Let's go outside and I'll tell you all about it."

"Myra, are you all right?" Danny asked, after John Masters and the boy left.

"Yes. I'm sorry. Mr. Mead, please continue. If you know the where-abouts of Phillip and my sisters, please don't keep me in suspense."

Danny leaned forward. "Myra, do you remember Wade Leigh?"

She thought for a few seconds. "Yes, that was my father's name. No, wait." She held her head in her hands and said, "Oh, let me think. Didn't I have a brother. Yes, Wade Jr., I remember. My father and brother both were named Wade. It's been so many years. So many years." Myra pulled a handkerchief from her dress pocket, held it to her face and began sobbing into it. "How do you come to know about my brothers and sisters, Mr. Toronto?"

"Danny, Myra. Please call me Danny. There's more. Go ahead, Jake. I think you should tell her the rest."

"Myra," Jake said as he leaned toward his sister, "do you remember at all the baby, Jacob Leigh?"

"Her face was wet with tears as her eyes reflected her emotional tension. "The baby on the train," Myra was gasping for air. "They wouldn't let me take him. He was mine. Is he—?" She stopped in mid-sentence, straightened her dress, took a deep breath, and forced herself to be calm. "Mr. Mead, my baby, what do you know about my baby?" she asked crisply. " Please."

"His name is now—Jake Mead," whispered Jacob huskily.

"Catch her, Jake!" Danny shouted as Myra began to swoon.

Danny grabbed the handkerchief from Myra's hand and hurried to the kitchen to look for water and rushed back just as Myra was straightening herself in her chair. Danny handed her the wet cloth.

"You," Myra looked at Jake. The room was filled with exquisite silence as she studied the handsome young man before her and gathered her tattered wits. A minute passed, two, then three. The silence was deafening.

At last, Jacob's face broke into an ear-to-ear grin as he regained control of himself. "I used to be Jacob Leigh, 'til the Meads adopted me back in 18 and 90."

Myra collapsed into uncontrollable sobs and buried her face in her hands. The magnitude of the disclosure was nearly intolerable.

Jacob and Danny sat for several minutes waiting for Myra to compose herself. She finally gathered herself together enough to speak again.

"Mr. Mead— I mean Jacob, how ever did you find me, and what about Phillip, and the girls, and Wade Jr.?

Jacob was eager to talk again and end the emotional flood tide that had welled up and swallowed them all in the little parlor. "Well, I ain't exactly found Wade Jr. yet, but I just spent three years with Phillip, Esther, and Elaine while I was going to school back in New York. Danny here's the one who found 'em and you, too, far's that goes. He writes for the newspaper back there, and darned if he's not a good detective to boot.

"Oh, yeah, I near forgot. I believe I know where Wade is, but there's one still missing. Do you remember Hiram? He was two years younger than you. He came right between you and Wade."

"Hiram?" Myra choked. "I remember him. Hiram and Wade were inseparable. I can recall one image of them now, almost is if I was looking at one of those moving picture shows playing in my head. I see two happy little boys with the whitest towhead hair, laughing and running for the front porch to get some cookies from Mama." A glowing smile crossed her face.

"And you, Jacob," Myra folded Jacob's hands in her own. "I remember as if it were yesterday. I held you in my arms for a thousand miles, all the way from back east. I never knew where we started from, but I held you.

"Mama and Papa made me leave you on the train." She swallowed hard and continued in a tight whisper. "I hated them for that. I grew up with a broken heart and, I guess a broken spirit.

"My arms ached for you even when I held my own boys, Jacob. As I watched them grow and run and play, I've always felt some mysterious emptiness. And now, here you are, and with news about Phillip and Esther and Elaine and Wade and maybe even Hiram. I feel as if I'm dreaming." She turned to Danny. "Tell me I'm not dreaming, Mr. Toronto."

Danny sighed and smiled, "All right, Myra, you can call me Mr. Toronto. But just for today, understand. Tomorrow, by gosh, you're to call me Danny." He became serious as he said, "Myra, this is no dream. Jake has his family back, and so have you. Welcome home."

John Masters stuck his head in the door. "Hey Toronto, got a minute?"

Danny rose and went to the door. "Sure, what's up?"

"Myra's got a lot to handle this afternoon, what with you two falling into her life and all. She isn't gonna feel like fixing supper, and she won't want you and Jake to leave either I 'spect. Listen, it'll be my treat. I want all of you over for dinner at the hotel tonight. Bring the boys and Mrs. Loder. Hank ain't as good a cook as Myra, but he's getting the hang of it."

"Thanks, Mr. Masters. I'll tell Myra. She'll appreciate it."

In an intimate and richly decorated private dining area of the hotel where wealthy and influential guests were usually entertained, the last of the dessert dishes were being taken away, except for Larry's and Frank's. They were each finishing their third helping of ice cream and apple pie. Jacob turned to Myra and asked about her plans for the future.

"I don't have any long term plans," she said, folding her napkin and smoothing it on the table in front of her. "I've got to think about the boys' schooling, so we need to settle permanently somewhere. Butte is a nice town." She hesitated and with a wry smile said, "Well, maybe it's a little rough, but I've got to consider that I have a good job and Mr. Masters is a kind employer."

"Would you consider going back to New York to settle?"

"New York?" she said with a nervous laugh. "No, I don't think so. Oh, but I would surely love to go back and get acquainted with my sisters and Phillip again. I'm doing well here and maybe in a year or two—. You never know. Where are you off to? Will we ever see you again?"

"I'm heading back to Idaho. 'Course that's where I was raised."

"You really are a cowboy then, aren't you?" She glanced at his boots.

"Sort of. We raise cattle, but we farm too. Grain, hay, and corn, and we have a few acres of apple trees, that sort of farming. Sure keeps ya busy. Growing up, I hardly ever got to town until I was grown, and my pa died."

"What sort of town is it?"

"Boomerang? Aw, heck, it ain't much of nothing. Just a wide place in the road on the way to Oregon."

Myra caught her breath. "Did you say Boomerang? Is it on the border by Oregon?"

"You've heard of Boomerang?" Jake asked, surprise evident in his tone. "You're the first person I've met in three years that's ever heard of it. I'll be danged."

"Jacob, I want to go to Boomerang with you!" Myra's cheeks flushed. "Right now. Tomorrow!"

"What. Why, for gosh sake's?"

"I met a wonderful old man named Del McBride. When he retired from the army he wanted to keep busy, so he became a bounty hunter, and now he's looking for my husband's killers." Myra took the letter she had received that afternoon from the purse sitting in her lap. "Here." She handed the letter to Jacob.

As he read the letter, Jacob's happy expression melted into a concerned scowl the instant his eyes hit the name Ed Frey.

"Danny," Jacob said, as pale as a ghost, "we gotta get to Boomerang. How soon is the next train to Boise. Myra, when did you get this?" he asked, turning to her abruptly.

"Just yesterday," she answered, her voice reflecting Jacob's anxiety.

"What's the matter, Jake?" Danny questioned.

"It's Ed Frey and Neil Browning is with him. I know it's them." Jacob turned to his sister. "Myra, your bounty hunter is looking for a cold-blooded killer by the name of Neil Browning. Danny?" Jake looked imploringly at his friend for help.

"Who is Neil Browning?" asked Myra.

"Neil Browning, and this fella Ed Frey, here in your letter, and three others came out to the ranch to rob us three years ago. They were fixin' to kill us too. What they wanted was the money my pa left us. We tussled with 'em some, and two were killed and we chased the rest of 'em off. They ran right into Tom Carpinelli, he was sheriff at the time, and he arrested 'em.

"They were waiting for Browning to die or get well enough to stand trial, but instead he killed his guard, Mason Crabtree, and escaped. Later on, two of 'em, Frey and Dan Davenport, were tried; Davenport was hanged for killing a cowboy up near Emmett, Idaho, and Ed Frey was sentenced to twenty-five years in prison. Frey escaped, and it looks like for sure he's with that man Foote, your bounty hunter mentioned.

"As I think on it, I remember Foote too." Jacob said thoughtfully. "I wasn't more than maybe four or five years old, but even way out of town we heard about Foote and his pal trying to rob the Moss payroll. It was the biggest thing that ever happened in Boomerang. They were still talking about it when I was grown. Three guards were shot, and my old friend Tom Carpinelli shot and killed one, and then wounded and captured Foote."

"How soon ya 'spose we can get outta here, Danny?" Jacob asked.

"I'll find out." Danny stood up and motioned for Jacob to follow him. Out of earshot he whispered to Jacob, "I'll send a telegraph while I'm at the station and let the Thorpe's know that we've found Myra and her family."

"Thanks, partner, my gosh, I should have thought of that myself."

As Jacob returned to the table Myra turned to her mother-in-law, her expression as firm as when earlier in the day she had announced to Danny Toronto that she was going to change and freshen up before receiving guests.

"Mrs. Loder, the boys and I are going to Idaho."

"Myra, those men are killers!" Jacob protested earnestly.

"We're going to Idaho, Mrs. Loder." Myra ignored Jacob's protest. "You're welcome to come or, if you wish, I will borrow money from Mr. Masters for a train ticket, and you can visit your sister until you decide if you would rather settle with her, or come back to Butte later and live with us. I feel we may be in Idaho for some time."

"Myra," Jacob persisted, "these men are terribly dangerous. I don't want you to risk your life or to risk harm to Larry and Frank by taking them on such a hazardous journey."

"Jacob, please try and understand," Myra said firmly, as she looked directly into his eyes. "Those men killed my husband and his father.

They killed my little boy's daddy and their grandfather. We deserve to be there when they're caught and punished. It's our right. I'll hear no more talk of danger."

Myra continued, "I understand your anxiety to protect us and your Idaho family, that's the foremost reason we're going with you. We want to protect you, Jacob. We're your family too."

"You'll need help with the boys," Mrs. Loder interjected. "And don't forget for a second, Myra, I lost a husband and a son. I'm not going to lose you and the boys as well."

Myra reached over and hugged the older woman. "I love you, Mrs. Loder."

CHAPTER 16

Neil Browning was sick. On the arduous ride from Butte, they had stuck to back trails as much as possible to avoid the more traveled roads, especially in Idaho. On a narrow trail outside of Ketchum, Neil's horse, exhausted by his rider's bulk, had slipped, fallen, and pitched Neil over the side of the trail and down some fifty feet into a ravine. A fallen log stopped Neil's fall, but something inside his guts had jarred loose, and now he was in trouble. For more than two months he had thrown up almost every day, and the pain in his stomach was growing worse.

From their hideout in a shaft of the old abandoned Blue Clay silver mine, a good fifteen or more miles west of Boise, Bruce Shotwell had made a couple of trips into Boomerang to gather supplies and information. The plan was for him to act like an ordinary citizen and not draw attention himself.

Neil's illness after returning to Idaho was delaying their plans, but it allowed Shotwell time to find out that the Mead ranch was nearly unguarded. Jacob Mead had left Boomerang some time ago, leaving just his mother and her hired hand on the place. Tom Carpinelli was dead of heart failure, news heartily welcomed by both Pross Foote and Neil Browning. And, finally, he found that Christian Moss was no longer associated with the Moss Brothers Company. Shotwell had thought Pross Foote would be disappointed at that news.

Pross was not deterred. On the contrary, he was elated. "Moss has sold out, eh. Good. Then we don't have to wait for no payroll train. He's probably got a million bucks stored right there in his house. That there just makes it easier!"

As the heat of mid-summer bore down on the land, conditions in the mine became nearly intolerable. Water was constantly dripping, the air was hot and dank, and nothing; bedding, saddles, food, or tack remained dry.

Neil Browning had undergone another metamorphosis during his two-month torment with the fever. More than a hundred pounds had melted off his frame, and his oversized clothes hung on him like rags. Under his beard, his puffy cheeks had melted, and his face had the pasty white look of unbaked bread, giving a mad expression to his piercing dark-rimmed eyes.

Pross Foote had come to be indisputably fond of his partner and worried about him constantly. "We gotta fetch a doctor fer ya, Neil. Dammit man, you look like hell. I kin have Shotwell fetch 'em next time he goes in to Boomerang."

"No dammit!" Neil had shouted, grimacing at the pain in his guts. "No Doctor. I licked this once, 'n I'll lick it again. You bring Doc up here, and that's the end of it, pal." Neil shifted his remaining bulk on a deteriorating davenport. "Bruce can bring me some lauduem next time he goes in.

"What the hell you think a doctor's gonna say when he gets back inta' town, fer chris' sake?" Neil mocked the imaginary doctor in a hi-pitched voice, "'I seen these fellas hid out up at the old Blue Clay and fixed one of 'em up. Real nice fellas.'"

"No, by dammit, no doctors. I ain't gonna die on ya, Pross. 'Sides, I'm feeling a mite better today, and the wait's been good fer us. We got a line on Christian Moss, and them extra guns Shotwell bought is gonna help. Next time he goes into town, have 'em get me some medicine, and I promise ya that by the end of the week, I'll be back on my feet."

"You've said that every week for the last two months. How long you think we can hide out here 'fore some kids or hunters stumbles onto us. We gotta hit 'em right away, Neil, this week. We're running outta money. Everything's going to hell in this mine and I want to get the hell out of here and down into Mexico 'fore I go crazy." Pross looked down at the sick man. "Friday night, old buddy. Friday night we're going into town, the three of us, Shotwell, Frey 'n me, and we're taking Moss."

"You ain't forgettin' the Meads, are ya Foote?" Browning asked, looking up slyly at his brutish looking partner. "Shotwell says there ain't but two of 'em out there on the ranch, just the old lady, her hired hand, and all that money. Don't it just make ya drool?"

"No, I ain't forgot your caper. I got a plan fer that one too. That's why I said Friday, instead of sooner. That'll give you an extra day to get your strength up.

"I figure we hit Moss early, right after dark, 'bout when everyone's bedding down. An hour or less, that's all it'll take to clean 'em out and we sneak out of town without raising no fuss. Afterwards, we meet you some place handy, so's you won't have to ride so far. Then, 'bout midnight or a little after, we hit the Meads. Slick as a whistle, we clean 'em out and head south."

Neil smiled. He liked the plan.

Pross elaborated, growing more enthusiastic as the plan materialized in his head. "See, we do 'em both the same night, quick, no hanging around, waiting for 'em to organize. And soon's we're done, we keep right on going down inta Nevada, 'n Arizona, and right on south till we get to Mexico."

Neil called to the man leaning against a support. "Hey, Eddie, com'ere."

Ed Frey walked over to where Browning was sprawled on the old davenport that had been left in the tumbled-down shack next to the mineshaft. The dry air had preserved it somewhat in the shack, but the dampness of the cave was causing it to deteriorate quickly. It kept Neil Browning off the floor of the cave, however, and for that it was adequate.

"Yeah?" Ed wasn't in the habit of talking a great deal to his companions, and they had come to expect little or no conversation from him.

"I know you ain't too hot on this Mead job, Frey, but I promise ya with the cash they got, you can get clear down to Mexico, hell, all the way down to South America, and live forever without no one looking fer ya. Whatta ya say, old pal, don't that sound good?"

Ed sighed and grunted in disgust. Saying nothin he retreated to his post at the entrance of the mine.

"You stick with us, Eddie boy, you'll see," Neil called to the departing outlaw. Beaming, Neil turned, looked at his partner, and winked.

"I don't like the way that piss-ant is acting," Pross whispered "Can we trust 'em?"

"Maybe," Neil said with a shrug. "But if he turns sour on us, well…" Neil made a slice motion across his throat. Pross raised his eyebrows and nodded in assent.

Ed Frey's fate was more firmly sealed.

The train had been waiting on a siding outside of Boomerang, Idaho, over two hours for the scheduled east-bound to pass.

"Sorry, folks," the conductor was explaining. "We usually don't get delayed like this, but after the Fourth of July celebrations it usually takes a week or two to straighten out the schedule again."

Jacob paced the narrow aisle nervously, as an eastbound freight/passenger train crept by. His nerves were on edge at the thought of Neil Browning in the Boomerang area. He turned and strode back to where Danny and Myra sat talking. Mrs. Loder was seated across the aisle playing with the boys.

"I'm about to bust, Danny," Jacob said.

"Come, sit here, Jacob." Myra slid over and patted the vacated bench in invitation. "I'm sure your family is all right. I think Mr. McBride would have written me if the outlaws had struck. They've probably moved on. Didn't you say two of them had family in Boise? Likely they visited family, and, if they are wise, they've left Idaho altogether. I shouldn't worry if I were you."

Jacob slid into the seat beside his sister. "I'm telling ya, Neil Browning ain't gonna leave Idaho until he gets another crack at the Mead ranch, and he's probably looking for me, too. I've dealt with that rattlesnake before, Myra. I think I've got every reason in the world to worry as long as he's in my part of the world. Soon's we get in, I'm heading out to the ranch. Danny can take you and the kids over to the hotel and put ya up till we can get it sorted out. Okay?"

"Don't we get to go out to the ranch and meet your family?" Myra asked in alarm.

"I'll be back tomorrow and fetch you all out there soon's I'm satisfied there isn't any danger."

The three of them, Jacob, Myra, and Danny, continued discussing the merits of Jacob's plan as their coach resumed its journey the last few miles into Boomerang.

Del McBride sat on the bench in front of the Bancroft Hotel in the same spot he had occupied for the last two weeks. He had yet to spot Bruce Shotwell, but others had seen him in town buying supplies, and he was sure that as soon as he could identify Shotwell, he would finally have the lead he needed to get to Pross Foote.

Harold Hermann crossed the dusty street from his store. "Morning, McBride. Getting an early start on yer sitting today, ain't'cha?"

"Morning, Harold," Del called, waving back. "Shotwell ain't been seen in town in over two weeks, so I figure he's about due back any day. I got to get an eyeball on 'em so's I know what the hell he looks like."

"I'll sure let ya know if he comes in the store," said Harold. "He missed me last time in."

The two men chatted for about a half an hour, and then Harold returned to his duties in the general store leaving McBride to sit and watch as the town began its daily rhythm.

The west-bound Union Pacific, nearly two hours late, pulled into the station on the north end of town at the same time Bruce Shotwell guided his horse across the tracks just in front of the huffing locomotive. It was well past 2:00 P.M., and he had been riding since just before daylight. He glanced to his left at the detraining passengers milling about and anxiously waiting for the baggage handlers to retrieve their trunks. Two motor trucks, still a curiosity to Bruce, were off-loading from a boxcar down the tracks.

A sandwich and a cold beer is what I need now, he thought, dismissing the activity at the train station. Heading for the Primrose, he noticed a lone man lounging on the bench in front of the Bancroft. Must be nice to be like that old fella 'n sit around all day and soak up the sun, he thought of the man who appeared to be napping with his hat covering his eyes. Wait till I get to Mexico, I ain't gonna do nothing but sit 'n soak up the sun and drink, what'd Eddie call that Mexican beer? — *cervesa*, all day, 'n drink tequila and pinch senioritas all night. Bruce chuckled at the prospects of such a bright, promising future.

Friday was just two days away, and Neil was going to need some medicine if he was going to be of any use to them. Shotwell felt a great deal of satisfaction and excitement in belonging to such a tough gang. It was his gang, and they seemed to like him.

As he was trying to refresh himself and gather information at the Primrose by talking to the bartender and a one of the customers, the day turned suddenly bitter for Shotwell. He had ordered his lunch and a beer and was in a pleasant conversation with a stranger, picking up a couple of nice bits of information, when some of the regulars came in for lunch and an afternoon beer.

"Hey. That you, Shotwell?" one customer called. "Heard you been slinking 'round these parts. Where ya been?" Another customer piped up, "I bet he ain't in town coon hunting." The room erupted in laughter at the obvious reference to Everett Koons.

The taunts spoiled his appetite.

"You out looking fer ol' Everett Koons?" one man called derisively.

"Hey," called another, "we heard he's looking fer you, too. Something 'bout stuffin' a horseshoe up your ass."

Another roar of laughter filled the bar.

"Ya'll try out to the Mead place. Hear there's a good looking widder out there." Like a pack of wolves, the men humorously vented their resentment on the hapless man.

With his ears burning, Bruce left his lunch and beer barely touched on the bar and stormed out of the saloon. He strode angrily over to Doc's place, his mind churning with embarrassment and hate. Once inside, he put on his best act for the doctor.

"Got the terrible stomach pains, Doc. Terrible. Can ya gimme somethin' fer 'em?" Shotwell's face was so flushed with anger and embarrassment that Doc Highsmith never questioned his claim to stomach discomfort. It was plain to see on his face.

Bruce stashed the medicine in his saddle bags, crossed over to Falk Mercantile, bought a few necessaries, and furtively headed back to the hideout, knowing he would likely have difficulties traveling in the dark later at night. He remembered again why he didn't like Boomerang.

Bruce tried to shut out the ringing jeers swirling in his mind by shouting at the empty prairie in an almost maniacal scream. "You sons-a-bitches!" He ranted again and again at the returning empty echo. "You rotten sons-a-bitches!"

The new sheriff was up in Emmett for a couple of days. That report would be helpful to the gang. Bruce wanted to get the news back to his friends, Neil and Pross Foote. "I'll fix them sons-a-bitches!" he shouted, his voice rising and falling. "All of 'em. We'll fix 'em all!" On the empty trail, alone with his thoughts, tears of rage and shame coursed down his thin, pallid cheeks.

Harold Hermann hurried back across the street as soon as he noticed the bounty hunter returning from the livery stable. "He's here, McBride. He just left the store, not five minutes ago."

"Yeah, I saw him come out." McBride stood with his arm over the saddle of his horse in front of Harold Hermann's store. "Figured it might be Shotwell when he rode through town a while ago. Been keeping an eye on him." He swung into the saddle. "See ya later, Harold."

McBride nodded a barely perceptible greeting to the group of people milling on the front steps of the Bancroft as he rode by. The two women, their backs to him, directing two small boys to carry bags into the hotel didn't notice him, but a dark-haired man in an eastern-style suit returned the sociable hail as the bounty hunter passed.

Del lowered his gaze and studied the fresh tracks of Bruce Shotwell's horse carefully. Shouldn't be any trick to follow 'em with a cracked shoe, he thought. Damn fool. Don't he know no better 'n to ride a cayuse like that?

The clattering of steel shod hooves crossing the bridge below the house drifted through the open windows and drew Ma's attention. She glanced at the clock on the mantel. "Past four o'clock," she mused. "Wonder who could that be?" She laid her needle work aside and walked leisurely out onto the front porch. Squinting in the bright afternoon sunshine, she could discern horse and rider, but the distance obscured his features. "Why'nt I ever remember to carry 'ma glasses?" she scolded herself, as the rider drew closer.

"Hi ya, Ma!" Jacob yelled, standing in the stirrups of his saddle.

She looked at the tall young man in fine clothes as he rode toward the house. "Jacob," she gasped. Then at the top of her voice she shouted, "Jacob! Everett, come quick, Jacob's come home he's home!" She rushed down the stairs of the porch and ran to greet him calling his name again and again.

Everett trotted out of the hay barn as fast as his old legs would carry him. He had a grin plastered from ear to ear. "I knew you'd hightail it home soon as ya heard the news," he said excitedly, as he joined Ma and Jacob. "Get down off that plug, and let's get a look at you, boy. Dang me, Ma, look at the size of that youngster. He's growed a foot. They'll have to retire that there horse 'n give it a pension just fer hauling him out here. Welcome home, son!"

Jacob dismounted and grabbed both Ma and Everett in a giant bear hug. His excitement wouldn't allow him to utter a sound, but his face said it all.

Jacob's forgotten horse wandered freely, munching grass on the front lawn while Jacob, Ma, and Everett sat on the porch. In the next hour, greetings were exchanged again and again, until emotions were finally corralled enough to permit normal conversation.

"Ma, I found my sister," Jacob said, his eyes bright with happiness.

"You sure did, Jacob. Imagine twins. I must'a read yer letter a hundred times 'bout the girls, 'n Phillip. That's wonderful, just like a miracle."

"No, not the twins, Ma, the other one. Myra. The one you said them boys talked about who was with me before you took me up off that Orphan Train back in '90."

"I plum forgot about her. She the one they said was with two boys 'n you on the train when it started?"

"Yep, and I brought her with me."

"Where is she?" Ma asked, sitting forward and scanning the road to the ranch with her weak eyes.

"Her name's Myra Loder. I found her in Butte with her two boys, and I brought the whole family with me. We put 'em up at the Bancroft till it's safe to bring 'em out."

Everett looked startled. "Safe? What the heck you talking about, safe? You don't think your ma and me—" he stopped in mid-sentence. "Come on, boy, hell, there ain't no place safer on earth than this here ranch. Your ma and me ain't seen no bears ner wild Indians neither since last time it rained."

"This ain't nothing to laugh about." Jacob's tone erased the smiles from their faces. "Remember Neil Browning?"

They both nodded.

"And Ma, you remember the time years back when a couple of fellas tried to rob the mill payroll and the three guards got shot?"

"I sure remember Neil Browning. I can't ever forget that day. Not sure about the payroll," said Ma.

"Well, Browning, and that other fella, the one who was in on that payroll robbery, are in Idaho. They were seen over in Boise, and I figure they're fixin to take another shot at us. And maybe they have one or two men riding with 'em. Looks like Ed Frey, for sure is one. And Everett, I 'spect you haven't forgotten a fella name of Bruce Shotwell, have you?"

Everett nearly choked at the name. "Shotwell, that sidewinder. You mean to tell me he's stupid enough to show up around these parts again? He's still got a damn good thrashing coming and I ain't so sure that's where I want ta' stop." Everett's face flushed with anger.

"See what I mean by wanting to see if it was safe?" Jacob said. "I've been worried sick ever since I saw Myra's letter. She's got a bounty hunter looking for one of 'em."

"Land sakes, what for?" Ma asked.

Jacob went on to explain about Myra's husband, the killings, the bounty hunter, and her letter.

"I'm sorely confused, Jacob. Everett, darling, you understand what he's talking about?" Ma asked, her brow furrowed.

Everett leaned across the table. "Jacob, you're feeding faster 'n we kin swallow. Slow down and give it to us a spoonful at a time, will ya?"

"Everett darling?" it was Jacob's turn to be confused.

"Your ma didn't tell ya?" Everett looked at Ma. "Didn't you put it in yer letter?"

"I started to, but I didn't know what to say. I'm sorry, Jacob."

"Sorry, hell!" Everett interrupted with a mighty smile and crows-feet wrinkle returning to his weather-beaten face. "She ain't sorry a'tall, Jacob. Oh, she may be sorry she forgot to write you we was married last year, but she's told me a thousand times she ain't sorry she asked me, and she said she ain't sorry I took her up on her offer. And ya know what, she ain't even raised ma' wages. Now them there's a gol-dern facts. Tell him, Evangeline."

Jacob looked at Ma, his eyes wide with surprise. He turned back to Everett, "You two are married?" He stared at them in stunned silence for several seconds.

Jacob suddenly yelled at the top of his voice, "Yahoo!" He smiled and in a normal tone said, "When'd you two tie the knot. This calls for a celebration. Wait till Danny hears. He'll have a fit." Jacob jumped up, pulled Ma up, and gave her a crushing hug. Then he reached across the table and grabbed Everett's giant mitt with both hands and, wordlessly, he gave Everett a broad smile, nodding his pleasure. Jacob caught his breath. "Wait a minute. Hold on there. Everett, what did you call my ma?"

"Just Evangeline. Why, that's her name, ain't it?" He swung his gaze from Jacob to Ma, mirth filling his eyes. "Well, ain't it? 'Cause that there's about the prettiest name I ever heard. And if that ain't yer real name, we're going to the courthouse first thing in the morning and get it changed from Ma to Evangeline."

Jacob couldn't believe his ears. He was twenty-two years old, and today he had heard his mother's proper name for the first time in his life. When he told the two listeners seated with him that he never knew Ma's given name until now, they all broke out in boisterous laughter. Troubles were forgotten as news of the past three years was exchanged, and the evening passed. They sat contentedly in the wicker chairs unmindful of the clouds gathering on the western horizon and the beautiful sunset they produced.

Jacob was home, and his house was full of delight. Later, as he lay blissfully in his own bed for the first time in over three years, he listened to distant thunder, and the steady light drumming of an uncommon summer rain falling on the roof of his loft room. Jacob whispered a fervent and thankful prayer for the end of his long journey and the safety of his family.

Miles away, Del McBride was forced to concede that further tracking would be impossible, as darkness and the steady drizzle obliterated the tracks of the horse with the split horseshoe. Three trails radiated in front of him into the low hills of the Snake River Valley.

"Well, hoss, might's well head back to town." McBride turned back toward Boomerang in the rain and cloud-hastened fading light. He ordinarily would have bedded down on the trail somewhere and begun tracking in the morning, but the rare summer rain made such plans useless.

"Hate to waste another week waiting on him to come back in," McBride told his horse in the absence of another human. "'Bout time I get a letter off to Myra again." He hunched his shoulders in the wet slicker. "Damn. I sure hate to disappoint her." It was past one o'clock in the morning when McBride stabled his horse and retired to the hotel and his room.

It was near one o'clock in the morning when Bruce Shotwell, emotionally devastated, dismounted in front of the dark mine entrance. Depressed almost to the point of suicide and unconcerned about his horse, he thoughtlessly tied the reins to a piece of rusting mine equipment and stumbled into the shaft. He dropped exhausted onto his sleeping pad, leaving the animal, wet, hungry, winded, and sore of foot, to stand in the clinging mud.

Chapter 17

Jacob awoke and lay staring at the dark ceiling. The sun wouldn't be breaking the horizon for another hour. Rain dripped off the eaves in disorganized rhythm as he rose and lit the lantern. Noise from the kitchen alerted him that Ma and Everett were already up.

Jacob rummaged around in the ancient bureau draws for some of his old clothes so that he could help Everett do morning chores.

When Jacob entered the kitchen, Ma turned and laughed at the sight of her son jammed into clothes he had so out-grown. Jacob stood for a moment chuckling himself and enjoying his mother's glee. He had been unable to fasten the top of his pants, his socks and shoes protruded awkwardly three inches below the cuffs of his trousers, his shirt strained to pop its buttons, and the sleeves came only to the middle of his fore-arms.

"Land sakes, Jacob," Ma cried, stifling her mirth with her hand, "ya'll can't go to the barn in that get-up. Everett an' me was talking, and we'd like to go to town early this morning and meet your sister and that friend of yours. Bring 'em out to the ranch fer a few days."

"They'd sure enjoy that. I need to go into Falk Mercantile today any-way and buy some better-fitting work clothes. Something happened to these whilst I was gone. They shrunk."

"I'll say," she chuckled as she handed Jacob a steaming cup of coffee. "Everett's down doing chores. He'll be up in a bit. Sit down, and I'll fix your breakfast."

"Never mind that. These old clothes can work one more day. I'm going down and help him. We'll all eat breakfast in town at the Bancroft later."

By 7:00 o'clock they were on the road. Boomerang was 12 miles away, so they would be there by eight.

Del McBride, as was his habit, strolled out onto the front verandah of the Bancroft Hotel to sit and soak up the morning sun. He was disappointed in himself. He held a pad of paper on his knee and one of those newfangled ink pens with a bladder that held a supply of ink in his left hand.

"What in the heck can I tell her?" he whispered. "I ain't done nothing but sit on my ass for two weeks. No, that ain't exactly true." Del mumbled out loud to himself, unmindful that someone was standing next to him also taking in the warm rays of the early morning sun. The man Del had seen a day earlier in the fancy suit smiled at the frontiersman.

"Morning to you sir. Bright warm sun will sure be welcome after last night's rain, eh?"

"Damn that rain last night," McBride snorted and looked up at the drummer or salesman, or whatever he was. "Hadn't been for that rain…. Aw, never mind, it don't concern you."

"I'm sorry. I thought rain once in awhile was welcome in these parts."

"As a matter of fact, that's normally true, except for last night. The night before last or tonight, it wouldn't have made any difference. Not a damn bit. Of all the nights it could have rained, why last night?" McBride looked up at the man and asked, "You staying here?" He motioned with his thumb back at the hotel.

"Yeah, I've got a partner who lives just outside of town. He's been gone for a long time, and I accompanied him home. We've come all the way from New York."

"What brings you to Boomerang Mr.—?"

"Danny Toronto. But call me Danny."

"Okay, Danny." Noticing Harold Hermann approaching McBride said, "Here comes one of the most important citizens in town. He checks up on me every morning." McBride introduced them. "Harold, meet Mr. Toronto. Mr. Toronto, this here is Harold Hermann, owner of this fine hotel and Falk Mercantile, that remarkable structure across the street."

"Mr. Toronto." Harold shook Danny's hand. "McBride does go on sometimes. Comes from spending too much time out on the trail alone, I 'spect."

"Morning to you, sir," Danny returned the greeting. Call me Danny." He turned to McBride. "Did I hear right. You wouldn't be Del McBride, the bounty hunter?"

Del looked at Danny and Harold with a perplexed expression. "The same. Why?"

"We're looking for you!" Danny exclaimed excitedly.

"Who's looking for me?"

"Jake Mead and me. I mean Jake Mead and I."

McBride cast a sideways glance out of the corner of his eye at Danny, and repeated Danny's initial reply. "Jake Mead and me? Who the heck is Jake Mead, and who the heck are you? And whatta you looking for me for?"

Danny smiled at the old bounty hunter. "I think the answer's just now arriving over by the train station."

Jacob, mounted on a Mead spread horse and leading the horse he had hired yesterday evening, was cantering across the tracks heading towards the hotel. Beside him rode Everett and Evangeline Koons in their wagon. They stopped in front of the Bancroft and Jacob dismounted.

Harold Herman greeted Jake with a firm handshake and a slap on the back.

"Welcome back, school boy. When'd you get home?" Before Jacob could answer, Harold continued, "Hey now, how come you went out to the ranch without stopping by my store and saying howdy?"

Everyone started talking at once, as Jacob led them into the hotel dining room, trying to explain everything to several people at once. Suddenly the chatter stopped as Del McBride fairly exploded at the sight of Myra Loder, Mrs. Loder, and Larry and Frank sitting in the dining room eating breakfast.

"Myra Loder!" he exclaimed. "I declare. What in heaven's name are you doing in Boomerang?"

There was pandemonium with everyone trying to talk at the same time. Eventually, however, rationality returned and Del McBride, Harold Hermann, Everett, and Evangeline were familiarized with the complex story as told, once again, by Danny Toronto of Myra Loder and her kinship to Jacob Mead and subsequent connection to the absent sheriff.

"He's due back on the noon train today," Hermann informed the group. "He's been up to Emmett a couple of days to see Quinabe. Quinabe's the town marshal up there. They get together couple times a year. They's pretty good pals. Grew up together over in Boise."

Harold looked at his turnip watch. "Whew, near ten. They'll be looking fer me over at the store."

"Harold, that watch. Tom Carpinelli bought me one just like his before I left for New York, remember?" Jacob asked. "Can I see it?"

"Sure." Harold handed his watch to Jacob. "Fact is, this is Tom's watch. He sent it back for fixin' when it quit on him, and he died 'fore it come back to the store. There weren't no one to claim it so I decided to keep it to remember him by. Damn, I sure miss that old boy."

Jacob examined the watch and handed it back to the storekeeper. "Thanks Harold. Come on out to the ranch on Saturday, we're fixin to have a wing-ding. We got some celebrating to do."

Pross Foote still lay snoring on his pad when Bruce Shotwell was shocked awake by a kick in the middle of his back. "What the hell time'd you get in last night, Shotwell?" Neil hissed in a demanding whisper.

"Past midnight, I guess. Why?" Bruce asked, his eyes filled with alarm and his voice craggy with sleep.

"Because, you damn fool, it looks like you ruined your horse." Neil was livid with anger. "His forefoot is split all the way to the quick. Didn't you know he was limping? Geez-us kee-rist, man. How stupid are you? Get your ass out there and tend to 'em. We gotta ride all night Friday, and you're gonna need a good horse under ya, or you're gonna hav'ta run all the way into town."

Bruce gathered his coat and shirt and, rubbing his bruised back, scurried out of the mine.

"What's up, Neil?' Pross called as he rolled out of his sack. He walked over to where Neil was glaring at the departing Shotwell. "Hey, man, good to see you up on your feet."

"Yeah, morning, Pross," Neil said disgustedly. "Shotwell may have wrecked the whole friggin' plan if you're still figuring on hitting 'em tomorrow night. The dumb bastard come in here last night with his horse on a split foot, and didn't even take the damn saddle off 'em."

Bruce came back into the mine and approached his cohorts. "It'll be all right, Neil. I think he'll be in shape by tomorrow night." Bruce stood back out of Neil's reach, aware that Neil's temper was not to be challenged.

"You bring that laudanum?" Neil asked.

"It's in my saddle bags." Bruce hurried out and came back with the medicine.

Without any thanks for the long ride or the procuring of the medicine, Neil grabbed the vial and shook his fist at Bruce. "You and that damn horse screw this job up Shotwell, and——." He left the threat hanging.

Bruce scampered out of reach and out of sight and hearing of the angry outlaw.

"Go to hell, all of ya," he muttered. "You think I'm sticking with you after this job is done? You can all go to hell."

"What's the matter, Bruce. Browning and Foote giving you a bad time?"

"Geez-us, Eddie, don't go sneaking up on a fella like that. Ain't nothing the matter, 'cept ma' horse is got a bad foot. Looks like he broke a shoe, and it split his hoof a little. Got any ideas how to fix it?"

The two misfit outlaws spent the rest of the day working at repairing the damage to Bruce's mount. Without the aid of a blacksmith and a couple of months' rest, there was little they could do for the animal.

Right at noon Danny Toronto, Jake and his family, and half the town waited for the train to slow to a stop.

A short, stocky young man, wearing a badge on his dark leather vest, stepped down from the passenger car and settled his hat on his head just as Harold Hermann rushed up to him and grabbed his elbow.

"Howdy, Harold. What's all the fuss about? Somebody leaving on the train?" he asked, as Harold led him to the group.

"Nope. These folks are all here to meet someone coming in."

"Who the heck would that be? Ain't but me and a couple of salesmen gitting off."

"Wade, there's some special people here to meet *you*, and I elected myself to introduce 'em." Harold pulled Jacob by the elbow and introduced him to Wade. "Jacob," he said, while he motioned to Myra to step closer, "Myra, this here's our sheriff, Wade Leigh, formerly of Boise, Idaho."

"Wade," Harold turned back to the lawman and, beaming with delight, said, "I'd like to introduce you to Jacob Mead, a long-time citizen of this here territory, just recently returned from an extended visit to the State of New York. And this pretty lady is Myra Loder, lately of Butte, Montana, and these are her sons." He bent and whispered in Myra's ear, "What's their names again?"

She whispered her reply.

"This here's Frank, 'n this here's Larry."

Wade looked over the newly introduced acquaintances with a baffled look. "All right, Mr. Mead, Miz Loder, I'm pleased to meet you. Would you mind telling me why?" But a sudden change in his expression revealed that his mind was racing ahead of Harold.

"Jacob and Myra are your brother and sister, Wade." Harold looked for a response from the sheriff.

"Myra Leigh?" Wade was stunned. He stared intently into Myra's eyes, then examined every curve of her face. "Of course you are. Look at you. Myra, I can't believe it?" They embraced in a tearful reunion of hearts and minds.

"Oh, Wade," was all Myra could squeak, in a tiny, tear filled voice. She held on to him for dear life, her face buried in the chest of the brother lost for twenty years.

Jacob stood back, tears of joy tracing glistening furrows down his cheeks. He wasn't the only one with tears in his eyes. Harold Hermann wiped his face unashamedly. Danny Toronto whipped out a handkerchief and blew his nose. Everett, like Jacob, paid no heed to the brimming moisture. Boomerang had never before had a homecoming quite like this one.

Wade turned to Jacob. "Mr. Mead, you'll forgive me, but my brothers' names are Hiram, and Phillip. I lost track of Phil when we were sent out West, but Hiram and I grew up together in Boise."

"I don't doubt you don't remember me," Jacob said. "I wasn't but a babe when we got separated, less that two years old. But Myra remembers me, and I went back and found her, and I found out about you too. You're named after our father, Wade Leigh, Sr. I've just come back from

New York, where I spent two and a half years with our brother Phillip Leigh, and our sisters Esther and Elaine. Do you remember them?"

Wade considered Jacob's question thoughtfully. "Weren't they about the same age—twins maybe? Yeah, I do remember 'em. My God, I haven't thought of 'em in years. Esther and Elaine; they were probably ten years older 'n me, maybe more.

"I don't remember a baby, though, but by damn, if you say you're my brother and you brought Myra back to me, then you're my brother." They grabbed each other in cheerful embrace.

"Wade, where's Hiram?" Myra asked. "You just said you grew up together in Boise. Do you know where he is?"

"Sure I do, we grew up next door to one another. His pa and my pa are brothers, and they wanted to keep us together, so they each took one of us. That makes us brothers and cousins at the same time," he said with a warm smile.

"Matter of fact, we were both with the police in Boise, till he took over as town marshal in Emmett. That's where I just came from. He and Ruth just had a baby girl less 'n a month ago, so I took some time off and went to see them 'n the new baby. Until about fifteen minutes ago, he and Ruth was all the family I had. Now look here, I got a whole railroad station full of family."

Jacob asked the next question as the diverse group walked toward the hotel and town. "Wade, if you was adopted, how come you go by the name of Leigh and not your folks' name?

"Well, that was my folks' fault. They're Quinabes, too, being as my pa and Hiram's pa are brothers. Ma and Pa never did get around to filing the papers to adopt me proper like, so when I went to work for the police department, I had to go by my old name. I got a little book somewheres with it printed inside. Hiram's still got his book, too, far's I know. Anyway, we both always did know what our names were. Hiram give his Leigh name up in favor of his ma and pa's when he was about ten or so.

"The folks didn't mind too much when I went back to Leigh, since by law I had to. They said I was too old to adopt by then anyhow. But," Wade added with a cheerful laugh, "Ma still says I'm still her little boy."

The rest of the day was spent getting acquainted, and re-acquainted. Jacob and Doc spent an hour or so exchanging news about Boomerang and the Highsmiths back in Ithaca. There were clothes to buy, friends to invite to the Mead family reunion, and a thousand details to fill the day.

In the Primrose later in the afternoon, the men hoisted a beer and toasted this very special day. Everett picked up change from his twenty-dollar gold piece and pocketed 17 silver dollars, one silver dollar in his shirt pocket, and 16 silver dollars in his pants pocket.

And what a glorious day it was. The previous night's rain had a refreshing effect on all the land. White fluffy clouds and bright sun made it seem like a new spring day. The temperature was twenty degrees cooler than it had been for the last month, a rare summer day in the Payette River Valley.

Wade made a telephone call to Emmett, Idaho. Hiram Quinabe, Ruth, the baby, and their boys would be at the wing-ding at the Mead Ranch on Saturday.

Bruce Shotwell's excitement at this day's, or rather night's, coming activity was consuming his thoughts. Fantasies of being free of Pross Foote and Neil Browning and having all the money he would ever need to live in Mexico were to be realized tonight.

Easy jobs, he thought. Ain't none of us gonna get hurt or caught, 'cause we ain't leaving no witnesses. Ain't but three of 'em, and we'll shut 'em all up permanently. Old Christian Moss and the two old idiots out at the Meads ain't got enough strength between all three of 'em to stop us. That's what they keep saying. Me 'n Ed can take off on our own after tonight. Hell, Ed likes me, I'll go with him. We can take care of one another.

Bruce rolled his blanket, stood up off his pad, dressed, and went out of the mine shaft to check on his horse in the corral where he had been released with the other three horses. Bruce's horse was dead.

"Oh, shit!" he cried. "Neil'll kill me. Where can I get a horse today?" Bruce was near panic. He called back into the mine for Ed Frey.

When Ed appeared, Bruce hustled him over to the corral and showed him the dead horse lying in the pool of muddy rainwater that had accumulated at the low end of the enclosure. Bruce pleaded with Ed Frey to help him extradite himself from the terrifying and dangerous situation.

"Hey, pal, don't look at me. Ain't nothing I can do for ya," Ed said indifferently.

"Yes there is, Eddie. Com'on man. Com'on, ya gotta help me. Ya can talk to Neil and Pross fer me and tell 'em it ain't my fault, can't ya? Geez-sus Ed, Neil will probably shoot me, and it really ain't my fault. You know that. You 'n me, we both tried to doctor that horse; he just wasn't much of a horse."

"He wasn't such a bad horse when you got 'em. Seems to me like you can't take care of business." Ed studied Bruce's terrified face for a moment. "All right, wait here. No, hold it a minute, I think you need to get out of camp. If I can't convince 'em to give you a break, I don't think you want to be around here, not with Browning being on the prod like he's been."

It took an hour to cool Neil Browning down to a point where he would even listen to a possible solution to the problem of the shortage of a horse. His first instinct was to grab his pistol. "I'll lay that son of a bitch out right next to that horse's carcass. Where in hell is he?"

Ed finally convinced Neil that he and Shotwell could ride double into Boomerang, do the Christian Moss job, then steal a couple of horses to get out to the Mead place before midnight. "It'll work out fine, Neil. We'll be in and out 'fore they even know we've been there."

Neil took a lot of convincing and more words than Ed Frey had spoken in the last two months, but eventually though reluctantly he accepted the plan.

When Ed left Browning and Foote alone, Neil called Foote nearer to him. "I want Shotwell the hell out of the way before daylight tomorrow. He may come in handy tonight, which I doubt, but just in case, we'll keep him around till after we finish with that Mead bunch."

"Gotta agree with ya. The longer I'm around 'em, the more he makes my skin crawl," Foote growled in a loud whisper of conspiracy. "What about Frey, he okay?" he asked as he helped Neil Browning to his feet.

"I'll let ya know by morning. So far as I'm concerned, he's just another share we gotta split with." Neil Browning felt no remorse for thinking about throwing away more then twenty-two years of comradeship. Pross Foote was his partner, and he knew he could count on him. Frey was another story. "If Ed can help, all right, if not..." Neil shrugged.

That settled, the outlaws spent the remainder of the day preparing for the night's assault.

Late afternoon and the sun was plastered against the western bowl of the sky. There remained no more than four hours of daylight when the outlaws abandoned their slovenly-kept hideout of the last two months.

Pross Foote and Neil Browning were mounted individually. Ed Frey and Bruce Shotwell were riding double, with Shotwell riding on back.

"For sure I ain't gonna miss that damn hole," Foote called back to the others riding behind.

"How's your nag holding up, Ed?" Neil asked.

"He's all right," Ed answered without elaboration.

On the way to Boomerang, Neil Browning dropped out of the group and concealed himself less than a mile from the Mead place to await their return. It was now completely dark with just a sliver of the new moon rising on the eastern horizon. His companions would be slipping into town in almost total darkness.

Christian Moss ate later on Fridays than he did the rest of the week. He was in the habit of eating out at either the Primrose or the Bancroft Hotel on Friday nights instead of having Iva, his cook, prepare his evening meal. Mrs. Hermann had prepared him a delicious steak, pink in the middle, tender and piping hot. The side dish had been a baked potato piled with butter, and a novelty followed the meal; ice cream. As he walked toward the Primrose for a nightcap, Christian patted his stomach with satisfaction.

He enjoyed an evening of conversation with friends, drank two stiff whiskies "neat," and headed for home and bed. It was 11:15 on the bedside clock as he turned over in bed to go to sleep.

CHAPTER 18

Abby Moss looked beautiful in her flowing garments of wind swept silk. Christian watched her fondly as she stood with waves of swirling haze enveloping her. She tarried, tantalizingly close but constantly out of reach, surrounded by Herculean pillars of snow-white marble. Flower petals mingled with torrents of crystal clear water cascaded from silver and gold portals, magically suspended in a deep blue, sunless sky that appeared dappled with billows of fleecy white clouds. She called to him. That's never happened before, Christian thought. She's never called out before. Even though he couldn't hear her loving voice, her musical tones played in his ears as clearly as church bells.

Everything abruptly disappeared in a blinding flash of blood-red insanity as Christian was jolted from the dreamy visit with his long dead wife.

"Wake up, you son of a bitch." Someone slapped the sleeping man again and again.

Christian struggled to defend himself, but his hands were pinned beneath his blankets. The faint light of an oil lamp, shielded in the pitch black, gave Christian little more than a ghostly image of a frightening face hovering above him.

"He's awake, Pross. Go easy, we don't want to kill him yet." another man whispered insistently.

The first man yanked the covers off and pulled Christian roughly from his bed and slammed him into the bedside chair. Pross Foote held the lantern next to his face and said, "'Member me, Mr. Boss Man. You remember who you sent ta prison fer twenty-five years?"

"Foote!" Christian exclaimed in a trembling voice.

"That's right, Mr. Boss Man, old Foote. Old Foote, who worked in your damn mill winters when it was so cold the drinking water froze," he slapped Christian with an open hand to emphasize his rage, " an' summers so damn hot you could fry eggs in the shade." Again Christian's head snapped back from another blow. "'N what'd I get for working my ass off for you and that lazy useless brother a yours? Thirteen years cooped up in a damn cage, after six lousy years of nothin' but sweat and nothin' to show fer it."

Christian glowered at his old foreman and replied in suppressed anger. "You were the best-paid foreman in the entire state of Idaho, Foote. You've got nothing to whine about." Christian dropped his voice as he regained control of himself and anger began to replace the panicked fear he had awakened with. He sneered contemptuously, "We even granted you a vacation which you used to try and rob us. Your own fallacious greed, not the injustice you imagined, is what earned you that cage, as you call it.

"Shut up, you son-of-a-bitch!" Pross hissed, striking Christian a vicious blow on top of the head, this time with a pistol that he'd pulled from his belt. "Where you hiding your money?"

Stunned but still alert, Christian slumped from the chair to the floor and feigned unconsciousness. He could hear the outlaws begin their search.

"Tear these rooms apart, you two. Look behind all them pictures, under the furniture, drawers, everywhere, and keep an eye on that bastard. I'll be right back."

Pross was gone for several minutes. With his ear to the floor, Christian could hear Pross destroying everything on the floor below in concert with the mayhem going on all about him.

Eventually, Pross re-entered Christian's bedroom, "You find anything?" he growled at his comrades.

"Some pocket money and his gun is all," Ed replied.

"He awake yet?" Pross asked angrily.

"He's stirred some. He's staying pretty quiet," Shotwell sneered.

"Get 'em on his feet, and fetch him down in the cellar. I'll make the son of a bitch talk. Hurry up, we're burning way the hell up too much time here." Pross headed out, followed by Ed and Bruce holding up Christian under his arms.

As he was being dragged, stumbling, unable to regain his feet, Christian Moss knew he was going to die tonight. It didn't matter if he revealed the location of his vault to these miscreants or not, he was still going to die. In his mind, there was no doubt and there was no fear. Christian managed a faint, grim smile.

As his head cleared and his thoughts calmed, Christian became aware of an enormous weight, as if an anvil were sitting on his chest. He found that couldn't breathe. He gasped in tiny breaths of air. His heart pounded like a blacksmith's hammer in anticipation of, what—fear of death? On the contrary, death meant peace. Death meant the end of his loneliness and, finally, a real reunion with his beloved Abby.

As the weight grew heavier and his arms began to feel as if they were being thrust into a smithy's fire, Christian's heart began to fail. What an astonishing prank to pull on a hapless fool, he thought. What incredible irony to die of heart failure, leaving my death on the hands of this evil man who will undoubtedly be hanged for it.

Once down in the cellar, Pross continued torturing Christian by slapping him again and again and shouting incoherent words that merely caused Christian to smile as the blows rocked him from side to side. The weight on his chest, and the pain in his arms were the focus of his consciousness. The impacts delivered by Foote were scant annoyances.

Minutes passed, a half an hour, an hour. Foote increased his pitiless assault on Christian Moss, but for Christian time ceased its relentless passage.

He became aware that he no longer felt his head being punished. The fires in his arms cooled the weight on his chest lifted as if it had been but a feather. His pounding heart, weary of its responsibility slowed softly to a halt.

Abby smiled her exquisite little crooked smile, reached for his out-stretched hand, and pulled him to his feet. Christian glanced back at the spectacle of his tormented body crumpled upon a pile of black coal and smiled at this final mockery. Abby led him away from his pain and lone-liness. "Come, Sweetheart," she said. "We've been waiting a long time for today."

"Pross. Stop it, dammit. Can't you see? You ain't getting nothin' out of him. He's dead." Ed Frey grabbed Pross' arm and tried to wrestle him away from the corpse slumped against the pile of coal.

"It's here, dammit!" Pross howled. "Its here someplace. Find it!" He grabbed Moss' limp shoulders and shook him violently. "Where in the hell is it?" he screamed.

Frantically, they rummaged through the cellar. Hours passed as they went back upstairs and again ransacked every room, every nook and hall of the huge house. It was Bruce Shotwell who suggested they move Christian's body and search the coal bin. In minutes, a gasp of satisfac-tion escaped their lips as Christian's safe, buried under the coal and sunk into the floor, was revealed. Tools were found, and the safe was dug from its hiding place.

"We ain't got time to open it here. We need a wagon," Pross said.

Ed Frey was sent to find something to transport the awkward cargo. He found a light buggy in back of a store and was able to man-handle it back to the Moss house. The night was getting away from them and Pross was frantic to secure his treasure and get out of town. Once loaded, he went himself to the livery stable and stole a horse and harness.

He whispered to Bruce, "Shotwell, you ride my horse, I'll drive the buggy. Let's get the hell out of here."

The gang rode out of town and found Neil peering out of his hiding place awaiting them. In the nearly total darkness of a setting new moon, the gang reunited. Laughing and backslapping, they admired the safe in the pallid gleam of the lamp Neil had brought along for light and comfort. It was nearly 4:00A.M. when they headed for the Mead ranch.

Jacob awoke and stared contentedly at the familiar loft ceiling. Dang me, it's good to be home, he thought. He rolled out of bed, dressed silently, and let himself out of the house to begin chores. Jacob looked up at the morning stars shimmering in the crystal-clear air as he walked toward the barn. They looked close enough to reach out and touch. He had missed the stars back in New York. Without barn chores, he had had no opportunity or excuse to rise so early in the morning to look at the heavens.

Off in the distance, the howl of prowling or playful coyotes pierced the final darkness, before the dawn began its dazzling rebirth.

Jacob knew Everett wouldn't be far behind, nor was it his intent to allow Everett the pleasure of sleeping late. He just wanted to get back into some of his old habits and be alone with the animals for a few minutes.

The docile draft horses met Jacob as he entered the corral, the heat of their breath warm in the early morning coolness. He patted their necks affectionately as they nuzzled him. When Jacob walked into the barn, they followed obediently into their respective stalls. Jacob tied their halters and went up into the haymow to throw hay into their feed cribs.

When he returned to the horse's stalls Jacob noticed that they were restless, stomping in their stalls, and looking around with eyes rolling white, straining to see behind them.

"What's the trouble, fellas. Coyotes spooking ya?"

A shiny glint flashed in the corner of Jacob's eye, then he heard the roar of a pistol shot that slammed a slug into his shoulder with the force of a charging buffalo. Jacob spun in an incomprehensible whirl of pain and confusion into one of the stalls and under the huge horse.

A crushing sensation and a resounding snap in Jacob's left leg were evidence that he was being trampled by the terrified beast, but there was no other place to hide. Blackness covered by even more intense blackness was dragging Jacob down. He fought to remain conscious. The fight sapped the last of his strength. He lay helpless under the horse. The pain was intolerable, but he dared not make a sound.

Everett had turned his lantern down to the smallest flicker possible in order to surprise Jacob in the semi-darkness inside. He was about to set the lantern down outside the barn door and stick his nose in, when the thunderclap of gunfire inside the barn halted him in his tracks. He slapped his hip, immediately aware that he was unarmed.

As he spun to retreat back to the house to protect Evangeline, Everett felt the presence of someone behind him. From the corner of his eye, even in such faint light, Everett recognized Bruce Shotwell. In one spontaneous motion, Everett whipped the lantern over his head like a club, smashing down with almost insane force.

Shotwell, disorientated in the unfamiliar surroundings, was taken totally by surprise as the lantern crashed against his skull. The welded seams of the lantern split and the reservoir of lamp oil spewed over his head and shoulders.

The force of the blow caused Bruce to squeeze the trigger of his gun, already cocked, and a thundering shot slammed into Everett's chest, robbing him of breath. He staggered off into the darkness, struggling for air, gasping, "Evangeline." He labored to keep his balance and get back to the house. "Evangeline," he wheezed, his direction becoming aimless as air was squeezed from his lungs.

Stunned by Everett's blow, Shotwell lay semi-conscious, unable to focus. The tiny flame, still flickering in the shattered lamp's remaining fuel, was no longer confined to its glass prison. As if guided by some form of intelligence, it wanted more. Slowly, the flames crept across the few inches of dry grass and nibbled at the edge of Shotwell's oil-soaked coat. With increasing appetite, it gathered strength, growing bolder and casting more light in the morning gloom. Suddenly, Shotwell became aware that he was on fire. He screamed in terror, leaped up, and began to run hysterically. Hungry flames, growing, burning, began consuming his hair, his face, his clothing. He struggled in vain with his coat; his hands were burning.

Unintelligible sounds escaped his throat. With each breath, inhaled flames fueled his panic. He ran, the flames raging, engorged on the fuel and the additional fresh air of the burning man's blind marathon. Shotwell continued to run irrationally; tripping, stumbling and falling, only to rise and run and fall again.

Ed Frey and Neil Browning watched in shock until finally the tortured Shotwell fell unconscious, the flames consuming the last of the fuel.

"We gotta help him Neil!" Ed said pleadingly.

"Help him, hell. Where's that old man. I seen just as he hit him." Neil turned from Shotwell's charred body and peered into the darkness.

"I didn't see 'em. Maybe this ain't such a good idea, what with Bruce hurt."

Neil grabbed Ed's coat collar and pulled his face within an inch of his own. "Shotwell was gonna get hurt anyway, Eddie. He just done us a favor."

Ed stood in shocked disbelief, trying to focus both his eyes and his mind on Neil Browning, his childhood pal and sometime partner.

"What about me, Neil?" he shouted. "You got plans to knock me off, too?"

"Hey, calm down, Eddie. We're buddies, you 'n me. Partners. Come on pal, we came here to get us some money." Neil pointed to the ranch house with his pistol, saying, "There it is, up there at the house, lots of gold. Let's go."

"I ain't going, Neil," Ed protested stubbornly. "I've had a gut full of this gang, 'n you, 'n killing, 'n being scared, 'n looking over my shoulder. It's over for me. I'm done." Ed turned toward his fallen comrade. "I gotta go check Bruce." Ed was in tears. "Shit, that was awful. I ain't never seen a man die like that," Ed cried, as his fear released a torrent of tears.

Shotwell lay on the ground, a dark shadow against the sunburned grass. Dawn was chasing the night away while a small flame still flickered on the shoulder of his coat. Ed leaned over the body. "Aw Geez-sus, Neil, he's still breathing. Whatta we gonna do?"

"Leave 'em?" Browning barked. He pressed his pistol against Ed's kidneys. "Get the hell up to the house. Now!"

"Foote, where are ya?' Browning called in a hoarse whisper. "Make a noise, man. You there?" The waning night had no answer.

Neil glanced around and shouted, "Shit. The son of a bitch took off, deserted us. He's gone!"

At the sound of the shots, Evangeline had grabbed one of Jess' old pistols and slipped out the back door. Still in her nightclothes, she snatched the best wrapping at hand to camouflage herself in the diminishing dark. It was the black coat Everett had worn when they got married. Like a shadow, she melted into the morning's darkness as quiet as a bird's wing. It would start to lighten quickly now. Already, a silver ribbon lay on the eastern horizon. She had to find Jacob and Everett and help them. For now she was nearly invisible, but it wouldn't last long.

Ma headed directly away from the house until she was sure she was well clear of the outlaws. Time was running against her as she edged around in a circuitous route towards the barn. Halting every few seconds in the stillness, she alarmed herself with the sound of her own heavy breathing, which to her sounded like the noon freight train over in Boomerang.

Something moving caught her eye, a movement where a movement shouldn't be. She crouched, making herself smaller, searching for a sign of recognition in the deep shadows. In a desperate move, she whispered softly, "Is that you, Jacob?" Her question was answered by the flutter of a startled bird that passed inches from her head. "Please, son," she implored, "answer me.

A slight noise was all the warning she got. Someone hit her a vicious blow with his fist on the side of her head. Bright lights flashed and blinding pain stabbed through her skull as the man grabbed a handful of her hair and yanked her head back.

He snarled in her ear, "Let's go, mama. It's time to open the bank. Come on, Eddie, let's go."

Evangeline felt herself being wrenched by the hair back up to her feet. Still groggy from the blow, she struggled to free herself only to feel the man's strength as he snapped her head back and slapped her across the cheek.

"Move, dammit?" His iron fingers dug deeply into her arm.

She stumbled toward the house, worried almost to death, not for herself, but for Jacob and Everett.

Pross Foote crouched in a thicket of brush at the edge of the creek. He glanced over his shoulder toward the ranch buildings. "Ain't no reason fer me to stick around, by damn," he said to himself. "I ain't getting shot on their account. I got mine." Pross chuckled to himself. "Let 'em go to hell."

When Neil Browning had shattered the stillness with his shot at Jacob, Pross had waited to see if there was any retaliation. The shot would surely alert the occupants of the house. A second shot, then silence, and finally the astonishing performance of Bruce Shotwell running around, screaming with flames swirling around his head, convinced Pross Foote that there was a lot more to be gained by slipping away than by staying in this nest of hornets.

"In two months I can be in Mexico. Sorry, Neil, old buddy, sometimes plans have to be changed."

Myra Loder had insisted Thursday afternoon on being invited out to the Meads' early Saturday to give Evangeline a hand with the preparations. The excitement of a family reunion, getting to know Jacob's family, as well having nearly half the town as company, was something she wanted to be fully involved in. Danny Toronto would follow later with the boys and Mrs. Loder, but Del McBride, instructed on how to get to the ranch, insisted on accompanying Myra out on her early morning ride. Evangeline's two sisters from Caldwell were coming as well.

Myra and Del McBride were still a considerable distance from the ranch but they could see the dark bulk of the buildings against the sun-dried grass when the first pistol shot hit their ears.

"Oh, Oh, trouble!" Del gasped. He grabbed her horse's bridle and brought her buggy to a stop. They listened intently but could hear nothing but the sound of crickets hailing the morning. Suddenly another shot rang out. "Myra, can you get yourself back to town from here?" Del asked.

"I'm sure I can," she replied.

McBride let out a gasp. Myra looked to see what had startled him.

A fiery phantom appeared to be floating amongst the buildings, disappearing and then reappearing. Screams of agony reached their, ears sending chills of dread coursing through both their bodies.

"Drive, Myra, drive like hell and find your brother and Harold Hermann. They'll know what to do."

Del wheeled his horse toward the ranch as Myra slapped the reins, and yelled, "Yaa!" to her team

McBride rode closer to the buildings and halted abruptly, listening for additional signs of trouble. Whoever had been running had disappeared. McBride glanced to the east to reckon the arrival of daylight. The eastern horizon was already bleeding red with the dawn's arrival as he dropped the reins and ran silently, ducking behind any shrub or post that helped conceal his progress. The bank of a small stream lay in his path. McBride stepped down into the trickle of water, and pressed, crouching against the other bank, concealed by a small bush. He held his breath and listened for clues to help him decide his next course of action.

Suddenly the figure of Pross Foote, trying to conceal his bulky body, but recognizable even in the faint light, loomed above McBride. Months of reading the wanted poster and memorizing the obviously accurate description left no doubt in McBride's mind that this was his man. When Foote stood up, not three feet from the experienced bounty hunter, McBride jumped up and drove his rifle butt viciously into the outlaw's crotch, crushing his manhood in a crippling stab that left Foote breathless and writhing like a wounded snake in the shallow water of the creek bed. McBride wasted neither time nor sympathy on the outlaw. As Foote rolled up, trying to regain his feet but helpless in his pain, McBride delivered a roundhouse blow to his head and followed it with a well-aimed kick to the center of his chest. Pross Foote lay as limp as wet laundry in the middle of the stream.

From a vest pocket, McBride withdrew several lengths of rawhide thongs, which he soaked in the stream. Kneading water into the fetters to soften the leather, he bound his prisoner's hands and feet, pulling the tethers into Pross' flesh with the knowledge that when the bonds dried, they would draw up and be almighty painful and exceedingly difficult to remove. It was not McBride's intention to torture his prisoner, but he wasn't about to suffer the embarrassment of losing $10,000. He had plans for that money. He was making damn sure that Pross Foote's outlaw days were over. Less than five minutes had passed since Del had jumped into the little stream.

The flame released by Everett's shattered lantern lay smoldering in the short tufts of trampled grass after Bruce Shotwell jumped up and ran off in his agony. It only required the faintest puff of a fresh morning breeze to cause it to sparkle, flare briefly, die, and flare again, creeping in an ever widening circle until it finally crawled to the generous undergrowth of parched grass surrounding the barn. With wild abandon, the flames bounded into the withered fuel, leaping, swirling, running, consuming. The stone foundation of the barn shielded the structure temporarily, but it was inevitable that the hungry flame would advance.

Inside the barn, barely conscious, Jacob stirred. In terrible pain, he lay still for as long as he could endure it, but he had to move his injured leg from its present position.

Suddenly, the horses began to prance nervously again. Jacob tried to make himself smaller under Harry's ponderous legs. Then it came to him, the faint, unmistakable odor of smoke. Jacob looked around for a shovel, a pitchfork, anything to hoist himself up.

Harry and Chub began to roll their eyes, and strain against the sides of their stalls. Harry pranced gingerly, aware that Jacob was under his feet, but alarmed by the acrid smoke wafting into his flaring nostrils.

The horse bumped against Jacob with his heavy steel-shod hooves, causing him additional distress. The big black horse swung his giant head around, the white in his eyes showing in bewilderment.

Grab the bridle. As the thought shot through Jacob's mind, he grasped the straps and hung on. Harry swung his head back around, easily jerking Jacob off the stall floor and onto his feet, pitching him against the feed crib. The pain was almost more than Jacob could stand. The veil of unconsciousness began to envelop him again. No. I'm not to going to pass out, his mind yelled in rebellion. I've got to get these horses out of here.

He could see the flickering flames at the other end of the barn. The ropes that held the horses' bridles were fastened near at hand. Jacob pulled the slipknot that released Chub in the next stall, then he freed Harry. Burning straw began falling from the haymow above them.

"Come on, Chub, back. Back, Harry, come on,boy, back." he gently urged the horses. "Now git." Jacob's commanding voice soothed the horses enough so that they anxiously backed out of their stalls. As Harry backed out of his stall, Jacob threw his good arm over the horse's back and hung on for dear life. Out of his stall, the horse made a turn toward the open door and the corral beyond, brushing Jacob from his neck and leaving him helpless once again on the floor of the burning barn.

A giant "swoosh" of hot air and blazing embers erupted down through the hay chute. In an instant, horses and man were surrounded by fire. Whinnies of fright burst from the terrified animals as they searched through the blinding smoke for the open door, snorting and trying to clear their nostrils of the offending fumes. Harry reared on his hind legs, gathering purchase to make a dash for the open air. Desperately, Jacob made a swipe at the horse's tail as Harry bolted out of the barn and across the corral, dragging the stricken man behind. Unintentionally, a hoof struck Jacob's head, knocking him unconscious, finally releasing him from his burdensome pain. He released his grip and rolled nearly 40 feet with the force of his wild exit, unaware of his surroundings.

"Geez-sus Neil, take it easy on her," Ed begged.

"Shut up, Frey!" Turning his attention back to Ma, Neil shoved her roughly to the floor of the kitchen. "Where is it?" he screamed. The stress was showing in the face of the sickly, fleshy man, protruding veins throbbed on his forehead as sweat poured down into his beard. It was light outside and they should have been miles from the ranch by now.

Ma looked dazedly at her captor.

Neil cocked his pistol against Ma's temple. "Ya got exactly two seconds to tell me where the money's hid."

Suddenly there was the roar that came from the open window.

At the sound of the shot, Ed Frey's eyes blazed with abrupt surprise and a loud gasp burst from his lungs. He slammed against the wall and stood for a moment with that shocked look in his eyes that he had seen in the eyes of his friend Pat Bracket nearly four years before. A trickle of blood oozed from the corner of his mouth as he slid to a sitting position, leaving a crimson smear on the wall where the bullet had exited his back.

Neil's reaction to the sound was to grab Evangeline and pull her to him tightly to use her as a shield. He fired blindly at the window, the roars of his gun almost a continuous roll of thunder so rapid were his shots. Ma, desperate to help or escape, flailed out and hit Neil's gun hand as he fired his last bullet. He struck her another cruel blow to the head, pulled a second pistol from his belt, and placed it against her temple as she sprawled in a rumpled heap in front of him.

Browning's savage plans were crumbling like a cake dropped in water. In desperation, he snapped Evangeline's head back and looked wildly for an avenue of escape that wouldn't cost him the money he was so desperate for. He dragged her to a corner next to the wounded Ed Frey. Even in the coolness of the morning's trapped night air, he was sweating like a workhorse, his hair hanging in long tangles, his shirt collar soaked with his flowing juices.

Ed Frey sat bleeding against the wall, watching the savageness of Neil's performance. He breathed in shallow gasps; the trickle of blood emerging from his mouth grew.

"Willie?" Ed whispered, looking intently through Neil as if he weren't there.

Neil turned to Ed and stared at him quizzically.

"Willie, is that you? Aww, Willie, you're dead," Ed was near tears, as he appeared to be listening to something.

Neil turned and looked behind him, almost expecting to see the ghost of Willie Frey hovering there. Then his finger tightened on the trigger of his gun tangled in Evangeline's tousled hair, Ed's rattling call to Willie startling and distracting him only momentarily. He looked once more with disdain at his dying partner. It was the final act in his evil life.

The roar of Ed's pistol sent a bullet hurtling at Neil Browning's heart. Neil, eyes wild with terror, grasp instantly the certainty that he faced eternity and that Eddie Frey had never forgotten or forgiven the accidental shooting of Willie.

"It wasn't my fault," he gasped, looking at Ed Frey in bewilderment, unable to understand why his best friend would shoot him. "It was a accident, Eddie," Neil whispered as life ebbed from his wicked heart.

It was over. Willie's death was avenged. Ed Frey surveyed the damage he had wrought in his life. He groaned in repentance as he slipped into his eternal rest.

Everett opened his eyes slowly. The sun was nearly two fingers over the horizon, blinding him with a welcome light, a light he was frankly surprised to see. He had heard the roar and felt the bullet strike him squarely in the chest. After staggering breathless into the darkness, his last thought was, I'm dying. To see the sun was a pleasure unexpected.

Everett sat up, and an enormous pain stabbed him in the chest. "I've been shot," he said out loud, as surprised at the fact that he could even utter such a statement, as he was to find himself alive. In spite of his pain, Everett couldn't avoid a humorous thought. "How in the hell come I ain't dead. What's it take 'ta kill me?" He felt a weight in his shirt pocket. Reaching in, he pulled out a battered silver dollar, the exact center dimpled by Bruce Shotwell's bullet.

"I'll be damned," he exclaimed, "it takes less 'n a dollar to kill me. Any more 'n that's probably too damn much too," he added ruefully.

Painfully, he heaved himself to his feet and surveyed the area to get his bearings. He must have been unconscious for a considerable time, because the sun had climbed above the horizon and bathed the earth in light. Out toward the orchard lay a man who appeared to be covered with tar or something, propped on an elbow, but otherwise immobile. Looking toward the corral, Everett spotted another person lying awkwardly, the team of draft horses standing over him protectively while a blazing fire consumed the barn a couple a dozen yards from them.

Everett recognized the new work clothes Jacob had been showing off just yesterday. Gingerly, for he was in great pain, Everett climbed through the bars of the corral, rushed to Jacob, and dragged him away from the heat of the fire. He sat down and propped Jacob's head in his lap. "Oh Jacob, hang on, son, yer gonna be all right. Yer gonna be all right."

Jacob's eyes opened and he smiled faintly. "Promise?"

McBride found the two men sitting in the corral, the horses still acting protective.

"McBride!" called Everett. "Where'd you come from. You get in on the shooting?"

"Me and Myra come early and heard it start. I sent her back to town to fetch the sheriff," McBride said, stooping to examine Jacob. "You hurt?" Del asked, turning to Everett.

"Naw, just bunged up some. What about the outlaws, they gone. Who's that over there?" Everett pointed to the burned man suffering his wounds, unable to move.

"You got that one yourself, with your lamp."

"I did?" Everett said with a raised eyebrow. "He still alive?"

"Yeah, looks like it. He's burnt real bad. Damn, he's gonna suffer. The rest of 'em kinda took care of themselves. I helped 'em a little. By the way, Evangeline was roughed up some, but she's doing fine. She's asking for ya. You all right?"

"I ain't never hurt this bad before," Everett grunted, as he stood up. Then with a wide grin he added, "But I ain't never felt better 'n I do right now, neither."

"Good!" McBride said, patting Everett on the back. "Get up to the house and see to your lady, I'll take over here till help comes."

Everett turned slowly and walked carefully up to the house, leaving McBride to tend Jacob.

McBride took off his duster, rolled it, and propped Jacob's head up and sat with him against the side of the corral. "Before long, this place will be teeming with help, pardner."

As he sat comforting Jacob, McBride mentally calculated the morning's work. Pross Foote, lying in the creek back a ways trussed like a pig ready for market, was money in the bank for both McBride and Myra. So were Ed Frey and Neil Browning.

He wasn't so sure about Bruce Shotwell. If he had any reward on him, it would have to come out later. Looking over at the charred figure still propped on one elbow, McBride thought, poor bastard, looks like he's suffering for his misdeeds right enough already. Del could see Shotwell was still alive, but he hadn't had a chance to go over and examine him.

Browning, apparently the leader of this pack, had been killed by one of his own men. That puzzled McBride some, but there was justice in there somewhere, he was sure of that.

The most satisfying of his reflections concerned Myra Loder's missing rosary. Pross Foote was still wearing it around his neck as he lay in his wet bed of trickling creek water. Myra Loder would finally be getting her rosary back. Del smiled at the satisfaction he felt.

"Yes, sir, Jacob, you 'n yer folks are gonna have some wing-ding today."

FINALE

August and half of September had passed and the Mead ranch had acquired a new barn in a community barn raising.

As Jacob and Everett sat in the kitchen one-day watching Ma make bread, Everett remarked that he was looking forward to fall again.

"Best time a the year, for sure. A fella can get some rest."

"Rest!" Jacob said jokingly. "You've been resting for two months. Ma, how we gonna get him to earn his keep?"

"All right now, you two, since yer both too stove up to work outside, ya'll kin start helping me right here in the house. There's dusting, cooking, n bringing in wood. Pick yer poison.

"Myra's planning on leaving fer New York first of October in time to catch the fall colors for her wedding. Danny says it's the prettiest time of the year back there," Ma said, smiling at the thought.

"Imagine Mr. McBride giving her and Danny a five thousand dollar wedding present so she can take her brothers and their families back to New York." She turned from her chore and scowled at her men, saying, "That means she ain't gonna be doing no more cooking and cleaning fer us."

"You know what, Jacob. I believe I got some mending to do down in the barn." Everett said, getting up to leave.

"Yeah, me too," Jacob said eagerly, as he grabbed his crutches and stood to leave. "I gotta rub Harry 'n Chub down. I ain't done that yet today."

"Jacob?" Ma called after him.

"Yeah, Ma," he turned to look at her.

"Didn't you tell me that Danny had a wife and family once?"
"Yeah."
"Whatever happened to 'em?"
Jacob shrugged. "I dunno; he's never said."